High-Tech Attack

The four Soviet SU-24s passed over the small Pacific atoll of Elu, on course to the target area held by the Americans. Captain Pavlyuk, flight leader, could see the sleek silver cylinder of his country's crippled satellite *War God* near the edge of the wooded plateau. But suddenly, a pale blue beam of light flashed up from the grounded space weapon and struck his plane. Billions of watts of perfectly focused gamma ray radiation struck the low flying SU-24, destroying its intricate electronic defense and navigational controls.

"Mayday! Mayday!" Pavlyuk radioed, frantically pulling on his controls without effect. Before he could give further commands, his plane hit the ground at six hundred miles an hour and vanished in a huge ball of orange flames.

ESPIONAGE FICTION BY WARREN MURPHY AND MOLLY COCHRAN

GRANDMASTER (17-101, $4.50)
There are only two true powers in the world. One is goodness. One is evil. And one man knows them both. He knows the uses of pleasure, the secrets of pain. He understands the deadly forces that grip the world in treachery. He moves like a shadow, a promise of danger, from Moscow to Washington — from Havana to Tibet. In a game that may never be over, he is the grandmaster.

THE HAND OF LAZARUS (17-100, $4.50)
A grim spectre of death looms over the tiny County Kerry village of Ardath. The savage plague of urban violence has begun to weave its insidious way into the peaceful fabric of Irish country life. The IRA's most mysterious, elusive, and bloodthirsty murderer has chosen Ardath as his hunting ground, the site that will rock the world and plunge the beleaguered island nation into irreversible chaos: the brutal assassination of the Pope.

Available wherever paperbacks are sold, or order direct from the Publisher. Send cover price plus 50¢ per copy for mailing and handling to Pinnacle Books, Dept. 17-436, 475 Park Avenue South, New York, N.Y. 10016. Residents of New York, New Jersey and Pennsylvania must include sales tax. DO NOT SEND CASH.

WAR
GOD

PATRICK F. ROGERS

PINNACLE BOOKS
WINDSOR PUBLISHING CORP.

To the officers and men of the 1st Australian SAS Regiment, the United States Army Rangers and the United States Army Special Forces, who will never get half the credit they deserve.

Most of the military units described in this book actually exist. Their organization, equipment, weapons, and strategic capabilities are described accurately. However, all the characters portrayed are fictional and any resemblance to any actual person living or dead is purely coincidental.

PINNACLE BOOKS

are published by

Windsor Publishing Corp.
475 Park Avenue South
New York, NY 10016

First printing: November, 1990

Printed in the United States of America

Chapter One

"Cosmos 2964 was placed in orbit on Thursday. The satellite is performing routine scientific observations in support of the Soviet space program. . . ." —*Tass*

Cosmos 2964, code named *War God*, was in orbit, a blunt cylinder weighing over fifty tons. Eight days before, it had roared up from Plesetsk on a pillar of white-hot fire. It was currently orbiting the earth once every ninety-two minutes. Now, two hundred miles above the earth's surface, it passed silently over North America.

American space surveillance radars noted its passing and flashed its orbital parameters to the North American Space Defense Surveillance computer. The computer crunched a few numbers and confirmed that *Cosmos 2964* was making another pass. No reason for alarm. In turn, *War God*'s attack warning sensors detected and classified the American radar. No need to take countermeasures; routine hostile surveillance only.

It was over Canada now, beginning to arch up over the North Pole at five miles per second. *War God*'s flight control computer confirmed that it was approaching the Soviet Union, passing over the coastline near Murmansk. At Plesetsk Cosmodrome, a powerful Soviet radar began tracking it, and a highly directional

1

radio antenna moved smoothly into position. *War God* could no longer be monitored from North America. It was time for the final test routine.

PLESETSK COSMODROME—PRIMARY CONTROL CENTER

Vladimir Sukhenkiy sat at his control console and sipped another cup of scalding-hot tea. Sukhenkiy was *War God*'s chief test conductor. His eyes were red rimmed, and he needed a shave. He had slept very little since the launch. All in all, things had been going very well these last eight days, perhaps too well. *War God* had performed perfectly so far, but Sukhenkiy believed devoutly in the oldest law of space flight taped to his console on a small card: "If It Can Go Wrong, It Will Go Wrong."

Sukhenkiy checked and rechecked his data displays. Everything was ready; there was no reason to delay. He lifted the red safety guard that protected the special button on his console which only he was authorized to push, the Initiate Attack button. He hesitated for a second or two. He was about to conduct a critical test. He might be ensuring peace for the next hundred years, or he might be starting World War III. It was a sobering thought. But, in for a kopeck, in for a ruble.

Sukhenkiy pushed the button on his control console, and the control center computer flashed a coded message into space. Aboard *War God,* the flight control computer ceased routine flight monitoring and responded to Plesetsk's commands.

—REPORT STATUS-
—ACKNOWLEDGED—ALL SYSTEMS OPERATIONAL-
—WEAPON SYSTEM STATUS?-
—CONFIRMED—WEAPON SYSTEM READY FOR COMBAT OPERATIONS-

The chief test conductor took a deep breath. *War God* had been amazingly successful so far, but this was the final test. The success or failure of the entire operation depended on what would happen next. There was nothing to be gained by waiting. Sukhenkiy reached out and pushed the second button. A second series of coded messages flashed into space.

—ARM WEAPON SYSTEM—PREPARE FOR FIRING-

—ACKNOWLEDGED—PREPARING WEAPON SYSTEM FOR FIRING-

—ATTACK TEST TARGETS 1 AND 2—ACKNOWLEDGE-

—ACKNOWLEDGED—PREPARING TO ATTACK TEST TARGETS 1 AND 2-

Sukhenkiy visualized a hatch opening smoothly at one end of *War God*'s blunt cylinder and the flight control computer aiming the laser at a point in space forty thousand miles away.

—TARGET ACQUIRED—WEAPON SYSTEM ARMED—REQUEST FINAL ATTACK AUTHORIZATION-

—ATTACK AUTHORIZED—DESTROY TARGETS 1 AND 2-

—ACKNOWLEDGED—ATTACKING-

—TARGETS 1 AND 2 DESTROYED-

Satisfied with the success of his mission, Sukhenkiy left the resumption of normal operation to his team and moved away from his monitor to celebrate.

EASTBIRD TWO

Eastbird Two was one of the key group of six U.S. satellites which formed the United States Threat Warning and Attack Assessment system. *Eastbird One* and *Eastbird Two* stared continuously at the Soviet Union, ready to transmit the first warning of a Russian attack

3

on the United States. Their sensitive infrared detectors would sense the immensely hot rocket exhausts of the Russian ICBMs as they roared out of their silos and streaked toward North America. Over the earth's oceans, the *Atlantic* and *Pacific Birds* maintained an unceasing watch for submarine-launched missiles. In the dangerous world of the 1990s, the security and continued existence of the United States might depend on how well those six satellites performed.

Eastbird Two was 22,300 miles above the earth's surface in a geosynchronous orbit. From the earth, it appeared to be standing still over a point on the equator, ceaselessly scanning the Eastern Hemisphere, reporting to its ground controllers any missile that flew from the Soviet Union. At the moment, little was happening.

Suddenly, an immensely powerful, pale blue beam reached *Eastbird Two.* To the billions of watts of perfectly focused radiation in that beam, *Eastbird Two's* reflective skin was completely transparent. *Eastbird Two's* electronics were destroyed almost instantly as wires shorted, transistors melted, and power supplies exploded. Blue-white sparks arced through the equipment modules. For five seconds, *War God's* primary laser beam blazed through its target. The last three seconds were overkill. *Eastbird Two* could not fall, but it was effectively dead.

There was one minor but vital exception. *Eastbird Two* was one of the latest models. It carried a small, heavily shielded module, an Attack Warning and Attack Characterization Sensor System. As *Eastbird Two* died, its AWACSS module survived for a fraction of a second and transmitted a short group of coded symbols. Then it, too, arced, shorted, and died. *Eastbird Two* hung in space, a useless piece of burned-out junk.

Forty thousand miles away, *War God's* lasers swung smoothly away from its third target and acquired *Pa-*

cific One. The pale blue beam blazed out again. *Pacific One* died like its twin and tumbled, burnt out and useless.

PLESETSK COSMODROME—PRIMARY CONTROL CENTER

—ATTACK ROUTINE CONDUCTED—TARGETS 3 AND 4 DESTROYED-

Svetlana Snastina was the weapons control engineer. She frowned at the message as it appeared on her control console display. Targets 3 and 4, what did that mean? Instantly, she hit the manual override button, commanding *War God*'s weapon system to go to the safe mode.

—WEAPON SYSTEM SAFE—SUBSYSTEM STATUS AS FOLLOWS-

A stream of coded symbols flashed down to Plesetsk. *War God* remained in perfect condition, ready, if ordered, to attack again. Without fanfare, *War God* resumed normal operations.

War God's controllers were not computers. Plesetsk Primary Control Center's calm scientific atmosphere exploded into cheers of glee and congratulations. Sukhenkiy was in danger of grave bodily harm as his team crowded around him, pounding him on the back and trying to shake his hand. Several bottles of vodka appeared from nowhere, and the control center echoed to toasts:

"Comrade Sukhenkiy!"

"Our team!"

And then with a roar that shook the center, *"War God!"*

It was against regulations, of course, but Sukhenkiy was not about to complain. They were the finest technical team in the Soviet Union. They had spent the last four years toiling on the project. Let them enjoy their celebration. Still, they were not quite finished with their tasks. They must bring *War God* back to earth, and any test conductor knows that reentry is always one of the most dangerous parts of any mission. Sukhenkiy pushed the Attention button, and a buzzer sounded. Instantly, the control center became quiet, and every face turned expectantly toward him.

Sukhenkiy was embarrassed. He dreaded any form of public speaking. Still, this was a historic occasion. He must say something. He lifted his battered teacup in a toast.

"Comrades. You have my respect and admiration for what you have accomplished. Today, we have given our beloved country the control of space. Soon, we will remove the threat of attacking nuclear missiles forever. I would also like to say that *War God* is not just the satellite in space. *War God* is also our team who designed and created it. I give you one final toast, *War God!*"

Cheers rang out again.

"Now, I must remind you that we are still on duty. Everyone to your test consoles. I want a status report on all systems in ten minutes. Commence reentry preparations. The time is now T-sixty minutes and counting."

"Excuse me, Comrade Chief Test Conductor, I have my system status now."

Sukhenkiy smiled. He knew that soft voice and formal style of address well. Svetlana Snastina was standing by his test console with a computer printout in her hands, peering earnestly at him through her thick glasses. A casual observer, looking at her slender figure and her blond braids, would have concluded that her function was to make the tea and take the minutes of the meetings. But Svetlana Snastina was the leading expert on high-frequency lasers in the Soviet Union. She had not created *War God*'s deadly laser single-handedly, but without her contributions it would not have existed. It was typical of Svetlana that she had checked her system status in the middle of a celebration.

Sukhenkiy was proud of her. He thought of her as one of his daughters, but he would never consider embarrassing her by speaking informally or affectionately while on duty.

"And what is our weapon system status?"

"Excellent, Comrade Chief Test Conductor. The power supply is stable. Main mirror temperature is 1.2 degrees higher than predicted but well within safety margin. We could fire again immediately if there were more authorized targets."

She sighed wistfully. Svetlana loved to fire her laser. She would cheerfully have destroyed every American satellite in space if only they would let her.

"However, there is one unusual factor. Telemetry indicates that the laser fired four times, not twice. It appeared that it was going to fire again. Therefore, I used manual override and shut it down. I have run diagnostics, but there are no abnormal indications. No further analysis is possible until *War God* has returned to earth. Therefore, I have secured for reentry."

Sukhenkiy relaxed. Nothing was wrong with the laser. An error in the command software, perhaps, but nothing serious. Sukhenkiy sensed her disappointment. There was really nothing more for Svetlana to do until *War God* returned to earth. Sukhenkiy smiled at her.

"Stay here with me, Svetlana. Watch what I do. When I am retired and resting my tired old bones, you will be the chief test conductor."

Svetlana beamed. If you told her she was brilliant, she would have nodded. She knew that. If you told her she was pretty, she would have blushed. She was not

7

sure of that. But if you told her that some day she would sit in Sukhenkiy's place, she would be your friend for life.

Eagerly, she watched as the lights on Sukhenkiy's console turned green. All subsystems were ready. It was time to bring *War God* back to earth. Sukhenkiy took a deep breath and pushed the Execute button. The coded command flashed up from Plesetsk. His instruments told him that *War God* was responding perfectly.

WAR GOD

War God rotated smoothly, end over end, until the main rocket engine pointed forward along the line of flight. The main propellant valves opened and monomethylhydrazine and nitrogen tetroxide flowed into the combustion chamber. They burst into flame on contact, and the engine roared into life. A white-hot lance of flame shot out, and *War God*'s velocity began to slow. Two minutes of firing, and *War God* would no longer stay in orbit but would reenter and land in the Soviet Union. At Plesetsk, the test team congratulated themselves. Everything was going according to plan.

Unseen and undetected, a handful of tiny objects flashed toward *War God*. They were small, inert pieces of metal, fragments of a long-forgotten American satellite. None of them weighed more than a few ounces. They appeared to be harmless pieces of space debris, but they were moving toward *War God* at ten miles per second. They were far too tiny for *War God*'s sensors to detect.

Their velocity made them incredibly lethal. One struck *War God*'s main communications antennas and tore them away. Another pierced the forward propellant tanks. Instantly, *War God*'s forward equipment bay was filled with fire and smoke as the propellants burst into flame on contact. *War God* vibrated as a high-pressure nitrogen tank exploded. The attitude control system failed, and *War God* began to tumble end over end, trailing great gouts of orange flame and greenish gray smoke. War God was out of control, helpless, burning and exploding.

But *War God*'s flight control computer was intact. Calmly and efficiently, it began to execute its emergency routines. It activated *War God*'s fire-extinguishing system, and high-pressure inert gases shot into the forward equipment bay and the fire went out.

War God's accelerometers told it that it was tumbling. Something seemed to be wrong with attitude control. Calmly, the flight control computer overrode and assumed control. At either end of *War God,* the auxiliary thrusters began to fire in short, precisely timed bursts. *War God*'s rotation began to slow.

The computer made a few quick calculations. Rotational torque would be zeroed out in approximately six minutes, plus or minus twenty-two seconds. To a computer, six minutes is an eternity. While the thrusters fired, the computer checked and rechecked *War God*'s status and its options.

—COULD ORBIT BE MAINTAINED?-

—NO—INSUFFICIENT VELOCITY—ORBIT DECAYING-

—COULD THE MAIN ENGINE REGAIN ORBITAL VELOCITY?-

—NO—INSUFFICIENT PROPELLANT REMAINING—MAIN ENGINE STATUS UNCERTAIN-

—OPTIONS?-

—NONE—REENTRY IS MANDATORY-

—SET EMERGENCY REENTRY MODE—REPORT SUBSYSTEM STATUS-

Data poured in. The flight control computer made a few quick calculations.

—PROBABILITY OF SUCCESSFUL REENTRY 78 PERCENT PLUS OR MINUS 10 PERCENT-

It waited until *War God*'s tumbling stopped and activated *War God*'s space-to-ground communications link.

—PLESETSK—*WAR GOD*—EMERGENCY—ACKNOWLEDGE-

There was no reply. *War God* transmitted the same message again and again. The flight control computer calculated.

—PROBABILITY OF SEVERE COMMUNICATIONS SYSTEM DAMAGE 99.9 PERCENT—COMMUNICATIONS WITH GROUND IMPROBABLE-

No help from Plesetsk. *War God* was on its own. The computer made its decision.

—PROPULSION—EXECUTE FINAL DEORBIT BURN-

The propellant valves opened, and the main engine roared back to life. The propulsion system computer sounded the alarm.

—ENGINE FIRING—FULL THRUST ACHIEVED—FUEL PUMP BEARINGS OVERHEATING—RECOMMEND IMMEDIATE SHUT DOWN-

—NEGATIVE—OVERRIDE—CONTINUE FIRING-

For another minute, the main engine continued to fire, blasting a steady stream of yellow white fire. Second by second, *War God*'s velocity dropped, and the huge satellite began to slant downward in a shallow dive toward the atmosphere below. *War God* was passing over China now, but the computer neither knew nor cared. All that mattered now was speed, timing, and the angle of reentry. The radar altimeter clicked on and began to report steadily.

—800,000—500,000—400,000-

At 400,000 feet *War God* began to encounter the upper fringes of the atmosphere. There were only a few molecules per cubic inch, but *War God* was moving at twelve thousand miles per hour. It was like slamming into a solid wall. *War God*'s structure began to creak and groan as the reentry stresses went up and up. *War God*'s heat shield began to glow red, orange, yellow, hotter and hotter, as superheated air flowed over *War God*'s hull.

—100,000—90,000—80,000-

The force of the passing air tore at *War God* like a giant hand. The holes and rents in *War God*'s skin generated standing shock waves. The unplanned loads threatened to tear *War God* apart or send it tumbling through the air out of control, but Sukhenkiy and his team had designed it well. *War God*'s structure held, and doggedly, determinedly, the flight control computer maintained control and fought *War God* down.

Now, *War God* was moving through the air at Mach 4, crawling along at a mere three thousand miles per hour. The flight control computer activated its radar and looked ahead. Water, a broad ocean area, stretched ahead. Here and there, the radar return indicated a few scattered islands, one significantly larger than the others.

—LANDING IMMINENT—SELECT LAND OR WATER LANDING SITE-

The computer made its final choice.

—HOLES IN OUTER STRUCTURE—WATER LANDING REJECTED—PREPARE FOR LAND TOUCHDOWN—EXECUTE-

At the aft end of the huge cylinder, hatches opened and giant orange-and-white parachutes deployed. *War God*'s forward movement stopped, and it swung at the end of its parachute shrouds like a giant pendulum. Touchdown! *War God* skidded along flat ground for two hundred feet and slid to a stop. The flight control computer issued one last order.

—DOWN AND SAFE—STANDING BY FOR RECOVERY—ALL SYSTEMS TO SHUTDOWN MODE—EXECUTE-

On *War God*'s upper side, a small transmitter began to send a short coded message into space over and over again.

—*WAR GOD* HERE—*WAR GOD* HERE—*WAR GOD* HERE-

A Soviet electronic surveillance satellite picked up the message and relayed it to Plesetsk. Seconds later, a passing American signal intelligence satellite recorded the message and flashed it to Fort George G. Meade, Maryland. *War God* was alone, but it would not be alone for long.

Chapter Two

"Therefore, leaders who understand strategy preside over the destiny of the people."
—Sun Tzu, *The Art of War*

ELU ISLAND—THE PLATEAU

Jack Cord sat in his old Land Rover, waiting for the sun to rise. Elu was, as Cord liked to say, "a thousand miles from nowhere." Entertainment was limited. Cord was often reduced to appreciating the wonders of nature. On Elu, these included sunrises and sunsets, and Miriam Foster. Miriam worked at the island's mission. Unfortunately, all Cord's blandishments had not lured her out of bed for a ride up the plateau road in the dark.

Cord took out his field glasses and looked around. He was about nine hundred feet above sea level. Dawn was near, but it was still dark. Far below, he could see the lights of the mission station and a few soft waves breaking on the beach. Idly, he scanned the horizon. There was really nothing to see but—. Suddenly, Cord stiffened. A bright yellow light had appeared in the darkness to the west. It was moving, growing brighter and brighter, slanting down across the sky, coming closer and closer. By God, it was coming straight at him!

Cord steadied his glasses. The thing seemed to dance in the field of view as he tried to follow its motion. He could see a glowing disc growing larger second by second as the thing flashed down from the sky. What was it? An airplane? No, planes don't look like that. A missile? Who would be crazy enough to fire a missile at Elu? There was nothing here worth blowing up.

Cord watched awestruck. He could see the thing with his naked eye now, huge and glowing, a great cylinder swooping down from the sky. Now, something shot out of the back of the cylinder and expanded rapidly. Parachutes! The damned thing was really going to land on Elu.

The parachutes were slowing it down rapidly. For a second, Cord thought it was going to go on over the edge of the plateau. Then, it touched down and skidded along the ground, crashing to a stop at the edge of a grove of trees.

It lay there on its side, emitting puffs of some strange vapor, cooling rapidly. Cord stared at the huge cylinder. The sun was rising now. Using his field glasses, Cord scanned the thing inch by inch. It was not like anything he had ever seen before; there were no wings, no sign of a cockpit or doors, and there was no indication of national markings or registration numbers. Cord watched for ten minutes. Nothing happened. The thing just lay there. It reminded Cord of a beached whale.

Well, duty called. Cord wore two hats on Elu. He was the local manager and caretaker for International Mines and Minerals, but he also had a second, secret job. He was a coast watcher for the Royal Australian Navy. He was supposed to report any unusual sea or air traffic around Elu to RAN Intelligence. Whatever this thing was, it was clearly something he must report.

14

He started the Land Rover and drove slowly toward the unknown cylinder's landing site. He stopped a hundred yards away and moved carefully forward on foot. Cord was uneasy. Suppose the damned thing was manned? He was armed, of course. His big 9mm Browning was in its holster at his side. After eight years in the Australian army's elite regiment, the SAS, Cord seldom went anywhere without a gun. But no one had ever briefed him on what to do in a situation like this. Suppose there were foreign astronauts inside. Should he arrest them or offer them some beer?

Slowly, cautiously, Cord moved in until he was two feet from the side of the cylinder. There were holes in the side. Cord unclipped his flashlight from his belt and peered inside through each hole he could reach. The inside of the thing was full of complex machinery, black boxes, metal spheres, electrical cables, and other things he could not identify. There was no one on board, and no place any crewman could have sat inside. All right, an unmanned space vehicle. A satellite. But whose satellite? And what was it doing on Elu?

The sun was up now. In the clear morning light, Cord could see what must have been access panels in the sides of the cylinder. He considered trying to open one and get a better look inside. There was a strange chemical smell in the air and an occasional crackling noise, like an electrical short circuit. No, he was not going to go inside. Let the government send some people who understand such things. Cord was paid to observe and report, not play around with space rockets. He went back to the Land Rover and drove toward the cave where his radio was hidden. Let RAN Intelligence figure out what to do next.

THE CRISIS CENTER—MOSCOW, USSR

The atmosphere in the crisis center seethed with tension. Vladimir Sukhenkiy had been speaking for two hours. Now, he was answering questions from the men seated around the long oval table. Svetlana Snastina sat in a row of chairs against the wall. She was proud of her chief. He had handled things extremely well, deflecting insinuations and accusations skillfully. But some of the questions! Svetlana was appalled. She knew the world was not perfect. Her mother had told her that most men are beasts. Her father had quietly taught her that not everything the Party said was true. But nothing had prepared her for the obvious fact that some of the most senior authorities of the Soviet Union were technically illiterate.

The questions ended. All eyes turned to the short, balding man who sat at the head of the table. He did not look important, but he radiated authority. He spoke quietly.

"Thank you, Comrade Sukhenkiy. Your presentation was complete and comprehensive. Comrades, we now have all the available facts. In an hour, I must brief the highest authorities. We must summarize what we know and recommend a course of action."

He paused and looked steadily around the table.

"Before I do this, I wish to say something to you all. I do not wish to hear any more childish bickering between organizations. This is not a KGB crisis or a GRU crisis, not a military crisis or a scientific crisis. It is a national crisis, one which conceivably could lead to war with the United States. We must act together as a team. Anyone who does not see this has no place in this room or in any position of authority in the Soviet Union. Do I make myself absolutely clear?"

There was total silence.

"Very well, comrades. I am happy to see that we are

16

in agreement. I shall proceed. First, we have established that the building and testing of *War God* were approved by the highest authorities. Second, the launch and testing were carried out with great success. Third, during the final test, the laser was fired and destroyed two Soviet test targets. Fourth, immediately thereafter, for reasons as yet unknown, the satellite attacked and destroyed two critical American warning satellites. It probably would have destroyed others except for the prompt actions of Comrade Sukhenkiy and his team. Shortly thereafter, the satellite was ordered to return to earth. There was some malfunction. It did not land in the Soviet Union as planned. It is on this island called Elu in the South Pacific. The island is under Australian control, but there are no Australian government facilities there. These are the facts. Are we agreed?"

Heads nodded around the table. He was not surprised. He was used to agreement.

"Very well. This leaves one critical question. Do the Americans know what has happened? General Galanskov, your opinion?"

Colonel-General Galanskov rose smoothly to his feet. He was an impressive figure in his uniform, with three stars gleaming on his shoulder boards and four rows of ribbons across his chest. His reputation was even more impressive. He was one of the highest ranking officers in the Directorate of Military Intelligence, the GRU.

Galanskov spoke precisely, choosing each word with great care.

"Certainly, they are aware that their satellites were attacked. Two identical satellites do not fail in two minutes from natural causes. And they know we did it, no one else has the capability. But I do not think they know *how* we did it. *War God*'s technology is very advanced. I do not believe they have anything like it. It is impossible to say what they know about *War God*, or if they will connect *War God*'s flight with the destruction of their satellites."

Galanskov paused and looked at the chairman.

"Very well, General, what are your recommendations?"

"We must assume the worst. *War God* contains revolutionary technology. It must not be allowed to fall into foreign hands. We must assume that the Americans know that *War God* destroyed their satellites and that they tracked its reentry. If this is so, they will attempt to seize the satellite. This must be prevented at all costs."

Galanskov glanced around the table. He saw no signs of disagreement, even from the detested officers of the KGB.

"My recommendations are as follows. Immediately, send personnel to Elu to secure *War God.* Allow no one else access to the satellite. Send naval units to the island and recover it if possible. If not, destroy the satellite. Destroy it utterly. Leave no evidence that *War God* ever existed. Do this as covertly as possible. Take action now!"

There was a murmur of approval as Galanskov sat down. The chairman glanced at his watch.

"Thank you, General. Now, I must be in the Kremlin in thirty minutes. There is little time for more discussion. Does anyone disagree with General Galanskov's assessment or recommendations?"

He looked slowly around the table. The KGB representatives looked unhappy. It was annoying to be upstaged by the GRU, but no one spoke.

"Very well. I will now go and brief the Defense Council. I will return in three hours with their decision. In the meantime, assume that General Galanskov's recommendations will be approved. Prepare for action. Alert units, ships, and aircraft. Move them toward the island.

Do not go beyond the point of recall until I return. Begin immediately. This meeting is adjourned."

ELU ISLAND—THE PLATEAU

Cord finished writing his message. He read it slowly and carefully again. Cord was convinced that what he had seen was important. He did not want to sound drunk or crazy. Australian folklore is full of tales of men who went spectacularly crazy on remote Pacific islands. He did not want his name added to that list. He changed a word or two and nodded. That was what he had seen. It was beyond him to say what it meant. Let the boffins in Canberra figure it out. That's what they were paid for.

Cord hit the starter on his emergency generator. For once, the damned thing started smoothly, coming on line with a hum of power. He turned on the radio and began to type in his message. He was not sending yet, the message was being stored in the memory of the minicomputer that ran the machine. Cord was a one-finger typist. After several minutes of hunting and pecking, the message was entered. Cord read the small, glowing, green letters on the display screen:

From: CW-44-Elu Island
To: Central Watch Officer
Priority: MOST URGENT—TRIPLE SEND
1. Large, unidentified space vehicle landed on Elu Island approximately 0545 hours today.
2. Vehicle approximately 4 meters in diameter and 12 meters long. It landed by using jets and large parachutes.
3. Vehicle appears to have suffered some damage during landing but is basically intact.
4. Have examined vehicle from outside and through holes in skin. No indications vehicle was

19

manned. Interior full of machinery and electrical equipment. There are no national markings or insignia.

5. Have not attempted to enter vehicle. Will continue to observe.

6. Request instructions immediately.

CW-44 (Cord) Elu

Good enough. Cord set the cipher dials carefully. It would not do to send in the wrong code. Satisfied, he pushed the send button. The computer transformed Cord's message into a jumble of meaningless symbols and transmitted it instantaneously. Two seconds later, it repeated the message twice and then switched to the guard-channel-and-receive mode.

Cord nodded to himself. All right, it was done. Now to settle down and wait for an answer.

THE CRISIS CENTER—MOSCOW, USSR

The buzz of conversation stopped as the chairman reentered the room and quietly sat down at the head of the table. Everyone looked at him expectantly. He reached inside his briefcase and took out a single sheet of paper.

"Comrades, I briefed the Defense Council. Our recommendations are accepted. Here is the authorizing directive. Now, I would like to hear your plans. But first, I have been gone for three hours. Is there any new information?"

Instantly, General Galanskov was on his feet.

"Yes, comrade. Our investigating team has discovered the cause of the incident. Captain-Engineer Cherenavin has just arrived from Plesetsk. With your permission, he will brief us now."

The chairman nodded.

"Proceed, Captain. What was the cause of the malfunction?"

Captain Cherenavin hesitated. He was a brilliant technical officer, but he was not used to briefing high-level party officials. He cleared his throat and began quietly.

"Comrade, with all respect, there was no failure or malfunction. *War God* functioned perfectly, exactly as directed by the flight control computer software."

The chairman frowned.

"Perfectly, Captain Cherenavin? Then, how do you account for the attack on the American satellites. Is that your concept of perfection?"

The captain flinched. He did like the look in the chairman's eyes. Still, he knew he was right.

"No, comrade, I do not mean that. Let me explain. In accordance with General Galanskov's instructions, I headed the software section of the technical investigation team. We have examined all the software involved in aiming and firing *War God*'s laser weapon. We—"

He paused and glanced around the table. Not everyone understood him completely, but no one was going to admit it. At least, the chairman was nodding in agreement.

"We have discovered a secret, unauthorized addition to *War God*'s fire control software. It directed *War God* to attack the American satellites, and it did so. There was no malfunction. *War God* did exactly as it was directed."

The chairman lost his icy calm. He was livid.

"What? How can this be? Surely, such things are carefully checked before a satellite is launched?"

"Comrade, the people who did this were very clever. This unauthorized software is activated only after the satellite experiences zero gravity in space. Unless you

21

know special passwords, it does not reveal itself in a ground test. If we had not been looking for something like this, we would never have found it."

"Who could have done this?"

Captain Cherenavin looked unhappy. He was a computer expert, not a security officer. Still, it was a direct question.

"It could only have been done by members of the *War God* team, specifically by senior members of the software programming and verification group."

"Sabotage! But why was it done? Who penetrated our most secret project?"

General Galanskov was instantly on his feet.

"Allow me to answer that question, comrade. The *War God* software group is headed by Comrade Vatsestis. He has six principal assistants, all citizens of the Soviet Baltic republics. Vatsestis himself is a Latvian. The others are Latvians, Lithuanians, and Estonians. They are men who want our Baltic republics to become independent nations. Fanatics. They will stop at nothing to achieve their aims. They have done this to damage the Soviet Union, perhaps in the hope that war with the United States will result and, somehow, the Baltic republics will become independent."

"Are you certain of this?"

"Yes, Comrade Vatsestis is attending a scientific conference in Rome. An hour ago he defected and requested political asylum. He issued a long statement denouncing Soviet tyranny and demanding freedom for Latvia, Lithuania, and Estonia. He was the head of the conspiracy. There can be no doubt. We have a video of his conference recorded from Italian television and relayed via satellite from our embassy in Rome."

Galanskov pushed a button. The room darkened, and the image of Professor Vatsestis appeared on the screen. He was a distinguished, older man, with curly gray hair.

He peered through steel-rimmed glasses and spoke earnestly into the camera.

"I will be accused of treason by the corrupt masters of the Russian government, but I am not a Russian. I am a Latvian! The Baltic republics have never been Russian. They were occupied and enslaved by Stalin in 1939 after he made a shameful agreement with Adolph Hitler. The present Russian government has refused to honor the promises made during the Gorbachev regime. I have chosen to flee to the West to expose their corrupt behavior. The Baltic republics must be free.

"I have also come to warn the West that the Soviet Union is developing advanced new weapons to seize control of space and dominate the earth. They are—"

The chairman slammed his fist against the table. "Enough! Shut that traitor off, Galanskov. This is treason! Treason! How did these traitors gain access to the *War God* project? Who authorized it?"

"All were cleared for the highest technical access level by the KGB," Galanskov said.

The senior KGB officer leaped to his feet.

"Cleared as individuals, not as a group! Their assignment to *War God* is clearly the responsibility of the GRU. They approved—"

Suddenly, the chairman stood up.

"Be silent! I will have no more of this. Sit down, both of you!"

They sat down. Galanskov resisted the temptation to sneer at the KGB officers. Let's see you wriggle your way out of this, comrades!

The chairman spoke in a voice filled with quiet menace.

"Very well, now we know what happened, treason and sabotage. Rest assured there will be a thorough investigation. The guilty will be found and punished. If anyone is guilty of negligence he will be dealt with severely. Do not doubt it."

No one did. He continued: "Now, I asked you to prepare plans and recommendations. What do you propose?"

The KGB director was on his feet in an instant.

"We have taken positive action, comrade. A KGB paramilitary team has been formed from our embassy personnel in Australia. They are in the air flying to Elu now. They will arrive in approximately eight hours."

The chairman stared at him coldly.

"I gave strict orders that no action was to be taken without my explicit approval."

"Exactly so, comrade. Your orders have been precisely carried out. The team is in flight, but for the next three hours they can be recalled if you so order. After that, they will not have enough fuel remaining to return. If they continue, they will be almost out of fuel when they reach Elu. However, they can land and secure the satellite until naval units arrive. The final decision is yours."

The chairman smiled.

"Excellent, a clever plan. You have done well. Order them to proceed."

Galanskov seethed. Paramilitary operations were the responsibility of the GRU, not the KGB. However, it did not seem to be the right time or place to say so.

The chairman went on without waiting for comments. "Now, what are the locations of our Pacific Fleet units?"

Chapter Three

"There is a time for the use of weapons."
    —Miyamoto Musashi, *A Book of Five Rings*

THE CRISIS CENTER—THE PENTAGON—
WASHINGTON, D.C.
The guards finished the ID check. Jim Brand followed the assistant secretary of defense into the crisis center. He scanned the room with the automatic, practiced stare of a man who has been an infantryman for twenty-five years. His feeling of uneasiness grew stronger. He had never seen so many stars in one room before. Lieutenant generals, major generals, and admirals seemed to be everywhere. As a brigadier general in the U.S. Army, Brand was used to attracting a little attention. In this group, he was totally outclassed. He wondered again why he was here. Maybe they needed someone to make coffee.

The civilians who sat at the long table did not appear to be impressed. They all wore expensive suits and ties and radiated assurance. Brand knew the civilian who sat at the head of the table. He had never met him, but he had seen him on television. He was the president's national security adviser. That did nothing to calm Brand's nerves.

The assistant secretary took a seat at the table. Brand slipped into a chair against the wall and tried to look inconspicuous.

A tall civilian in a tweed sport coat stepped up to the speaker's console.

"Gentlemen, I'm John Oliver, chairman of the technical assessment team. We have completed our analysis. For the benefit of those who did not attend the initial meeting, I will summarize the situation.

"Approximately eleven hours ago, two of our six Early Bird warning satellites were attacked and destroyed. Perhaps destroyed is not the proper word. Physically, the two satellites still exist, but they are totally nonoperational.

"The possibility of natural causes has been considered and rejected. Both satellites failed in an identical manner within ninety seconds. No other U.S. satellites were affected. We have been analyzing all available data intensively to determine the type of attack and its origin." He paused. "Are there any questions, gentlemen?"

There were none. Everyone waited for him to drop the other shoe.

"All right. Fortunately, one of the satellites carried a new Attack Warning and Attack Characterization Sensor System. The AWACSS data indicate that *Eastbird Two* was attacked by an immensely powerful beam of coherent gamma radiation. The radiation intensity levels detected were equivalent to that generated by a twenty-megaton thermonuclear weapon detonated within ten miles of the satellite."

The air force lieutenant general slammed his fist on the table. "Jesus Christ, are you saying the Russians used hydrogen bombs against our satellites? That's an act of war!"

Oliver smiled with the tolerant air of one who must explain great mysteries to the ignorant.

"Of course not, General. I merely said the radiation levels were equivalent. But, gentlemen, it might have been better if they had."

A murmur of disbelief ran round the table.

The national security adviser frowned. Scientists are extremely useful people, but there are times when they are very annoying.

"Dr. Oliver, please summarize your findings. Quickly, please, time is short."

"Yes, sir. The team concludes that our satellites were destroyed by a directed-energy weapon operating at gamma ray frequencies. Analysis of satellite orbits and the angles of attack indicate that the weapon was onboard an orbiting Soviet satellite, *Cosmos 2964*.

"Immediately after the attack, the satellite reentered and returned to earth. There appears to have been a malfunction. It landed on Elu Island, an Australian trust territory in the Southwest Pacific. We know it came down intact. We have monitored recovery beacon transmissions."

"Doctor, you said it would have been better if the Russians had used nuclear weapons. Just what did you mean by that?" the national security adviser asked.

"We understand nuclear weapons. We have them. We could use them now if we had to. We don't understand this. In theory, a gamma ray laser is possible, but we don't know how to build one. It's not just another laser. It operates at much higher frequencies than anything we've tested. And they must have something entirely new for their power supply. Not even a large nuclear reactor could deliver power like that. They must have achieved a major technical breakthrough. There's no way to shield a satellite or a missile against those frequencies and that power level. If they had a dozen of these weapons in orbit, they would control space. They could knock out every satellite we have and destroy any missiles we launch."

"Thank you, Doctor. Do you have any recommendations?"

"Sir, we must get the technology on that satellite. Ideally, we should bring the satellite here to the United States for study. At a bare minimum, our experts must examine the key components in detail. If we don't, I am not exaggerating, the security of the United States will be threatened."

"Thank you, Doctor. Is the Intelligence Committee assessment ready?"

An air force major general moved quickly to the speaker's console.

"Yes, sir. The CIA, NSA, and the DIA have been analyzing the situation. All national surveillance assets have been monitoring activity in the Soviet Union. We don't understand what we see. Their actions just don't make any sense. Knocking out two Early Bird satellites does not destroy our early warning capability. The remaining four provide adequate coverage. If they intended to attack us, they would have taken out all six.

"Also, there are no signs of preparations for an attack. Their strategic rocket forces are not on a high-alert state. All detectable military activities are routine. We can see no rational purpose for this attack. All they have done is alert us to the fact that they have an advanced new weapon. It just doesn't make sense."

"Anything else, General?"

"Yes, sir. We concur totally with the recommendations of the technical assessment team. The United States must get that satellite. The survival of the United States may be at stake."

"I concur. I am ready to recommend to the president that we seize the satellite. Is there any disagreement?"

A distinguished-looking man in an expensive gray suit spoke immediately.

"John Marston, State Department. Gentlemen, I can hardly believe what I hear. Are you really going to recommend to the president that U.S. forces attempt to seize a Soviet space vehicle from Australian territory?"

The national security adviser smiled bleakly. "Yes. There is no viable alternative."

"But, surely, there must be some alternative. Can't we contact the Russians? Discuss what has happened? Perhaps there was some mistake, some kind of mechanical malfunction. What you propose could create a grave crisis with the Soviet Union. It could lead to war. I must strongly recommend that there be no military or paramilitary action."

"I have considered that. But there already is a serious crisis with the Soviet Union. The technology demonstrated by this satellite threatens to upset the balance of power. Our actions will be as covert as possible. We will try to prevent an all-out confrontation, but we must have the technology on that satellite. The security of the United States *is* at stake. Are there any other comments?"

No one spoke.

"All right, gentlemen. I am going to call the president on the secure phone. I will recommend covert military action to seize the satellite. While I am gone, start your contingency planning."

He pointed at Jim Brand's boss.

"I believe most of you know Chuck Martin. He is the assistant secretary of defense for special operations and low intensity conflict. Secretary Martin will coordinate the operation. All branches of the armed services

29

and all government agencies will give him complete co-operation."

Jim Brand no longer wondered why he was there. The assistant secretary might be going to coordinate, but it was going to be up to Brand to come up with the plan. They were handing him the hot potato, or maybe it was the live hand grenade.

He stared at the huge map on the wall. A yellow flag marked Elu. The damned island was a long way from any U.S. base. He began to check off what he had available in the Pacific—Special Forces Teams, Rangers, SEALs, Marine Force Recon.

Brand hardly noticed when the national security adviser left the room. His mind was concentrated on what he had to do. How could he move men and equipment to Elu? What help could he get from the navy? Could the air force—?"

Suddenly, there was absolute silence as the national security adviser came back. He did not waste time on speeches.

"All right, gentlemen. The president says go. Let's get moving, we're going in."

ELU ISLAND—THE PLATEAU

It was hot and humid in the cave. Cord was almost asleep when his radio emitted a soft chime. He stared at the screen. The receive/decoding light was on. Fascinated, he watched the display as the first lines of decoded text came up on the screen as the radio's computer decoded the message.

From: Central Watch Officer
To: CW-44 Elu Island
Priority: MOST URGENT
1. Your message regarding landing of unidentified space vehicle on Elu received and acknowledged.

2. You are hereby directed to secure the vehicle and hold it until Australian Government Personnel arrive to investigate.

3. Allow no other persons access to the vehicle. Allow no components of the vehicle to be removed from Elu. You are authorized to use force to prevent this if necessary.

4. HMAS *Darwin* is en route to Elu. Captain Crossman will assume command upon arrival Elu.

5. You are hereby recalled to active duty with 1st Australian Special Air Service Regiment with rank of Sergeant. Pay and allowances commence as of this date.

6. These orders are to be carried out at all costs. National Security is at stake.

> [Good luck, Cord.]
> —Central Watch Officer

Cord read the message again. It was clear enough what they wanted him to do. It was not clear how he was to do it. Just who was coming to Elu? Other Australians? The Russians? How would they come, and how many? Suppose the whole U.S. Pacific Fleet sailed up and landed a brigade of marines?

Cord would be glad when HMAS *Darwin* arrived and Captain Crossman could do the worrying. In the meantime, the military might of Australia on Elu consisted of Sergeant John H. Cord, Number 2 Squadron, Australian SAS. He was back on active duty, with an independent command. What more could he ask for?

Cord opened a footlocker, and took out his government issue weapon, an Owen gun. It was deceptively light and looked like a child's fragile toy. Actually, it was one of the deadliest submachine guns ever made, reliable, accurate, and lethal. If it came to a fight at close quarters, there was no better weapon. Cord also had his own personal weapons, his rifle and his pistol.

Perhaps he was being paranoid. Probably, nothing was going to happen. But Cord was an old soldier. He did not like the words in the next to the last sentence, "at all costs." When the Brass start to talk like that, life is likely to get grim and nasty for sergeants. He took out the spare magazines for the Owen gun and began to fill them with 9-mm cartridges.

EN ROUTE TO ELU ISLAND

Barsukov sat in the Grumman Albatross's copilot's seat trying to stay awake. It was hard to do. They had been in flight for over ten hours, and the steady roar of the engines was hypnotic. Barsukov was the team commander, but at the moment there was nothing for him to do but worry. He was not a pilot and knew very little about airplanes.

Linkin was flying. He knew that Linkin was a dependable man and a good pilot. Linkin had better be good. They were long past the point of no return. If they missed the island, they were going down in the largest ocean in the world in an area where few ships ever went. Barsukov did not like that thought. Still, all he could do was depend on Linkin.

He glanced back into the cabin. His eight men seemed to be sleeping in their seats. Good. They might need all the rest they could get. He looked at the ninth person in the cabin. Irina Yakoleva was asleep in her seat. As usual, she was making a shameless spectacle of herself in her tight T-shirt and faded jeans.

Barsukov did not like Irina Yakoleva. He was one of those Russians with a deep puritanical streak, and he found her behavior disgusting. She paraded around in decadent Western clothes, had love affairs, and drank too much. Only off duty, to be fair, but Barsukov had heard that her consumption of vodka was remarkable. Worst of all, she was not a member of the KGB, but an officer of the detested GRU.

Barsukov wished she were not on the mission, but she was the only qualified medical technician he could get. It would be reckless to go on this type of mission without a medic, and Barsukov was not a reckless man. Well, he would keep an eye on The Yakoleva. If she stepped out of line, he would—

Suddenly, Linkin was shaking his shoulder and pointing ahead. Yes, there ahead, on the horizon, was a dark speck, an island.

Barsukov took out his field glasses and scanned the island as the Grumman flew closer. He felt a surge of relief. It looked like the pictures he had been shown at the briefing. The northern half of the island was a broad, flat plateau eight or nine hundred feet above sea level. The southern half was flat, and low lying, mostly covered with tropical rain forest. There should be a small harbor near the southern tip. Yes, there it was. There could not be two islands like that. It must be Elu.

He clapped Linkin on the shoulder and motioned to circle the island and make a low pass over the plateau. Linkin looked at his fuel gauge and nodded. They were approaching Elu from the west. Linkin throttled back the engines and started a slow, low pass over the plateau.

Barsukov scanned the plateau eagerly. Yes, there it was, a huge silver gray cylinder lying on its side near the southern edge of the plateau. *War God.* Barsukov scanned the rest of the plateau. He saw a man and a woman in a jeep. The man was carrying a hunting rifle.

He motioned toward the harbor. Linkin nodded and pulled the Grumman into a final approach. The water was smooth and calm. Linkin's landing was perfect. The seaplane settled down into the water, and Linkin began

33

to taxi toward the harbor. Barsukov sighed with relief. The KGB team had arrived at Elu.

ELU ISLAND—THE PLATEAU

Cord was talking to Miriam Foster. Cord liked to talk to Miriam. She was an attractive young woman, with long, dark, curly hair and a splendid figure. Since she was the only white woman on Elu, Cord found her irresistible. So far, unfortunately, Miriam had not found Cord to be irresistible. He'd have to work on that.

Miriam had driven up the plateau in her jeep. Father Paul had sent Miriam up to the plateau to find Cord and see if he knew anything about the strange thing which had come down from the sky.

"I was asleep when it happened, but Brother Edward saw it. He said a great glowing light came down from the sky and seemed to land on the plateau. It scared our parishioners to death. They've run away into the bush, muttering about evil spirits and taboos. Some of them say it's a sign from the gods that something terrible is about to happen. You know how talk like that upsets Father Paul."

Cord smiled. He thought that Father Paul was a good man, but quite a lot of things upset him, including Cord's sinful and worldly ways. However, Cord was ready to help. It was certainly an excellent chance to impress Miriam.

"It's nothing much. Just a large satellite that came back down from space and landed here. I looked it over. There's no danger. It's all taken care of. I reported it to Canberra. Would you like to see it?"

"Oh, yes, Jack, please."

Cord was not surprised. This was the only exciting thing to happen on Elu in a long time. Naturally, Miriam wanted to see it. They drove to the satellite in

Miriam's jeep. Cord happily pointed out the parachutes and the rocket nozzles and let Miriam peer inside through the holes in the skin. Cord really knew very little about *War God,* but Miriam knew nothing at all, and he impressed Miriam with his sophistication and vast technical knowledge.

They were about to start back when Cord heard airplane engines. For a moment, he could not believe it. There was no airfield on Elu. Planes never flew there. But the sound persisted, and Miriam heard it, too. Cord did not hesitate. With the caution that had kept him alive through eight years in the SAS, he started the jeep's engine and drove under the trees. He did not like it. It was too much of a bloody coincidence. First the satellite, and now a plane. The two must be connected.

Cord looked at the plane through his field glasses. It was a seaplane, some kind of Grumman, he guessed. No military insignia, only civilian registration numbers. The plane came lower and lower and made a slow, low pass over the plateau. Probably looking at the satellite, Cord would have bet a month's pay on that. Now, it was circling out to sea and losing altitude steadily.

Cord moved carefully to the edge of the plateau. Miriam followed him, a few feet behind. They were about a mile east of the road. There, a projecting finger of the plateau towered over the harbor and the small cluster of buildings that formed the village.

He calculated the angle to the sun carefully. He did not want a reflective flash from the lenses of his glasses to give him away. Cord intended to see but not be seen. Satisfied, he brought up the 20-power naval glasses and scanned the harbor area.

The Grumman seaplane was tied up at the pier. No one seemed to be on board. Well, there was really only one place for anyone to go. Cord looked at the mission. Yes, there they were, a group of about ten men. They were talking to Father Paul and Brother Edward. Father Paul seemed to be angry. It looked as if he was blocking the mission door, refusing to let the strangers in. One of the men who seemed to be the leader gestured angrily.

Cord passed the heavy field glasses to Miriam Foster.

"Take a look, Miriam. Have you ever seen that plane before? Do you recognize any of those men?"

Miriam looked carefully, trying to hold the heavy glasses steady.

"I don't think I ever saw an airplane like that before, Jack. I know I've never seen any of those men before."

Cord had been afraid of that. The last hope, that it was all a bloody coincidence and the men from the plane were there on mission business, faded.

Cord took the glasses.

He stared carefully at the little group in front of the mission. There was nothing unusual about them, but Cord's nerves began to crawl. If they were there on mining company business, he would have gotten a message from the company. If they were from the Australian government, his message from RAN Intelligence would have mentioned it. There was no good explanation.

They were still arguing with Father Paul. Cord was not sure about what. Perhaps they—

"Jesus Christ!" Cord stiffened.

Almost casually, a tall, thin man in a red-and-white shirt had drawn a flat black automatic pistol and fired at point-blank range. Father Paul and Brother Edward crumpled to the ground. Cord had seen men shot before. Father Paul and Brother Edward were almost certainly dead.

"Bastards! Bloody murdering bastards!"

Cord had shot men, but that had been in combat. This was cold-blooded murder.

The tall, thin man made sure. Carefully he shot each one of them through the head. Then, he took out a spare magazine and calmly reloaded.

Miriam was getting frantic, but Cord had no time to talk. Now, the strangers were pulling things out of the canvas kit bags they carried. Cord swore again as he recognized silenced submachine guns. Three of them went inside the mission. Four more headed for Cord's house, weapons ready. It was just as well Cord was not home. It did not look like a social call.

"Please, Jack, what's happening? What's wrong?"

Cord was too startled to be kind. Besides, he could not think of any kind way to say it.

"Those bastards from the plane, they shot Father Paul and Brother Edward. They killed them both, the murdering bastards!"

Miriam began to cry. She had no doubts. There was something in the tone of Cord's voice that carried absolute certainty.

Time to get moving. Cord was sure that he would have company on the plateau in an hour or two. He had better be ready. He took one last look through his glasses, staring at the man in the red-and-white shirt. Cord was not given to making melodramatic speeches.

"All right, mate, I owe you one."

That was enough. Cord always paid his debts.

Miriam had stopped crying, but she was still pale and shaking.

"I don't understand, Jack. Why? Why did they kill them?"

Cord did not like his answer, but it was the only explanation that made any sense.

"They're intelligence agents. They're here because of the satellite. They are going to get it, or something very valuable out of it. They won't stop at anything to get it. And they don't intend to leave any witnesses. They'll kill us in a second if they get a chance."

Miriam turned pale again. Cord did not blame her. It is not pleasant to hear that ten professional assassins are coming to kill you.

"Listen, Miriam, you can't stay here. Work your way back down to the harbor. Stay fifty yards off the road in the bush. Don't go back to the mission. Stay in the bush and hide. There's an Australian warship coming. They'll take care of you when they get here."

Cord went to one of his footlockers and took out a spare set of fatigues and an old bush hat.

"Here, these will make you harder to see. Take this canteen and these rations. One other thing."

He handed Miriam the Owen gun. She looked at it as if it were a snake.

"It's an Owen gun. Best little submachine gun ever made. See, here, this little lever is the selector switch. This is safe, this is fire. Just pull the trigger. Don't shoot all the rounds in the magazine at one time. If you need to reload, just take this magazine out and put a new one in. It's simple, really."

"But, Jack, I've never shot a gun. I don't think I could shoot anyone."

"Take it anyway, Miriam. If they find you, they'll kill you. Now, you'd better get going."

Miriam looked dubious.

"But where will you be, Jack? What are you going to do?"

Cord smiled. It was not a pleasant sight. Miriam shivered.

"Fight."

Chapter Four

"Who dares, wins"   —The motto of the SAS

ELU ISLAND

Barsukov looked at his team. He knew several of them had never seen men shot before, but they all seemed to be reacting well, including that bitch, Irina Yakoleva. Good. Time to get things underway. He spoke formally:

"Comrades, the plan is simple. We will take the mission truck. We will install the canvas top. Linkin will drive. I will ride beside him. The rest of you will be concealed in the back. Linkin and I will carry only pistols concealed. When we reach the plateau, we will approach this Australian, Jack Cord, casually, saying that we are interested in buying the mining property. If possible, we will capture him for interrogation. However, we will take no risks. If he is armed or offers any resistance, kill him. As soon as he is taken care of, we will secure the satellite and wait for the navy."

Barsukov paused and looked at his team again. He was proud of the briefing. It was done by the book, the way they teach you at the KGB academy, short, simple sentences focused on single thoughts which cannot be misunderstood. He closed with the standard phrase, "Are there any questions or comments, comrades?"

Irina Yakoleva took a deep breath and prepared to speak. Barsukov sighed to himself. Now, we are going to hear again about The Yakoleva's experiences in Afghanistan. It was a great pity the Supreme Command had not had the benefit of her military genius. Russia might have won the war.

"I have one or two comments, Comrade Barsukov, on the details of your plan. First, it would be a serious error for all of us to ride in the truck. This man, Cord, has a high-powered rifle. It will shoot through this truck with ease. If the driver is killed on the mountain road, the truck will go out of control and the whole team may be lost. Also, as I learned in Afghanistan,"—Barsukov winced—"it is extremely easy to ambush one vehicle. I recommend that we use one of the jeeps to lead. The main party can follow in the truck, keeping two hundred meters behind. That way, this man, Cord, cannot ambush both vehicles simultaneously. If the men in the jeep are pinned down, the main party can come to their assistance. I volunteer to ride in the lead jeep; the sight of a woman will keep this Australian off his guard."

Barsukov sighed. He hated to admit it, but the Yakoleva was right. He still detested her, but a good officer must be fair.

"Those are excellent suggestions, Comrade Yakoleva. We will adopt them. Lvov, take one man, and lead in the jeep. The rest of you men, into the truck. We have wasted enough time talking; let's move out."

"Comrade, it would be better if I rode in the lead jeep. I have been in combat before, and—"

Barsukov stopped her with an angry gesture.

"Comrade Yakoleva, you are not here because I asked for you. You are not here because of your lovely

40

figure and charming personality, nor because you won the war in Afghanistan single-handed. You are here because you are the only qualified medical technician I could get. If we have wounded, you must treat them. You cannot do that if you are in the lead jeep, charming this Australian. Now, get your medical kit, get into the other jeep, and follow the truck. Do not stand there. Carry out your orders!"

Irina Yakoleva snapped into a rigid military brace and saluted with a precision which would have done credit to a Guards Airborne officer.

"At once, Comrade Officer! Exactly so! I carry out your orders without question!"

Irina grabbed her medical kit bag and ran for the jeep. Barsukov sighed. Somehow, he doubted that her salute had been a gesture of respect. Perhaps he had been too hard on her in front of the others. Barsukov knew that he was too rigid at times. He always tried to be fair. As the rest of the team climbed into their vehicles, he walked over to Irina's jeep. Irina's face was flushed with anger. She looked away as Barsukov approached.

"I did not wish to speak harshly, Irina, but I must make the decisions. We are on a mission, and I am in command. You must not question my orders."

"Of course, Comrade Barsukov, you are in command. I do not mean to question your orders."

That was better, assuming she meant a word of it. Barsukov continued in a conciliatory tone.

"Your suggestions about the vehicles were excellent. I will mention that in my report. In the meantime, let us not be so tense. After all, we are going against one man armed only with an obsolete hand-operated rifle. There are eleven of us armed with modern automatic weapons. He stands absolutely no chance against us."

"Perhaps so, comrade," Irina said in a low voice,

"but I saw what the Afghans did, armed only with obsolete hand-operated rifles. We had better be careful, very careful."

Without responding, Barsukov went to the truck, gave the signal, and climbed into the cab. The KGB team started their engines and moved out, toward the plateau road.

ELU ISLAND—THE PLATEAU

Cord shrugged into his 1958 Pattern web equipment, slipping his arms through the suspenders and fastening the web belt. Without conscious thought, he began to feel for and check each item of equipment. "There is a place for every bloody thing, and every bloody thing had damned well better be in its bloody place," as Sergeant MacNair so eloquently put it.

After four years in the Royal Australian Regiment and eight in the SAS, Cord could check his equipment night or day, drunk or sober. Quickly, he checked the items on his web belt, feeling each pouch to make sure that it was full:

Left-hand ammunition pouch—120 rounds of .303 rifle ammunition—Check!

Right-hand ammunition pouch—80 rounds of .303 rifle ammunition—and rifle cleaning kit—Check!

Water bottle pouches—water bottles full—Check!

Kidney pouches—first aid kit and canned rations—Check!

Holster—Browning 9-mm automatic pistol, loaded, cocked, and locked—Check!

Four spare magazines for same—Check!

Haversack—sniper's smock, face veil, camouflage cream, 60 spare rounds of .303 rifle ammunition—Check!

Poncho roll—Check!

Knife—Check!

42

Cord could live and fight for seventy-two hours with his weapons and the contents of his 1958 Pattern web equipment, providing he did not run out of ammunition, of course. But something was missing. Cord smiled wryly. Grenades. He would have cheerfully paid one hundred dollars a piece for some L2 hand grenades just now, but there were no friendly ordnance men in the vicinity to take his money. Well, he would just have to make do without them.

Cord opened a long wooden case and took out his rifle. To the casual eye, it appeared old fashioned, almost quaint. It was a hand-operated bolt-action rifle whose design dated back to 1900. A military small arms expert would have identified it as a British caliber .303 Lee-Enfield Rifle Number 4. It lacked the sleek, deadly metal-and-plastic look of an M16A2 assault rifle. Its hand-rubbed walnut stock surrounded the barrel, extending all the way to the front sight, giving it a thick, heavy appearance. It did not look like a particularly deadly weapon, more suitable for deer hunting, perhaps. But a real connoisseur would have noticed the walnut cheek piece screwed to the stock and the mounting bracket for the telescopic sight and known it instantly for what it was, a Mark I (T) sniper's rifle, one of the deadliest weapons of World War II.

Cord's grandfather had used it against Rommel's Afrika Korps in North Africa and against the Japanese in New Guinea. His father had carried it in Korea with the Royal Australian Regiment. Cord could not remember a time when he had not known that old rifle and listened with awe to the family war stories about it. Cord's father had taught him to shoot with it, slowly, carefully, patiently, until Cord seldom missed what he aimed at. There are few really excellent riflemen in the modern world, but Cord was one of them.

Cord took the Number 32 Mark II telescopic sight from the case. Slowly, he slipped the scope into the mounting bracket and carefully tightened the clamping screws until it was mounted on the rifle. Next, he opened a flat brown cardboard box stamped Small Arms Ammunition, Calibre .303 Mark VII. One by one, he took the cartridges out, checking each brass cartridge case and pointed, copper-jacketed, .30 caliber bullet. Then, he pressed ten cartridges into the Lee-Enfield's magazine, closed the bolt, and pushed the safety lever into the safe position. He placed the remaining ten cartridges in his shirt pocket. You can never have too much ammunition.

Cord lugged several rocks from the side of the road and placed them strategically in the center of the road. Then, he took his position along the right side of the plateau road. He was about two hundred yards from the fourth bend in the road. He would let them come to him. When nothing happened at the first three turns, they might get a little careless.

Cord's position was excellent. Cord thought of it as his "hide," and he was well concealed. Nobody could detect him until he opened fire. Even then, it would not be easy. He settled down to wait.

The minutes crawled by. The rocks Cord had placed in the road were no real obstacle, but no smart man would try to drive over them without checking first to see if they were mined.

Cord began to swear softly to himself. Where the hell were they? Then, he heard engines. Trembling a little, with pre-action nerves, Cord reminded himself of the nicest thing anyone had ever said about him in the SAS. Sergeant MacNair had once told the squadron commander, "Cord is a bloody awful little man. He drinks too much and all he thinks about is girls, but he certainly can shoot."

44

Cord smiled to himself. Wish old MacNair were here. Wish the whole bloody SAS were here! Cord took a deep breath to steady his nerves. Then, a jeep came round the bend.

The jeep ground to a stop. Cord watched as Lvov got out and moved toward the rocks. The three-power magnification of Cord's Mark II telescopic sight showed every detail of the jeep and its two passengers. The Mark II's sighting reticule was a vertical post and cross hair combination. The vertical black line of the post extended upward from the bottom to the center of the field of view. The bullet would strike where Cord placed the tip of the post. The thin black line of the horizontal cross hair told Cord that the rifle was level, not canted to the right or left. Cord placed the tip of the post against the center of Lvov's chest.

Lvov did not seem to be armed, but that did not matter to Cord. He recognized the red-and-white shirt. That was the man who had killed Father Paul. Cord felt that he owed Lvov something for that, and Cord was a man who always paid his debts.

Cord was in a steady prone position, ideal for accurate long-range rifle shooting. The big Lee-Enfield rested in a V formed by the palm of his left hand. His wrist was straight and locked, and his left elbow and forearm were directly under the rifle barrel. His right hand kept the stock pressed firmly back against his shoulder. His face was pressed against the smooth walnut cheek piece. It is the steadiest shooting position in the world if you do it right, and Cord did.

Lvov was two hundred yards away, and Cord's sight picture was perfect. He pushed the Lee-Enfield's safety off and began to apply a slow, steadily increasing pressure to the big rifle's trigger. All right, Cord, do it right! Don't jerk the trigger, squeeze it, squeeze it, squee—. The Lee-Enfield bucked and roared. A giant, invisible hand seemed to slap Lvov back toward the jeep. Lvov died instantly. He never knew what hit him, but it was a 174 grain .303 caliber full-metal-jacketed bullet moving at twice the speed of sound.

Cord's right hand moved with the speed of a striking snake. His palm cupped the Lee-Enfield's bolt handle and drove it up, backward, forward, and down in one smooth, continuous motion as he chambered a fresh cartridge and fired again, driving another bullet through Lvov's body. Cord was not particularly vindictive, but he liked to make sure.

Cord worked the bolt again as he swung his scope to the right. The driver had reacted instantaneously, rolling over the left side of the jeep and taking cover behind the hood. That was clever. Only the engine block provided the slightest protection against a .303 bullet. Cord placed the the cross hairs of the Mark II scope across the top of the jeep's hood and waited. The ball was in the stranger's court.

Cord did not have to wait long. The driver leaped to his feet, snapping a deadly black submachine gun to his shoulder. Cord found himself looking down the cold, black maw of its silencer. Through the Lee-Enfield's scope, it appeared to be pointing directly at Cord's face. Suddenly, the submachine gun spouted yellow-orange fire as the driver fired a long burst. He had deduced where Cord must be and was saturating the area with bursts of full automatic fire. Cord felt the casual contempt of a true professional for an amateur. A short-range submachine gun against a scope-sighted rifle at two hundred yards! It was brave, but it was stupid.

Nevertheless, Cord kept his head down as 115 grain full-metal-jacketed 9mm bullets tore through the trees around him. There are such things as lucky hits! The nearest bullet missed Cord by five feet. Quickly, he peered through the Mark II scope again. The jeep driver had run dry. His magazine was empty. He was drawing a long black magazine from a belt pouch as Cord squeezed the Lee-Enfield's trigger and placed a .303 bullet through his chest. The driver staggered. The silenced submachine gun suddenly seemed too heavy for his hands to hold. He fell heavily and lay still. Cord took no chances. Smoothly, he worked the Lee-Enfield's bolt and put another round through him. The driver's body jerked from the impact, but he was already dead.

Everything was still. Automatically, Cord opened the Lee-Enfield's bolt and pressed four fresh cartridges into the magazine. He placed his scope on the edge of the bend in the road. Who knows, someone just might be stupid enough to look around it. Someone was. A man's face appeared suddenly, peering up the road. Cord did not think the man was going to stand there and admire the view. He snapped off a quick shot, and the .303 bullet buried itself in the dirt four inches from the man's face. A ton of kinetic energy blasted a fountain of rock and gravel into the man's face. He vanished instantly behind the cover of the bank. Cord smiled. He would have bet a hundred dollars that there was a very unhappy man behind that embankment. He had probably not hit him, but as Sergeant MacNair so eloquently put it, he had "bloody well demoralized the bloody bastard."

Well, time to go. They were not stupid enough to try coming up the road again. They knew approximately where he was. You did not have to be a military genius to see what would happen next. They would try to flank him, moving on both sides of the road through the bush. If three or four of them could get in close with those bloody submachine guns, he was probably finished. Cord rolled to his feet and began to run steadily up the slope toward his next hide. He smiled as he ran. The score was Australia two, Visitors nothing. The home team was still in the game!

ELU ISLAND—THE ROAD TO THE PLATEAU

Barsukov was in a cold rage as he wiped dust, blood, and bits of gravel from his face. His look around the bend had been short, but long enough for him to grasp the situation. The lead jeep had been ambushed. He had lost two men. He knew that he, himself, had been within inches of instant death. His men were looking at him, waiting for him to give the orders. Very well, the situation was obvious. Cord must be killed, and the team must reach the plateau. It was also crystal clear that any one who drove or walked up the road was going to certain death.

Barsukov forced himself to speak calmly despite his anger.

"Comrades, Lvov and Belyi are dead. This Australian, Cord, was in an ambush position. By now, he has probably moved and is in another. We cannot move up the road against his sniper's rifle. He would pick us off, one by one. So, we will flank him. Karpov, take your section and move up the left side of the road. Slutsky, take your section and go to the right. Linkin and I will stay here and guard the road. We must not let him slip behind us. Take no chances. When you find him, take advantage of your automatic weapons. Pin him down, get him in a crossfire, and kill him."

Barsukov looked around him. His men were grim faced and angry as they checked their weapons, but he saw no signs of panic. Good!

"Any questions? No? Very well. Remember your training. Do not bunch up. Cover each other. Conserve your ammunition; do not fire until you have a target. Use cover and concealment. Now, let us get a little revenge for Lvov and Belyi."

There was a growl of agreement as the two sections faded into the bush. Barsukov took out his field glasses and started to do the hardest thing of all, wait.

Cord was running steadily up the right side of the road, steadily but not happily. He was ten yards in from the edge of the road. The ground was rough and uneven and overgrown with typical tropical rain forest trees, bushes, and vines. The going was hard. The temperature was over ninety degrees, and the humidity was close to one hundred percent. Already his fatigues were soaked with sweat. Cord was carrying an eleven-pound rifle, a pistol, and fifty pounds of gear. He could feel the strain before he had gone fifty yards. He was not in nearly as good a shape as he had thought when he laid his plans. Too much beer and not enough exercise. Worst of all, he felt the first familiar twinges of pain in his bloody left knee. He had injured it two years before in a practice parachute jump. The doctors had done their best, but it was never going to be quite right again. No amount of willpower was going to make it right. If that would work, Cord would still have been in the SAS. No two ways about it, he was not going to make it very far at any pace faster than a quick walk. If they caught him moving, without cover, he was a dead man. He might get one, perhaps two, with his rifle, but the others would cut him to pieces.

All right, Cord, you military genius, your bloody brilliant plan isn't going to work. What do you do now? Take them by surprise and kill them. Easy to say, but hard to do. Think now, what are they looking for? What do they expect to see? A man with a rifle, a sniper waiting in ambush. All right, then, show them that.

A few yards ahead, there was a small clearing. At the far edge, there was a tangled clump of bushes, the kind a sniper might use for his hide. Quickly, Cord took off his bush hat and sniper's veil and pushed them into the bushes so that they hung a foot above the ground, just where his head would be if he were hiding there in ambush. Then, he slid the Lee-Enfield into the bushes, bracing the stock until the big rifle's muzzle pointed menacingly down the trail. He hated to risk his rifle, but that was what would make his trap convincing. They would not believe that Cord would abandon his rifle.

Cord moved to the right edge of the clearing and stood behind the trunk of a large banyan tree. He drew his Browning Highpower from its holster and checked the big pistol. A 9mm round in the chamber, thirteen more in the magazine, two spare magazines on his belt, ready for a fast reload. He held the Browning in both hands, palms vertical, his left hand cupping his right. He took a few deep breaths to steady himself and waited, listening intently. He did not have long to wait. Cord heard the sounds of people trying to move silently through the bush without knowing how. Cord sneered. Bloody amateurs! They were probably wonderful at murdering people in telephone booths, but they would never have made the cut in the SAS!

The point man entered the clearing. He looked disarmingly normal, except for the deadly silenced Beretta Model 12 submachine gun in his hands. He saw Cord's rifle barrel pointing at him. He fired from the hip, three long, silenced bursts. Full-metal-jacketed 9mm bullets tore through the clump of bushes. Splinters filled the air. Cord saw an invisible hand snatch his bush hat away and throw it through the air. The man yelled loudly in a language that Cord did not know. Excitement and triumph made his voice hoarse.

Two more men men dived into the clearing, coming low and fast, one to the left, and one to the right. They rolled into hasty prone positions and fired simultaneously. Two long bursts riddled Cord's false hide. A deadly crossfire of 9mm bullets tore through the bushes. Cord was impressed. It was fast and neat, not at all amateurish. If Cord had been there, he would have died instantly. Someone barked an order. The first man was reloaded now. He covered the clump of bushes while the other two reached for fresh magazines. That gave Cord all the advantage he was going to get. Now use it! Cord stepped around the banyan tree, the big Browning Highpower ready in his hands.

Cord could see his front sight clear and sharp against the first man's khaki shirt. He pulled the trigger, and the big Browning roared. He kept his wrists and elbows locked against the recoil, and instantly pulled the trigger again in the deadly technique that serious pistol shooters call the double hammer. The two shots were so close together that they sounded like a single blast as Cord fired both shots in a quarter of a second. The two 9mm bullets struck the first man almost simultaneously. The impact was terrible. The stranger dropped his Beretta and started to fall.

Cord could see the right-hand man's face distorted by fear and surprise as he saw Cord swinging the Browning's muzzle toward him. His submachine gun was reloaded and ready to fire, but he was facing forward, toward Cord's ambush. He had to turn ninety degrees to fire at Cord. Cord could see the black cylinder of the Beretta's silencer swing toward him in a deadly arc.

Too late. Cord needed to turn only a few degrees. His upper body swung smoothly, like a gun turret, head, arms, and the big Browning staying perfectly aligned. The instant the Browning's front sight was on target, Cord fired again and again. The double hammer struck, and the man staggered and slowed, but he did not go

51

down. Instantly, Cord fired again. Two more 9mm bullets smashed into the second man, and he went down hard.

The third man had turned toward Cord, ready to fire. He had to hesitate for a second, because his teammate was in his line of fire. Now, as his comrade fell, he had a clear shot. As Cord swung his Browning toward him, the man fired a ten-round burst from the hip. With an AK-47, it would have been fatal, but the Beretta submachine gun was not well balanced for that kind of shooting. He should have taken another half second and used his sights. Still, he only missed by inches. Cord could see the yellow-white muzzle flash inside the silencer, and splinters flew from the banyan tree behind him. Now, Cord's sights were on, and he fired rapidly, two double hammers, as fast as he could pull the Browning's trigger.

The man started to fall forward. He was pulling the Beretta's trigger as he fell, and a dozen 9mm bullets tore into the ground halfway between him and Cord. He was probably dying as he fell. Cord did not lack compassion, but he could take no chances. Kill or be killed means exactly what it says, and the man still had the Beretta in his hands. Cord shot the third man twice more, and he went down heavily and lay still.

There was a sudden, deafening silence. Cord swung the Browning in a rapid arc around the clearing, but there was nothing left to shoot. Automatically, without thinking, he pushed the button on the side of the Browning and dropped out the magazine. He pulled out a fresh magazine from his belt pouch and snapped it into place. Cord stared at the used magazine in his left hand. There was a single 9mm cartridge between the feed lips and one more in the chamber. He had fired twelve shots. Another double hammer and he would have run dry. It had been close. Too damned close! Cord began to shake as reaction hit him. He was lucky to be alive. Cord snapped back to reality. He was not going to stay alive much longer if he did not get moving. He holstered the Browning, snatched up his Lee-Enfield, and faded into the bush.

Karpov was leading his section up the left side of the road. They were making good progress. The vegetation was thinner on the down slope side. There were fewer possible places for an ambush. Still, Karpov made certain that his men moved carefully and kept their weapons ready for action. Suddenly, Karpov stopped. Shots! He heard shots. Someone was firing rapidly, not far away. It was coming from across the road and nearby.

Karpov made his decision instantly. Quickly, he led his men to the right, moving rapidly until they reached the edge of the road. For a second, he hesitated. It was certain death to go out there if Cord was waiting in ambush. What the hell, you don't win if you won't take chances.

"Petrov, stay here and cover us until we are across. Kochetov, follow me. Ready? Go!"

Karpov leaped to his feet and ran forward. Kochetov followed, a pace behind. Suddenly, a figure burst out of the bush on the opposite side of the road and came straight at them. A man in dirty green fatigues, with his face painted in strange green-and-brown patterns, and a big rifle in his hands. Cord! Karpov snapped up his submachine gun, ready to fire.

Cord moved rapidly up the right side of the road, moving at the fastest pace he thought his knee would stand. There were more of them, he was sure of that. They would have heard the shots, and they would be coming. He must be under cover and take them by surprise. He reached his second hide and risked a quick around. Nothing. He would be able to see back down the road much better if he crossed over to the other side. It was taking a bit of a chance, but he could be across the road in five seconds. Come on, Cord, you know the SAS motto, "Who dares, wins." Let's dare!

He leaped to his feet and ran forward. He had not gone ten feet before two men leaped out of the bush and came straight at him across the road. Cord did not stop to think. Bullets were shooting by him. Despite the awful shock of sudden surprise, he leveled the Lee-Enfield and fired. The heavy .303 bullet tore through the leader, and Karpov went down. No time to stand there and work the Lee-Enfield's bolt. Cord dropped his rifle and threw himself down and to the right, drawing his Browning as he went. A burst of 9mm bullets tore through the place where he had been. Cord swung the Browning up as Kochetov aimed a second burst. Kochetov was not used to moving targets. He hesitated a fraction of a second to be sure that he was on target, and Cord fired first, pulling the trigger of the big Browning again and again. It was not pretty shooting, but it was good enough. Hit half a dozen times, Kochetov went down.

Cord scrambled to his feet and started to dive back toward the right side of the road, driven by the infantryman's basic instinct to get under cover during a firefight. He had not seen Petrov, nor did he hear the silenced Beretta as Petrov squeezed off a burst. Something smashed into Cord's right side with immense force. Cord staggered. Petrov fired again. Something hit Cord on the right side of his head. Stunned by the impact, Cord dropped the Browning, spun around, went down on his back, and lay there unable to move. He heard footsteps approaching. The Browning was lying on the ground five feet away. He considered rolling toward it.

"Go ahead," someone said calmly, "but you won't make it."

Cord blinked. A tall, thin man was standing a few feet away. There was nothing at all remarkable about him. You would have passed him on the streets of Sydney without a second glance. Cord's attention was forcibly attracted to the muzzle of a Beretta Model 12 submachine gun pointed steadily at the center of his chest.

"You are Cord?" the man asked quietly.

Cord nodded. There seemed to be no point in denying it.

"Petrov. I am Oleg Petrov, KGB, Department 8, Active Measures. What are you, Cord, CIA paramilitary, a Green Beret? It is not important, but I would like to know."

"Not bloody likely. I'm an Australian, Number 2 Squadron, Australian SAS."

"Ah, the SAS. Yes, that explains a great deal. Well, Cord, you did your duty today. Your regiment would be proud of you."

They stared at each, two professionals.

"Well, Cord, Barsukov said to shoot you. That is really best. You do not want to be interrogated. It is always better to go quick than slow."

Cord stared in amazement. Six feet behind Petrov a strangely shaped bunch of bushes was rising from the forest floor. It was Miriam Foster, almost lost in a pair of Cord's old fatigues. She had tied branches to her hat and her arms and legs in an attempt at camouflage. Her face was white, and she was trembling. In her hands, she held Cord's Owen gun, pointing it at the middle of Petrov's back. The Owen's muzzle moved back and forth in small arcs as Miriam shook with fear.

Jesus Christ! Miriam was as helpless as a baby against

55

a pro like Petrov. In a minute she would speak, and Petrov would whirl around and cut her in two. He had to do something quickly. Cord snapped his eyes back to Petrov's face. Too late, he had stared at Miriam too long. Petrov had noticed Cord's glance. Petrov smiled bleakly.

"You are a clever man, Cord, but I know that trick. I am supposed to think that there is someone behind me and turn around while you go for your pistol. It is an old trick, but you did it well. An amateur would have said something stupid, you merely stare and look back. Very convincing. Who knows, if I did not know you were alone, I might have believed you. You are a clever man, Cord, clever but dangerous. I am going to kill you now. If you are a religious man, say your pray—"

The Owen gun roared into life as Miriam jerked the trigger. She had never fired a gun before. Dazed by the muzzle blast and frightened as the Owen shuddered and shook in her hands, she froze on the trigger. Thirty full-metal-jacketed 9mm bullets tore through Petrov's body in less than three seconds. He died instantly, falling forward over Cord's knees.

Miriam stared in horror at Petrov's body and the Owen gun in her hands.

"I—I killed him, I killed him," she stammered.

"Too right you did, Miriam!" Cord said admiringly. "You put thirty rounds through the bloody bastard and blew him to hell. You were great, just great!"

Miriam looked dubious.

"I didn't want to shoot him, Jack. But when he said he was going to kill you, I knew he meant it. I had to do something. I tried to do what you said, push the lever and pull the trigger. I don't think I did it right. You told me not to shoot all the bullets at one time."

"It's all right, Miriam, you did fine."

Miriam's attention shifted from Petrov to Cord.

"You're hurt, Jack, your head is bleeding."

This was something that Miriam knew how to deal with. She snapped open her first aid kit, took out a bandage, and took a quick look.

"You were lucky, Jack. It's just a crease, a flesh wound along the side of your head. I'll clean it out and bandage it."

"No time for that. We can't stay here. Just stop the bleeding. Then you go get the Land Rover, come back, and meet me here."

Miriam did what she was told. Cord watched her go with a smile. He was beginning to think that Miriam was a wonderful girl.

Cord liked girls, but he had other things on his mind. He picked up his Browning, reloaded it and put it in his holster, and retrieved his Lee-Enfield. He moved to the left side of the road and took his position in the drainage ditch. He looked down the road. There was a bend in the road about four hundred yards away. Cord set his scope for 400. There was someone behind that bend, Cord was sure of that. Someone who had heard the shooting and must be frantic to know what was going on. Someone who just might get a little careless.

Cord settled down to wait. His head began to throb. He opened his first aid kit and took a painkiller. His right side ached. Suddenly, Cord remembered, something had hit him there. He stared at his web belt. Exactly in the center of his right-hand ammunition pouch was a neat, round hole. Cord opened the pouch. Nestled among the .303 cartridges was a 9mm bullet. Cord could see the the fresh rifling marks on the bullet's metal jacket. It had smashed through two rows of .303 cartridges and stopped in the third.

Cord began to laugh. He laughed harder and harder until his whole body shook. Got to hand it to old Mac-

Nair. He always said "carry extra ammunition Cord: it may save your bloody life." And he was bloody well right!

Cord saw a flicker of motion through his sight. Instantly, he stopped laughing. First, one man came around the bend, then another. The first man was using field glasses, looking up the road toward Cord. Cord put his sights on the center of his chest, took a deep breath, let half of it out, and began to squeeze the Lee-Enfield's trigger.

Irina Yakoleva was still seething as she drove up the road. That stupid man Barsukov was an excellent example of what was wrong with the Party! Give him a little authority, and he thought he was Stalin! Just because she was a woman, he patronized her and refused to accept her capabilities. She had seen too many men like him in Afghanistan.

The memory of Afghanistan was like a sudden chill. Steady down, Yakoleva! You are not on a holiday drive in the mountains. There is a man out there who will kill us all if he can. Driving along like a fool, cursing Barsukov, will get you nothing but a bullet through your pretty blond head. Irina did not like that thought at all. Think now, what are your options?

She must obey direct orders, but what exactly had Barsukov ordered her to do? Get her medical kit, take the jeep, and follow the truck up the road. He had not specified any particular distance or method. As long as she followed orders, she could use her own initiative, and Irina was good at that. There were several sharp bends in the road as it reversed to snake up the mountainside toward the plateau. As you came round the bend in a vehicle, you must slow to a crawl to make the turn, and you could see nothing beyond the bend until you made the turn. Those were the danger points. At one of them, Cord would be waiting, hidden, camouflaged, with his sniper's rifle. Irina shuddered. She would not give a ruble for the chances of the two men in the lead jeep.

Very well then, Yakoleva, slow and careful does it. As she approached the first bend, she stopped, shut off her engine, and listened. She could hear the truck's engine growling as it ground up the road ahead. She started her engine and drove on, stopping and listening at each bend. She was starting to feel a little foolish as she stopped at the third bend. Then she heard the flat roar of the Lee-Enfield firing four fast shots. There was a short pause, then a fifth shot. Then, silence.

Irina got out of the jeep and walked the final twenty feet to the bend. She drew a small steel mirror from her jacket pocket and used it to look around the bend. She could see the truck stopped just short of the next bend. She could see Barsukov gesturing, giving orders. Next, two three-man teams slipped into the bush on each side of the road. That was logical. Cord had ambushed the lead jeep. Barsukov was trying to flank him.

Irina waited and listened. For a few minutes, nothing happened. Then, she heard the flat, repeated bark of a 9mm weapon being fired very rapidly, a pistol, perhaps, or a submachine gun on semiautomatic. Her team's 9mm submachine guns were silenced. She could not hear them firing. Perhaps Cord had a 9mm pistol. The flanking teams had probably caught him, and he was making a desperate last stand. Irina began to feel better. Perhaps Cord had not been as dangerous as she feared. She waited another minute or two and then turned toward her jeep. Suddenly, she heard the Lee-Enfield firing again. After a pause, Irina heard the staccato bark of a 9mm submachine gun firing on full-automatic, a long ripping burst of twenty-five or thirty rounds. Irina felt a cold knot in her stomach. They had been wrong, Cord was not alone!

Irina thought quickly. She could go forward, and join Barsukov at the truck. However, she could see no wounded to treat, and nobody had signaled her to come forward. She decided to stay where she was. She did not think Barsukov was wise to stay behind the hood of the truck. It only provided cover in one direction. If Cord decided to flank Barsukov, he was a dead man. Irina waited. Her nerves began to crawl. Cord could be circling wide. In that case, she had no cover, either.

Suddenly, Barsukov made a decision. He moved around the bend, field glasses in hand. Linkin followed him, a few feet behind, submachine gun ready to fire. Irina winced. Most unwise, comrade, most unwise. She waited for a few seconds, then heard the sound of Cord's Lee-Enfield firing again, four fast shots, then silence. Linkin staggered back from around the far bend. Irina could see a great splotch of blood on his shirt. He took two more steps and fell heavily.

Irina saw his arms and legs twitching. Linkin was still alive. Irina swore. She had to go out there and try to help him. Irina was no angel of mercy, but you do not let your comrades down in combat. Quickly, she laid down her submachine gun and her pistol, took off her jacket, removed the holder from her ponytail, and shook her shoulder-length blond hair. She had lived in Australia for four years. She thought she knew Australians well. If Cord was a typical Australian, he would not shoot an unarmed woman. He would kill her in a second if she came at him with a weapon, but Cord's scope would show him every detail, and in her tight T-shirt and faded blue jeans she was obviously a woman, and obviously unarmed.

She stepped around the bend and walked to Linkin. Irina resisted the temptation to run. If Cord was watching, that might trigger a shot. She reached Linkin, but he was dead. Two full-metal-jacketed .303 bullets had torn through his chest. She hesitated for a second, listening. She heard a low moan, then another. Barsukov was still alive, a few meters around the bend. Irina found herself trembling.

Cord might not be able to see her here, but he had just shot two men around the bend. She would be in his sights the instant she stepped around the next bend. Perhaps he would shoot her. She had never heard anything good about the capitalist elite troops, the American Rangers, the Green Berets, and the SAS. The political officers had told her that they were the scum of the earth, drug-crazed homicidal maniacs and sadists, who delight in committing unspeakable atrocities! Irina was not stupid enough to believe everything that the *Zampolits* said, but who knew, Cord might shoot her in the belly, and laugh while she writhed in agony. It did not make any difference. She detested Barsukov, but she had to go. Irina took a deep breath and stepped around the bend.

She walked slowly, careful to do nothing that might startle Cord. Irina knew he was there. Her skin crawled. She could feel his cross hairs centered on her chest, but her plan seemed to be working. Cord did not fire. She reached Barsukov and knelt down to examine his wounds. Irina shook her head. He was bleeding to death, and she could not do anything to save him. He needed a doctor and massive blood plasma transfusions. Still, she had to try. She tore open a trauma dressing and began to bandage his chest. Barsukov opened his eyes and looked at her. He seemed stunned and disoriented.

"Lie still, comrade," Irina said in her best bedside manner. "I will bandage your wounds and then give you something to kill the pain."

"Thank you for coming, Irina, but do not bother. I am dying. You know it, and I know it. I think that that damned Australian has killed the whole team. You are the only one left. I think"—he stopped and coughed. Irina winced. She had heard men shot through the lungs before. She felt a wave of anger. Until now, the situation had seemed like a tactical exercise. Now, with Linkin's and Barsukov's blood on her hands, she was filled with cold fury.

"Do not worry, comrade. I will track down this Cord and kill him for you. I will put a magazine through him and laugh while he dies!"

Barsukov smiled weakly. Whatever you might say against The Yakoleva, she was not a delicate flower. He summoned up the last of his strength and spoke as clearly as he could.

"No, Irina, do not do that. It makes no difference if you kill this man, Cord. He is of no real importance now. The mission is important, only the mission. Stay alive. The navy is coming. You must brief them and lead them to the plateau. Secure *War God.* Promise me that you will do—"

"Very well, comrade, I will not go after Cord. I will wait for the navy. I will carry out our mission."

Irina was talking to herself. Barsukov was gone. Time for her to get out. Cord might be circling to cut off her retreat. She got to her feet and moved quickly to the jeep, started the engine, and drove as fast as she dared back toward the village. Very well, Comrade Barsukov, I will carry out the mission, but that does not mean that I will not kill this man, Cord, if I can!

ELU HARBOR

Cord was feeling better. Miriam had carefully cleaned and bandaged his wound. While she was not looking, Cord had medicated himself with two cans of

Foster's lager beer. The combination had worked wonders. He needed rest, but he needed to know what was happening in the village. He drove to the edge of the plateau and left Miriam in the Land Rover. He walked to his lookout. From there, he had a panoramic view of the plateau road and the village.

Cord scanned the village through the Japanese naval glasses. The 20-power optics showed every detail. Cord searched carefully. He had seen ten or eleven strangers in the village before, but that did not mean he had seen them all. The blond he had failed to shoot might be headed back for reinforcements. He saw no sign of movement. The village appeared deserted. Cord was about to put up his glasses when something caught his eye. There, out in the harbor, was a huge patch of frothing white bubbles, and a great, gray shape began to rise menacingly above the surface. Cord looked through his glasses and felt a knot in his stomach. The Australian navy had nothing like that. Cord tried to remember the photographs from his training classes two years ago. Suddenly, it came to him. He was looking at a Soviet Echo class nuclear attack submarine!

Chapter Five

"He who is skilled in defense hides in the secret recesses of the earth, making it impossible for the enemy to find him."
—Sun Tzu

LENINGRADSKI KOMSOMOLS—ELU HARBOR

The launch came smoothly alongside the huge gray submarine. Irina Yakoleva gripped her seat with both hands. Her knuckles were white. She did not like small boats, but she loved the submarine. The last two hours, alone on Elu, had not been pleasant. She had searched Cord's house and the mission and had kept moving, her submachine gun ready.

She knew what Cord looked like now from the pictures she had found while searching his house. She could not help imagining Cord creeping up behind her slowly, quietly, knife in hand, waiting for her to make a mistake. Now, she was no longer alone. The submarine was solid proof that the might of the Soviet Union was behind her.

Lieutenant Pavel Shpagin shouted an order from the launch. A sailor on deck threw down a rope ladder.

Irina followed Lieutenant Shpagin up the ladder to the deck. He pointed to an open hatch.

"Down there, comrade, the captain will want to see you at once."

Irina clambered down a metal ladder into a narrow corridor. There was a faint smell of oil and the low hum of machinery. She followed Lieutenant Shpagin into a small compartment. There was a steel table in the center of the room.

A slender, gray-haired man sat at the table. Irina was not good at recognizing naval insignia, but she had no doubts. The man radiated quiet authority. He must be the captain.

Shpagin saluted.

"Captain, this is Irina Yakoleva. She is a Senior Lieutenant in the GRU. Comrade Yakoleva, allow me to present Captain Khrenov."

"Welcome to *Leningradski Komsomols,* Lieutenant Yakoleva. Please be seated. Pavel, please assemble all officers not on watch here in the wardroom."

Irina sat at the table. Captain Khrenov stared at her briefly. She was an attractive woman, but his attention was drawn to the bloodstains on her clothes.

"Some tea, Lieutenant Yakoleva? You look as if you have had a hard time."

Irina nodded. She would have sold her soul for a cup of hot, strong tea. Khrenov poured steaming tea into a chipped china mug. He produced a bottle of vodka and poised it over the cup.

"A little something to strengthen it?"

Irina hesitated. She knew she drank too much, but she only drank off duty.

"Thank you, Captain, I would like it, but I am on duty and—"

"Nonsense! It is not for pleasure, it is medicinal. I prescribe it."

Irina did not argue. She took the cup and sipped the hot tea and vodka gratefully.

There was a knock at the door. Lieutenant Shpagin came in followed by seven other officers. They seated themselves at the table and stared amazed at Irina Yakoleva. Tall blonds in tight T-shirts and faded jeans are unusual on nuclear attack submarines. Not unwelcome, but definitely unusual.

Khrenov did not waste time. "This is Senior Lieutenant Irina Yakoleva. She is a member of the Soviet team we were to contact when we reached Elu. She will brief us and explain the situation on the island."

Irina took a deep breath to steady her nerves. It was important that these men regard her as a cool, professional officer, not as a hysterical woman. She spoke quietly, choosing her words with care. She described everything which had happened since the KGB team reached Elu, covering every detail she considered important. When she finished she looked around the table. Good. She had held their attention. No one looked skeptical.

"That is what happened, comrades. Are there any questions?"

Captain Khrenov shook his head.

"Your entire team was killed by one man? You make this man, Cord, sound like the devil himself. How is this possible?"

Irina took a color photograph out of her pocket and placed it on the table. It showed four soldiers in uniform. One held a rifle with a telescopic sight. A second soldier held a target with ten bullet holes clustered in the center of the bull's-eye. The man with the rifle was being congratulated.

"I found this picture in Cord's house. The man with the rifle is Cord. I know this from other pictures in the house. He shot that target at six hundred meters. It is framed and hanging on his wall. I think that is the rifle

66

he used today. The man is a master sniper. And look at their headgear in the picture."

"They are wearing berets, but what of that? Many soldiers do."

"Look at the color of the berets, light tan, the color of sand, and see the cap badges. A winged dagger. You cannot read the motto, but I know what it says, 'Who dares, wins.' Cord was in the Australian SAS."

Khrenov frowned. "SAS? What is that?"

"The Australian Special Air Service. They are the elite regiment of the Australian Army, the Australian *Spetsnaz.*"

She did not need to say anything more. Every Russian has heard of *Spetsnaz,* the blue berets, the elite troops of the Soviet army. If Cord was Australian *Spetsnaz,* he was a dangerous man, indeed.

"Cord is alone? He did this single-handed?"

"We thought so. Our information was that only Cord and three missionaries were living on Elu. We may have been wrong. Most of the firing I heard was from a high-powered rifle. But I also heard a submachine gun firing. Ours were silenced. I could not have heard one of them. Someone, perhaps two or three people, may be with Cord. But he did most of the killing with his rifle. Believe me, the man is deadly."

"We believe you. The bloodstains on your clothes are very convincing."

Khrenov turned to his officers.

"You now know the situation. This meeting is adjourned. Lieutenant Samsonov, I will send a message to Pacific Fleet headquarters via satellite in fifteen minutes."

The officers filed out. Khrenov took a pad of paper from the table. He wrote steadily for ten minutes. Irina Yakoleva sipped her tea and tried to stay awake.

Khrenov looked up at her. There was a faint smile on his face.

"This may seem unfriendly, Lieutenant Yakoleva, but do you have any proof that you are who you say you are?"

Irina smiled.

"I do not carry a card that says 'I am a Russian secret agent,' but here."

She wrote ten numbers on the pad.

"That is my personal identification number. Have them send it to GRU headquarters in Moscow. They will confirm my identity."

Khrenov nodded.

"Very well. I will send the message immediately."

NATIONAL SECURITY AGENCY FACILITIES— FORT GEORGE G. MEAD, MARYLAND

Leningradski Komsomols's satellite antenna locked on a Soviet communications satellite in geostationary orbit twenty-three thousand miles above the earth. Lieutenant Samsonov pushed the send button, and Captain Khrenov's message flashed skyward at the speed of light. The communications satellite received the message and re-transmitted it. A few seconds later, it was received at Soviet Pacific Fleet headquarters.

The Soviet satellite was not the only one which received Khrenov's message. An American signal intelligence satellite also received and recorded it. In seconds, it was relayed and downlinked to the NSA facility at Fort George G. Meade, Maryland. A few seconds later, one of the most powerful computers in the world was dissecting it, analyzing every characteristic.

A light flashed on a monitoring console. The operator glanced at the display and beckoned to the watch officer.

"Another SATCOM transmission from a Priority One surveillance area, Elu Island."

"Is it that Australian coast watcher again?"

"Negative, different type of transmitter, different code."

He stared at his screen as the display changed.

"Preliminary analysis coming up. Russian naval transmitter, type normally carried on Echo I or Echo II class submarines. It's in a code we haven't cracked yet. Analysis is confirmed. No doubt about it. Soviet Echo class submarine transmitting via SATCOM from the vicinity of Elu."

The watch officer nodded. He picked up a secure phone.

"Get me the Pentagon, the Crisis Center, General Brand. General, this is Dick Bronson, NSA. We have just detected a Soviet nuclear attack submarine transmitting from Elu. No, there is no doubt. No other country operates Echo class submarines. Yes, we will continue to monitor."

LENINGRADSKI KOMSOMOLS—ELU HARBOR

Irina Yakoleva was tired, and vodka in the hot tea affected her more than usual. She was dozing in a wardroom chair. She woke up with a start as Khrenov and Shpagin entered the room. Captain Khrenov had a sheet of paper in his hand. He sat down at the table and began to read. He looked surprised.

"Well, we have gone up in the world. This is from navy headquarters in Moscow. It is signed by Admiral of the Fleet Voznesensky, himself. Listen to this. 'Attack and sink any non-Soviet ship or submarine which attempts to approach the island of Elu.'"

Lieutenant Shpagin whistled softly.

"The war order? Are we at war with the United States?"

"No, the order applies only to the area around Elu, but it is quite clear. If time allows, we are to confirm with Pacific Fleet headquarters; but if that cannot be done, we attack anyway."

"That is enough war for one submarine. Very well, Captain, I will—"

"Wait, there is more. We are ordered to form a landing party and seize and hold *War God* until Soviet surface ships arrive. Lieutenant Yakoleva's identity is confirmed. She is temporarily assigned to *Leningradski Komsomols* and is directed to give us all possible assistance. I am ordered to remain on board. You will command the landing party. The admiral states that this operation is of vital importance to the security of the Soviet Union. He has the utmost confidence in us."

Khrenov and Shpagin stared at each other. In the entire history of the Soviet submarine service, no submarine had ever been ordered to form a landing party and seize something on shore. It sounded insane, but there could be no doubt, the order was authentic.

Khrenov was amazed. He got up and poured fresh tea into three mugs.

"Well, orders are orders. Now, we must plan. I am afraid we know very little about fighting on land. You have fought on Elu. What advice can you give us, Lieutenant Yakoleva?"

"Well, Captain, first, I need to know more about your weapons and their capabilities. For example, can your cannon reach the top of the plateau?"

Khrenov and Shpagin looked at her and smiled. Irina knew she had said something stupid, but she could not imagine what.

Captain Khrenov continued to smile as he spoke. "We have no cannon, Lieutenant Yakoleva. No submarine I know of carries a cannon anymore. *Leningradski Komsomols* is a nuclear-propelled attack submarine.

70

We carry eight large antiship cruise missiles with a range of nearly three hundred miles. With a skilled attack and a little luck, we can sink any ship that floats. For close-in work, we have twenty-one–inch torpedoes. They are effective against surface ships or other submarines. Unfortunately, we have nothing that can be used against land targets. Those are all the weapons we have."

Khrenov's smile broadened.

"But wait, I forget, we do have the contents of our arms room. Lieutenant Shpagin, show Comrade Yakoleva our arsenal."

ELU ISLAND—THE PLATEAU

Khrenov was not the only one who was planning. Cord was thinking hard. The submarine had put a small party ashore in some kind of motorized life raft. They had contacted the blond he had seen on the road. Cord was beginning to feel he had made a mistake when he had not shot her. Then they had gone back to the submarine. Cord did not think they were having a tea party. There was no use hoping that they would stay put until the Australian navy came and chased them away. No, they wanted the bloody satellite. They would be coming after him.

There was only one way they could come at him—up the road. All right, Miriam could watch the submarine. Time to prepare a few surprises, unpleasant surprises.

LENINGRADSKI KOMSOMOLS—ELU HARBOR

Irina Yakoleva followed Lieutenant Shpagin back into the wardroom. She had been disappointed in *Leningradski Komsomols*'s small arms. A nuclear-propelled, cruise missile–armed submarine seemed like a marvel of modern technology. She had expected to see the latest weapons. Instead she had seen a small arms museum, fifty AK-47 rifles, the old model, not the newer AK-74s, a half-dozen Tokarev pistols, and four PPSH-41 submachine guns. PPSH-41s! Irina's grandfather had carried one of those at Stalingrad. He had killed half the German army with it if his stories could be believed.

She had hoped for some machine guns and, particularly, an SVD sniper's rifle, but there had been nothing like that. Irina was beginning to understand that infantry weapons and tactics were not very important in the Soviet submarine service.

Captain Khrenov looked up and smiled.

"Well, Lieutenant Yakoleva, what do you think of our arsenal?"

Irina put a smile on her face. No use complaining about what can't be fixed. *Leningradski Komsomols*'s crew would have to fight with what they had.

"Good, sound weapons, Captain, and in excellent condition, very well maintained."

"Yes, Warrant Officer Moiseev takes care of them. He was in the naval infantry before he transferred to submarines. He understands such things. Very well, now to make our plans. What are your recommendations?"

Irina spoke carefully. It was important that they take her advice.

"Send the strongest possible landing party. Arm them with the AK-47s. Send your man who was in the naval infantry. He will be useful. One other thing, no one should wear any insignia of rank."

Khrenov looked at her curiously.

"Cord will try to kill the officers first to demoralize your men. I know. I have had sniper training. That is what I would do if I were in his place. I will accompany

72

the landing party. My medical training may be very useful."

Khrenov and Shpagin looked at each other. It was not going to be a picnic on that damned island. Khrenov nodded.

"Very well. We have one hundred officers and men. We will send fifty ashore. Pavel, you will command the landing party. It is starting to get dark now. We will go ashore at first light."

Chapter Six

"We have good corporals and sergeants, and those are
much more important than good generals."
—General W. T. Sherman

ELU HARBOR

Irina Yakoleva climbed down *Leningradski Komsomols*'s side into the launch. She felt better. A few hours'
sleep and a hot meal had done wonders for her morale.
Things seemed to be going well. The weather was clear
and sunny, and the sea was calm. *Leningradski Komsomols*'s crew was efficent and well organized. Twenty
men were already ashore, and nothing had happened.
That was only logical. Irina did not expect Cord to fight
in the harbor area. The plateau road would be where
he would make his stand.

The launch pulled away from *Leningradski Komsomols*'s huge gray hull and headed toward the shore.
Irina glanced at the sailors in the launch. They were
dressed in dark gray coveralls. Each man clutched an
AK-47 and wore a web pouch which carried his spare
magazines. They did not appear frightened. Most of
them looked excited. Going ashore on a tropical island

74

was different, a real adventure. She knew how they felt. She remembered her excitement when she got her orders to go to Afghanistan. She had learned there that certain kinds of adventures can be extremely hazardous. If Cord decided to fight, some of them would not live to see nightfall.

The harbor was a pretty picture, bright blue waves crashing on a wide sandy beach, with a lush, green tropical rain forest in the background. Not everything was pleasant. It was already getting hot, and the humidity was high. It would have been a wonderful day for Irina to wear her prized string bikini and have a small party on the beautiful white sands. But she was not on Elu to have fun.

The launch pulled alongside a rough log pier. Moiseev was there, checking each man as he clambered out of the launch, telling them to chamber a round and set the selectors on their AK-47s to safe. He nodded to Irina Yakoleva and pointed toward the mission building. Lieutenant Shpagin had set up headquarters there. He smiled as she approached.

"Good morning. Things are going well. Another half hour and the entire landing party will be ashore. Then we will be ready for our stroll up the mountain."

It is nice to be cheerful, but Irina did not think that the morning's activities would be a stroll. Already she could feel the heat and the humidity. That would be a disadvantage.

"If I may make a suggestion, let us form an advance party and start now. We may need all the daylight we have. Besides, I want to try this."

She lifted a canvas carrying case. "I brought this portable loudspeaker from the submarine. My English is excellent. Perhaps I can talk Cord out of fighting. He may not be fighting to defend the satellite. I think that he saw the missionaries shot. He may have thought we would kill him and simply fought in self-defense. Perhaps I can persuade him to stay away from us while we recover *War God*. After all, what we want is the satellite. If we get it, it doesn't matter if Cord lives or dies."

Lieutenant Shpagin looked dubious.

"Perhaps, but Cord does not sound like a man who will be easy to persuade. However, it costs nothing to try. I will be very happy if we can finish this mission without getting anyone killed. Give it a try."

ELU ISLAND—THE ROAD TO THE PLATEAU

Irina Yakoleva stepped round the first bend in the road to the plateau. She had the loudspeaker in one hand and kept her white flag prominently displayed in the other. She brought the portable loudspeaker up and pushed the button.

"Cord. Jack Cord. I am Irina Yakoleva. I am an officer in the Soviet armed forces. What happened yesterday was a mistake. There is no need for any more fighting. Come out and talk."

Her amplified voice echoed off the cliffs that formed the southern edge of the plateau. Nothing moved. Everything was quiet. Well, she had not really thought Cord would be stupid enough to show himself.

"Very well, Cord, if you do not want to come out, stay where you are and listen to me. This is not an invasion. We are not trying to take the island away from Australia. The satellite which landed on the plateau belongs to the Soviet Union. We must recover it. Then we will be gone. I am not asking you to surrender. I am not asking you to do anything. Just stay away from us while we recover our satellite. Be reasonable. There is no need for any more bloodshed. Think about it, Cord. What do you say?"

Silence.

"Do not be a fool, Cord. We outnumber you ten to

one. If you try to stop us, you will be killed, and we will recover the satellite anyway. There is no way you can stop us. Why die for nothing, Cord? You cannot—"

Five yards in front of her, the ground suddenly exploded in a shower of dust and dirt as a .303 full-metal-jacketed bullet tore into the ground at twice the speed of sound. A fraction of a second later, Irina heard the crack of Cord's rifle. The answer was clear.

Irina swore quietly. All right, Cord, you made your choice. Now we will kill you. She knew she was right. Even if Cord was the devil himself, he could not beat the odds against him. Still, it was going to be a long, hard, hot day.

Cord opened the bolt of his Lee-Enfield and pushed a fresh .303 cartridge into the magazine. He thought the blond had gotten his message. A .303 rifle bullet makes a very eloquent argument. What had she said her name was? Irene something or other. Well, Irene, maybe that will teach you not to make so much bloody noise so early in the morning.

It was interesting to know he was up against the Russians. But, the trouble was, the bitch was right. He had seen forty or fifty men come ashore from the submarine, all armed with AK-47s. He could probably hold them up for a while, kill some of them, but the odds were that he was not going to stop them. He—.

Something moved in the field of view of Cord's Mark II telescopic sight. Two men in dark coveralls dashed around the bend and took cover in the drainage ditches on each side of the road. All right, they had cover, but they couldn't stay there all day. Cord placed the cross hairs and post on the place where the man to his left had disappeared. He took a deep breath and let half of it out.

Steady down, Cord, steady down. Suddenly, the man was on his feet, ready to dash forward. Cord squeezed his trigger and the Lee-Enfield roared. The man dropped in his tracks. One down! But Cord knew it was going to be a long, hard day.

Leningradski Komsomol's landing party was pinned down at the third bend in the road. Irina Yakoleva was seething with frustration. Fighting Cord on this damned road was like fighting a ghost. He stayed under cover and changed his position often. The landing party never saw him, never got a shot, but anyone who got a little careless was in mortal danger. They could not use their superior numbers effectively.

None of their attempts to flank Cord had been successful. He simply faded away to another position and resumed his deadly sniping. He was not interested in being heroic and shooting it out with them. He was simply conducting a superb delaying action. That made Irina nervous. It must mean that Cord knew something that they did not. Irina was afraid that Cord expected help to arrive. If he held them off long enough, the landing party might be wiped out. Cord was bad enough. Suppose the Australians landed an SAS squadron behind them!

In three hours, they had advanced less than a quarter of the way to the top. And they had suffered seven casualties. At this rate, the only question was whether they would run out of men or daylight first. There must be something they could do, but what? If they could get close to Cord, pin him down and use their automatic weapons, it would all be over, but Cord knew that. It was hard to think. The temperature was over ninety degrees, and the humidity was brutal. Sweat was trickling down her back and between her breasts.

Lieutenant Shpagin dropped down into the drainage ditch by Irina Yakoleva.

"It does not go well. How many bends are there on this damned road?"

Irina tried to remember what she had seen from the KGB plane.

"Nine or ten. The road was built so that trucks could haul ore from the mines down to the harbor. The twists and turns keep the grade from being too steep. Unfortunately, it is ideal for ambushes, and Cord knows the ground. We must change our tactics and try something new."

Lieutenant Shpagin nodded.

"Tell me what you think best and we will try it. Frankly, I do not understand this kind of fighting. Well, at least one thing is in our favor, Cord is not as good a shot as we feared."

Irina looked blank. She never wanted to be shot at by anyone who was a better shot than Cord.

"I mean he has hit seven of our men. Two are dead, but five are only wounded. Should not a master sniper shoot better than that?"

"If he is shooting to kill. He may not be. Think. If he kills a man, that is the end of it. If he wounds a man, we must take care of him, get him back down the mountain and to the submarine. Wounded men sap our strength. Cord may not be shooting to kill."

That was an unpleasant thought. Lieutenant Shpagin did not like it.

"Very well. What shall we do next?"

Irina sighed. Lieutenant Shpagin would lead the men, but it was obvious that she must come up with the plan. She smiled to herself. Well, Yakoleva, yesterday you wanted to do the planning for Barsukov. Do not complain now that you have the responsibility.

She felt a breeze on her face. Off to the west a line

of low-lying, fast-moving clouds was approaching the island. Irina could smell moisture in the air. Rain! This might be it. If Cord could not see well, he could not shoot well. If they could get a few men behind him and pin him down, Cord would be finished.

"Let us take a chance. When the rain hits, have Moiseev take half the men and rush him. The rain will hamper Cord's shooting. We will put down heavy suppressing fire, and try to get around the next bend. If only a few of us get behind him, I think we will have him. He cannot fight in two directions at the same time."

"Very well, I will give the orders. When the rain hits, we go."

Cord was waiting around the bend, about two hundred yards up the road. He did not like waiting, he preferred action. Things had been quiet for ten or fifteen minutes. He did not like that. They were planning something, he could feel it. He checked his weapons again. The Lee-Enfield was ready, ten rounds in its magazine. The Owen gun was ready, too. It was extra weight to carry, but if he made a mistake and they got in close, he would need his Owen gun.

He wiped the sweat from his face. He was not comfortable. His head ached, his damned knee throbbed, and he was feeling the mounting tension of steady moving and fighting. A breeze began to blow from the west. Well, at least that was something. Perhaps it would get a little cooler. Cord watched as the line of clouds swept over the island. It was nothing unusual. Tropical rain showers were common on Elu.

Scattered drops of rain began to fall. Cord took off his bush hat and placed it over the telescopic sight on his Lee-Enfield. Better to get his head wet than his scope. Now the rain came down in sheets. Cord was protected a little by the trees around him, but it was obviously he was going to get soaked. Well, he had been wet before. The SAS teaches you a certain amount of disdain for minor discomfort.

He glanced down toward the bend in the road as the rain came down harder still. Bloody hell! He couldn't see the bend in the road. He could barely see fifty yards. Cord snapped his Owen gun to his shoulder and pushed the selector to automatic. If they had any sense, they would be coming now.

Cord saw dark shapes moving through the rain. They were learning; they kept three or four meters apart. He looked through the sights of the Owen gun and squeezed the trigger. The Owen roared into life and spat six full-metal-jacketed 9mm bullets at the Russians. Cord swung the Owen along the road, firing burst after burst as he changed the mantra of a good submachine gunner to himself as he fired. Short bursts! Short bursts! Short bursts! Some of the dark shapes fell. Cord could not be sure whether he had hit them or not. They might be taking cover in the drainage ditch. With a click, the Owen ran dry as the thirty rounds in its magazine were exhausted. Quickly, Cord reached for another magazine.

Suddenly, an AK-47 opened fire from the ditch. Then another, and another. Steel-jacketed .30 caliber bullets ripped through the trees and ricocheted off the ground. They were not quite sure where Cord was. They simply blasted any place Cord might be. He ducked as a ten-round burst came unpleasantly near. Predictably, they all emptied their magazines simultaneously. Bloody amateurs! But the damage had been done. Some of them had vanished up the road, invisible in the rain. Time to break contact and move out.

Cord snapped the Owen gun to his shoulder and fired a quick series of short bursts, raking the lip of the ditch. That should make the bloody bastards keep their heads down. Cord grabbed the Lee-Enfield and faded into the bush.

Irina Yakoleva was going with Moiseev's group. She had picked up an AK-47 from a wounded sailor and put on the web equipment. The AK-47 was a real weapon. She had had enough of that stupid KGB silenced submachine gun. The rain was pouring down now. Irina was soaked to the skin, but she hardly noticed. Moiseev looked at her inquiringly. She nodded and Moiseev shouted the order.

The assault group got to their feet and rushed round the bend. Irina felt her stomach tighten as she ran up the road. Cord had had two chances to shoot her before, and hadn't. Now, she was carrying an AK-47 and wearing web equipment. She knew that Cord would not hesitate to squeeze the trigger if he got her in his sights. Of course, she was ready to return the compliment, if she could just get him in her sights!

They were moving rapidly up the road. Irina had long legs. A stride for her, when she was running, was close to a meter. She counted to herself, 50 meters, 100, 150; perhaps Cord wasn't there. Then she heard the rapid chatter of a 9mm submachine gun firing on full auto. Bullets tore into the road or whined by as Cord raked the advancing group. Two men fell. Others, following Moiseev's orders, took cover in the drainage ditch, and began to lay down covering fire.

The submachine gun stopped firing. The AK-47s continued to fire. Irina kept counting, 200 meters, 250, 300. Good! They were past the point where Cord could see them. Now, if they could just cut him off and pin him down. She heard the 9mm submachine gun open fire again, burst after burst. Then, silence. Suddenly, the rain stopped, and, within moments, the sun came out. Instantly, Irina took cover. Cord and his sniper's rifle were back in the game.

She waited, hopefully, for the sound of more firing. None came. She had a sinking feeling that Cord had faded away. The rain shower was gone; they no longer had its cover. They were back to fighting Cord for the road. Irina swore to herself.

Chapter Seven

"Let your plans be dark and impenetrable as night, and when you move, fall on the enemy like a thunderbolt."
—Sun Tzu

THE CRISIS CENTER—THE PENTAGON—
WASHINGTON, D.C.

Brand was briefing the national security adviser. He was tired and irritable. So was everyone else in the room. The civilians had no experience with the problems of moving men and weapons over long distances. They thought things were proceeding very slowly. The military felt that they were being asked to move at an impossibly rapid pace.

Brand's stomach was acid. Too much Pentagon coffee and not enough sleep. Still, for the first time he was going to tell them something they wanted to hear. He pointed at the map. A long yellow line now stretched from Guam to Elu.

"Gentlemen, this is Task Force Eagle. The Task Force consists of nine B-52Gs from SAC. They are carrying thirty-eight officers and men from the 1st Special Forces Group and two civilian scientists. They refueled from KC-10 tankers approximately three hours ago. The B-52s will drop the landing force and weapons and supplies. Our men will use precision parachute landing techniques to land on the plateau. One B-52 is configured for the low-altitude antishipping role. She is carrying a surprise for that Russian submarine the NSA detected. Task Force Eagle will arrive over Elu in approximately one hour. Unless we recall them, they're going in. Any questions?"

The man from State raised his hand.

"These Special Group soldiers, are they first-class troops?"

Brand blinked. Working with Washington civilians was not always easy.

"Well, sir, they are from the 1st Special Forces Group, they're Green Berets. I believe we can assume that they are competent."

There were a few chuckles at that.

The national security adviser smiled bleakly.

"They'd better be good. They're going in."

TASK FORCE EAGLE—EN ROUTE TO ELU

The first camouflaged B-52G flew steadily on, its eight Pratt & Whitney J57-43W turbojet engines maintaining an altitude of 38,000 feet and a cruising speed of 560 miles per hour. Behind the leader, eight more of the huge aircraft followed in a loose formation.

Captain Andy Carter sat in a small pressurized compartment just aft of the lead B-52's flight deck. The compartment was crowded with nine other soldiers and their weapons and equipment. The other men, like sensible soldiers, were asleep. But Carter was the commanding officer. He stayed awake and worried.

There were plenty of things to worry about. Carter didn't like this mission. He and his men were going to make a High Altitude–High Opening jump. All of his men had made HAHO jumps before, but none of them had ever jumped from a B-52. The near airflow, the disturbance in the air as it flowed over the B-52's huge fuselage and wings at two hundred miles per hour, would be bad. It would be like dropping into a hurricane. And they were jumping heavy. Every man had an M16A2 rifle in a jump case, and they were festooned with spare magazines, grenades, and assorted knives and pistols.

Jumping with all that gear was not the safest thing in the world, but Carter had decided they must take the risk. No one knew what the situation was on that damned island. He and his men had to be ready to fight the moment they hit the ground.

The compartment door opened. An air force sergeant came in. He carefully picked his way to Carter. He clearly believed in letting sleeping Green Berets lie. He was a smart man. There were several men in his detachment that Carter, himself, would not have wanted to startle.

"Major Banford says we're twenty minutes out. You and your men should get ready to jump. Please come to the flight deck when you're ready."

Carter nodded and started rousing his men. The next ten minutes were hectic as the ten men struggled into their helmets, chutes, and gear. Some strong opinions were expressed about the air force, in general, and B-52s, in particular, but Carter's men were old hands, and somehow they got it done. Carter checked each man's oxygen tanks and mask personally. At thirty-eight thousand feet, the outside air was so thin that anyone whose mask or tanks failed would be unconscious in thirty seconds. Carter finished his check. He was satisfied. He and his men were ready.

The air force sergeant reappeared. He looked anxious. "Major Banford says please come to the flight deck now, sir!"

Carter followed him slowly and carefully, moving clumsily in more than a hundred pounds of bulky gear. There was a cold knot in Carter's stomach. The sudden summons almost certainly meant something was wrong.

Major Paul Banford looked up from his instruments as Carter stood behind the pilot's seat.

"Captain, we're sixty miles out, on course, ETA is nine minutes, but the electronic warfare officer has picked up an air search radar operating on or near Elu. It could be a warship with surface-to-air missiles. I'm going to go into a holding pattern and send *Eagle Nine* down to investigate. Sorry for the delay. Keep your men ready to jump. I'll let you know what happens"

LENINGRADSKI KOMSOMOLS—ELU HARBOR

Captain Khrenov was unhappy. Any submarine captain is unhappy when he is on the surface in a danger zone. But Khrenov had to stay on the surface to maintain communications with the landing party. That meant he was a sitting bird for any patrol plane or surface ship that happened by.

There was only one thing he could do. *Leningradski Komsomols* had an excellent air surveillance radar. It could detect any approaching aircraft. But, if he turned it on, its pulses could be detected by hostile electronic intercept equipment. Then, his own radar would act as a beacon to lead the enemy to him. On the other hand, if he left it off, he could be surprised and—to hell with it! Better to do something than sit here and do nothing.

"Radar, stand by to search. Sweep the horizon for sixty seconds, then shut down unless you detect something."

The radar officer nodded.

"Understood, Captain, starting search now."

The antenna of the Snoop Slab radar mounted on top of *Leningradski Komsomols*'s conning tower began to revolve smoothly, sending pulse after pulse of high-frequency radio energy out toward the horizon. The radar officer stared at his scope. He did not expect to see anything, but orders are orders. Khrenov was a cool and cautious commander, and that is the best kind to have if you want to live to draw your pension. Suddenly, he stiffened.

"Captain! Aircraft detected! Eight of them, bearing starboard 43, strong returns, large aircraft, altitude 38,000 feet, speed 550 knots."

Eight aircraft? Damn and blast! Khrenov wasted no time wondering who, what, or why. He made his decision instantly.

"Engineering! Emergency! Give me full power now!"

The engineering officer wasted no time asking questions. The control rods slid smoothly out of *Leningradski Komsomols*'s twin reactors, and steam flashed to the turbines. Her huge propellors began to revolve, and *Leningradski Komsomols* began to move out to sea toward deeper water.

"*Stand by to dive!*" Khrenov would take her down as soon as he had two hundred feet of water under the keel.

"Captain!" The radar officer shouted the alarm. "There is another one. Bearing starboard forty-four. He's diving hard. He's making a run straight at us!"

EAGLE NINE—OFF ELU

Eagle Nine was diving hard. The old airframe shuddered and shook as five hundred thousand pounds of airplane plunged down through the thicker, lower air. Like all B-52s, she was an old airplane. She was more than thirty years old, older than her pilot and her crew, more than old enough to vote! Capt. Ray Chavez was in the pilot's seat. He kept his eyes on his instruments, and his hands on the control yoke. He wanted to get down fast, but it would be embarrassing if he pulled the wings off.

Chavez eased the yoke back, and *Eagle Nine*'s nose came up as the huge aircraft leveled off at a thousand feet. Chavez spoke into his intercom mike.

"EO?"

"He's still radiating, air search pattern, dead ahead."

"Weapons?"

"All Harpoons checked out and ready for launch."

No use waiting any longer.

"Fire One and Four!"

The weapons officer pushed the button.

Two AGM-84D Harpoon cruise missiles dropped from beneath *Eagle Nine*'s wings and started their J402 jet engines. Quickly, they dived to sea-skimming altitude and roared toward Elu at Mach .75.

Four minutes later, their PR-53/DSQ-58 homing radars clicked on and began their programmed search patterns. Yes, there was a target, a large one, moving fast. Their homing radars locked on, and both missiles roared toward the target.

LENINGRADSKI KOMSOMOLS—OFF ELU

Khrenov was sweating blood. The charts showed 180 feet, but charts can be wrong. *Leningradski Komsomols* was a big submarine. A fast dive in shallow waters would be dangerous. But could he wait any longer?

"Radar! Where's that plane?"

"We've lost him, Captain, he's below our radar horizon."

Now, what was he doing? Was he coming in on a bombing run? Or was he—?

Suddenly, the electronic warfare officer was shouting.

"Captain! Radars detected. Hostile cruise missiles incoming, bearing starboard forty-four. Terminal homing mode!"

Instantly, Khrenov pushed his intercom button. His amplified voice rang through *Leningradski Komsomols*'s hull.

"Emergency dive! Dive! Dive! Dive!"

Leningradski Komsomols shuddered as hundreds of tons of seawater roared into her ballast tanks. *Leningradski Komsomols* began to slip beneath the surface as she grew heavier and heavier. She was going down, but not fast enough.

Khrenov snapped his orders.

"Planesman, negative twenty degrees on the bow."

Leningradski Komsomols was moving at more than twenty knots. As the diving planes pointed the bow downward, 40,000 horsepower began to drive her 5,200-ton hull under. *Leningradski Komsomols* shook and vibrated as she plunged downward. The attack center crew stared at their gauges in horror. If *Leningradski Komsomols* struck the bottom at this speed—

"Planesman, level her off, zero degrees angle on the bow!"

Leningradski Komsomols began to level off, like an airplane coming out of a dive. Khrenov glanced at the depth gauge. Two hundred feet. There had been no margin for error.

Radar pulses will not penetrate water. The Harpoon homing radars lost their target as *Leningradski Komsomols*'s huge hull vanished beneath the surface. They returned to search mode, but there was no longer any target for them to detect. They roared over *Leningradski Komsomols* and streaked on toward Elu. It had been close, but *Leningradski Komsomols* had survived.

EAGLE TASK FORCE—OVER ELU

"Eagle Force, this is *Eagle One. Eagle Nine* attacked a hostile submarine. The submarine dived. No further radar emissions detected. We're going in. Prepare to drop troops two minutes from now."

Eight huge B-52Gs began a wide, shallow turn and headed straight for Elu.

Chapter Eight

"Place your force in deadly peril, and it will survive; plunge it into desperate straits, and it will come through safely."
                                                              —Sun Tzu

DETACHMENT—1ST SPECIAL FORCES
GROUP (AIRBORNE)—ELU

Captain Carter and his men stood in the forward bomb bay of *Eagle One*. Carter was acutely aware that they were standing on the bomb bay doors. When they opened, there would be nothing below him but thirty-eight thousand feet of air.

The one-minute warning light was on. The bomb bay was not pressurized. Carter and his men were breathing oxygen from their bail out bottles, the individual oxygen tanks that would keep them alive until they were below ten thousand feet. Carter was acting as his own jump master. He gave each man a final check. Their faces and heads were covered by their helmets and masks. Gloves, boots, masks, and insulated jumpsuits protected the rest of their bodies. It was 70 degrees below zero outside, and the air would be blowing past the B-52's fuselage at 150 knots when they jumped. It would be like stepping into an icy hurricane. Any unprotected skin would suffer almost instant frostbite.

Carter made a thumbs-up gesture at his men. Each man returned the gesture with his own thumbs up. Good. No one was having breathing problems or trouble with his gear. Carter pointed upward, and each man gripped the nylon drop net. The Green Berets were spaced around the outer edges of the net. When it was released, the heavily weighted center would pull them down rapidly through the airflow around *Eagle One*'s huge fuselage.

The thirty-second warning light came on. There was a sudden change in the roar of the engines as Banford throttled back. He would hold *Eagle One* as close to stalling speed as he dared in order to minimize the airflow around the fuselage. When he was satisfied, he would push the ten-second warning light. That would activate the drop sequence. Unless Carter called an abort, they would go.

Eagle One began to shudder and shake as her speed dropped to within a few knots of stalling. Satisfied, Major Banford pushed the button. The ten-second warning light came on, the standby order, the last warning before the jump.

Eagle One's bomb bay doors swung smoothly open. Carter and his men were hanging from the drop net, with nothing beneath their jump boots but thirty-eight thousand feet of air.

Carter felt a quick surge of fear. He was always frightened at the instant before he jumped, but he always went. Looking down, he saw a God's-eye view of Elu. At least they were in the right place! Nothing left to do now but pray.

Suddenly, the go light was on. There was a loud cracking noise as tiny explosive devices cut the drop net free. The weighted center of the net dropped instantly through the bomb bay doors. Carter and his men were buffeted by the airstream as the net pulled them down and clear. Three, Two, One! Release! The net dropped away. Carter and his men were in free-fall. Looking up, Carter could see the huge wings and fuselage of *Eagle One* glinting in the sun as she pulled away. Her aft bomb bay doors were open, and cargo drop containers were falling into the slipstream.

Carter used his arms and legs to assume a face-down position. He was counting to himself without thinking as he glanced quickly to the left and right. He could see *Eagle Two* and *Eagle Three* clearly. Dark shapes were falling free below the huge B-52s.

Eight, Nine, Ten! Carter pulled his ripcord. His pilot chute deployed, pulling his special high-performance, ram-air canopy out of its pack and into the air. The canopy blossomed, and Carter felt a strong jolt as the canopy filled with air and slowed his fall. Quickly, he slipped his hands into his steering loops, ready to maneuver if he had to. A collision with one of his men could ruin his whole day! Rapidly, he looked around and counted, seven, eight, nine. He felt a surge of relief. Everyone's chute had opened. He estimated the dispersion of his group at less than one hundred meters.

Their special chutes could be flown like hang gliders, allowing them to fly down at angles as great as forty-five degrees if they had to. They should be able to come down close together on the assembly point. Good. Carter had no real idea of the situation on Elu. They might have to fight for their lives the instant they hit the ground.

At the moment, things were almost peaceful. The sun was shining, and the air was clear. The roar of the B-52's engines faded into silence. All Carter could hear was the sound of his demand-regulated breathing and the air sighing through his canopy's suspension lines.

Looking down, he could see Elu below him. From this altitude, it looked lovely, lush green forests, clear blue water, and white waves breaking softly on the beach. Carter had the dismal feeling he was going to hate it when he got to know it better. That is the trouble with a HAHO jump, it leaves you with too much time to think. It would be fifteen minutes before Carter and his men hit the ground.

There was a brief crackle of static, and Major Banford's voice sounded in Carter's earphones.

"Talon Leader, this is *Eagle One. Eagle Two, Three,* and *Four* report all personnel and cargo containers cleared their aircraft. *Eagle Five* and his flight are standing by. We are running short of time and fuel. Do you want them to drop? If so, designate area. Over."

Carter was Talon Leader. He wondered, not for the first time, who the hell it is who makes up these names?

"*Eagle One,* this is Talon Leader. Uncertain of situation on ground. Over."

"Roger, Talon Leader. *Eagle Nine* is still down low. He will make a low-altitude pass. Stand by, out."

EAGLE NINE—OFF ELU

Eagle Nine was thirty miles east of Elu at two thousand feet. Ray Chavez grinned when he got the message.

"Roger, *Eagle One,* going in."

"Come on, Bill," Chavez said. "Let's show the peasants some real flying, full power."

The roar of the eight J57-43W turbojets deepened as the copilot pushed the throttles home. He wondered for the thousandth time what maniac had chosen Ray Chavez to fly bombers. He was a born fighter pilot if there ever was one, and the fact that *Eagle Nine* was a B-52, not an F-15, did not bother him in the slightest. Oh, well, flying with Ray was seldom boring.

Chavez pushed *Eagle Nine*'s nose down and leveled off at a hundred feet. The big plane vibrated and shuddered as she shot over the water at 550 miles per hour.

"Terrain avoidance radar on."

The forward-looking X-band radar began to scan ahead. An alarm sounded as it detected Elu. Things happen fast at ten miles per minute.

The radar altimeter indicated ninety-five feet. Good enough, they were usually accurate to twenty-five feet.

Elu seemed to grow larger and larger in the windscreen.

Chavez and his copilot gripped their control yokes. This was no time to make a mistake. The plateau road rose in front of them. A little right rudder, and *Eagle Nine* roared straight for the point where the road reached the top of the plateau. Chavez relaxed. They were going to clear it by forty or fifty feet.

ELU ISLAND—THE ROAD TO THE PLATEAU

Irina Yakoleva felt a surge of triumph. Cord had not been able to stop them this time. Five or six of *Leningradski Komsomols*'s sailors had made it onto the plateau in the last rush. She could hear their AK-47s firing, punctuated by the louder crack of Cord's Lee-Enfield. At last, they had gotten off this damned road. With room to maneuver, they could bring their superior numbers to bear. All they had to do now was—

Something strange was happening. The air around her seemed to be vibrating, and there was a dull roar, like a distant waterfall. The roaring noise grew louder and louder. The trees and the ground began to vibrate. Irina glanced to her right and froze in amazement. Something gigantic was coming through the air, coming straight at her! For a moment, her mind was paralyzed. Then, her training took over. She was, after all, an intelligence officer. It was a plane. A gigantic plane coming head on at treetop level.

She saw the big oval fuselage, the huge swept-back wings, two dual engine pods under each wing, and a great vertical stabilizer towering above the fuselage. Nothing else in the world looks like that. It was a B-52! An American B-52 bomber!

Irina threw herself down. With an immense roaring noise, the B-52 flashed over the road, clearing it by less than fifty feet. A few hardy souls brought up their AK-47s and fired as the B-52 flashed by. Irina saw four bright yellow lights flashing from the B-52's tail. For half a second, Irina was puzzled. Then, 750 grain .50 caliber full-metal-jacketed bullets tore through the treetops as the B-52's tail gunner returned the compliment. Then, the B-52 was gone, roaring off toward the other side of the island.

Irina kept down. There are such things as retarded bombs that take many seconds to drop, but nothing happened. Lieutenant Shpagin threw himself down next to Irina Yakoleva.

"What in the name of the devil was that?"

"An American B-52."

Lieutenant Shpagin was impressed. When he was a child during the Vietnam War, the news had been full of the horrible atrocities committed by the American B-52s. Lieutenant Shpagin was too intelligent to believe everything the government told him. But after what he had just seen, he was ready to believe that a B-52 was a very dangerous airplane, indeed.

He snapped up his binoculars.

Irina was curious. "What is he doing?"

"Going on out to sea. It does not look as if he is coming back."

That was a relief. Irina had seen enough of that B-

52. She would be quite happy if she never saw another B-52 in her life.

Lieutenant Shpagin was puzzled.

"But why did he do that? He dropped no bombs. He did us no damage. What was he trying to accomplish?"

Irina Yakoleva was puzzled, too. It made no sense to her.

"I don't know, he must have been trying to do something. But what?"

EAGLE TASK FORCE—OVER ELU

Ray Chavez's voice came clearly through Maj. Paul Banford's earphones.

"Eagle One, this is *Eagle Nine.* Low-level pass completed. Approximately forty men along the road just below the plateau. Visual observation confirmed by the ASQ-151 infrared. And they are not nice people. They shot at us!"

"Roger, *Eagle Nine."*

Quickly, Banford switched channels.

"Talon Leader, This is *Eagle One. Eagle Nine* reports approximately forty hostile personnel where the road intersects the plateau. That's approximately eight hundred yards from your target. We have to do it now if we're going to do it. What's your decision?"

Carter did not hesitate. He needed something to provide cover as his team hit the ground.

"Eagle One, this is Talon Leader. Do it!"

Banford nodded.

"Eagle Five flight, did you copy that?"

"Roger, *Eagle One."*

"Execute."

Aboard *Eagle Five, Six, Seven,* and *Eight,* the crews checked their computers. The bomb bay doors slid smoothly open. Streamlined olive-drab shapes began to drop from the bomb bays and arc down toward Elu.

They were Mark 83 1,000-pound low drag bombs, 108 of them.

ELU ISLAND—THE ROAD TO THE PLATEAU

The B-52 had vanished, flying off to the west. But that did not mean it was gone. Perhaps it would climb, circle back, and attack them.

Irina Yakoleva turned to Lieutenant Shpagin and spoke urgently.

"We must get the rest of the men up on the plateau. We are vulnerable to an air attack here on the road, and that B-52 may come back."

Whatever doubts Lieutenant Shpagin had concerning Irina Yakoleva's tactical advice were long gone. He shouted an order, and the men began to move up the road. They stayed three meters apart and kept close to the drainage ditches at the side of the road. Good. They were learning.

Irina checked her AK-47 and moved forward. Well, Cord, you have had your fun on this damned road. Once we have you in the open it will be our turn to—. She stopped. There was a strange whistling-sighing sound. It was growing louder and louder. She had heard that sound before, in Afghanistan.

She hurled herself toward the drainage ditch, screaming at the top of her lungs.

"Bombs. Bombs! Take cover. Take cover! Bombs!"

Leningradski Komsomols's sailors had learned to take Irina Yakoleva's advice seriously. They dove for the ditches. Boom! Boom! *Boom!* A giant was stamping through the forest, closer and closer to the road. The ground shook, and the air vibrated. Huge gouts of dust and dirt filled the air. The noise was intolerable. Irina clapped her hands to her ears and screamed as the explosions walked across the road. A giant hand seemed to slap her entire body again and again. Dust and smoke obscured everything, and the acrid smell of burning explosives filled the air.

There was a sudden deafening silence, broken only by the sound of rocks and branches raining back to earth. Irina was dazed and shaken by the repeated blasts. She tried to think. She knew what had happened. She had studied such things at the academy. There had been other B-52s. Unseen and unheard, they had dropped their bombs from high altitude.

She struggled to her feet and looked around. All right, Yakoleva, you are a brilliant intelligence officer. Someday you can write a book on military history. At the moment, you are standing here like a fool, in the middle of a battle. Well, just don't stand there. Do something!

Half the bombs had exploded up on the edge of the plateau. The air must be full of smoke and dust up there, too. That was it! Cord would not be able to see them! The best sniper in the world is helpless when he cannot see his targets.

Irina waved and pointed up the road.

"Come on, men. Lets go! The smoke hides us. Cord cannot see us now! Go! Go! Go!"

The men were dazed, but a voice they knew was telling them what to do. Clutching their AK-47s, they got to their feet and ran up the road. Irina felt a sudden flush of embarrassment. She had assumed command and was screaming orders at Lieutenant Shpagin's men. He might be very angry.

But Shpagin was laughing as he ran up the road. The next time someone told him that all women were weak and timid, he would tell them about Irina Yakoleva.

DETACHMENT—1ST SPECIAL FORCES GROUP (AIRBORNE)—ELU

Carter glanced at the altimeter on his wrist. He was

at eight thousand feet now. He unsnapped his oxygen mask. He could feel the warm, humid air on his face below his goggles. There was little or no low-altitude wind. Good. The critical thing was to get his men down together and ready to fight before the enemy could react.

The scene beneath his boots was no longer peaceful. Fascinated, he watched *Eagle Nine* roar across the island. He had given *Eagle One* the execute order. Now, he waited tensely. Carter hoped the B-52s did not take too long. He did not like the idea of landing in the middle of an air strike.

He checked his altimeter again: 5,500 feet. What the hell was taking them so long. Then the world beneath his boots exploded. Carter watched, awestruck, as 108 1,000-pound bombs exploded in 60 seconds. He had heard the old timers talk about B-52 ARC LIGHT strikes in Vietnam and the incredible destruction they produced. Now, as he watched the huge cloud of dust and smoke below him, he had no trouble believing them.

There was no way to tell how many casualties the bombing had caused. But the Russians must be dazed and disorganized. Now, to get his team down and organized for combat before they could recover and react.

Carter scanned the plateau below him. He could see *War God* now, a massive silver-gray cylinder to his left. He pulled on his steering loops and tilted his canopy in a slow turn to the left, toward *War God.*

He glanced at his altimeter again: four thousand feet. He pulled down on his steering loops and went to full brake. Carter lost all forward thrust from his canopy and hung on the edge of a stall. As he lost forward motion, his rate of descent increased. The surface of the plateau seemed to shoot upward toward him.

All right, Carter, do it right. You are going to feel

extremely stupid if you break an ankle. *War God* was directly below him. He went to half brake and turned to the right. He wanted to land two hundred meters to the east of *War God,* toward the plateau road. He completed his turn and went to full brake. Now, he went straight down.

He was no longer a detached observer. He was down amongst them. He could hear rifle fire, AK-47s and something heavier he could not identify. At one hundred feet, Carter pulled the release and felt his equipment pack drop away and dangle below him. The ground came rushing up to meet him. Carter hit, rolled, and came back to his feet. He felt a thrill of relief. He was down and safe.

Carter pulled his quick release handles and slipped out of his harness. He was in the open with no cover. He did not like that. No infantryman does. No time to bother with his chute. He unclipped a red smoke grenade from his web equipment, pulled the pin, and threw it. The red smoke would mark his position for his team.

Carter opened the jump case and pulled out his M16A2 rifle. Quickly, he pulled the charging handle to the rear, chambering a round. He dropped into a prone position. He could still hear AK-47s firing, but no one seemed to be shooting at him. He looked around rapidly. Parachutes were raining down from the sky as cargo containers and soldiers hit the ground.

He had organized his team as three rifle squads and a support squad. To his left, Carter saw a yellow and then a green smoke plume, and to his right, a blue. Good, all his squad leaders were down. Now, if they could just get organized before the Russians counterattacked.

Coughing and cursing, *Leningradski Komsomols*'s landing party struggled through the smoke and dust. They could only see a few feet ahead, but Irina Yakoleva could feel that the ground beneath her feet was flat, no longer sloping upward. They were no longer moving up the hill, they were on the plateau.

Irina moved forward carefully. The dust and smoke were getting thinner. She could hear rifles firing ahead of her, AK-47s firing steadily and the occasional louder roar of Cord's Lee-Enfield. Careful now, Yakoleva, it is time to be cautious. It would not do to stroll casually out into the sunshine and have Cord put a bullet through your head.

She dropped down and crawled the last few meters. She blinked as she emerged into the bright sunlight and looked around. In a second, her eyes adjusted. Thirty meters ahead was a clump of low rocks. Moiseev was crouched behind the rocks with five sailors, firing their AK-47s at something ahead of them. They were firing semiautomatically, one shot at a time, not wasting ammunition. Good, Moiseev was maintaining fire discipline. Irina wriggled forward to the rocks and crouched by Moiseev. The warrant officer grinned and pointed at a clump of trees, two hundred meters ahead.

"We have him, Lieutenant Yakoleva, he is pinned down in those trees. He has no more cover to retreat to. Cord is a dead man."

A .303 rifle bullet smashed into the rocks a foot above Moiseev's head. Rock dust and splinters flew. Moiseev grinned again.

"Well, perhaps he is not quite dead yet, but we have him. Let's bring up some more men, surround these trees, and finish him."

Irina shook her head.

"No, Cord is not important now; *War God* is our objective. We must secure the satellite. Keep Cord pinned down here. The rest of us will go to *War God* and establish a defensive perimeter. You just keep Cord pinned down."

"Understood, Lieutenant, but you will not mind if I shoot Cord if I can?"

Irina Yakoleva grinned wickedly.

"Not in the slightest, Moiseev. You have my full and complete permission."

Irina ran back toward the road, keeping low in case Cord fired at her, but no shots came. Moiseev and his men were keeping Cord occupied. Lieutenant Shpagin had his men lying down, grouped in a rough arc. Their rifles were pointed outward, across the plateau, ready for action. Shpagin was learning. Irina briefed him quickly.

"I think we should move on the satellite immediately, as rapidly as we can. But we must go carefully. Whoever was with Cord yesterday may be guarding it."

Lieutenant Shpagin nodded. "Very well, I will give the orders."

It took a minute or two, and some shouting and swearing, but *Leningradski Komsomols*'s landing party formed a loose skirmish line and began to trot toward *War God.* Irina was good at estimating range. The satellite was about eight hundred meters away. She felt a thrill of anticipation. A few more minutes and they would have *War God!*

Suddenly, one of the sailors stopped and pointed upward. He was shouting something. For a moment, Irina could not catch the word. Then, it came loud and clear.

"Desantniki! Desantniki!"

Desantniki? Paratroops! Irina looked up. The sky was full of parachutes, raining down between her and *War God.* Some of the men stopped and began to fire their AK-47s. That was foolish. Only pure luck would let even the best shot hit a falling parachutist at four hundred meters.

Lieutenant Shpagin looked stunned. Nothing in his naval officer's career had prepared him for a situation like this. Irina knew what they must do. No time to explain or argue. She filled her lungs and shouted.

"Forward! Attack. Hit them before they can organize. Come on, men! Come on!"

Without waiting, she ran forward, toward *War God*. Behind her, she could hear Lieutenant Shpagin shouting orders. For a moment, Irina Yakoleva had the chilling thought that they might not follow her. But *Leningradski Komsomols*'s crew were brave men. Cord had given them a hard time on that damned road. Fighting him had been like fighting a ghost. But here were men they could see, and fight, and kill. With the deep, instinctive, wordless shout that has been the Russian battle cry for a thousand years, they surged forward.

DETACHMENT—1ST SPECIAL FORCES GROUP (AIRBORNE)—ELU

Carter started to get to his feet. He changed his mind rapidly as a .30 caliber rifle bullet whined by his head. Quickly, he used his field glasses. About four hundred meters away, a skirmish line of thirty to forty men was advancing, moving rapidly in his direction. They were wearing some kind of dark uniform which Carter did not know, but he could recognize their AK-47s and was absolutely certain they were not the welcoming committee from the Elu Chamber of Commerce. Damn! Someone on the other side knew what they were doing. An immediate counterattack is the thing the commander of any airborne operation dreads.

Carter's men had not had time to form up in squads and fire teams. Some of them were still coming down. It was going to be a soldier's battle, no brilliant decisions from the high command. But Carter's men were well trained and experienced. Immediately, without waiting for orders, his riflemen opened fire, and the spiteful crack of M16A2s answered the duller boom of the AK-47s. The Russians came on. As the range fell to three hundred meters, Carter heard the "blup" of M203 grenade launchers as his grenadiers lobbed 40mm high-explosive grenades at the enemy.

Carter stared through his glasses. Give the SOBs credit, they were coming on. Suddenly, Carter stiffened in disbelief. For a second, he thought he saw a tall blond woman in civilian clothes leading the attack. Sober up, Carter, you've made too many damned HAHO jumps on oxygen!

Carter sighed with relief as he heard first one, then several SAWs open up. He had six of the deadly little 5.56mm Squad Automatic Weapons. They were light machine guns, firing the same cartridge as his M16 rifles, but they were firing burst after burst of full automatic fire from two hundred–round belts. Now, he heard a louder, deeper roar as his two M60 machine guns opened fire and sent burst after burst of .30 caliber full-metal-jacketed bullets at the advancing Russians. The guns were not perfectly placed. They did not have carefully selected interlocking fields of fire, but they were enough. Under the sustained fire of eight machine guns, the Russian attack wilted. They no longer came on, but dropped to the ground, taking advantage of what cover there was, and fired back with their AK-47s.

Carter thought rapidly. They showed no signs of going away. Logically, he ought to counterattack, but his men were still fighting as individuals. There was no way to organize an attack under fire. Leaping up and yelling, "Charge!" would get him nothing but a lot of casualties. Perhaps he could—

Tube noise! A mortar firing. It is the ugliest sound

in the world or the loveliest, depending on whether it is your mortar or theirs. The sound was coming from behind Carter. His one and only M242 60mm mortar was in action, firing as fast as the three-man crew could drop the 60mm bombs down the muzzle. The bombs arced high into the air and plunged down on the Russian positions. The 3.5-pound bombs seemed almost like toys, but they were lethal toys and they sprayed *Leningradski Komsomols*'s landing party with lethal fragments. There was no cover on the open plateau against mortar fire coming straight down. It was too much. Through his field glasses, Carter could see them start to fall back and withdraw. They did it in good order, some men providing covering fire while others withdrew, then alternating. They were retreating toward the road, back off the plateau.

ELU ISLAND—THE PLATEAU

Cord was waiting in his last position. Too right, it was his last position. He had intended to hold them where the road entered the plateau, then fall back toward the trees near *War God*. He had waited too long. Two or three of them had gotten in the rocks about two hundred meters away and were firing steadily. They didn't know exactly where he was, but it didn't really matter. If he left the cover of the trees, he was a dead man. If he stayed put, they would infiltrate more men, surround him, and he was finished. He checked his Owen gun. It never occurred to Cord to try to surrender. He did not think they were interested in taking prisoners. Let the bastards come. He would take some of them with him.

For some reason, Cord thought of his mother. She was deeply religious and always said if you do your duty the best you can, God will help you when you really need it. There was a loud roaring noise, and a huge green-and-brown camouflaged aircraft roared across the edge of the plateau, fifty feet above the ground. Cord recognized it instantly, a B-52. This did not look like divine intervention, more like the American air force. But when you are fighting alone and outnumbered, it is very encouraging to find that the U.S. Air Force is on your side.

Cord heard the sound of falling bombs and watched in awe as the edge of the plateau seemed to explode in dust and smoke. Unfortunately, they had not dropped one on those bastards in the rocks, and they were still shooting. Still, their mates on the road were not going to feel like coming after Cord for a few minutes.

Cord listened carefully. For a few minutes, nothing happened. Then he heard a number of AK-47s firing rapidly. That was strange. They weren't firing at him. Just who were they shooting at? Cord risked moving to the edge of the trees. Some of the Russians were shooting upward. The sky seemed to be full of parachutes. Cord snapped up his field glasses. He had jumped before. He knew the drill. Some of the chutes were for equipment, but others were carrying men. Cord liked what he saw. He recognized American leaf-striped camouflaged uniforms and the funny new American helmet that looks like the ones the Germans wore in World War II.

It almost seemed like time to celebrate, but Cord was cautious. Not everyone who wears an American uniform is an American. He fell back toward the center of the trees. Suddenly, Cord heard a snapping, crackling noise. One of the jumpers was crashing down through the branches. He was a big man, wearing the American uniform. He released his harness, and pulled a rifle from his jump case. He was facing away from Cord.

Careful, now, Cord. It would not due to get your

head blown off by a friendly visitor. You would both regret it. The man was swearing, fluently and in English. Even Cord was startled. It really did not seem possible that the designer of the parachute had done all those peculiar things with his female relatives. Cord took cover behind a fallen log. He reminded himself to sound as Australian as possible.

"G'day, mate."

The man whirled in a perfect response right, the flash hider of his M16A2 pointed in the direction of Cord's voice. Cord sighed with relief. The man was nearly six and a half feet tall, he was covered with weapons and ammunition, there was a ferocious snarl on his face, but he was black. The only black Russians Cord had ever seen were poured into glasses in bars.

"Who the hell's there?"

"Easy, mate, I'm Cord."

Cord reached into his haversack and took out his last can of Foster's lager beer. He raised it slowly above the top of the log. It was the friendliest gesture he could think of.

"Cord?"

"Right, mate. Jack Cord, Number 2 Squadron, Australian SAS. Welcome to Elu. How about a beer?"

The American began to shake. He laughed harder and harder, almost doubling over. He stood up and wiped his eyes.

"Jesus Christ! I've jumped on more God damned DZs than I can remember, but this is the first one where anyone ever offered me a beer. I'm Frank Jackson, glad to meet you, Cord!"

ELU ISLAND—THE VILLAGE

Irina Yakoleva sat in the mission sanctuary. She had finished treating the wounded. In a few minutes, the launch would take them out to *Leningradski Komso-*

109

mols. She was writing a message. Carefully she described the day's events on Elu. Her last paragraph would be critical. Slowly, she wrote: "American elite troops now hold *War God.* Naval landing party cannot hope to recapture it. Recommend *Spetsnaz* or VDV Air Assault troops be sent to Elu immediately.

         —Senior Lieutenant I. A. Yakoleva, Elu."

She thought for a moment. She must be certain the message got to someone who could do something about it. Irina was not timid. She addressed her message to Colonel-General S. P. Galanskov—Immediate and Personal. He was the highest-ranking GRU officer whose name she knew.

Lieutenant Shpagin sat nearby. He was pale and shaken. He had taken an M16 bullet through the shoulder. Irina handed him the message.

"Please ask Captain Khrenov to send this to Moscow immediately via SATCOM."

Lieutenant Shpagin nodded.

Irina hesitated for a moment. General Galanskov was an important man. His staff officers would screen his messages. They might pay no attention to a message from a mere Senior Lieutenant. She took the message back and printed, Priority—War God—Elu, at the top and bottom. There, that ought to get some action!

Chapter Nine

"Above all else, show no zeal."   —Talleyrand

THE CRISIS CENTER—MOSCOW, USSR

General Galanskov entered a small office near the crisis center conference room. The chairman sat inside at a small oak desk. His suit was rumpled, and he looked tired. Galanskov was on guard, alert for trouble. A sudden summons from officials of the chairman's rank can be extremely hazardous.

"You wished to see me, comrade?"

Yes, General, I need to talk to you."

The chairman gestured toward a bottle and glasses on the table.

"Do you drink vodka, Stepan Pavelovich? This is a Polish herb-flavored vodka. It has an excellent taste."

Galanskov relaxed a bit. You do not call a man by his first name and offer him vodka if you intend to dismiss him or have him shot.

"Thank you, comrade, I would like a glass."

Actually, Galanskov thought that flavored vodka was effete and decadent, but it did not seem to be the time or place to express his opinion.

The chairman poured.

"It is about this cursed *War God* affair. Things do not go well. Have you seen the latest reports, General? The KGB team was slaughtered. We have a submarine off Elu. A landing party was sent ashore, but the Americans put elite troops on the island, and the landing party was defeated. The Americans hold the plateau and *War God.* The situation is grave. What are we to do next? Speak frankly. We must do something to retrieve the situation."

Galanskov sipped his vodka. It really was not so bad, herbs or no herbs. He already knew everything the chairman had told him as a result of a well-written report from this useful person, Senior Lit. Irina Yakoleva. She was a credit to the GRU. He made a mental note to see that she was promoted to captain, provided she lived through this affair. Now, he must play his cards carefully.

"Comrade, what I am about to say could be misunderstood. It might appear that I am attacking the KGB or the navy. This is not the case. I am merely giving you my analysis of the situation, and my best advice, as you have requested."

He paused and looked at the chairman. The chairman nodded. "Go on, General."

"Very well. The problem is that we have made wrong decisions, attempted to accomplish our objectives with the wrong personnel."

The chairman frowned, but Galanskov had his attention.

"Explain."

"Modern warfare is very complex, comrade. No one man or group of men can be expert in all types of operations. For example, it was not a bad idea to send the KGB team to Elu. Had there been no military opposition, they could have dealt with the civilians there and

112

secured the satellite. But there was military opposition. They had the wrong weapons and the wrong training. Two or three elite Australian soldiers killed them all. I do not doubt that the KGB agents were brave men. I am sure that they tried to do their duty, but they were not elite soldiers. Against the Australian SAS they stood no chance. They were slaughtered to a man."

The chairman nodded and poured himself a second glass of vodka.

Galanskov continued smoothly: "Similarly, to send the submarine, *Leningradski Komsomols,* to Elu was a brilliant move. She can attack and sink any ship that tries to approach the island. Admiral Milshtcyn says her captain is an excellent officer with a well-trained crew. But to send them ashore to fight elite American troops was most unwise. We have confirmed through GRU channels that forty to fifty members of the American Special Forces, their Green Berets, are now on Elu. Our sailors stood no chance against such men."

"You have made your point, General. What are you recommending?"

"Paramilitary operations are the responsibility of the GRU and the army, and we are organized and prepared to conduct them. We have men who can deal with American elite troops, our own special purpose troops, *Spetsnaz.*"

The chairman nodded. He had heard about *Spetsnaz.* It was said they had done astounding things in Afghanistan.

"You have a plan?"

It is underway as we speak, comrade. I have assembled a picked *Spetsnaz* team under a highly qualified officer, Colonel Viktor Ulanov."

"Ulanov, Viktor Ulanov. Somehow, that name seems familiar."

"He was in the news some years ago. He led the counterattack at Mazar-e-Sharif in Afghanistan. Ulanov was a captain then. He saved a battalion of the 360th Motorized Rifle Division from certain destruction. He was awarded the Order of the Hero of the Soviet Union for that action."

"Yes, the press made much of him at the time. From what you say, it seems that it was not undeserved. But are you sure he is the man for this job?"

Galanskov hesitated for a second. He must express himself carefully, very carefully. His reputation was on the line.

"I believe so. He is a brilliant officer. He has combat experience, and he is a good leader. They say in *Spetsnaz* that the men will attack hell itself, if Ulanov is leading them."

"So, a perfect officer?"

"No. He has one fault. He will never be a marshal. Ulanov is unorthodox. He comes up with unusual maneuvers and different tactics. That is very useful in combat, but it makes our orthodox generals very nervous."

The chairman smiled. "Ah, yes, I see. You are a clever fox, Stepan Pavelovich. Elu is an unorthodox situation. It calls for an unorthodox officer."

Galanskov nodded.

"Exactly so. In my opinion, Ulanov is the best officer we have to command this operation."

"Where is he now?"

"In flight to Vietnam. The *Spetsnaz* team is assembling there. All that is required is your approval."

The chairman spoke in his official voice.

"Very well, General Galanskov. You will assume command of the *War God* operation. Send in Ulanov and the *Spetsnaz* team. Give the orders immediately."

General Galanskov stood up and turned to leave.

"One other thing, Stepan Pavelovich: Do not fail!"

*   *   *

General Galanskov sat at the conference table, sipping a mug of strong, hot tea. He allowed himself to relax. Things were going well. He had outmaneuvered the KGB. The orders to Ulanov and the *Spetsnaz* team had been sent. The navy and the air force were being cooperative. Next, he would—.

Suddenly a navy officer was coming rapidly across the room. It was trouble, Galanskov would bet his last ruble on that.

The officer arrived and saluted.

"Sir, I am Captain Bezobrazov, naval intelligence. I have an urgent report from Pacific Fleet operations center. An American warship is approaching Elu."

Galanskov winced. That is all we need! First, their B-52s, then elite troops, now, their damned navy. He resisted the temptation to swear aloud.

"You are certain of this, Captain?"

"Yes, sir. Here are photographs from one of our reconnaisance satellites. There can be no doubt."

Galanskov was fascinated. It still seemed amazing that a satellite in space could take clear photographs of an object hundreds of miles below.

"It is clearly an American guided missile frigate of the Oliver Hazard Perry class."

"What are its capabilities?"

"It is primarily an antisubmarine ship, but it is also armed with antiaircraft missiles and antiship missiles."

Galanskov did not like the sound of that. "So, if this ship reaches Elu, it can attack *Leningradski Komsomols* and shoot down our aircraft when they arrive."

"Exactly so, General."

Galanskov did not hesitate. This must not be allowed to happen.

"Are *Leningradski Komsomols*'s missiles effective against ships of this type?"

Captain Bezobrazov smiled.

"Sir, her missiles are effective against any ship in the world."

"Then contact *Leningradski Komsomols* immediately. Order her to attack at once!"

Chapter Ten

"A single submarine is capable of destroying a major surface ship with a single salvo of cruise missiles."
—Sergei G. Gorshkov, Admiral of the Fleet

LENINGRADSKI KOMSOMOLS—OFF ELU

Captain Khrenov sat in *Leningradski Komsomols*'s control center, fighting to keep awake. With half his crew killed, wounded, or trapped on that stinking island, he had been forced to order his remaining officers and men on back-to-back watches. The endless routine of four hours on duty, four hours off to eat and sleep, then four hours back on duty again wore out the strongest men. It did not help that there were a dozen seriously wounded men on board. Submarines are either intact or blown to bits as the pressure hull fails under the first hit. Submarine designers do not provide facilities for treating large numbers of wounded men. Khrenov's crew was demoralized, and there was nothing he could do about it.

Orders were orders, and he must remain on the surface off this damned island, a sitting bird for any American submarine or patrol plane which might wander by.

Meanwhile, the remaining members of his landing party were being slaughtered by elite American troops. He commanded a powerful nuclear attack submarine, but none of his weapons were effective in this insane situation. His long-range cruise missiles and torpedoes were designed to be used against hostile ships and submarines. There was no way to use them against land targets. It was ironic: *Leningradski Komsomols* was a major threat to the largest and most powerful ships in the U.S. Navy. She could do nothing against a handful of Green Berets. Khrenov nodded in the captain's chair. There must be something he could do. Something . . .

"Captain! Captain! A message from Fleet headquarters. *Urgent—first priority!*"

Khrenov found himself looking into the face of *Leningradski Komsomols*'s junior communications officer. At least, he had not said, "Wake up, Captain." There was something peculiar about that young man's expression. For a moment, it eluded Khrenov as he struggled to wake up. Then he had it; the junior communications officer did not appear demoralized and ready to drop from exhaustion. Instead, his face blazed with excitement.

Khrenov took the message and began to read. His dazed, exhausted expression changed to a savage snarl of satisfaction. He reached for the intercom mike and began to speak. His voice echoed through *Leningradski Komsomols*'s compartments. His men stared up in apprehension. Not another detail to go ashore on that rotten, stinking island!

"Men. This is the captain speaking. I have just received a message from Fleet headquarters. An American warship is approaching, less than two hundred miles away. We are ordered to attack and sink her!"

A spontaneous cheer rang through *Leningradski*

Komsomols. There was a note of fierce anticipation in the sound.

Khrenov smiled. He seldom used the word "comrade." It reminded him too much of political officers. When he did use it, he meant it.

"Yes, comrades, the Americans have had their fun on that God-forsaken island. Now, it is our turn! We will get something back for our slain comrades. *Battle stations!*"

Khrenov stopped. He was almost embarrassed. Cool, quiet Khrenov did not make melodramatic speeches to his crew. He looked around quickly. No one was laughing. The adrenaline was flowing. The men in the control center moved rapidly to their battle stations. They were excited and clapping each other on the shoulder. *Leningradski Komsomols* was going to war, and it was her kind of war, at last!

The captain spoke again. Cool, quiet Khrenov was back.

"Engineering, both reactors on line as soon as possible. Torpedo rooms, load antiship torpedoes in all tubes, fore and aft. Weapons Officer, prepare all missiles for launching. All hands prepare to dive; we are going down as soon as we have fifty meters of water under the keel."

Down in the engine room, the chief engineer watched his gauges as the control rods in the twin reactors slid smoothly out to their full-power positions. Within the reactors, the nuclear fission reaction began to build. Superheated steam flashed from the reactors to the turbines. *Leningradski Komsomols*'s huge propellors began to revolve, and the great, gray hull started to move smoothly through the water. As she cleared the shore, water frothed around the hull, filling the ballast tanks, and 5,200 tons of submarine vanished under the waves. *Leningradski Komsomols* was on her way to battle.

Two hundred miles away, HMAS *Darwin* moved steadily toward Elu. *Darwin* was a guided missile frigate, a sister ship of the American navy's FFG-7 Oliver Hazard Perry class. *Darwin* was moving rapidly, with both of her General Electric LM2500 gas turbines on line, delivering 40,000 horsepower, to drive her 3,600 tons through the water at 29 knots.

Darwin's 185 officers and men knew that something was up. Their routine training voyage had suddenly been interrupted by a satellite message from Fleet headquarters. They had been running southeast at full power for two days toward an unknown destination. The captain might know what was going on, but if so, he was not talking.

The captain was Bruce Crossman, Commander RAN. Unfortunately, he knew little more than his crew. He sat in the captain's chair on *Darwin*'s bridge and tried, for the hundredth time, to figure out just what in the hell was going on. Slowly, he read his orders again:

From: Headquarters—Royal Australian Navy
To: Captain—HMAS *Darwin*
1. Proceed immediately to Elu Island at maximum speed.
2. Secure and hold the island until relieved.
3. Hostile ships, submarines, and aircraft may be encountered.
4. You are hereby authorized to engage and destroy them.
5. Unauthorized persons may be encountered on Elu. Arrest and detain. If resistance is offered, use all necessary force.

6. Nothing, repeat, nothing is to be removed from Elu without Australian Government permission.
7. Maintain radio silence until otherwise authorized.

—Good luck and God speed: Carson,
Captain(D)

Crossman sighed. His orders made no sense, no sense at all. He knew Elu. It was a small, out-of-the-way island, of no real use to anyone. But just how, in the name of God, was he supposed to "secure and hold it"? *Darwin* was designed for antisubmarine and antiair warfare. She had no big guns and no marines.

It was baffling, but it was totally trivial when compared to sentences 3 and 4. "Hostile ships, submarines, and aircraft may be encountered. You are hereby authorized to engage and destroy them." Crossman stared at the blunt words. He knew "Bloody Bill" Carson well. If Carson said, "Engage and destroy," that was what he damn well meant. Australia must be close to war. With those maniacs in Canberra running the new government, that was not surprising. But with whom? Who was he supposed to fight, the whole bloody U.S. Pacific Fleet?

Someone coughed discreetly. Tom Randall, *Darwin*'s executive officer, was standing at his side. There was a peculiar expression on Randall's face.

"What's up, Number One?"

"Sir," Randall said formally, "a message has just been received on the OE-82 SATCOM. I thought you should see it immediately."

A message via military communications satellite, what the bloody hell now?

"What do our lords and masters in Canberra want now?"

Randall held out the message form.

"Wherever it's from, Captain, it's not from Canberra."

Not from Fleet headquarters? Who the bloody hell else would be on the OE-82 SATCOM? He took the message and read it.

URGENT—URGENT—URGENT—
To: Captain HMAS *Darwin*
Electronic surveillance indicates Soviet Echo II nuclear cruise missile submarine operating off Elu.
—A Friend

"Is this a joke, Number One?"

But, of course, it wasn't. Randall liked practical jokes, but he did not play them on his captain, not when they were on duty.

"Well, sir, if it is, the joker owns an Australian navy cipher machine and a communications satellite."

"This was in code?"

"Yes, sir, it was in WOMBAT-6."

"WOMBAT-6! Bloody hell! That was last month's code. Why is it in WOMBAT-6?"

The captain was not happy, Randall could tell. He glanced at the overhead for a second. Still, it was a direct question.

"Well, sir, perhaps 'A Friend' hasn't cracked WOMBAT-7, yet."

That was an unpleasant thought. The idea that someone was merrily intercepting and decoding secret Australian navy messages gave Crossman a chill. Was he heading into a trap? He would not put it past the bloody CIA to try and provoke a fight between *Darwin* and a Russian submarine. Still, his orders were quite clear. Go to Elu, Russian submarine or no Russian submarine.

"Well, sir, do we take this message seriously?"

"Too right, we do, Number One. Sound General Quarters!"

LENINGRADSKI KOMSOMOLS—OFF ELU ISLAND

Leningradski Komsomols moved smoothly through the water at a steady six knots. Captain Khrenov was much happier now. No nuclear submarine commander is ever happy when he is on the surface in a danger zone. *Leningradski Komsomols* was at four hundred feet, well below the thermocline, the layer that sharply divides the surface layer of the ocean which is heated by the sun from the much colder water below. The thermocline acts as a barrier which confuses and distorts sonar signals. He was certain that the American frigate could not detect *Leningradski Komsomols* until the range fell to twenty miles or less, and Khrenov was going to make sure that that never happened.

He ordered a passive sonar search in all directions. Slowly and carefully, *Leningradski Komsomols*'s sonar operators scanned the surrounding water, listening carefully for any unusual sound that might betray the presence of another submarine. That was the real threat. Khrenov was sure that *Leningradski Komsomols* could destroy the American frigate, but if an American attack submarine was following him in the disturbed water in *Leningradski Komsomols*'s wake, the first warning he would have would be the approaching whine of Mark 48 torpedoes. Khrenov waited impatiently for the report. Still, he was not fool enough to rush his sonar operators. There are simpler ways of committing suicide than that. At last, the sonar officer reported.

"All clear, Captain. No contacts in any direction."

"No contacts, whatsoever?"

"Well, Captain, there are six whales passing by twenty kilometers to starboard. I am sure that they are neutral whales, not American whales."

"When I want more idiotic humor to interfere with the operations of this ship, Lieutenant Gagarin, I will call on you. You seem to be an expert in such things. In the meantime, report like a naval officer!"

"No contact in any directions, sir!"

Some of the old hands grinned circumspectly. That would teach the new lieutenant to annoy Khrenov when he was planning his next move.

Khrenov had already forgotten the unhappy Lieutenant Gagarin. His mind was concentrated on his final decision, how many missiles to launch. *Leningradski Komsomols* carried eight giant SS-N-3C antiship missiles in four huge launchers built into her upper deck. The forty-foot-long missiles were the size of fighter planes. The launchers must be loaded before *Leningradski Komsomols* sailed. She carried no reloads. The eight huge SS-N-3C missiles were a deadly threat to any surface ship in the world, but when they were gone, the nearest replacements were four thousand miles away.

Khrenov must be cautious, but not too cautious. To launch too few was as bad as to launch too many. He must fire enough to overwhelm the frigate's defenses. He considered his orders. It was clear he must stop the frigate from reaching Elu at all costs. Very well, then, he would launch four missiles. That would give the Americans something to think about!

"Weapons Officer. Stand by to launch One and Two, and Seven and Eight."

He pushed the intercom button. His voice echoed through *Leningradski Komsomols*'s compartments.

"Stand by for surface action-guided missiles. Battle

surface!" Compressed air roared into *Leningradski Komsomols*'s tanks and began to force hundreds of tons of water out into the ocean. As her ballast tanks emptied, *Leningradski Komsomols* became lighter and lighter and rose menacingly toward the surface. The long, gray hull surfaced in a pool of frothing white bubbles. *Leningradski Komsomols*'s crew exploded in a frenzy of activity. Hatches slammed open. Orders rang out.

"Man the bridge!"

The lookouts swarmed up the ladder and emerged on the bridge at the top of *Leningradski Komsomols*'s conning tower and began to scan the horizon with their binoculars. Khrenov was right behind them. He believed in radar and sonar, but there is no real substitute for the human eyeball.

"All Clear!"

Khrenov waited a moment until his own binoculars confirmed the lookouts' report. Conditions were almost ideal for a launch. The sea was calm, and there was almost no wind. Khrenov suppressed a shiver of nervous excitement. He was about to command the first Soviet naval combat action since World War II. All right, Khrenov, do it right!

"Commence launch operations!"

There was a dull rumble of machinery, and *Leningradski Komsomols* seemed to start to come apart. Locking lugs withdrew, and the entire front of the conning tower rotated smoothly to the right, exposing the antennas of the missile guidance and tracking radars. Four huge missile launchers emerged slowly from their stowed positions flush with *Leningradski Komsomols*'s deck. They rose slowly upward twenty degrees and locked in place, ready for firing. The final countdown checks began.

Khrenov began to sweat. This was the bad part, the

one great tactical weakness of Echo II class submarines. *Leningradski Komsomols* had to surface to launch her missiles. Even after they were launched, she must remain on the surface to provide missile guidance and final midcourse corrections. While the conning tower was open and rotated and the launchers were erected, she could not dive. Khrenov glanced repeatedly at his watch. The second hand seemed to crawl around the dial. Would the damned missiles never be ready for launch? But, at long last, the report came.

"Weapons officer to captain. Ready for missile launch as ordered."

Khrenov snapped his orders.

"Prepare for missile launching! Clear the bridge!"

Quickly the bridge party swarmed below, and the hatches were closed and dogged down. *Leningradski Komsomols* must be tightly sealed before firing. The blasts of flame and white-hot gases from the missile boosters would sweep the deck, giving, for a few short seconds, a very convincing imitation of hell.

Khrenov manned the periscope and trained it toward the forward launcher.

"Fire One and Two!"

There was a tremendous roar. *Leningradski Komsomols*'s 5,200 tons shook and vibrated, as two solid propellant rocket motors fired and accelerated missile Number One out of the launcher and into the sky, trailing huge plumes of gray-white smoke. Four seconds later, the intervalometer sent the second firing command, and Number Two's booster motors fired, and the second huge missile roared from the launcher. Khrenov watched, fascinated, as the two missiles roared upward, moving faster and faster as the boosters accelerated the missiles toward ramjet ignition speed. Khrenov found himself holding his breath. This was the critical moment. The slightest malfunction now, and the missiles would be lost.

As Khrenov watched, the twin boosters fell away from beneath Number One's wings, and the ramjet ignited and the huge missile roared upward at 1,500 miles per hour. Now, Number Two dropped its boosters, and its ramjet roared into life.

Khrenov remembered he was the only man who could see what was going on.

"Missiles away, on ramjets and on trajectory!"

"And responding to guidance commands!" the weapons officer added.

Khrenov rotated the periscope and stared into the aft launcher. It was like looking into the muzzles of two giant cannons.

"Fire Seven and Eight!"

Khrenov stared in awe as Number Seven roared out of the launcher and seemed to come right at him. He fought the impulse to duck and counted to himself, one, two, three, four, five, six—where the hell was Number Eight?

"Abort! Abort!" Khrenov heard the weapons officer shout. "Guidance malfunction on Number Eight!"

"Abort Eight. Fire Number Six!"

The weapons officer reacted instantly.

"Switching to Six. Stand by. Launching Six in sixty seconds!"

Khrenov swore. His perfectly coordinated launch was ruined!

"Six ready!"

"Fire Six!"

Number Six roared out of the launcher and vanished from Khrenov's view as it soared over *Leningradski Komsomols*'s conning tower and out of the periscope's field of view. Quickly, Khrenov rotated the periscope and looked forward again. In the distance, he could see the yellow-white exhausts of One, Two, and Seven as they climbed out and roared downrange toward the enemy. Closer in, he could see Number Six drop its boosters and follow the salvo downrange. It was perhaps a minute behind the first three, but at ramjet speeds, a minute is twenty miles. Well, not a perfect launch, but it would do.

Khrenov could do nothing now but wait. The missiles were climbing higher and higher, waiting for their final commands as they roared toward their target. The weapons officer consulted his fire control computer, nodded, and pushed the button.

"Sir, final guidance commands computed and sent. All missiles responding!"

"Prepare to dive! Secure launchers and conning tower!"

Khrenov took one last look through the periscope. Already, the missiles were nearly out of sight as they roared away toward the target. A good launch. Look out, Yankees, here comes a message from *Leningradski Komsomols!*

HMAS DARWIN—OFF ELU ISLAND

On *Darwin,* Commander Crossman was reviewing his options. If he was about to fight, he had three weapon systems he could use. Forward of the bridge, he could see *Darwin*'s single Mark 13 missile launcher. It could be used to launch either Standard SM-1 Block 6 surface-to-air missiles or Harpoon antiship missiles. Both types of missiles were highly effective against their particular targets. That, as the Yanks say, was the good news. The bad news was that some idiot in the Pentagon had decreed that the Mark 13 launcher should have only a single arm. Only one missile at a time could be loaded and ready to fire at any one time. He could have a Standard SM-1 SAM ready or a Harpoon, but not both. If he could get close to the Echo II and catch her on the surface, he could blow her out of the water with Harpoons. But his Harpoons had a range of only sixty-eight miles. *Leningradski Komsomols*'s SS-N-3C missiles had a range of nearly three hundred miles. If it was going to be a missile action, Crossman had a dismal feeling he knew who was going to attack first.

Aft, *Darwin* had a Mark 15 Phalanx 20-mm Close-In Weapon System. The Phalanx System was self-contained, with its own search and fire control radars and a General Electric M61A1 Gatling gun. This was a truly remarkable weapon, capable of firing 6,000 rounds per minute. It provided *Darwin*'s final defense against an incoming cruise missile. Unfortunately, its maximum effective range was only 2,000 yards. That was a weakness, but Crossman was extremely glad he had it.

Amidships was *Darwin*'s one and only gun, a Mark 75 3-inch gun. The U.S. Navy had selected the Italian OTO Melara 76-mm Compact dual-purpose naval gun for their FFG-7 frigates and, for some reason, renamed it the Mark 75. By either name, it was an excellent cannon, but it was only a 3-inch gun. Crossman would much rather have had a longer-ranged, more-powerful U.S. 5-inch/54, but no one had asked him. Like many a ship's captain before him, he was going into combat with what he had. Well, it was up to him to make the best possible use of the weapons *Darwin* had.

Quietly, Crossman issued his orders.

"Load a Standard 1 on the missile launcher. Man the gun mount, and load antiaircraft ammunition in the Mark 75. Set Phalanx on automatic. Full surveillance and warning mode on the SLQ-32."

The SLQ-32(V)2 Electronic Warfare System was not, strictly speaking, a weapon system, but it might be the critical element in *Darwin*'s defense. It could provide warning, identification, and direction of approach of threatening antiship missiles as soon as they turned on their homing radars. Even more important, the SLQ-32 controlled *Darwin*'s electronic countermeasures and the Mark 36 Decoy Launching System.

Now *Darwin* was ready for combat. Was there anything else he could do? Perhaps fly off a helicopter to scout ahead and—A bloodcurdling alarm suddenly sounded. Someone in the Combat Information Center (CIC) wanted to speak to the captain immediately!

"Randall here, sir. Another message from 'A Friend' on OE-82 SATCOM."

URGENT—URGENT—URGENT-
To: Captain—HMAS *Darwin*
Vampire! Vampire! Vampire!

—A Friend

Jesus Christ! Crossman had trained with the American navy. He knew instantly what that cryptic message meant. Hostile cruise missiles detected, incoming! He pushed the alarm button and spoke into the intercom. Crossman's amplified voice rang throughout *Darwin:*

"General quarters—all hands man your battle stations! General quarters—all hands man your battle stations!"

Darwin's crew exploded into superbly organized confusion. The weapons were already manned, but there are other final preparations to be made before combat. Watertight doors were slammed shut and dogged down. Crewmen struggled into their anti-flash burn gear. Below decks, the surgeon laid out his instruments and started to wait for the wounded he devoutly hoped would never come.

On the bridge, Crossman decided to gamble. *Darwin* was headed straight for Elu. If the Russian submarine was off Elu, then the missiles were almost certainly headed straight for *Darwin*'s bow. Head on, *Darwin*'s superstructure masked both the 3-inch gun and the Phalanx against attacks from that direction. If he turned broadside toward the attack, *Darwin*'s radar signature would be significantly increased. The incoming missiles would be able to detect her quicker. But, if there were more than one or two missiles coming, *Darwin* would need all her weapons to survive. There really was no choice. Crossman snapped the order, and *Darwin* began to turn rapidly to starboard. One last thing. There was no use maintaining radar silence anymore. Another order, and *Darwin*'s SPS-49 long-range search radar began to scan the horizon. Now, there was nothing left for Crossman to do but wait and pray.

He did not have long to wait. Reports began to flow from CIC.

RADAR CONTACT—THREE TARGETS BEARING 270 AT 4,000 FEET AND DIVING—STRONG RETURNS—POSSIBLE HOSTILE AIRCRAFT-

But Crossman knew that they were not aircraft.

INCOMING CRUISE MISSILES!—INCOMING CRUISE MISSILES!—SLQ-32 REPORTS THREE SOVIET SS-N-3C SHADDOCKS INCOMING— BEARING 270—IN FINAL SEARCH MODE-

Crossman snapped up his binoculars and looked. The sun was bright, and the air was clear. Forty miles away, he saw a sight few men have ever seen, the three round, silver dots of three huge Soviet SS-N-3C missiles coming straight at him at more than ten miles per minute. It would make a wonderful story if he lived to tell it. As he watched, the missiles slanted down toward the water in a shallow dive. They were going into the terminal-attack sea-skimming mode. They would come at *Darwin* at less than 100 feet and at 1,400 miles per hour.

The Mark 13 launcher rotated smoothly and elevated to firing position. The Standard SM-1 SAM loaded and was ready for the firing command.

INCOMING CRUISE MISSILE! INCOMING CRUISE MISSILE—SLQ-32 REPORTS ONE SOVIET SS-N-3C SHADDOCK INCOMING—BEARING 272 IN FINAL SEARCH MODE.

Bloody hell! Not another missile salvo. Did they think *Darwin* was the whole U.S. Pacific Fleet? Crossman snapped up his binoculars and looked again. Yes, there was one more round, silver dot, another Soviet SS-N-3C missile was coming straight at him. Tactically, it made no sense, but Crossman had no time to worry about that. Suddenly, the bridge was flooded with reports.

RADAR CONTACT. THREE TARGETS BEARING 272 AT 75 FEET—CLOSING RAPIDLY!

INCOMING CRUISE MISSILES! INCOMING CRUISE MISSILES!—SLQ-32 REPORTS THREE SOVIET SS-N-3C SHADDOCKS INCOMING—BEARING 272 IN FINAL TERMINAL HOMING ATTACK MODE—MISSILES HAVE RADAR LOCKON—COUNTERMEASURES INITIATED!

Crossman raised his binoculars and looked again. There they were! The three huge missiles roared over *Darwin*'s horizon, less than seventy-five feet above the water, moving at supersonic speeds. Behind each missile, two rooster tails of white water shot high into the air, as the shock waves tore into the ocean's surface. Crossman heard a series of dull thumps from amidships as the SLQ-32 fired the Mark 34 chaff launchers and canisters of rapid-blooming chaff toward the oncoming missiles.

There was a dull, rumbling roar from the bow as the first Standard SM-1 blasted off the Mark 13 launcher and shot toward the SS-N-3Cs, trailing gray-white smoke. Immediately, the Mark 13 launcher rotated back to the reloading position, and the next Standard SM-1 missile began to move up from the magazine, but it would be twenty-five whole seconds before *Darwin* could launch again!

Number One, Number Two, and Number Seven were attacking under ideal conditions. *Darwin* was a single ship in the middle of a broad ocean area. There were no other targets to create confusion, no land to cause radar clutter. The missiles achieved radar lockon instantaneously, and the three missiles roared directly at *Darwin* at maximum attack speed. But the ideal conditions did not last long, as *Darwin*'s SLQ-32 Electronic Warfare System flashed into action. To the human eye, nothing seemed to be happening, but in the radar spectrum, the sky exploded as the SLQ-32 responded with every dirty trick its designers had been able to imagine and program into its software.

Darwin's rapid-blooming chaff blossomed, creating clouds the SS-N-3Cs' homing radars could not see through. A dazzling array of false targets appeared, false radar return pulses flooded the radars' receivers, and Hycor anti-infrared rockets exploded in great flashes of heat, confusing the missiles' backup infrared sensors. But the men who had designed the SS-N-3Cs knew how the game was played. Their electronic counter-countermeasures responded instantly, and the missiles fought back with every trick in the book.

Momentarily, the three missiles lost radar lockon. Undismayed, they switched to Home On Jam mode, and came on toward *Darwin,* homing in on the signals from her radar jammers.

Darwin's first Standard SM-1 missile roared toward the oncoming three missiles at 1,600 miles per hour. Its X-band mono-pulse homing radar locked on Number One, and the two missiles flashed together at four times the speed of sound. Both vanished in a huge orange ball of fire as their warheads detonated simultaneously.

Number Two and Number Seven came on. *Darwin*'s Mark 13 missile launcher was reloaded now, and the second Standard SM-1 missile roared off the launcher and shot toward the SS-N-3Cs, trailing gray-white smoke. Immediately, the Mark 13 launcher rotated back to the reloading position, and the third Standard SM-1 missile began to move up from the magazine, but Crossman knew it was too late. *Darwin* would not have time to launch a third missile before the oncoming missiles struck.

Now, the two missiles were less than ten miles away. From amidships, the Mark 75 3-inch gun began to fire in one long, sustained roar, pumping out a 3-inch 14-pound antiaircraft shell every second. The 3-inch shells began to explode in front of and around the oncoming missiles. As each shell burst, 630 grams of Compound Three exploded and blasted 4,660 tiny tungsten spheres at the oncoming missiles. Through his binoculars, Crossman could see tiny yellow flashes blossom on Number Two and Number Seven. They must be inflicting damage, but still the damned things came on!

Now they were two thousand yards away, and the Mark 15 Phalanx 20mm Close-In Weapon System roared into action. There was a sustained ripping sound, like a huge piece of canvas being torn in two, and the Phalanx spat a hundred-round, one-second burst at Number Seven, radar ranged on the outgoing burst, corrected, and fired again and again, a hundred shots per second.

Crossman could see the yellow-white flashes of metal striking metal at velocities over 4,000 feet per second. Phalanx was getting hits, but the heavy steel casing of Number Seven's warhead protected the missile's vital parts. Number Seven came on. Another burst struck.

Number Seven staggered in flight and began to drift to the left. Phalanx fired again, and more than thirty 20mm rounds smashed into Number Seven's left wing root. Two rounds tore through the main wing spar, which failed instantly under the immense aerodynamic loads of low-altitude supersonic flight. The left wing tore away, and Number Seven began to roll, out of control, and the huge missile nosed down and smashed into the water at 1,200 miles per hour. The 3,300-pound warhead fused and fired. A tremendous fountain of white water shot upward, and hundreds of fragments rained down. *Darwin*'s bridge crew cheered spontaneously. Score one for Phalanx.

Instantly, Phalanx swiveled and began firing at Number Two. The first burst missed, but the Phalanx system corrected, and Phalanx's Gatling gun spat precise one-second, hundred-round bursts at Number Two. Crossman could see the yellow-white flashes as some of the 20mm rounds struck home. Another burst ripped into Number Two, but the heavy steel casing of the warhead stopped most of the hits. Crossman could feel his stomach tighten. The bloody thing seemed to be invulnerable, nothing could kill it!

Crossman watched in horror as Number Two came on, trailing flame and smoke, straight for *Darwin*'s bridge. Number Two was dying as it came. A fire was raging in its engine compartment, one wing was damaged, and its radar altimeter was out. A pilot would have ejected, but cruise missiles are fearless. Number Two came on.

The Phalanx System got off one last burst. Crossman could see the yellow-white flashes as the 20mm shells struck. Number Two nosed up slightly and drifted to the right as the 20mm projectiles tore through it, but still it came on.

Number Two struck *Darwin*. There was a tremendous grinding roar and the shriek of tearing metal as the 3,300-pound steel-cased warhead hit the metal tower that mounted *Darwin*'s SPS-49 Search Radar and tore it away. Only one thing saved *Darwin* then. Number Two's warhead had been designed to destroy American aircraft carriers. It did not detonate instantaneously on contact. Its fuse incorporated a delay element designed to let the warhead penetrate into the vitals of a large warship before exploding. Number Two's warhead ripped the open metal latticework of the radar tower away and smashed into the water fifty feet beyond *Darwin*'s starboard side.

The warhead detonated. The hydrostatic shock from the explosion struck *Darwin*'s hull like a giant sledgehammer. Crossman was hurled off his feet. The whole ship shuddered and groaned. Hundreds of tons of water fountained into the air and cascaded down onto *Darwin*'s deck. Crossman jumped to his feet. All that remained of the SPS-49 radar was the twisted stump of the radar tower. There was minor fragmentation damage to the deck here and there, but the damage control parties were reacting smoothly. Crossman felt a surge of pride. His crew had reacted superbly. *Darwin* had survived!

But Crossman had forgotten about Number Six. Unfortunately, Number Six had not forgotten *Darwin*. The SLQ-32 had momentarily confused its guidance unit. Radar lockon had been lost. Number Six's computer instituted the target reacquisition mode. The huge missile began a series of graceful turns as its radar searched for *Darwin*. Number Six steered around a dissipating chaff cloud and saw *Darwin* straight ahead, a beautifully defined target against an uncluttered background. Instantly, Number Six's computer set the attack mode, and the huge missile went to full power and roared forward, straight for *Darwin*'s stern.

The Phalanx system computer sent the fire command, but there was no response. The Phalanx magazine was empty. The missile launcher and the 3-inch gun could not fire, they were masked by *Darwin*'s superstructure. Instantly, the SLQ-32 flashed into action, trying to jam Number Six's homing radar, but it was too late. Number Six was too close. At point-blank range *Darwin*'s radar return was too strong. Number Six flashed across *Darwin*'s stern and crashed into and through the helicopter hangar doors, smashing through the helicopters, and rupturing their fuel tanks. The 3,300-pound warhead fused and detonated. There was a tremendous blast, and the helicopter hangar vanished. The blast wave tore the Phalanx system away, hurling it hundreds of feet into the air. The explosion blasted into the main engine exhaust stacks, and red-hot flames and choking black smoke filled the engine room. *Darwin*'s two turbines flamed out, and she slid to a stop as all power was lost.

For a moment, there was a deafening silence. Then auxiliary power kicked in, and a dozen alarms sounded through out the ship and the damage control parties fought to put out the fires and stop leaks. On the bridge, Crossman listened grimly as the damage reports poured in. Main engine room out. Fires burning aft. Forward missile launcher jammed. Phalanx system gone. Search and fire control radars out. Crossman added it up. *Darwin* was badly damaged, but she was not going to sink. With the help of God and a little luck she would survive. That was fine, but Crossman knew that Russian Echo class submarines carry eight SS-N-3C missiles. The Russian captain had launched four. If he decided to attack again, *Darwin* was not going to survive. She was going down.

Chapter Eleven

"A Prince must, as already stated, avoid those things which will make him hated or despised."
—Machiavelli, *The Prince*

THE PRIME MINISTER'S OFFICE—CANBERRA, AUSTRALIA

The prime minister sat behind his desk, seething quietly. The last thing he needed now was another crisis. His new social justice tax bill was in trouble in Parliament. His party was split on the new immigration laws, and now this insane business on that insignificant island. The minister for defense and the military seemed hell bent on dragging Australia into a confrontation with the Soviet Union. Well, he would bloody well stop them!

There was a knock on the door, and his secretary ushered in the minister for defense and the service chiefs. The minister for defense was a member of his own party, but the prime minister did not trust him. He was too ambitious, by far. The prime minister knew where he stood with the military men. They despised him and his new social justice coalition government. He had stopped them from squandering billions on new weapons Australia didn't need. They would never forgive him for that.

He smiled his best political smile and asked them to be seated.

"Good day, gentlemen. Is there anything new on this Elu affair?"

The minister for defense nodded. The prime minister did not like the look on his face. He knew he would not like what he was about to hear.

"I am afraid so, prime minister. The situation has become extremely serious. I have asked Admiral Graves to brief you."

Admiral Graves moved to the large map on the wall. "Prime Minister, gentlemen. Approximately two hours ago, HMAS *Darwin*, on her way to Elu, was attacked and badly damaged by a Russian submarine."

The prime minister turned pale. "What? Are you sure, absolutely sure?"

"Yes, sir. *Darwin*'s electronic warfare system identified the attacking missiles as Soviet SS-N-3Cs. That is confirmed by the visual observations of *Darwin*'s officers. No other navy in the world operates that type of missile. It has to be the Russians."

"Surely there must have been some mistake. Could *Darwin* have taken some action the Russian submarine captain thought was hostile?"

"No, sir. *Darwin* was attacked at a range of over two hundred miles. She was no possible threat to the submarine at that distance. It was an unprovoked attack on an Australian warship on the high seas."

The prime minister could see it coming. They were trying to paint him into a corner. They would do anything to destroy his policy of peace and nonalignment.

"Nor is that all, Prime Minister. We have positive information that a KGB intelligence team flew to Elu.

There, they murdered two Australian citizens in cold blood. Fortunately, they were defeated by Australian military reservists. Subsequently, a Soviet submarine sent a landing party ashore and is attempting to seize control of Elu. Our people are resisting, but the issue is in doubt."

The prime minister was trapped. He made one last effort to dodge the bullet.

"All right, gentlemen. I will call in the Soviet ambassador and make a strong protest. I will demand an explanation of these actions."

The minister for defense nodded.

"A good diplomatic beginning, Prime Minister. But we must also take military action immediately."

"Military action? Are you insane? Are you suggesting we go to war with the Soviet Union? In case you have forgotten, they have intercontinental ballistic missiles and hydrogen bombs!'

"No one is suggesting all-out war with the Soviet Union, Prime Minister. Their actions constitute a limited attack. We should respond in kind. We must reinforce Elu, defeat the Russians, and drive them from the island."

"How do you propose we do this?"

"That is the problem, Prime Minister. Unwise decisions of this government and previous governments have reduced our military capability. We no longer have an aircraft carrier since HMAS *Melbourne* was scrapped. None of our military aircraft can reach Elu without aerial refueling, and we have no long-range tanker aircraft. Sending another destroyer or frigate is senseless. She could be attacked just like *Darwin.*"

The prime minister began to relax. If there was nothing which could be done, he could not be blamed for doing nothing.

"So, there is nothing we can do?"

The minister for defense smiled faintly.

"By ourselves, no. But, we are not without friends. I know the American ambassador quite well. I took the liberty of talking to him this morning. The Americans remember that we stood by them in Korea and Vietnam. He assures me that the United States stands ready to assist us. They will supply long-range tanker and transport aircraft and will also support sending a joint Australian-American force to Elu."

Behind his smiling mask, the prime minister raged inwardly. I just bet they are! And you, you flaming bastard, cozying up to your friends in the CIA. You think you have me. Well, we'll just see about that. Outwardly, he kept his best smile on his face and spoke calmly.

"Gentlemen, military action is out of the question. Sending *Darwin* to Elu was a serious mistake on your part. It invited a Russian attack. It is obvious to me that the Russians are merely trying to recover their satellite, *and it is their satellite.* Let them have it, and this unfortunate affair will be over."

"Prime Minister, I must protest! Australia will not—"

"You may protest if you like. I will not allow Australia to be drawn further into this affair!"

"But—"

The prime minister was no longer smiling.

"There is nothing more to discuss. There will be no military action. That is my final decision. This meeting is over. Good day, gentlemen."

The minister for defense did not stand up. He slipped his hand inside his coat and drew out five envelopes.

"Not quite, Prime Minister. Here is my resignation, and that of the chief of staff, and those of the service chiefs. They are effective immediately."

The prime minister slammed his fist against the table.

"Damn you! This is intolerable. It's mutiny! You are trying to overthrow the government."

The minister for defense smiled.

"Prime Minister, I am shocked at such intemperate language. Mutiny, indeed. You know very well, sir, that when a minister or a senior serving officer is told by the government to do something dishonorable, it is his duty to resign, and to say why he resigned."

He paused for a second to let his words sink in.

"Of course, there will be a parliamentary inquiry. After we have testified, there will be a motion for a vote of no confidence in the government. You will lose, and you will be out of office. But it will be perfectly in accordance with the law, sir, and you know it."

The prime minister was shaking with rage, but there was nothing he could do. He was not prepared to be forced out of office over this stupid incident. He took a deep breath, put his best smile back on his face, and forced himself to speak calmly.

"I had no idea you gentlemen felt so strongly about this matter. There can be no possibility of my accepting your resignations. The country needs you. Now, just what do you propose?"

THE CRISIS CENTER—THE PENTAGON— WASHINGTON, D.C.

Brand was briefing again. He was getting very tired of endless briefings. He wished he were a Ranger battalion commander again. At least, in those days, he was sure he knew what he was doing. Around here, he only felt like that when he went to the latrine. Well, at least he had good news. They were going to be happy.

"Gentlemen, we have just received messages from *Eagle One* and Talon Leader. All aircraft reached Elu. The drop was successful. We hold the plateau and *War*

God. Our scientists will start examining it shortly. Mission accomplished, gentlemen!"

There was a roar of approval. Brand continued. "The navy informs me that we have a large amphibious ship, the *Wasp,* returning from a visit to Singapore. We will divert her to Elu. *Wasp* operates CH-53E heavy-lift helicopters. They will lift *War God* and fly it to the ship. *Wasp* will bring *War God* to the United States for detailed analysis. That's all, gentlemen."

Brand stepped down from the speaker's console. The assistant secretary clapped him on the shoulder. "Damn fine job, Jim, I knew you could do it!"

Brand smiled politely.

Someone handed Brand another cup of coffee. He stared at the situation map. It wasn't a good idea to have the *Wasp* out there by herself. Perhaps the navy could—

He looked up. A navy captain was shoving a piece of paper at him.

"General, there's a new development. Admiral Askins asked me to brief you immediately. The NSA has just decoded these satellite intercept messages. The Russian submarine off Elu attacked and badly damaged the Australian frigate HMAS *Darwin.*"

Brand whistled softly. "Well, that ought to put the Australians on our side."

"Yes, sir, but the Russians probably thought *Darwin* was one of ours. She is an Oliver Hazard Perry guided missile frigate. The U.S. Navy operates fifty ships of that class. I doubt that any Russian recon satellite could have told them she wasn't an American ship."

Brand waited for the captain to drop the other shoe.

"This creates a problem, General. The Russian submarine used long-range antiship cruise missiles against the *Darwin.* The Australian message indicates she fired four. That class of submarine carries eight. She can attack again."

"She's a threat to *Wasp?*"

"Yes, she can probably blow *Wasp* out of the water when *Wasp* gets within three hundred miles of Elu."

"We'll have to do something about that. What do you have that can get to Elu before *Wasp?*"

The captain checked his clipboard.

"The best bet is the *Los Angeles*. She is about eight hundred miles south of Guam. If she makes a high-speed transit, she can reach Elu before *Wasp.*"

Brand waited, but the captain seemed to be finished.

"That sounds fine, captain, but is the *Los Angeles* able to take on this Russian submarine?"

The captain looked startled.

"Of course, sir, she's a 688."

Brand suppressed a strong desire to strangle the captain.

"Captain, just what the hell is a 688?"

"I mean she is an SSN-688 class submarine, one of our latest and best nuclear attack submarines. There's no finer antisubmarine platform in the world than a 688."

"Good. Then tell them to get their ass in gear and get to Elu as fast as they can."

It was not standard wording for a navy ship movement order, but the captain had no doubt what Brand meant.

"Yes, sir. Right away!"

USS LOS ANGELES—CENTRAL PACIFIC

Los Angeles was running at antenna depth, her 359-foot-long, teardrop-shaped black hull slipping quietly through the water. Only her antennas and periscopes were above the surface. Normally, she would have been several hundred feet deeper. Once each hour she came up to antenna depth to receive or send messages.

Things were calm in *Los Angeles*'s attack center. Lieutenant Commander Paul Jones had the con. He sipped a cup of coffee strong enough to peel paint and glanced around the narrow rectangular compartment. Good. All boards were green. *Los Angeles* was going smoothly about her business.

He glanced at his watch. Two more minutes and he would take her down. *Los Angeles* was on a routine mission. He had not really expected a message.

A radioman materialized at Jones's elbow.

"Message from SUBPAC, sir. Its got every damned priority there is."

Jones smelled trouble. He read the message quickly, then pushed the intercom button.

"Engineering, this is the executive officer. Give me full power immediately!"

The engineering officer did not ask questions. The control rods slid smoothly out of *Los Angeles*'s S6G reactor to the full-power position. High-pressure steam flashed to her twin turbines. *Los Angeles*'s huge propeller began to turn faster and faster, and the long black hull began to pick up speed as 35,000 horsepower drove it through the water.

"Johnson, go call the captain. Navigation, give me a ROUTE CALC to Elu Island, speed thirty knots."

The navigation officer was astounded.

"Thirty knots? They'll hear us all the way to Vladivostok."

"Jim, this order is signed by the chief of naval operations. You want to argue with the CNO?"

"Thirty knots, aye, aye!"

KRASNOGVARDETS AND 70 LETT USSR—
VLADIVOSTOK NAVAL BASE

A cold, biting wind howled down from the north and blew across *Krasnogvardets*'s great gray hull. A U.S. Naval Intelligence Officer would have recognized her instantly as a Victor III class nuclear attack submarine, one of the newer and deadlier submarines in the Soviet Pacific fleet. Captain 2nd Rank Pallitsyn stood on her deck and suppressed another shiver as he listened to what he devoutly hoped were the admiral's final words.

"I do not need to repeat, Captain, that this mission is of vital importance to the security of the state. You must accomplish it at all costs. Proceed to Elu with *Krasnogvardets* and *70 Lett USSR* at maximum speed. Reinforce *Leningradski Komsomols*. Prevent any foreign ships from approaching the island. Have you any questions?"

"None, sir. I carry out your orders without question!"

The admiral smiled. "Very well. Get underway as soon as possible, and good luck, Mikhal."

Pallitsyn was astounded. He would have sworn that the admiral did not have a human feeling in his body. He saluted and watched as the admiral's barge pulled away, then turned and climbed down through the hatch into *Krasnogvardets*'s hull. Thank God he was out of the wind. He moved quickly into the control center.

His executive officer spoke immediately. "Ready to get underway, Captain." Pallitsyn nodded. "Good. Contact *70 Lett USSR* and tell her to get underway. Course for the island of Elu, speed thirty knots."

"Thirty knots, Captain? They will hear us in Pearl Harbor!"

"It is a direct order from the admiral. Do you wish to discuss it with him?"

"No, Comrade Captain, thirty knots! I carry out your order without question!"

Chapter Twelve

"The only way to safety is to rely on the indestructible might of the Soviet Armed Forces."—Yuri Andropov

CAM RANH BAY AIR BASE, VIETNAM

Colonel Viktor Ulanov awoke with a start as the Ilyushin IL-76 jet transport touched down. He glanced out the window. He had never been in Southeast Asia before, but there was really nothing to see. The Ilyushin was taxing down the runway of a huge military airfield that might have been located anywhere in the world.

The big plane turned off the runway and stopped. Ulanov moved toward the aft door. The stewardess handed him his kit bag with a smile. She was a pretty girl and obviously impressed by a Hero of the Soviet Union. It was a pity he had no time to become better acquainted.

The door opened, and Ulanov started down the stairs. The heat struck him like a blow. It must have been a hundred degrees or more. At least he had had the sense to wear his summer uniform. A naval rating was waiting near the foot of the stairs. A vehicle was standing nearby. Ulanov was amused to see that it was an American jeep, tastefully repainted in Soviet navy colors.

The sailor glanced at the medal hanging from Ulanov's throat and saluted smartly. He also respected a Hero of the Soviet Union. Most Russians do. That was why Ulanov was wearing his summer walking out dress uniform and his ribbons. Soviet regulations require that the actual Hero of the Soviet Union medal be worn, not just the ribbon. No one could call him vain for wearing it. The medal attracted instant attention and respect, and he would need every advantage he could possibly get before this strange mission was over.

He returned the sailor's salute.

"I am Colonel Ulanov. Take me to Soviet naval aviation headquarters immediately."

"Exactly so, Comrade Colonel, at once!"

Ulanov looked around as they drove. Ahead was a large building. In front of it, the hammer and sickle hung limply from the flagstaff. To the left was what he had come to see. A dozen huge, gray aircrafts were parked in a row. He could see the sixteen-foot-diameter propellers, the four engines, the swept-back wings, and the giant tails. He nodded to himself: Tupolev TU-95 bombers, the longest-ranged combat aircraft in the world. Absolutely nothing else looks like that.

The jeep stopped at the building. Ulanov was ushered into an office. A sign on the wall proclaimed that the office belonged to Captain 2nd Rank Ivashko. A warrant officer handed Ulanov a cup of tea and told him the captain would arrive at any minute.

Colonel Ulanov sipped his tea and wandered around the office. The walls were decorated with pictures of TU-95s in flight. He glanced in a cracked mirror on the wall. He saw a tall man with dark blond hair. An American might say he had rugged good looks. There was a thin, white scar on his left cheekbone, a souvenir of Afghanistan. The doctors had told him it could be removed, but he rather liked it. It showed the world he was a combat officer.

His brown summer uniform was a little wrinkled, but it would do. There is no *Spetsnaz* uniform. Ulanov's shoulder boards, collar tabs, and cap band were a pale blue, showing that he was an officer in the *Vozdushno Desantnaya Vayaska,* the Soviet airborne assault force. Since all *Spetsnaz* officers and men must be airborne qualified, they normally wear the uniform of the VDV.

Ulanov turned as Captain Ivashko came in, a small, dark man in a flight suit. As quickly as possible, Ulanov briefed the captain. When he finished, Ivashko nodded.

"I see. You and a few men must get to Elu. You want me to fly you there in a TU-95. There is no airfield there, so you will jump. Well, TU-95s were not designed as troop transports, but I believe we can manage that. Correct?"

Ulanov smiled.

"Not exactly, Captain. My party consists of two hundred forty officers and men. We must move them and their weapons and supplies to Elu. Once we are there, we will need logistics and bombing support. It must be a sustained effort, perhaps for several days."

Captain Ivashko smiled. "I do not doubt that your mission is important, Colonel, but that would take every TU-95 in the Pacific Fleet. It would completely disrupt naval aviation operations. We could not do that unless it were authorized by the Defense Council in Moscow."

Ulanov slipped a copy of his orders across the table. Ivashko glanced at them. His eyebrows rose as he read the signatures.

"Well, yes, exactly so! Very well, I will give the orders at once. The devil alone knows what the admiral will say."

The phone rang. Ivashko answered.

"Your men are arriving, Colonel. We will assemble them in Hanger Four."

Colonel Ulanov stood quietly just outside the back door of Hangar Four. For a few minutes, he wanted to see and not be seen. The hanger swarmed with hard, competent-looking men wearing the mottled brown summer camouflage uniforms and blue berets of the VDV. The hangar buzzed with purposeful confusion. Men were checking weapons and gear, loading cargo containers, and distributing rations and ammunition.

Ulanov had changed into his own camouflage uniform. The men he was about to meet would not be favorably impressed by his walking out dress uniform. They would be much happier with a colonel who wore their own uniform.

A captain with a clipboard was at the center of the uproar. Someone pointed out Ulanov. The captain hurried over and reported.

"Colonel Ulanov? I am Captain Chazov. I am your executive officer. Captains Gromov and Kamenev are the company commanders. They are checking weapons and loading equipment. Do you wish me to assemble the men?"

Ulanov shook his head. "Let them keep on with their work, at the next break will do."

He noticed a hard-faced major standing to one side. He was observing Ulanov and Captain Chazov intently.

"Who is that major?"

"That is Major Yegor Mamin, the intelligence officer."

As he spoke, Captain Chazov made an odd gesture with his left hand, extending three fingers. Damn! Ulanov knew what that meant. KGB Third Directorate, the branch of the KGB which controls all military political officers and spies on the officers and men of the armed forces. Mamin was a KGB political officer. He had hoped to go on this mission without a dammed *Zampolit* looking over his shoulder. Ulanov shrugged. Since the bastard was here, there was little he could do about it. Still, combat can be very dangerous. Perhaps Major Mamin would have an accident.

"What of the men and equipment, Captain?"

"We have two hundred forty officers and men selected from the Second *Spetsnaz* Brigade. As you requested, as many as possible have combat experience. About half of them fought in Afghanistan."

Chazov stopped for a moment and checked his clipboard, then continued.

"As for the weapons, they are good standard models, what the men are used to, AKD-74 rifles, BG-15 grenade launchers, RPK-74 squad automatic weapons, PKM machine guns, and RPG-7D rocket launchers. We are carrying large quantities of ammunition, spare weapons, and grenades in the cargo carriers."

Ulanov nodded. He approved. Nothing fancy, just good, standard, reliable weapons. Chazov smiled and pointed to one corner of the hangar, where a dozen men were checking two heavy weapons.

"And there are your heavy mortars, M1943 120mms."

Ulanov smiled. They certainly were not pretty. An unkind Soviet general had once described them as "pieces of sewer pipe mounted on manhole covers," but they were some of the deadliest infantry weapons in the world. Ulanov had demanded them. If he had to blast the Americans out, he would need those 120s.

A bell rang, and the frenzied activity stopped. Well, now Viktor, it is time to impress the troops.

"You have done well, Captain Chazov. Let the men get their tea, and then I will speak to them."

Ten minutes later, Ulanov was well into his briefing. He tried to avoid flowery words and phrases. Better to be straightforward and honest with men like these. He finished quietly. "So you see, comrades, this mission is of critical importance. The enemy is already on Elu, American Rangers or Green Berets."

There was a murmur of excitement. American Rangers or Green Berets! This was the capitalist's first team. It would not be like fighting the ragheads in Afghanistan.

"We will take the island, secure the satellite, and hold it until navy ships arrive. Now, finish checking your equipment and get some sleep. We leave in nine hours. One thing more. I need you all. Check your equipment carefully. No one is to kill themselves in stupid accidents when we jump. I warn you, if anyone kills himself, I will have that man court-martialed and shot!"

Some of the men chuckled. It was an old *Spetsnaz* joke, but it made its point.

"Very well, men, do you understand your orders?"

Captain Chazov was on his feet instantly.

"Exactly so, Colonel. We carry out your orders without question! Dismissed! Back to work."

The men dispersed, all except one. He planted himself in front of Ulanov and delivered a salute that would have honored a Marshal of the Soviet Union.

"*Starshiy Serzhant* Sharypa is honored to report to the Colonel!"

Sharypa was a small, slender man. He hardly fit the image of a rugged *Spetsnaz* sergeant. Ulanov was not fooled. He knew that Sharypa was deadly with an AK-74 rifle and a magician with a knife. He returned Sharypa's salute with equal precision.

"Colonel Ulanov is honored to receive Senior Sergeant Sharypa's report."

He relaxed and clapped Sharypa on the shoulder.

"How are you, Sharypa?"

Sharypa beamed. "Very well, Colonel, very well indeed. I am very pleased to see you. It will be like old times with you in command. If you will excuse me, Colonel, I must get back to the men."

Ulanov nodded. Chazov smiled.

"A good man, Sharypa, the best senior sergeant in the brigade. He certainly thinks well of you. It would have taken a Guards tank division to keep him from coming on this mission when he heard that you were to command."

Ulanov smiled.

"He is a good man. He was my company sergeant in Afghanistan. He was with me at Mazar-e-Sharif. There is no better sergeant in the army than Sharypa. I am glad he is here."

Ulanov was glad indeed that Sharypa was there. He would spread the word that Ulanov was an excellent officer, and the men would believe him. That would not hurt.

He turned to Captain Chazov. "Now we must plan. The navy tells me that they can carry twenty men per aircraft. How do you propose to divide the team?"

Nine hours later, Viktor Ulanov stood on the flight line. Sixteen huge TU-95s waited in a long row, silent and menacing. Ulanov's men, loaded down with parachutes, rifle cases, ammunition bags, and rucksacks, were slowly climbing aboard the first twelve planes. The other four TU-95s would carry bombs.

Captain Ivashko pointed to the first TU-95 in the

line. The sun was starting to rise now, and it gleamed off the silver-gray wings and the large red stars.

"This is my plane, old *98*. She will get us there. You know the Americans call TU-95's 'Bears.' It is not far from wrong. They are strong, fast, tough, and reliable."

Ulanov certainly hoped so. They were about to fly four thousand miles over water. It was good that Ivashko had confidence in his aircraft.

Ivashko looked down the flight line.

"Well, the loading is complete. It is time to go."

Ulanov followed Ivashko up the ladder into the big TU-95's enormous fuselage, moving slowly under the load of ninety pounds of weapons and equipment. They emerged on the flight deck. Ivashko slipped into the pilot's seat. He pointed to a small folding seat behind his own. Ulanov wedged himself in with a sigh. The TU-95 was not designed as a troop transport. It was going to be a long nine hours.

Ivashko and his copilot held a short, incomprehensible conversation. Ivashko nodded and the copilot hit the starter button. Ulanov heard a steadily louder whine, and then a roar, as the first Kuznetsov 14,795-horsepower, NK-12M turbine engine caught and the giant, sixteen-foot propellers began to turn faster and faster. The TU-95 vibrated as, one after the other, the other engines came on line.

Ivashko released the brakes, and *Number 98* began to taxi out toward the runway. Behind her, fifteen other planes began to move. *Number 98* turned on the runway and began to roll as Ivashko went to full power. The four engines roared as *98* moved down the runway faster and faster. Ivashko pulled back on his control yoke, and 375,000 pounds of airplane soared into the sky. The *Spetsnaz* team was on its way to Elu.

Chapter Thirteen

"Everything must be made as simple as possible, but
not one bit simpler."   —Einstein

ELU ISLAND—THE PLATEAU

Andy Carter stared at *War God.* Even from a hundred meters, the great silver-gray cylinder was impressive. *War God* looked like a weapon that could dominate space. He was not about to go near it. He had
issued strict orders for his men to keep away. Investigating *War God* was a job for the team's two scientists,
if he could find them. He was not surprised that they
were lost. They were qualified parachutists or they
wouldn't be on the team, but there had been no time
to train them adequately on the high-performance
HAHO chutes.

In the meantime, all Carter could do was improve
his position and wait. He had established a defensive
perimeter with half his men. The others were busy collecting and opening cargo containers. There were a few
little surprises for the Russians in case they tried to retake the plateau: two .50 caliber Browning machine
guns, a spare M242 mortar, some Claymore mines, even

a few shoulder-fired, antiaircraft Stinger missiles in case the Russians tried anything nasty with their seaplane.

It was not the Russians who were on Elu who worried Carter. He could deal with them. It was the ones who were almost certainly on the way. If this damned satellite was really as important as everyone said, the Russians were not going to accept with a smile his capturing it. Well, whatever they sent, he would have to handle it. His orders were clear, hold *War God* at all costs. Carter had never liked that phrase. It tends to be used by people who are not going to be there to help do the holding or pay the costs.

PLESETSK COSMODROME—PRIMARY CONTROL CENTER

Vladimir Sukhenkiy sat at a small table in one corner of the control center. Svetlana Snastina sat with him. She appeared to be in a trance. Actually, she was studying some blueprints. Captain-Engineer Cherenavin was talking to Moscow on the secure phone. His end of the conversation consisted mostly of "Yes, sir, no, sir, and immediately, sir." Sukhenkiy was an old hand at these things. He knew the call was trouble.

Cherenavin hung up. He was shaking his head as he sat down. "That was Colonel-General Galanskov," he said. "Things do not go well. The Americans dropped parachute troops on Elu. They hold the plateau and *War God.* Worse still, one of our agents in America says that two American government scientists almost certainly accompanied their troops, a Dr. Edward Gregory and a Dr. Laura Walsh. Do either of you know them?"

Sukhenkiy shook his head.

Suddenly, Svetlana spoke. "Laura Walsh? Yes, I know her, that decadent American bitch! She considers herself to be a great expert on high-frequency lasers."

Sukhenkiy was startled. He had never known Svetlana to speak harshly of anyone.

"You know this Laura Walsh, Svetlana?"

Svetlana's face was flushed. "Yes, I met her at the high-frequency laser symposium in Geneva last year. She read a paper on new concepts in X-ray lasers. There were several errors in her thinking. I pointed them out to her at the reception that evening. She did not accept my criticisms in a comradely or scientific manner. She called me 'a flat-chested refugee from a rag bag, who did not know a laser from a screwdriver!' Well, it is true that I am not built like a cow, and I do not dress like a whore!"

Captain Cherenavin had the look of a man who finds himself tiptoeing through a mine field. Still, duty called. He spoke softly. "It is obvious that she is a vulgar and uncultural woman. But is she a person the Americans would consider an expert on lasers? Would they be likely to send her to investigate *War God?*"

"Perhaps I should forgive her. She was obviously drunk, making a shameless spectacle of herself, falling out of her whore's dress and making eyes at—. What? Oh, yes, the Americans would send her. They think the bitch is marvelous."

Cherenavin continued quickly. "General Galanskov asked me to inquire if there is anything you can do to block or obstruct an American investigation of *War God?*"

Sukhenkiy spoke quietly. "Yes, there is something. It is already in place. The technology on *War God* is extremely critical to the security of the Soviet Union. We took the precaution of installing anti-intrusion devices. Only the members of the recovery team and I knew this. Anyone who attempts to enter *War God* without knowing the proper techniques is in for some unpleasant surprises. Also, we began repositioning *Cos-*

mos 2009 yesterday. It is an advanced communications satellite. In a few more hours, we will have continuous communications with *War God.*"

"Excellent, Comrade Sukhenkiy. Is it a destruct system? Can you blow up *War God* if you must?"

"No. We never fly destruct systems on our military satellites. It is too great a risk. If we did, and the Americans were to break our codes, they could command our satellites to destroy themselves."

"Very well, I understand. I will inform General Galanskov of this. He will be pleased to learn about the anti-intrusion devices."

"One moment, comrade," Svetlana said quietly. "I am working on an idea. I believe, if it comes to that, I can detonate the laser's main power supply."

"If you were to do so, would it destroy *War God* completely?"

"Comrade, it would destroy everything within several kilometers of the satellite."

Cherenavin was surprised. "Surely, not kilometers, Comrade Snastina. Surely, you must mean meters?"

Svetlana frowned. She was normally good natured, but she did not like to be corrected when she spoke about technical matters.

"Comrade Captain, when I state a fact, I state a fact! If I can detonate the laser power supply, the explosion will destroy everything within three thousand to ten thousand meters. The exact radius of destruction depends on the rate of the energy release, which is hard to calculate precisely. If the value of delta is between five and ten, while the omega factor is less than two, all living things on the island will be destroyed. On the other hand, if delta exceeds ten, which is quite possible, the entire island may be completely destroyed, and if—"

"I understand, comrade, *kilometers.* I will inform

General Galanskov at once. He will be extremely interested."

ELU ISLAND—THE PLATEAU

Carter's scientists had been found. He watched as they trudged up, guided by a corporal from the third squad. They did not appear happy. Dr. Gregory was limping, and Dr. Walsh moved as if she were bruised and aching. Carter was not surprised. To make your first HAHO jump from a B-52 on to a combat drop zone is a rough way to start.

Neither of them looked like brilliant scientists, but Carter had never known any brilliant scientists. Gregory was a small, wiry man in his fifties. Laura Walsh was more spectacular. She had dark, auburn hair and filled out her blouse and jeans remarkably well.

Carter smiled as they arrived. "Pull up a rock and sit down."

Gregory grinned. "Don't mind if I do. I'm afraid I sprained my ankle when I landed. Sometimes, I think I'm getting too old to jump out of airplanes."

Laura Walsh winced at the thought. "No, thanks. I'll stand. My legs got tangled up in the suspension lines of your God damned high-performance chute. I landed hard. I have bruises all over my ass."

Carter admired the injured part of Laura's anatomy. He wondered if she would like some immediate and personal medical attention. Oh, well, he was on duty, and there was probably something against it in the regulations. Carter smiled and pointed. "There's your satellite. I've given orders that no one is to touch it but you. What do you want to do?"

Gregory and Walsh stared at the huge silver-gray cylinder. Bruises and fatigue were forgotten. There it was, and they were about to get their hands on it. They picked up their equipment bags and started walking toward *War God.* Carter told his executive officer to take over and followed them.

"Who's in charge, and what's the plan?"

Gregory smiled. "Technically, I am, but we have to work as a team. I'm a satellite systems engineer. That means I know a little bit about everything, but not much about anything. Laura is a specialist in high-frequency lasers. You really ought to have a team of fifty people for this job. But what you see is what you've got."

They stopped twenty feet from *War God.* Gregory and Walsh took tool kits and instruments from their equipment bags. Gregory took a black box with a silver probe on a long black cable and began to walk slowly around *War God.* He shook his head in awe.

"Look at the size of this thing! It must be wonderful to have boosters as big as theirs. Look at those holes in the skin! Something hit it in space, that's probably why it landed here."

He walked back toward the far end of the satellite, where the parachute suspension lines were connected. The black box in his hands began to emit a slow clicking noise.

"What's he doing?" Carter asked.

"That's a Geiger counter. He's checking for ionizing radiation. The clicks mean he's detecting some, probably from a nuclear power source."

Carter was not amused. "Can it detonate? Is there a radiation hazard?"

Laura Walsh smiled tolerantly.

"Of course not. It's either a small nuclear reactor or a radioactive isotope power supply. Neither one is anything like a nuclear weapon. It can't explode, that's completely impossible."

Thank God for small favors! Carter did not think he

was making a good impression on Laura Walsh, but he pressed on. He had to know.

"What about the radiation, is it hazardous?" He hoped that was not a stupid question. Apparently it was not.

"No, Ed's detecting very low levels of radiation. That means the shielding of the device is intact. As long as that's true, there's no radiation hazard."

"All right, that's good. What's next?"

"We go in. That's Ed's department. Once we're in, I try to figure out the payload. We think there's a very advanced high-frequency laser onboard."

Gregory returned. He had put away his Geiger counter and was speaking into a tape recorder. He finished talking and slipped the tape recorder into his pocket. He opened up a large and elaborate tool kit.

"All right, it's time to do it. Let's open this baby up."

SPACE—GEOSYNCHRONOUS ORBIT TORUS— COSMOS 2009

Cosmos 2009 was twenty-three thousand miles above the equator, drifting steadily eastward. At Plesetsk, its controllers monitored its every action. The test conductor checked his console and gave his commands to his crew.

"Stand by for orbital correction burn in thirty seconds."

Coded signals flashed from Plesetsk to *Cosmos 2009.* Aboard the satellite, propellant valves opened, and the small rocket engines of the reaction control system flared into life. Yellow-white flame shot from the nozzles. *Cosmos 2009*'s eastward velocity dropped steadily toward zero. The rocket engines stopped. *Cosmos 2009* appeared to be standing still above the equator. A few minor corrections were made, and the controllers were satisfied. Communications antennas were locked on and checked.

The test conductor smiled and beckoned to his assistant. "It's done. Call Comrade Suhkhenkiy. Tell him he now has continuous, broad-band communications capability to his precious *War God.*"

Chapter Fourteen

"The most important thing to do in solving any problem is to begin."   —Frank Tyger

ELU ISLAND—THE PLATEAU

Ed Gregory looked at *War God*'s left-side access hatch and shook his head. "I don't like it. There's too much power on. It just doesn't feel right."

Laura Walsh sighed. Gregory grinned. "Laura is a real scientist," he said. "She doesn't believe in superstitious nonsense like worrying about how things feel. Me, I was a tunnel rat in Vietnam, with the 56th Engineer Demolition Team. I'm still alive to do crazy things like this because I worry about how things feel. Why don't you and Laura get behind those rocks over there before I start on this hatch. We'll keep in touch by radio."

Laura was about to say that she would stay when she saw Carter moving rapidly toward the rocks. She had never been in combat, but that did not mean that she was stupid. Carter seemed a little dense when it came to technical matters, but he was an experienced soldier. If what Ed Gregory said worried Carter, perhaps she should worry, too. She followed Carter quickly and took cover behind the rocks.

"Ed never talks much about the war," she said. "What is this tunnel rat business?"

"In Vietnam, the Viet Cong dug huge, underground tunnel complexes. They used them to hide troops from air attack, store supplies, or conceal troops before attacks. When we found them, we had to blow them up. Tunnel rats were American soldiers who went down into the tunnels, searched them for intelligence information, and set the charges to blow them up. If the VC were there, they tried to blow your head off. If they weren't home, there would be booby traps, lots and lots of very bad booby traps. Any tunnel rat who lived through the war was very smart or very lucky, probably both. When an ex–tunnel rat tells me something doesn't feel right, I look for cover."

"All right," Gregory said into his walkie-talkie, "here we go. I'll tell you what I'm going to do before I do it. Take notes, Laura. You'll want to know what I was doing if I do something wrong."

Gregory's voice changed. He spoke in dry, precise, emotionless tones, like a doctor describing an autopsy. "I am now going to attempt to open the satellite's left-side, forward-access hatch. I am checking the hatch and the surrounding structure with a multimeter. There are no detectable indications of electrical activity. There is a small panel, approximately three by four inches, inset in the center of the hatch. It appears to be hinged to open upward. I will now attempt to open this panel."

Gregory pressed himself against *War God*'s hull, carefully keeping out from in front of the access hatch. He drew a long-shafted screwdriver from his equipment roll. Carter found himself holding his breath. There was a small metallic click.

"I have opened the panel. I see a keypad. There are

sixteen keys. Twelve are numbered from one to twelve. The other four have no numbers, but are colored, one red, one yellow, one green, and one blue. I can see no reason for such a device on a spacecraft except to control an anti-intrusion device. There is almost certainly a number-color sequence which allows safe access. I, of course, do not know that sequence."

Gregory paused. He seemed to be thinking hard. Carter did not blame him. He and Laura Walsh were twenty yards away from *War God*. Would that be enough if the entire satellite exploded? Probably not. He leaned over and whispered in Laura Walsh's ear. "Do you think he can break the code?"

Laura looked startled. Was Carter serious? Apparently so.

"No, of course not. There is no code. There will be a sequence of numbers and colors randomly selected. Surely you can see what the odds are?"

Carter looked blank. Laura was disillusioned. It was hard to believe that the leadership of the United States Army was technically illiterate. She sighed and went on. "Look. You have to pick the first number. There are twelve numbers, so there is one chance in twelve that you are right. You do see that, don't you?"

Carter nodded. That did seem reasonable.

"Good. Now you must pick the second number. The chance that you got both right is one in one hundred forty-four. Now the third number and your chances are one in four hundred thirty-two. If the correct sequence is twelve numbers and one color, your chances of guessing right are approximately one in two billion, but of course, you see that."

Carter nodded wisely. "Of course."

Gregory spoke. "There is no possibility of deducing the correct sequence. I am going to proceed on the basis of the following assumptions. First, the anti-intrusion

166

device will not be intended to destroy the satellite, only to kill the intruder. Second, the device must be light in weight to be used on a spacecraft. Therefore, it must be directional and will operate so as to strike anyone in front of the door. I will stand to one side and activate the keys in a random pattern, starting now."

Gregory used his screw driver to press the keys, making sure that his hand was not in front of the door. "One, two, three, four, fi—." *Bam!* The door shot forward out of *War God*'s side. It whined through the air, struck the ground thirty feet from the satellite, and bounced away. Gregory looked at the gouge in the ground.

Gregory smiled. "I can now state that the access hatch is open. I will now use the multimeter and recheck the hatch frame." He touched the multimeter's two probes to the hatch frame. There was a sudden sharp, crackling noise, and blue fire blazed between the two probes. Gregory dropped the multimeter. It lay on the ground, forlornly emitting white smoke and a scorched smell. Gregory bent over and read the meter. "Off scale at fifty thousand volts. Now, that's not nice. Somewhere, there's somebody who doesn't like me."

PLESETSK COSMODROME—PRIMARY CONTROL CENTER

Vladimir Sukhenkiy heard a chime from his test console. The event-monitoring computer wanted to tell him something. Quickly, he checked the display. Someone was trying to open *War God*'s Number Two access hatch. A light flashed. The hatch anti-intrusion device had fired. Sukhenkiy threw a switch. A coded command flashed upward into space to *Cosmos 2009* and was relayed to *War God* in a fraction of a second. *War God*'s reactor went to full power. Fifty-five thousand volts surged through *War God*'s Number Two hatch frame.

167

The needle of a meter on Sukhenkiy's console suddenly slammed against the top. Someone or something had touched the hatch frame. If someone had touched it with his hand or an uninsulated metal tool, someone was very dead.

It gave Sukhenkiy an odd feeling. He did not think of himself as a man who fought battles, but unless the Americans were very clever, he had just killed two or three people he had never seen. He watched the console display intently. For several minutes nothing happened. Then the display changed. Someone was working on Number Three hatch. An indicator light flashed. Number Three's anti-intrusion device had fired. The hatch was open.

Sukhenkiy sighed. The Americans were in. He had no more tricks to play. It was up to the specialists now. Perhaps Svetlana could come up with something extremely clever.

ELU ISLAND—THE PLATEAU

Gregory finished opening the third hatch. He was sweating profusely. He wiped his face on his sleeve. "That does it," he said. "We're in. Come on, Laura. Take a look, but be careful."

Laura Walsh was shaking with excitement. High-energy laser development is some of the most secret research in the world. Laura had never seen a high-energy Russian laser. Now she was about to get her hands on the most advanced laser the Soviet Union could produce. It was this chance that had persuaded her to volunteer to fly eight thousand miles and jump out of a B-52. It was the chance of a lifetime.

She moved forward to *War God*'s side and joined Gregory. Carter followed her. He stayed out of the way and was careful to touch nothing. Gregory and Walsh peered into *War God*'s forward equipment bay. They began to talk to each other excitedly. Carter presumed that they were speaking English although he understood only one word in three. Finally, Carter could stand it no longer. "Is this it?" he asked.

Laura Walsh's face was flushed with excitement. "Is it? Look! Just look at it! Look at the size of the primary mirror. And the cooling system. They're using liquid hydrogen. The power of that laser is fifty times greater than anything we've tested. And it operates at gamma ray frequencies! No wonder it destroyed those two satellites in seconds. No doubt about it. They've made a major technical breakthrough!"

"You're right, Laura," Gregory said softly, "but how do they pump it? Where do they get the power?"

Carter was startled. "I thought Laura said it has a nuclear reactor?"

"It does. I've looked at it. It's just a standard Soviet 100-kilowatt reactor. They use it on all their large spacecrafts. It couldn't produce a tiny fraction of the power that's needed to drive this thing. No"—he pointed with his screwdriver—"that must be it. It can't be anything else."

Carter peered. "That" looked like a squat, black, oversized hot-water heater. "What is it?" he asked. "Damned if I know," Gregory said. He took out a 35mm camera. "I'm going to get some pictures while the light's still good. Laura, you'd better report to the technical assessment team. Tell them they were right. It's an extremely high-powered high-frequency laser, and it's miles ahead of anything we've got. Do we have voice communications with Washington, Captain?"

Carter nodded. "We've got an AN/PSC-3 satellite communications radio. You can talk directly to Washington via SATCOM."

"All right, Laura, tell them where we are. The good news is that we have the laser. The bad news is that

169

it's worse than they thought. This thing can destroy anything we put in space, satellites, missiles, space shuttles, anything. Ask them what the hell they want us to do next."

Chapter Fifteen

"Never give the Russians time to dig in. They become very stubborn once they are dug in."

—Colonel-General Von Rhinegau

DETACHMENT—1ST SPECIAL FORCES GROUP (AIRBORNE)—ELU

Cord followed Sergeant Jackson across the plateau. The light was starting to fade. Jackson moved slowly and carefully.

"We're getting close to where the captain was going to set up the perimeter. Take it easy. Some of these troopers are God damned trigger happy."

"Flying!" someone shouted.

Jackson threw himself down. Cord followed him instantly.

"Flying, God damn it. Flying! Give the response, or I'll fire!"

"Tiger!" Jackson shouted. "Tiger! Ortega, you fire that God damned SAW at me, I'll twist it around your scrawny throat for a necktie!"

"Sergeant Jackson. Why didn't you say so? The captain's been wondering where the hell you were. Come on in."

Jackson and Cord crawled forward. They found themselves staring down the muzzle of a wicked-looking light machine gun. The gunner peered at Cord suspiciously. "Who the hell's he?"

"He's Cord," Jackson said. "He's an Australian. The captain wants to see him. Where's the CP?"

"Over there, in the edge of the trees, near that Russian rocket."

Jackson nodded. "Come on, Cord."

Cord hesitated. "Wait a minute," he said. Cord looked at his fatigues and boots. He did not need a mirror to know he was a bloody mess. His fatigues were dirty, dusty, wrinkled, and smudged with powder fouling. His boots were bloody horrible. Australians are not in love with military pomp and circumstance, but here on Elu, Cord was the Australian SAS. He must uphold the honor of his regiment. He brushed himself off. It did not do much good, but it was the principle that mattered. He took his sand-colored beret from an inside pocket, buffed the winged dagger badge on the cleanest spot he could find on his sleeve, and set his beret on his head at the exact angle prescribed by the regulations. It was not parade dress, but it would have to do.

Jackson chuckled. "You look great, man, come on."

Cord followed Jackson. Carter sat on a rock, studying a map. He glanced up as Jackson and Cord approached. Cord snapped to attention and saluted with the precision of a Grenadier Guardsman at Buckingham Palace.

"Sir. Sergeant John H. Cord, Number 2 Squadron, Australian SAS."

Carter was startled. He had heard that the Australian military were informal. That did not seem to be the case. He returned Cord's salute.

"Captain Andrew Carter, 1st Special Forces Group, United States Army. I am in command of all U.S. forces on Elu."

Carter looked at Cord. From the condition of Cord's uniform and the Lee-Enfield rifle slung over his right shoulder and the Owen gun over his left, he knew that Cord had had a busy day.

"Glad to meet you, Sergeant Cord. You are the commander of the Australian forces on Elu?"

Cord thought that over. Well, he must be. There was no one else, and his orders said he was. "Yes, sir, I am."

"Good. How many men do you have? How are they armed and where are they?"

"There's just me, Captain. Well, there's Miriam Foster. Miriam's a nice girl, but she's not much for fighting."

"There's just you, Cord? Would you mind telling me what the hell's going on around here?"

"Well, sir, this bloody Russian satellite landed on Elu. Then ten bloody KGB bastards flew in here in a seaplane. They killed Brother Edward and Father Paul at the mission. They had submachine guns, the bloody murdering bastards."

Carter nodded. "Sounds like KGB paramilitary. You're right, they are. Where are they now?"

"Dead, I killed them. I had my orders."

"You killed them, Cord? All by yourself?"

"No, Miriam shot one. She did it in self-defense. She's a nice girl."

Carter stared at Cord.

"Then what happened?" Carter asked.

"Well, then this damned Russian submarine arrived. They put fifty men ashore early this morning with AK-47s. That crazy blond Irene seemed to be in command."

"What did you do then, Cord?"

"Well, they bloody well had me outnumbered. There

really wasn't much I could do, but I had my orders. I fought a delaying action."

"You fought a delaying action? Just you?"

"Yes, sir. I had Miriam hide. I didn't want her mixed up in a fight like that. I held them up for six or seven hours. They really weren't very good, bunch of bloody amateurs. But there were too many of them, they were winning in the end. That crazy bitch Irene knows her business. I was really glad to see your planes. You got here just in time. That's really all there is to it."

Carter stared at Cord's sand-colored beret and the winged dagger badge. "Who dares, wins." They seemed to take that very seriously in the Australian SAS.

"Sit down, Cord. Have a cup of coffee and take it easy for a few minutes. Then, we need to do some planning. In the meantime, is there anything you need?"

Cord thought for a moment.

"Well, Captain, do you have any hand grenades you could spare?"

Sergeant Jackson laughed softly.

"Lord, remind me never to go to war against no Australians."

ELU ISLAND—THE VILLAGE

Irina Yakoleva watched the launch pull away from the pier and head for *Leningradski Komsomols*. She had done her best for the wounded, but she did not deceive herself. They would be better off on the submarine, but some were going to die. The knowledge was depressing.

She looked up. Warrant Officer Moiseev was standing at her side. He put his hand on her shoulder and spoke softly. "You did your best for them." He paused for a moment and then went on. "Let me also say that you did your duty today. No one could have done more."

Irina shook her head. "Perhaps so," she said bitterly, "but we failed."

"That was not your fault, or Lieutenant Shpagin's fault, or mine. Our men are simply not trained or equipped to fight American elite troops. How could they overcome elite troops with mortars and machine guns?"

Irina nodded. That was true. Still, there must have been something she could have done. But who could have predicted the B-52s? The Americans were clever and deadly foes. They had modern technology and efficient weapons.

"What is the situation, Moiseev?"

"I have not been idle while you were treating the wounded. We have about twenty men fit for action. I have posted six to guard the road. The rest are outside. We are low on ammunition, but I sent a message on the launch with a request for all available 7.62mm ammunition. Other than that, we must fight with what we have. The captain cannot send any more men ashore and still be able to fight *Leningradski Komsomols*. I fear we must do the best we can with what we have."

Irina thought for a moment. If she were the American commander, she would not let the landing party stay on Elu, controlling the harbor. The Americans would not sit idly on the plateau and wait for something to happen. No, they were coming. She could feel it.

"We do not have the men or the weapons to try to retake the plateau. We must hold the harbor area."

Moiseev agreed. Irina could sense the relief in his voice. He did not want to try to go up that road again. "Very well," he said. "We can fortify the mission and Cord's house. That should give us some advantages."

Irina shook her head. "No, Moiseev, that would be most unwise. The walls of those buildings are made of thin wood. The Americans have .30 caliber machine guns. Full-metal-jacketed .30 caliber bullets will go through wooden walls as if they were paper. And they

175

have 40mm grenade launchers. If we fight from inside the buildings, they will be death traps."

"What shall we do, then?"

"Send men to search every building in the village. Have them gather tools, picks, shovels, anything that will move dirt. My grandfather fought at Stalingrad in the Great War. He used to say that there are times when a spade is a better weapon than a rifle. I think this is one of those times. We will dig in."

"Very well, I will give the orders." Moiseev smiled. "We stopped the Germans at Stalingrad. Perhaps we will stop the Americans here."

Irina nodded. "Perhaps."

ELU ISLAND—THE PLATEAU

The joint American-Australian Command on Elu was having a conference. Andy Carter was talking to Cord. "I don't think it's safe to let the Russians hold the harbor. Another Russian submarine or surface ship could arrive at any time. As long as they hold the harbor, they can land men and equipment rapidly. I think we ought to hit them tonight."

Cord nodded. It made sense to him. He was feeling better. A hot meal and a little rest had given him his second wind.

"The problem," Carter continued, "is how we do it. I have a feeling your friend, Irene, is smart enough to guard the road. If they ambush us there, things could get nasty. Is there any way we can get down to the village without using the road?"

Cord thought for a moment. "Well, they had to drill and blast to build the lower part of the road. There's a trail about halfway down to the village. It was wide enough for mules. Nobody has used it for years. I think we can get down it. There's a three-quarter moon tonight. It will be two or three hours of hard slogging, but I think we can make it."

"Good." Carter turned to his executive officer. "Goldberg, I'll take Blake's squad, and Tarantino's, and Sergeant Mendoza's M60 machine-gun team. Just in case they get cute with that seaplane, have Blake bring a couple of Stingers. We'll use Cord's Land Rover as a backup vehicle. Bring it down when I fire two flares, a yellow and a red. OK, tell the men to get some rest. We'll start as soon as it gets dark."

ELU ISLAND—THE HARBOR AREA

The sun was beginning to set. *Leningradski Komsomols*'s sailors were digging enthusiastically. They knew that if the Americans came, the trenches that they were digging would be their own, personal cover. They remembered the Americans' automatic-weapon fire on the plateau. They thought digging in was a splendid idea.

Irina Yakoleva moved from one position to another. She had not tried to do anything fancy, just basic two-man fire trenches, two meters long, a meter wide, and as deep as the armpits of the tallest man. The trenches were to the south of the village, toward the harbor. She and Moiseev had selected the position of each fire trench with great care. The fields of fire interlocked nicely. If the Americans were a little bit careless, they might get a nasty surprise.

Moiseev was distributing fresh ammunition and cold rations from *Leningradski Komsomols*. Russian cold rations have an unfortunate taste, but Irina had learned in Afghanistan that cold food is much better than none. She ate hers gratefully. Everything seemed to be in order. She longed desperately for some mines, barbed wire, machine guns, and hand grenades, but she was not going to get them. Well, let the Americans come, if they were going to. She had done her duty.

DETACHMENT—1ST SPECIAL FORCES GROUP (AIRBORNE)—ELU

The moon was beginning to rise. The raiding party moved silently down the road. Carter had personally checked each man to be sure that there was nothing that could rattle or click. Cord and Jackson took the point. Carter was moving with the first squad, reinforced by Mendoza's M60 machine gun team. They were the assault group. The assault group would make the actual attack. The second squad was the security group. They would cover the assault group during the attack and its withdrawal if something went wrong.

Cord moved cautiously. He did not think the Russians were going to try to stage an ambush on the upper road, but "I didn't think they would" are famous last words. Cord was glad Jackson was backing him up. The big sergeant was carrying an M16A2 rifle with a 40mm M203 grenade launcher clipped under the barrel. Cord was carrying his Owen gun. It was a better weapon than his Lee-Enfield for a close-quarters fight in the dark.

Cord was nervous. A night raid always looks easy on TV, where the heroes have the scriptwriter on their side. The real thing can be very different. If the slightest thing goes wrong, total confusion can occur in few seconds. Then, you must depend on the men around you. That was the problem. Cord was willing to believe that Carter and his men were competent. Most things he had heard about the American Special Forces were complimentary. Still, he had never served or fought alongside any of these men. That kept his nerves on edge.

Slowly, steadily, the raiding party moved down the road. The moonlight made it easy going. They reached the fourth bend in the road above the village. Cord remembered his fight with the KGB and smiled. He had not done half-bad there, if he did say so, himself. Sergeant MacNair would have been proud of him. Cord held up his hand in the signal to halt. He looked around. Yes, there it was, a large gray-white rock by the side of the road. Cord pointed and stepped off the road into the bush. One by one, the raiding party followed him toward the trail.

ELU ISLAND—THE VILLAGE AREA

Irina Yakoleva was waiting tensely. She could think of nothing else to do. They were dug in and ready. She had left the mission generator running. Light shone from the mission's windows. Now, if the Americans would only be so kind as to attack the mission, they might get some hard knocks.

Moiseev put his hand on her shoulder. "You must get some sleep. The Americans may not come for hours, if they come at all. It will do no good for you to be dead on your feet. Get some rest. I will wake you if anything happens."

Irina knew Moiseev was right. She also knew she would not go to sleep. Well, at least she could get a little rest. She sat down with her back against one end of the fire trench and put her head on her knees. She couldn't go to sleep, she was too tense, but she would. . . .

Moiseev looked at Irina and smiled. She was sound asleep and snoring softly. Well, let her get her sleep. She might need all the rest she could get.

ELU ISLAND—THE OLD TRAIL

Cord swore softly. The trail was far worse than he remembered. And he had walked it in daylight. In the dim moonlight filtering through the trees, the raiding party was having trouble. The ground was rough and uneven, difficult going for men carrying sixty pounds

179

of weapons and gear. Vines and bushes were catching men's legs and equipment. Nerves were taut, and tempers were frayed. They were hours behind schedule, and there was nothing to be done about it. Trying to move faster only made things worse.

At last, Cord could feel flat ground under his feet. They were off the slope and only two hundred or three hundred yards from the village. Cord raised his hand and gave the halt signal. He moved the selector lever of his Owen gun forward from safe to automatic and moved forward slowly and as quietly as he could. Logically, there was no way the Russians could have known about the old trail, but Cord had learned the hard way that life is not always logical.

He reached the edge of the trees and dropped into a prone position. He could see all of the buildings in the village. Only the mission showed signs of life. Cord could hear the hum of the mission generator. Light was shining from the mission windows. He took out his field glasses and scanned the building carefully. He saw no one. That made him nervous. He did not expect the Russians to be peering out the mission windows, but where were their sentries? He did not think Irene was stupid enough not to post sentries.

He moved back a few feet into the trees. Captain Carter and Sergeant Jackson came up quietly. Cord briefed them quickly, describing exactly what he had seen.

"I don't like it," Cord said. "It looks too damned easy, all of them in the mission with the lights on and no sentries I can see. If they're all in there, it's a piece of cake, if not"—he shrugged his shoulders. It was Carter's decision now.

"All right," Carter said. "We won't take any chances. If they're in there, we'll smoke them out. Jackson, bring up the security team. I want their grenadiers on the firing line." Jackson slipped away. "We're going to do a reconnaissance by fire, Cord. That's a fancy way of saying we're going to blow it apart. We'll use the M203 grenade launchers."

Cord agreed completely. He had been taught in the SAS that, when you are going to attack a building, grenades are better weapons than rifles.

The Special Forces soldiers began to move past Cord, silently taking up their positions along the edge of the trees. Carter whispered to Sergeant Jackson. "Have all the grenadiers load a WP. As soon as those are in, fire three HE grenades per man as fast as they can."

Cord watched as the nearest grenadier depressed the barrel latch on his M203 grenade launcher, slipped the barrel assembly forward, and pushed in a 40-mm white phosphorus grenade. Then, he flipped up the special grenade sight on the forestock of his rifle and gave the ready signal. Cord had seen M203 grenade launchers fired before. The WP grenades would throw particles of burning white phosphorus in all directions and produce dense, choking white smoke. The high-explosive grenades would add explosions and lethal fragments to this devil's brew. If the Russians were inside the building, setting a trap, they were going to be extremely sorry.

Captain Carter raised his hand, poised it, and swept it down.

"Fire!"

Cord heard the "blup" as four M203 grenade launchers fired together. The 40mm grenades arched through the air at 250 feet per second and sailed through the mission windows. There was a series of yellow-white flashes as the grenades detonated. Burning phosphorus fragments filled the inside of the building, and dense white smoke began to billow out the windows.

Mendoza opened fire with the M60, sending a

hundred-round belt of .30 caliber full-metal-jacketed bullets tearing through the walls a foot above the floor. As fast as they could, the grenadiers reloaded and fired 40mm high-explosive grenades through the windows. The old building shook and shuddered as grenade after grenade detonated inside. Cord was impressed. He would not have given two cents for the chances of anyone caught inside.

ELU ISLAND—THE VILLAGE AREA

Irina Yakoleva woke up with a start. The sound of explosions filled the air. Moiseev was pointing toward the mission. The building was burning and exploding. Burning yellow-white particles were arcing through the air, and explosions were detonating inside the building, again and again. A .30 caliber machine gun was firing steadily. Irina could see its muzzle flash and streams of red tracers tearing into the mission. Moiseev did not have to tell her; the Americans were here.

Simultaneously, she heard the "clack" of AK-47 selectors being pushed to the fire position, and the sudden sustained roar as twenty AK-47s opened fire. Green tracers flew toward the American position. The Americans must have been surprised, but they reacted quickly. The edge of the banyan trees near the mission was suddenly filled with bright, flashing yellow lights as they shot back with automatic rifles and light machine guns. Red tracers streamed toward the Russian position. To Irina, it seemed that they were all coming right at her. Now, she felt the shock waves as 40mm grenades began to fall and explode among the Russian fire trenches.

Irina was dazed. She had never been in a firefight at night. The lights and sounds were dazzling. It was hard to think. Bullets were striking and ricocheting around her, but the fire trenches were providing good protection from the bullets and grenade fragments. Well protected, and with visible targets to fire at, the sailors of the landing party poured fire on the American positions.

Suddenly, she sensed a change in the firing. Not so many Americans were shooting. Irina knew what that meant. They were attacking, using fire and maneuver tactics, the basic technique of modern infantry combat. One fire team in a squad would pour in covering fire while the other team advanced. Then, they would alternate, moving steadily closer in short rushes. When they got within hand grenade range, it would be bad.

There really was nothing Irina could do. *Leningradski Komsomols*'s sailors lacked the training for maneuvering at night, and they had no hand grenades. Well, at least she could shoot. She snapped her AK-47 to her shoulder and looked for targets. The light was surprisingly bright. The mission was burning rapidly now, flames and smoke were streaming upward. Irina saw dark figures leap up and rush toward her. A light machine gun seemed to be firing straight at her. Red tracers flashed past her head. Irina shot back, firing short bursts, until her thirty-round magazine was empty. She ducked beneath the lip of the trench and snapped a fresh magazine in place.

She popped back up, ready to fire. There was a sudden change in the volume of fire. The Americans had stopped shooting. Things had changed. The smoke from the burning mission was beginning to drift down over her position. Why had the Americans stopped firing? She did not think they had gone home for breakfast. They had not liked attacking head on into twenty-two automatic rifles. Very well, if she were the American commander, what would she do? The answer was obvious: flank attack. The Americans would hit them on one end of the firing trench line or the other, taking out one

183

trench at a time. The smoke was getting thicker and thicker. It was hard to see more than ten yards. The Americans would use it as cover to get within hand grenade range. Then it would all be over.

Perhaps not. If the smoke gave the Americans cover, it could do the same for her. "Moiseev," she said urgently, "we must withdraw. We will use the smoke for cover. Tell the men to head for the trees to the east of the mission. Let's go, now!"

Jackson was leading the flank attack. Cord was moving with him, three yards to the right, his Owen gun ready in his hands. Jackson had his M16A2 with a thirty-round magazine in the rifle and an antipersonnel round in the M203 grenade launcher. Cord did not like the situation. A flank attack was tactically sound, but the smoke from the old mission was so thick it was hard to see twenty feet. They might stumble on the Russians before they saw them. Stumbling on people armed with AK-47s can be extremely hazardous. Maybe they should—

Two men in dark uniforms suddenly appeared through the smoke, running straight at Cord and Jackson. They weren't wearing helmets. All the Americans were. Russians! Cord squeezed the trigger of his Owen gun and fired from the hip assault position, sending a six-round burst of 9mm bullets into the man on the left. The Russian went down before he could fire.

Desperately, Cord pivoted in a response to the right, twisting from the hip to swing the muzzle of the Owen on. The Russian made the mistake of jumping to turn. His AK-47 seemed to explode in Cord's face as a ten-round burst of 7.62mm bullets tore by, missing by inches. Before Cord could fire, Jackson pulled the trigger on his M203. The antipersonnel round was like a

184

giant shotgun shell. A dozen projectiles struck the Russian, and he died where he stood.

Cord could hear bursts of automatic fire to his right and left, but he could see nothing to shoot at. Suddenly, everything was quiet. He and Jackson kept their weapons ready, but nothing happened. Cord realized what had happened.

"They weren't counterattacking, Frank," he said, "they were pulling out."

Jackson smiled. "Yeah, man, you're right. We won, I think."

Chapter Sixteen

"When a commander makes no mistakes in war, it is because he has not been at it long."
                    —Marshal the Vicomte de Turenne

SPETSNAZ TEAM—OVER ELU

Colonel Viktor Ulanov awoke with a start. The steady sound of the engines had changed, and the flight deck was tilted. The huge TU-95 was losing altitude steadily.

Captain Ivashko grinned and pointed forward through the windscreen. Ulanov stood up and moved forward until he could look over the captain's shoulder.

"There is your island, Colonel, right on schedule."

Ulanov peered through the windscreen. Yes, there was a dark blur ahead on the horizon. Well, Ivashko had done his part, now it was up to *Spetsnaz.*

"We are six minutes out, altitude eight thousand feet and letting down. We will send your men to their jump stations now."

Ulanov nodded and automatically checked his parachutes and equipment. This was not going to be easy. The TU-95 was not designed to carry or drop troops.

He and his men would have to go one at a time out the side-access doors. It would be slow, and, inevitably, they would be scattered and disorganized when they hit the ground. He resisted the temptation to go check his men. Sergeant Sharypa was acting as jump master. He would take care of that. Now, Ulanov had one final, critical decision he must make.

Major Mamin came on the flight deck. He had two mugs of hot tea in his hands. He passed one to Colonel Ulanov. "Compliments of the navigator, Colonel. It seems that he is also the cook on this flying resort."

Ulanov was surprised. It was a friendly gesture. Perhaps the *Zampolit* was not such a bad fellow, after all. He sipped the hot tea gratefully.

Mamin stepped forward and peered through the windscreen. Elu was looming larger and larger as the TU-95 approached the island at eight miles a minute.

"There it is, Elu. Allow me to congratulate you, Colonel. A most ingenious plan. It was unorthodox, but it has worked perfectly."

Ulanov smiled modestly. "So far, so good, Major. I will call it perfect when we are all down and safe. Then we can—"

Captain Ivashko interrupted. "We are here, comrades. The other planes are orbiting. Do you want your low pass now, Colonel?"

Ulanov nodded. "Yes, over the plateau."

"Very well, here we go, low and slow."

"Not too low, and not too slow. The Americans may be in a nasty mood."

Captain Ivashko smiled as he spoke. "And how will these ferocious Green Berets attack a TU-95?"

Ulanov frowned. It is well to be confident, but it is foolish to be overconfident. "Stingers, Captain. They could have Stingers."

Stingers! The smile vanished from Ivashko's face.

187

Like all Russian pilots, he had heard of Stingers, those deadly, American, shoulder-launched, heat-seeking, antiaircraft missiles which had caused such havoc in Afghanistan. Instantly, he was on the intercom.

"Electronic warfare, this is the captain. Stand by for infrared countermeasures, on my command."

He turned to Ulanov. "Good advice, Colonel. Well, here we go, one thousand feet and three hundred knots."

Ivashko pulled *Number 98* into a sharp bank to the left, and the huge TU-95 roared over the plateau.

"Countermeasures, now!"

Behind *Number 98,* infrared flares burst in bright flashes of heat intended to baffle any infrared missile's heat seeker. Colonel Ulanov and Major Mamin peered intently through the side windows.

There! Ulanov stiffened with excitement. There it was! A huge silver-gray cylinder, lying on its side, near the edge of a small forest. *War God!* It could be nothing else. Quickly, Ulanov scanned the rest of the plateau. Nothing. It appeared to be deserted, but he knew the Americans were there, dug in and camouflaged, waiting.

The TU-95 swept across Elu's east coast and out to sea. Ivashko looked at Ulanov. "Another pass?"

"No. Not over the plateau. Take us in over the harbor."

Ivashko nodded and pulled *Number 98* around, heading toward Elu's southern tip. The southern half of the island was covered with a thick, green, tropical rain forest. Ulanov could see a road snaking up the plateau and a small cluster of buildings. He looked for the submarine, but did not see it. The captain had probably dived as soon as he detected approaching aircraft.

Nothing moved in the village. There were two or three vehicles parked near the buildings. One building was burnt and smoldering, as if it had recently been on fire, but there was no sign of life. If the Americans were there, they were under cover. Well, he could delay his decision no longer. In a way, it was obvious. The Americans would concentrate their forces to defend *War God.* The empty look of the plateau could be a deadly trap. Better safe than sorry. He would take the harbor area first.

"What is your decision, Colonel? Fuel is starting to run low. I cannot keep my planes here too much longer."

"Very well. We will drop on the harbor area. One plane at a time until we see how the jumping works."

"What?" Major Mamin shouted. His face was flushed with anger. "That is insane! We must jump on the plateau. We must recapture *War God* immediately!"

Viktor Ulanov frowned. He was not used to having his orders questioned in the middle of a mission. Still, you must be careful how you pull rank on a political officer. He spoke loudly to be sure Captain Ivashko and his copilot heard every word. He might need witnesses later.

"We will drop on the harbor area, Major Mamin. The plateau is as flat as the top of a table. We would have to land in the open. We must jump slowly, one man at a time, from twelve different planes. It would be many minutes before we could be organized and ready to fight. If the Americans know their business—"

Mamin broke in furiously. "But we outnumber them five or six to one. True, there will be casualties, but we will have *War God.* That is all that counts. You must change your order. Do it now!"

"Do not be a fool, Mamin. Lieutenant Yakoleva's message says the Americans have eight or ten machine guns and mortars. Have you ever been in combat, Major?"

Mamin shook his head angrily.

"I thought not. If you had, you would know what machine guns and mortars can do to men caught in the open without cover. The plateau is as flat as a table where there are no trees. It is a perfect killing field if the Americans have their weapons properly placed. We are up against the American *Spetsnaz*. I do not choose to gamble."

Sergeant Sharypa entered the flight deck. He stood quietly behind Major Mamin. Only Colonel Ulanov noticed that Sharypa's fingers were casually curved around the handle of his fighting knife.

Mamin was still furious. "I had not thought that Heros of the Soviet Union were so timid."

It was Ulanov's turn to be furious.

"This is not a debate before a political committee, Major. It is a combat operation, and I am in command! Do not question my decisions. Go to your jump station immediately. That is an order!"

"Exactly so, Comrade Colonel. I carry out your orders without question!"

Mamin stamped off the flight deck. Sergeant Sharypa casually drew his fighting knife and carefully tested the point and edges. Ulanov smiled bleakly. Sharypa's knife was always sharp.

"The *Zampolit* is becoming troublesome, Colonel. Perhaps he will have an accident as he goes out the door."

It was certainly a tempting thought, but Ulanov shook his head. Too many witnesses. Perhaps later, if Mamin continued to cause trouble. Who knows, perhaps some well-intentioned American would do Ulanov a favor and blow Mamin's brains out.

"Be sure everyone is ready to jump, Sharypa. I will be there in a second."

He turned back to Captain Ivashko. "I wish to thank

you for your support, Captain. I could not ask for better. You and your men have done your duty."

Captain Ivashko smiled.

"Carrying passengers is easy, Colonel. I am glad you liked the ride. I try to be better than Aeroflot. The next time you fly with me, I shall have beautiful blond stewardesses and serve champagne and caviar."

Colonel Ulanov stood in the TU-95's aft door. The door was open. The air howled by at 150 miles per hour. *Number 98* was at five hundred feet, heading in from the ocean, making her run from east to west. All Ulanov could see was blue water flashing by. There were no jump lights. They would have to depend on Ivashko for the jump signal. One of the TU-95's crewmen stood by Sharypa's shoulder, listening intently to the intercom. Suddenly, he spoke to Sharypa.

"Ready?" Sharypa was shouting to be sure Ulanov heard him over the sound of the air rushing by and the whine of engines.

Ulanov placed his right foot forward, his hands lightly touching the door frame. He nodded. He was as ready as he would ever be. Now he could see a blur of green through the door. They were over land. Any second now. Time seemed to crawl. At times like these, Ulanov wondered why he had ever wanted to be a *desantniki* and wear the blue beret. He wondered if—

"Go!" Sharypa's hand slapped him on the shoulder. Ulanov dived through the door. It was like jumping into a hurricane. He waited tensely for the tug of the static line as it opened his main chute. When it came, it was an immense bone-jarring jolt. Ulanov was dazed. He was no longer falling. What was happening? His back slammed hard against something. He twisted his head against the force of the airflow. What had he hit? He

191

gazed in horror at the huge gray fuselage of the TU-95 three feet away.

The static line had failed to open his parachute. The canopy of his D-5 main chute had not deployed. He was still attached to the TU-95, being towed along at 150 miles per hour by his nylon static line. He could feel his parachute harness cutting into his chest under the deadly pull of that damned line. He swung toward the TU-95's fuselage again. Desperately, he kicked off with both feet. The impact jolted his entire body. The constriction of his harness grew worse and worse. He gasped desperately for breath. If he passed out now, he was a dead man. He would be battered to death as his body slammed again and again against the TU-95's huge fuselage.

Ulanov remembered his training. Only Sharypa could save him now. He would be looking out the door, but Sharypa could do nothing unless he knew that Ulanov was still conscious. Desperately, straining every muscle, he forced his left arm with fist clenched over his head. That was the "I am conscious" signal. Now, if Sharypa could cut the static line quickly, before——. Ulanov swung toward the fuselage again. This time, he struck across his parachute pack. The impact was numbing. He could not last much longer. Hurry, Sharypa, hurry!

Suddenly the static line parted. Ulanov shot backward, toward the TU-95's huge tail. He missed the horizontal stabilizer by a foot or two, as he turned over and over in the giant aircraft's slipstream. Quickly, he tried to use his arms and legs to slow his rotation. He was starting to fall as he lost forward velocity, and it does not take long to fall five hundred feet. His rotation slowed.

Now or never! He jerked his reserve chute's release ring. The pilot chute deployed and pulled the canopy of his Z-5 reserve chute out of its pack. The canopy opened, and Ulanov felt the jolt through his harness. But he was not complaining; it was the most beautiful sensation he had ever felt.

Now, his canopy was fully open. He was past the drop zone, coming down toward the trees to the west of the village. He pulled on his suspension lines and tried to miss the trees. Too late. His Z-5 reserve chute did not have the divert capability of the high-performance American parachutes.

His boots struck the treetops, and with a crackle and a crash, Ulanov fell through the upper branches of a big banyan tree until his canopy caught on something solid. He was dangling twenty feet in the air from a branch of the huge tree, but he was down and safe. Officially, Ulanov was an atheist, but his mother prayed for him every day. He was not going to smile at his mother's prayers anymore.

He pulled himself up on his suspension lines until he could hook a leg over a solid branch. Carefully, he worked his way into a sitting position and released his harness. First things first. He opened his rifle case and took out his AKD-74, snapped in a magazine, and chambered a round. Ulanov had fitted a BG-15 40mm grenade launcher under the barrel of his rifle. It was not an orthodox weapon for a colonel, but if he had to fight, he intended to attract the enemy's attention forcibly.

Now he was ready to fight, but he was still sitting twenty feet up in the air. *Spetsnaz* training does make you resourceful. He fastened his parachute harness around the branch and opened the pack of his D-5 main chute. The canopy spilled down to the forest floor. He climbed down the canopy and dropped the last three feet to the ground.

He listened intently. He could hear the screaming whine of TU-95 engines. Presumably the drop was underway. He could hear no firing. The Americans were not resisting the landing. But he was badly out of position, a team leader without a team. He had better get to the village area quickly. The devil only knew what would happen if that idiot, Mamin, tried to take command. Well, at least Sharypa would have sense enough to shoot Mamin if it came to that.

ELU ISLAND—THE HARBOR AREA

Irina Yakoleva sat with her back against a tree, slowly cleaning her AK-47. She was a filthy mess, her blond hair was damp with perspiration, dirty and tangled, and her clothes stained with dirt, sweat, and blood. She was hungry, and her muscles ached with fatigue. So much for the glamorous life of a GRU officer. She was thoroughly miserable.

The worst part of it was that she had failed. She had tried hard to do her duty, but they had not recaptured *War God*. Now the Americans had driven them from the village and held the harbor. The remains of *Leningradski Komsomols*'s landing party had no food and were low on ammunition. Their morale was shattered. There was no use planning a counterattack. The sailors did not have it in them.

She wondered if she would be court-martialed when she got back to Moscow. Assuming, of course, that she lived to get back to Moscow. That made her think of her famous message to Colonel-General Galanskov. If it had ever gotten to Moscow, no one had paid any attention.

She knew she was feeling sorry for herself, and that made her angrier still. Well, she would think of something. She——. There was a noise that cut through the bird calls and the wind blowing in the tree branches. Engines! Airplanes approaching. Not those damned American B-52s again! No, the sound was different. Not the dull, rumbling roar of B-52 engines, but a higher-pitched screaming whine. The sound grew louder and louder.

Irina glanced upward through a break in the trees. She saw a huge gray aircraft roar by a few hundred feet above the treetops, then another, and another. She saw the huge fuselage, the swept-back wings, and the giant propellers turning so slowly you could almost see the blades. She did not need to see the red stars on the wings and fuselages. She knew. Nothing else in the world looks like that. Russian TU-95s!

She was on her feet, laughing and dancing around. Moiseev stared at her as if she had gone insane. Plane after plane roared by. Their bomb bay doors were open, dropping dozens of cargo containers. From the fuselage doors, *desantniki* were jumping, their parachutes filling the sky, hundreds of them.

Irina shrieked with glee. "TU-95s, they are ours, men, ours. *Spetsnaz* is here!" She could see the sailors' faces light up. They began to cheer.

Irina felt a spasm of savage glee. All right you Green Berets, and you, Cord, with your damned rifle. The odds are even, now. Let's see how you do against *Spetsnaz!*

Chapter Seventeen

"When victory seems certain, tighten your helmet
strings."
                                    —Samurai proverb

*THE CRISIS CENTER—THE PENTAGON—
WASHINGTON, D.C.*

Brand was furious. He slammed his fist against the
conference table. "I don't believe this. God damn it,
I can't believe this!"

The national security adviser flinched. He had the
feeling that he might be in danger. Perhaps he was.
Brand had killed more than one man with his bare
hands. "I'm sorry, General," he said. "I disapprove of
the decision as much as you do. It certainly was not my
idea. It was the secretary of state. He went to the president and argued that the whole *War God* operation is
a major mistake. He says it will destroy our credibility
in the United Nations and ruin our standing in world
public opinion. He argues that we should take the matter to the United Nations Security Council and ask that
a United Nations peacekeeping force be dispatched to
Elu. The president is thinking it over. In the meantime,

196

he has directed that no more offensive operations of any kind be conducted on or against Elu."

"What the hell does that mean?"

"We are not to enlarge our forces on Elu. There are to be no more B-52 strikes. Actually, it's not so bad. Carter and his men control *War God*. All he has to do is hold on until the *Wasp* gets there. Then, it will all be over."

Brand took a deep breath and forced himself to speak calmly. "With all due respect, sir, this is insane. I'm a soldier, not a rocket scientist, but you and your technical people have told me that this damned satellite is the most important thing in the world to us and the Russians. They aren't going to quit because Carter defeated their naval landing party. I'll bet a year's pay that there's a Russian strike force on the way to Elu right now, and it won't be a bunch of sailors off a God damned submarine. They'll send in *Spetsnaz* or their air assault troops. What the hell is going to happen to Carter? What happens when he runs out of ammunition? Do we tell him to throw rocks at *Spetsnaz?* We sent him there. We've got to support him, resupply and reinforce him. If we don't, we'll lose Carter and *War God.* Surely, the president must see that!"

The security adviser sighed. He was not sure that the president did. After all, the president did not have a military background. Tactics, strategy, and logistics were not his strong suits.

"I understand, General. What is the exact situation, now, at this moment?"

Brand paused and thought. He would have to play this carefully.

"The navy has the *Wasp* and the nuclear attack submarine, *Los Angeles,* en route to Elu. They won't be there for days. The immediate problem is Eagle Force.

They have three B-52s en route to Elu now. They will arrive in the next hour."

The national security adviser frowned. "What are they carrying, General?"

"Reinforcements and supplies for Carter, and an engineering survey party."

"No bombs?"

"No, but we have a bombing flight ready to take off from Guam within the hour."

The national security adviser cleared his throat. Somebody was going to have to bite the bullet. It looked as if he was somebody. "Don't worry about the ships. Keep them heading for Elu. Hold the bombers on Guam. Go ahead and send the B-52s in flight to Elu, and let them drop the men and equipment. I'll take the responsibility."

Brand nodded. He looked at the national security adviser with new respect. The national security adviser noticed the change in Brand's attitude and smiled to himself. Yes, General, you like to see a politician with guts enough to not pass the buck, but you may be talking to a new national security adviser tomorrow.

Aloud, he said, "Keep things under control here, gentlemen. I'm going back to the White House and see if I can get the president to change his mind."

1ST SPECIAL FORCES GROUP (AIRBORNE)— ELU

The sun was up on Elu. Carter was surveying the area and counting the cost. He had four dead and four wounded. He had found eight dead Russians and two wounded, who were now prisoners, though God only knew what he would do with prisoners. The team medic was treating Russian and American wounded alike, and loading them into the back of Cord's Land Rover. Carter had decided to evacuate the village. He would be stretched too thin if he tried to hold it. He wondered where in hell his reinforcements were. They should have been here by now. They—

What was that noise? Aircraft engines. B-52s? No, the sound was different, a high-pitched whine. Off to the west, sunlight flashed on metal. Carter raised up his field glasses. A huge gray airplane was coming straight at him. Whatever it was, it was not a B-52.

Carter did not hesitate. "Everybody under cover. Now! Move it!" His men dispersed rapidly, running for the edge of the trees. Carter snatched another look. The plane had turned slightly. It was making a low pass over the plateau. As it turned, Carter could see the side of the huge gray fuselage and the bright red star painted on the side. That was all he needed to know; the Russians were here.

He shouted his orders. "Jackson, we've got to get out of here. Move them out!"

SOVIET 32ND NAVAL AIR REGIMENT—OVER ELU

Ivashko was pleased. His confidence in the men and aircraft of his regiment had been justified. They had certainly done their duty. Perhaps it would soon be Captain 1st Rank Ivashko. In the meantime, fuel was running low. They could not stay over Elu much longer, and he had four TU-95s loaded with bombs. Presumably, the army wanted them dropped on something. He pushed the button on his air-to-ground radio. "Ivashko to Ulanov. Come in Colonel."

A voice answered, but it was not Ulanov's.

"Captain Ivashko, this is Captain Chazov. Something happened to the Colonel when we jumped. I am in command."

"Chazov, all your men have jumped and all of the

199

cargo has been dropped. I have four TU-95s loaded with bombs. Where do you want them dropped?"

Ivashko could almost here Chazov thinking. It is lonely to suddenly find yourself in command in the middle of a mission.

Chazov answered quickly. "Drop them along the edge of the trees near the satellite. But keep them at least two hundred meters away from the satellite. The devil only knows which one of us they will shoot if you blow it up."

Ivashko smiled. "Probably they will shoot us both. But do not worry. The 32nd Regiment is noted for the incredible precision of its weapons delivery. We will attack at once." He switched to air-to-air frequencies and gave the order. Rodinov was a good flight leader. He would get the job done. Ivashko watched as the four TU-95s turned and lined up for their run. It was going to be very unpleasant for the Americans if they were down there. The TU-95s were carrying 1,100-pound bombs.

Rodinov was sending in one aircraft at a time. Ivashko could see the infrared countermeasures flares flickering in their wakes. He watched as the bombs dropped free and saw the flickering flashes as the bombs detonated. Trees and branches flew through the air. Now, the second and third planes dropped. Good! Bombs right on target. Now the fourth TU-95 was—. What was that?

Something small and fast flashed from the edge of the woods and rocketed toward the fourth TU-95. Stinger! Ulanov had been right. He saw a yellow-white flash as something detonated against the TU-95's right wing. Instantly, the inboard engine was a mass of orange flame. Ivashko watched helplessly as the pilot fought to retain control. A second missile flashed from the edge of the woods. It struck the TU-95 in the cockpit and detonated. Ivashko watched horrified as the huge plane rolled slowly to the right and fell. A huge ball of fire blossomed as the TU-95 struck and fuel and bombs went up together. There were no parachutes. Ivashko had lost the plane and its crew.

SPETSNAZ TEAM—ELU ISLAND—THE VILLAGE

Colonel Viktor Ulanov moved quickly through the trees. He must be near the edge of the forest. Careful, now, Viktor, it would not do to get your head blown off by one of your own men. He could still hear the whine of TU-95 engines. Ivashko's planes were still on station. Now he heard the dull, rumbling boom of bombs exploding in the distance.

He reached the edge of the trees and took a quick look with his field glasses. Excellent. His men were obviously in control of the situation. Everywhere he looked he could see purposeful groups of men in the mottled brown camouflage uniforms of the VDV. They were collecting equipment containers and unloading ammunition and supplies. Chazov was standing in front of the smoldering ruins of a building, giving orders to a small group of officers and men. He smiled broadly as Ulanov came up.

"There you are, Colonel. We were beginning to be concerned."

Ulanov smiled. "I am hard to kill, Captain. Only the good die young. What is the situation?"

"Sharypa is leading a reconnaissance patrol up the road to the plateau. The First Company is assembled and ready to move out. I have the Second Company collecting weapons and supplies. Your mortars are being assembled and checked out."

"Excellent. Where is Major Mamin? What is he doing?"

"The *Zampolit?* Well, I cannot complain. He made no effort to take command. He has told the men that this is a vital mission and they must follow their officers and do their duty. It is hard to argue with that."

"No," Ulanov agreed, "but we must be careful, Chazov. That man is a fanatic. Such men are dangerous on combat operations." He pointed to the smoldering ruins. "What happened here?"

"A serious firefight. We found eight dead bodies wearing Soviet navy uniforms. There are many fired cartridge cases. And look at this."

Chazov held up a black automatic rifle. The plastic stock had been shattered by bullets. "An M16A2. There can be no doubt. The Americans were here."

Ulanov frowned. It appeared that the Americans had attacked and wiped out the navy landing party. Then they had retreated back to the plateau when the TU-95s arrived. Well, that was logical. It was what he would have done if he had been the American commander.

Now if——. A corporal with a radio on his back was speaking.

"Colonel, a message from our planes."

Ulanov took the headset. Captain Ivashko's voice was clear. He no longer sounded cheerful. "I can stay no longer, Colonel. We have just enough fuel to get home. You were right about the Stingers. I lost *Number 73* and her entire crew. It seems our countermeasures are not effective against a head-on attack. We have other planes preparing to fly out from Cam Ranh Bay. I will be back, myself, as soon as I can. I will enjoy bombing the Americans who shot down *Number 73.* Until then, good luck."

THE CRISIS CENTER—THE PENTAGON— WASHINGTON, D.C.

Brand was still seething. He had seen too many good men killed when operations were ruined by political interference. Against his better judgment, he poured himself another cup of coffee. Well, at least *Los Angeles* and *Wasp* were still on their way to Elu, but Carter was in a bad spot if the politicians kept Brand from reinforcing him. There ought to be something he could—.

An air force colonel was moving rapidly across the room. Brand did not like the look on his face. It was not the expression of a man bringing good news. The colonel arrived and saluted. "General, we just received a message from *Eagle Ten.* The B-52s reached Elu and dropped personnel and cargo successfully, but—"

Brand had known there would be a "but."

"—they observed heavy air activity over Elu, fifteen large multiengined aircraft tentatively identified as Russian TU-95s. They report hundreds of parachutes. A major air landing operation appears to be underway."

"All right, Colonel, I understand. I want you to coordinate with the navy. Is there any way we can get air force or navy fighters to Elu?"

The colonel saluted and was gone. Brand reached for the secure phone. He would call the White House and—. An army major interrupted.

"General, we have a message coming in via SATCOM from Lieutenant Goldberg on Elu."

Goldberg? What the hell had happened to Carter? "Put him on the loudspeaker."

The AN/PSC-3 satellite communications radio was working perfectly. Goldberg might have been in the next room.

"—many parachutes dropped. Enemy now holds

203

harbor and village areas. We urgently need reinforcements. We—"

Goldberg was interrupted by a series of rumbling roars growing louder and louder until a final *boom!* which nearly shook the loudspeaker off the wall. For a moment, there was a stunned silence. Then Goldberg's voice came through again.

"Washington, we are under heavy air attack! I say again, *heavy air attack!* Hunter, get those Stingers going! Look out! Here comes another one! They're—"

Another series of blasts shook the loudspeaker.

"Where the hell are those God damned Stingers? Shoot, God damn it, shoot!"

Goldberg was no longer talking to Washington. Brand heard the roar of a small rocket motor and then another. The urge to ask questions was almost overpowering, but Brand knew better than to bother men who are fighting.

"Got him! Hit the bastard! Look at that, he's on fire! He's going in! He's—"

Brand heard another tremendous blast.

"He blew up. Look at that fireball! Good work, Hunter!"

There was a moment's silence. Brand picked up the microphone and pushed the button. "Lieutenant Goldberg, this is General Brand. What is your situation?"

"Yes, sir. I'm sorry, I got a little excited when they started bombing us."

"Steady down, son, and tell me the situation."

"Yes, sir. We have established a defensive perimeter around the satellite. We are dug in. Captain Carter took two squads and a machine gun team and raided the village area. I am defending the satellite with the third squad, the other machine gun team, and the mortar team."

"Right. Now where is Captain Carter and the raiding party now?"

"I don't know, General. I think the raid was a success; we must have had some casualties. The captain signaled me to send down a vehicle. Then all hell broke loose. About fifteen large Russian aircraft arrived. They dropped hundreds of parachutes. I estimate two hundred fifty to three hundred troops and many equipment containers. They dropped on the village area. Captain Carter may have been cut off, I don't know. Then four of them made a bombing attack on my position. We suffered no casualties. I think they were trying to miss the satellite. We got one with Stingers."

Brand could feel the tension knotting his stomach. Goldberg was defending the satellite with fifteen or sixteen men. Even if Carter got back, it would be less than 40 Green Berets against 250 or 300 *Spetsnaz* or crack VDV troops. Carter's men were good, but not that good.

"General, we've got to have reinforcements."

"I know you do. Listen, three B-52s flew over you during the Russian air attack. They dropped thirty men HAHO. They should be landing in your area in a few minutes. Twenty of them are from the 1st Special Forces Group. The others are a Combat Engineers team. Add the Special Forces troopers to your defense. Hold on. You're in command until Carter gets back. If he doesn't make it, you are in command, period. I will get you reinforcements as soon as possible."

"Yes, sir. What are my orders if the Russians make a large-scale attack?"

Brand hated what he was going to say next. He had heard those words too many times before, and too many good men had died because of them. Now, there was no way he could avoid saying them. "Hold them," Brand said. "Hold them as long as you can."

There was a moment's silence. Goldberg was not a child; he was a Special Forces officer. He knew instantly what Brand's words meant. He and his men were expendable. They were to fight to the last man.

"Yes, sir."

"Hang on, Goldberg. I'll do everything I can to reinforce you as soon as possible."

Brand put down the microphone and picked up a secure phone. "This is General Brand. Get me the White House, the national security adviser. It's a major emergency."

Brand thought carefully about what he was going to say. It was highly possible that he would be a retired brigadier general by this time tomorrow. Still, he had sent Carter and Goldberg and their men to Elu to fight and die. He was willing to risk his career for them. The national security adviser came on the line. Quickly, Brand briefed him. He finished describing the situation on Elu. Now, to put it on the line.

"There is no way Carter and Goldberg can hold out with what they have. Even if Carter gets back, he will be outnumbered five to one. There's no way in hell he can win against those odds. We will lose them, and we will lose the satellite. We have to reinforce Carter and give him all possible air support. We have to do it now. Please impress the gravity of the situation on the president. Tell him we must have a decision now!"

There was a long silence. Then the national security adviser spoke quietly.

"I understand the situation, General. But I cannot get an immediate decision. The president had a heart attack twenty minutes ago. They are taking him to Walter Reed now. I have contacted the vice-president. *Air Force Two* is bringing the vice-president back from San Francisco now. It will arrive in Washington in approximately four hours. Until the vice-president is briefed and agrees to change the president's orders, there is nothing I can do."

Brand was stunned. There was nothing he could think to say.

"Brand, assume the vice-president will say go. Have everything ready. In the meantime, I authorize you to take any defensive action you can think of to protect our men on Elu. Get them fighter cover if there is any way you can. One other thing. Better see if you can develop a viable evacuation plan. We may need a way to get Carter and his men off Elu quickly."

Chapter Eighteen

"There is only one tactical principle which is not subject to change. It is to use the means at hand to inflict the maximum amount of wounds, death, and destruction on the enemy in the minimum amount of time!"
—General George S. Patton

ELU ISLAND—THE ROAD TO THE PLATEAU

Sweating and swearing, the raiding party crashed through the bush as they moved as rapidly as possible up the old trail. They could see nothing through the canopy of trees which hung over the trail. The sounds they could hear were not reassuring. The whine of aircraft engines seemed to come from all directions, and now they heard explosion after explosion. Somebody was getting it, and Carter was afraid he knew who. The heat was brutal, and the humidity was worse. Their fatigues were soaked with sweat as they tried to keep up the pace, weighed down with weapons and ammunition. Cord's knee was killing him. The rest of the raiding party were not in much better shape. They were going to have to stop soon, or men were going to start dropping in their tracks.

Sergeant Jackson suddenly held up his hand in the halt signal. They were almost to the road, thank God. There was no time for celebrating. They checked their weapons quickly. If the Russians were ahead of them, it was going to be grim and nasty.

Jackson crept forward to the start of the trail. He looked carefully up and down the road and then gave the all-clear signal. A wave of relief swept through the raiding party. They weren't cut off. Carter motioned to Cord to follow him and moved forward to join Jackson. They dropped down into the prone position beside Jackson and scanned the road. Carter was thinking hard. Cord took the opportunity to take out his water bottle and have a drink. He reminded himself to swallow slowly; he did not want cramps.

Carter turned to Cord. "Is there any way they can get up to the plateau in force except up this road?"

Cord thought it over. "They might get a few men up, but they'd have to be damned good at climbing. Any number of troops with equipment have got to move up the road or alongside it."

Carter made his decision. "All right. They'll probably feel us out with a patrol before they commit their main body. We'll ambush their lead elements here. Sergeant Jackson, you take command here and set up the ambush. I've got to get back up the plateau and contact Washington. We have to have reinforcements."

He paused for a minute. Cord was not really under his command. "What do you want to do, Cord, go with me and talk to Australia or stay here with Jackson?"

Cord had recovered his Lee-Enfield from the Land Rover. He unslung it and checked his telescopic sight. He really had nothing to say to Canberra, and Jackson was going to need all the help he could get. Besides, he could not go much farther without resting his knee. "I'll stay here," he said. "I might get a shot or two."

Carter stood up and started to move out. He paused for a second. He and Jackson had served together for years. Jackson knew his business, but there was one more thing Carter had to say.

"Don't be a hero, Frank. Hit them as hard as you can and then fall back. Don't get cut off. And remember this. I don't want you to die for your country. I want you to help them die for theirs."

SPETSNAZ RECONNAISSANCE PATROL—ELU ISLAND—THE ROAD TO THE PLATEAU

Sharypa was moving cautiously but steadily up the road. His patrol consisted of three nine-man squads, himself, and his radioman. The first squad was leading. Sharypa and his radioman moved with the second squad. He did not deceive himself. He was going to be ambushed. The only question was where and when. He did not think he was going to enjoy it. He had read the intelligence manual on American infantry weapons during the flight to Elu. It was obvious that American small units had a lot of firepower.

Well, he had picked good men for the patrol. Most of them had fought in Afghanistan. They would—. Sharypa heard a peculiar thumping ripping noise. He had heard it a thousand times in Afghanistan, the sound a high-velocity, full-metal-jacketed bullet makes as it tears through a human body. He saw his radio operator spin and start to fall. Instantly, instinctively, Sharypa threw himself down and rolled for the drainage ditch on the left side of the road, yelling as he went, *"Ambush! Take cover! Ambush!"* He heard the crack of a high-powered rifle, and half a second later the "thu-thu-thu-thu" of a .30 caliber machine gun firing short, precisely aimed bursts down the road.

Sharypa knew what was going to happen next. It was a classic line ambush. From the trees to the right side

of the road, automatic rifles and light machines opened
fire, and hundreds of .223 caliber, high-velocity, full-
metal-jacketed bullets sprayed the patrol. If most of
the *Spetsnaz* troopers had not been combat veterans,
they all would have died then. But reflexes learned the
hard way took over, and they hurled themselves into
the ditch. Now their training took over. They must
shoot back. They did. Sharypa heard the spiteful crack
of AKD-74 rifles and RPK-74 squad light machine guns
as his men opened fire and high-velocity .215 caliber
bullets shot toward the American position.

Sharypa risked a quick look. There were bodies in
brown mottled camouflage uniforms sprawled in the
road. The radioman's body lay still a few feet away. He
knew a sniper had killed his radioman. The sniper was
probably waiting for someone to try and get that radio.
Sharypa was right. He was still alive because Cord had
not been able to identify the patrol leader, so he had
shot the radioman. Sharypa was wearing the same uniform as his men. He was not stupid enough to wear the
shoulder boards of a senior sergeant while leading a
combat patrol. But the sniper would know the radioman would have been moving close to the patrol leader.
He would be watching and waiting, his finger on the
trigger.

Now 40mm high-explosive grenades began to land
and detonate as the American grenadiers tried to drop
their lethal projectiles in the ditch. Things were not
going well. The Americans had four or five .223 SAW
light machine guns against two RPK-74s, and that
damned .30 caliber machine gun made things worse.
Sharypa considered his options. He could try to counterattack the main American position. No, the Americans had too much firepower, and that damned .30 caliber machine gun would pour in deadly flanking fire as
they tried to cross the road. Retreat? No, the Ameri-

211

cans would cut them to pieces as they tried to move out. No way out, he must try to get the radio, but first he had one card to play, and the Americans would not like it.

He glanced to his right. Dudorov, the second squad's rocket grenadier, was crouched in the ditch, the three-foot-long, tubular shape of his RPG-7D rocket-propelled grenade launcher ready for action. Sharypa risked pointing and yelling. "Dudorov, get those damned machine guns!"

Dudorov nodded and peered for a moment through his PRO-7 optical sight. He pulled the trigger, and Sharypa saw a streak of gray-white smoke as the 85mm OG-7 antipersonnel rocket grenade whooshed towards the American position. The five-pound warhead detonated in an orange-yellow flash. One of the American SAWs stopped firing. There was another whoosh as the first squad's rocket grenadier joined the party. A second yellow-orange blast bloomed in the American position. Sharypa looked to his right. Dudorov was slipping a fresh OG-7 grenade into the muzzle.

Sharypa shouted. "Dudorov. Yell when you are going to fire."

Dudorov nodded. He was a cool, stolid man, with the temperament a man needs who may be called on to engage a fifty-ton tank with a hand-held rocket launcher. He lifted his RPG-7D to his shoulder and picked his target through his PRO-7 optical sight.

"Ready, Sharypa, three, two"—Sharypa crouched, ready to run—"one"—whoosh!

Sharypa sprang from the ditch as Dudorov fired. He reached the radioman's body in three quick strides and grabbed the web straps of his pack harness. He heaved with all his strength and dragged the body back toward the ditch. Sharypa heard a loud crack and his bush hat jumped off his head and flew through the air. He reached the lip of the ditch and threw himself in. There was another crack and the radioman's body shuddered as another .223 bullet struck. Sharypa yanked the radioman's body into the ditch. It was a hard way to treat a comrade's body, but Sharypa had to have the radio.

A fountain of dirt suddenly erupted on the edge of the ditch as a .303 full-metal-jacketed bullet struck at 2,200 feet per second. Sharypa crouched deeper. Damn! That sniper was the very devil! Well, perhaps Sharypa could arrange a little entertainment for him. He pushed the microphone switch. Now, if the damned radio still worked! There was a reassuring hum of static. Then Sharypa heard Colonel Ulanov's voice.

"Blue Four, Blue Four. What is your situation, Blue Four?"

"Blue One, this is Blue Four. Ambush! We are under heavy automatic weapon and grenade fire. We need support now!"

"Steady, Sharypa. Give me the exact coordinates of the American position."

Sharypa pulled out the photo map of Elu. He read the coordinates carefully. He knew what the colonel was going to do. If Sharypa made a mistake, his mother would be mourning her only son.

"443-562, Colonel. I say again, 443-562."

"Acknowledged, Sharypa. Stand by."

Sharypa moved six feet down the ditch. He risked popping up for another look. Nothing had changed. His men and the Americans were still exchanging bullets, rifle grenades, and curses. Dudorov and the first squad's rocket grenadier fired again. Two more 85 mm rocket grenades streaked through the air and detonated in the American position. Good, the Americans would not like that, but RPG-7D rocket grenades weigh fifteen pounds. Not even a strong man like Dudorov could carry more than five rounds. When they were gone, things would get grim.

"In the air, Sharypa, stand by."

"Two smoke rounds, ten, five, three, two"—unheard over the din of rifle and machine gun fire, two 34-pound 120mm mortar bombs plunged down out of the sky and struck at the edge of the trees. Clouds of gray-white smoke began to spread rapidly.

"On target! On target!" Sharypa yelled gleefully. "Pour it on them!"

Colonel Ulanov used a little more military precision, but it meant the same thing. Sharypa heard his voice on the radio. "Section! Sight settings correct. High-explosive bombs! Sustained fire!"

Sharypa heard the "thung, thung, thung," as the mortars fired as fast as their crews could load them, twelve bombs a minute from each mortar. He did not need Colonel Ulanov's reassuring, "In the air, Sharypa, stand by."

He waited impatiently. Then the mortar bombs arrived. Two thirty-four pound high-explosive bombs every five seconds plunged down out of the sky and began to blast the American position. Dust, dirt, and tree branches filled the air, lit by continuous yellow-orange detonations. The *Spetsnaz* patrol watched fascinated, as the heavy mortar bombs tore the American position to pieces.

1ST SPECIAL FORCES AMBUSH PARTY—ELU ISLAND—THE ROAD TO THE PLATEAU

Jackson ducked as an RPG-7D rocket whooshed over his head and detonated in the trees behind him. Fragments from the 85mm high-explosive warhead whined through the branches overhead. He spotted the cloud of dust stirred up by the rocket launcher's back blast. He fired an answering burst from his M16A2 and saw the dirt fly as his bullets raked the edge of the ditch. These God damned rockets were something else. Maybe it was time to think about pulling—. Something smashed into the ground twenty feet in front of Jackson. A fountain of dust and dirt erupted and dense gray-white smoke began to billow upward. Another something smashed into the ground. Mortars! Heavy mortars!

Some one was yelling, "Incoming! Incoming!" But Jackson already knew that. He knew what was happening. The first two rounds were smoke for spotting. You have to do that when you fire heavy stuff close to your own troops at long range. But the HE bombs were next, and they might already be on the way. The time of flight would be thirty or forty seconds, not much time, but maybe just enough. Jackson filled his lungs and yelled loudly. He could yell very loudly when he had to. "Break contact! Break contact! Pull out!" He emptied his rifle's magazine at the Russians and fired the 40mm grenade from his grenade launcher, turned, and ran deeper into the trees. He could hear his men blasting out heavy fire to keep the Russians' heads down as they attempted to break contact and retreat into the trees.

There was no increase in answering fire. The Russians were not pursuing; they were staying put. Jackson God damned well knew what that meant. There was a large fallen log ahead. Jackson threw himself behind it as a giant coughed and the world started to blow up. Blast after blast rocked the log. Lethal fragments whined through the air. Dirt and broken branches rained down. He hoped to God his men had found cover. Anyone who hadn't was probably dead.

The explosions stopped. Instantly, Jackson was alert. The Russians might be coming right behind their mortar barrage. He listened intently. He could hear an M60 machine gun firing steadily in the distance. Mendoza was reminding the Russians that an attack across the road was still extremely hazardous. Jackson watched and counted as his men began to filter back through the trees. He counted Cord and eight of his men. Damn it! They must have killed a dozen Russians, but he had lost six men. No use trying another ambush. Those heavy mortars would blow him to hell if he tried that again. Time to fall back to the plateau and make a stand there. But how the hell were they going to stop two or three hundred Russians there? Well, Carter would have to come up with something. He was the captain, after all; that's what they paid him for.

1ST SPECIAL FORCES GROUP(AIRBORNE) DETACHMENT—ELU ISLAND—THE PLATEAU

Carter pushed on up the road, running a few hundred yards and then slowing to a fast walk. The heat was murder, and the humidity was worse. His fatigues were soaked with sweat. He resisted the impulse to try to go faster. A captain with heat prostration was not going to do his men or his mission any good. At last, he was close to the top. He slowed down and went carefully. It would not do to be killed by his own men.

He reached the edge of the plateau. Ahead, from a large clump of rocks, the challenge rang out. Carter gave the reply and came on in. Lieutenant Goldberg emerged from the rocks and came to meet him. There was a noticeable look of relief on Goldberg's face. He had not enjoyed being in command in this crazy situation. Quickly, he briefed Carter on what had happened in the last few hours.

"We've got twenty reinforcements and there are eight combat engineers and two air force types running around on the plateau. The bad news is that there's some monumental screwup in Washington. General

216

Brand may not be able to reinforce us. The general says we hold them as long as we can. I've set up our defenses here to try to keep them off the plateau. If that doesn't work, I figure we fall back and fight around the satellite as long as we can."

Carter nodded. Goldberg was a competent officer. He had done what Carter would have done. No need to change anything. Still, he wanted to check the machine gun and mortar positions before the Russians arrived. That did leave one question. "What are these combat engineers doing?"

"They haven't told me. It's supposed to be hush-hush. But it's pretty damned obvious. They're filling holes, blasting rocks, and laying out markers. They're setting up an airstrip. Maybe the general is going to try and evacuate us if things get too rough."

Carter nodded. "Maybe so." But he doubted it. He had served with Brand before. When Brand said, "Hold them as long as you can," that's what he damn well meant. There wasn't going to be any evacuation. There was no use discouraging Goldberg. "Let's check things one more time. There are two or three hundred *Spetsnaz* troopers on the way. We'd better be ready."

SPETSNAZ TEAM—ELU ISLAND—THE VILLAGE AREA

"Cease fire! Cease fire!" The mortar section stopped dropping bombs down the muzzles of the 120mm mortar tubes. Colonel Ulanov hoped he had given the Americans a bloody nose. Now, it was time to conserve ammunition. The nearest replacement 120 mm mortar bombs were in Cam Ranh Bay. He knew he might need every round he had when the team went up the plateau road.

It was time to do that. He knew where the Americans were. They were ready to fight for the plateau and *War*

217

God. It was an interesting situation. He had numbers on his side, but the terrain favored the Americans. Well, he must get his men up the road and do it quickly. The daylight would not last forever.

"Chazov, tell Captain Gromov to move out. He is to take the First Company to Sharypa's present position. Second Company is to follow in ten minutes. We will use that truck to move the mortars and their ammunition. You and I and the Command Group will move with the Second Company. Understood?"

"Exactly so, Colonel, I will issue the orders immediately."

Ulanov turned. A *Spetsnaz* sergeant was leading a small group of people toward Ulanov and Chazov. Ulanov could see why Chazov was startled. The leader of the group was a tall blond woman dressed in decadent Western civilian clothing. She was wearing web equipment and carrying an AK-47 rifle. Ulanov smiled. There could be no doubt. This must be the famous Irina Yakoleva.

The tall woman approached and gave Ulanov a superb salute. "*Starshiy Leytenant* Irina Yakoleva, GRU, reporting, and this is Warrant Officer Moiseev of the Soviet submarine *Leningradski Komsomols.*"

Colonel Ulanov was impressed. If only more GRU officers looked like this! He returned her salute with equal precision. "I am Colonel Viktor Ulanov, *Spetsnaz.* We are glad to see you, Lieutenant Yakoleva. You are here just in time. Chazov, hold the movement order. Assemble the officers and senior sergeants. Senior Lieutenant Yakoleva will brief us on the situation."

The officers and men of the Command Group stared at Irina Yakoleva. Colonel Ulanov's luck in attracting pretty women was legendary in *Spetsnaz,* but here, on Elu, in the middle of a combat operation? Astounding!

The officers and senior sergeants gathered quickly.

Irina began her briefing. She was used to giving briefings; after all, she was an intelligence officer. But this time she was self-conscious and embarrassed. Her clothes were filthy, and her hair was a mess, but worst of all, she was briefing battle-hardened leaders of the Soviet Union's elite troops on a tactical situation. She was afraid they would laugh at her. Actually, her appearance worked for her. Had she been clean and scrubbed, and wearing her best walking out dress uniform, they might have sneered and called her an empty-headed blond. But they knew what people who have been in sustained combat look like. Her dirty, bloodstained clothes and the AK-47 slung over her shoulder told them she was one of them. And she had done one thing they had not. She had fought against elite American troops. They listened intently. The smallest thing she told them might be the difference between life and death.

Irina finished. There were a few questions. It was hard to believe this sniper, Cord, could be as dangerous as she said. Still, the bloodstains on her clothes were very convincing. The American B-52s sounded particularly unpleasant. They were painfully aware that the *Spetsnaz* team had little air-defense capability. Well, now they knew what they were up against. It did not alter their determination to do their duty. They would not have been in *Spetsnaz* if they lacked courage and determination.

Colonel Ulanov spoke quietly. "Thank you, Lieutenant Yakoleva. An excellent briefing. Have you anything else that you should tell us?"

Irina thought for a moment. "Only this, comrades. Be on your guard. The Americans are clever and deadly foes. They are well armed and well trained. We outnumber those who are here on Elu five to one. But the Americans want *War God*. More of them are probably on the way, and those B-52s could return at any minute."

Ulanov nodded. Good advice. Well, they had talked about it. Now it was time to do it. "Comrades, Captain Chazov will issue your orders. Then rejoin your units. Be prepared to move out in ten minutes. Lieutenant Yakoleva, you will accompany the Command Group. I will need your advice." He smiled. "You had better turn in your AK 47 for an AK 74. I fear we brought no ammunition for AK 47s. There are spare weapons in the equipment canisters."

Moiseev stepped forward and saluted. "What do you wish us to do, Colonel? We are ready to go with you if you need us."

Ulanov looked at the thin line of dirty, exhausted sailors. He returned Moiseev's salute sincerely. "That will not be necessary. Return to your submarine. Your captain needs you. We will take care of the American army. You keep their navy off our backs. One thing more, you can be proud of what you did here. Without you, the Americans might have escaped with the satellite. You did your duty."

Moiseev saluted, and the survivors of the landing party started for the harbor.

Ulanov turned as Irina Yakoleva came back. She had a new rifle in her hands, but it was not an AK 74. It was an SVD sniper's rifle, complete with telescopic sight.

"You prefer an SVD to an AK 74, Lieutenant?"

Irina Yakoleva smiled. Ulanov liked to see a pretty woman smile, but there was something cold and deadly in Irina Yakoleva's smile. "Yes," she said softly, "I have had training as a sniper. It may be that I shall see Cord before he sees me."

SPETSNAZ TEAM—ELU ISLAND—THE ROAD TO THE PLATEAU

Grimly, determinedly, the *Spetsnaz* team toiled up the plateau road. Viktor Ulanov marched along with his men. His uniform was soaking wet from sweat. Inwardly, he was seething. He had miscalculated. The march was brutal. His men were carrying their weapons, six hundred rounds of ammunition, grenades, food, and water—more than sixty pounds of gear per man. The steady upward slope of the road made marching difficult.

He had expected that. He had not considered the weather. The temperature was over a hundred degrees and the humidity well over ninety percent. His men had flown from wintertime in central Russia to summertime in the Southwest Pacific. The sudden change in the climate was devastating. His men were tough and in excellent physical condition, but already half a dozen of them had collapsed by the side of the road, nauseated, weak, and dizzy as they succumbed to heat exhaustion. Willpower and determination were not enough. Many of his men were not going to make it to the top of the plateau. Those who did would be in no condition to fight. He could not attack today; he must change his plan.

He gave the order to halt and fall out. Gratefully, his men collapsed by the side of the road. Captain Chazov came up in one of the mission jeeps. He had several large metal water cans in the back. Good. Chazov was using his head. The men desperately needed more water. So, for that matter, did Ulanov. Chazov approached and handed Ulanov a full canteen. Ulanov drank gratefully. He would have made Chazov a major on the spot if he had had the authority.

"How does it go, Chazov?"

"The mortars are emplaced. One of Captain Gromov's platoons and four machine gun teams are in place near the top of this damned mountain. I sent them up on the truck as you ordered. The cork is in the bottle. The Americans cannot get out. But, the rest of it does not go well. As you see here, the heat is deadly. I recommend we slow down and rest. If we are in position by dark, we can rest the men and attack tomorrow morning."

Ulanov did not like it, but there was no alternative. He nodded agreement. "You are right; give the orders. Have you been to the top? What does the position look like?"

"Yes, I went up with Captain Gromov's platoon. Unfortunately, the American position is very strong. There is a large outcropping of rocks that dominates the entrance to the plateau. If the Americans dig in properly, it will be very hard to push them out."

"I do not intend to try and push them. We will blast them out. Do you have the R-350M SATCOM radio in the jeep?"

Chazov nodded. "Good," Ulanov continued. "Have the operator get me Captain Ivashko in Cam Ranh Bay." Ulanov drank more water and rested until the radio operator beckoned. He took the headset. SATCOM never ceased to amaze Ulanov. Captain Ivashko's voice was as clear as if he were a mile away, rather than over four thousand.

"How does it go, Colonel?"

"Well enough, Ivashko, but the Americans are proving stubborn. I intend to attack the plateau in the morning. I will need all the support I can get. I want as many TU-95s with bombs as I can get. I want to blast them out. One other thing. I need many more 120mm mortar bombs and at least four AGS-17 grenade launchers with large amounts of ammunition. Get them from our Vietnamese friends if necessary, but get them here as soon as possible. Understood?"

"I understand, Colonel, one moment while I check things out."

Ulanov waited a few minutes until Ivashko spoke again. "Very well, Colonel. We can give you what you need. My planes are in maintenance, I cannot fly tonight, but Captain Pavlovsky's 44th Regiment has staged in from Vladivostok. They will be ready to go in two or three hours. Of course, the 44th Regiment is not as outstanding an organization as my 32nd, but they are quite good in their way. They can put up sixteen TU-95s. Twelve will be loaded with bombs. The other four will carry your weapons and ammunition. It will take a little time to get them here and get them loaded. The takeoff will be delayed a bit, but the 44th should be over Elu two hours after dawn."

"Excellent, Ivashko, but do not fail us. I must attack tomorrow morning, no matter what. The planes must be here."

"Exactly so, Colonel. Do not worry, the 44th Regiment will be there. The Americans will have 1,100-pound bombs for breakfast."

THE CRISIS CENTER—THE PENTAGON—
WASHINGTON, D.C.

The air force colonel shook his head. "I'm sorry, General, I can't get you the fighter cover you need. It just isn't possible. I could get some F-15Cs to Elu for an air strike, but I'd have to have tankers refuel them going in and coming out. Even then, they would only have enough fuel to stay over the island for twenty or thirty minutes. That's long enough to attack something on the ground, but what you want is air cover, defensive patrols, fighters over the island for hours at a time. There's no airfield on Elu. We can't land planes and refuel and rearm them. What you need is planes that can fly to Elu and stay there, in the air, for hours. Believe me, there's no fighter plane in the world that can do that."

Brand believed him, but he didn't like it. He turned to the navy captain, who sat listening intently.

"Can the navy do anything, Captain? Our men on Elu have got to have air cover."

"Yes and no, General. If we fly from land bases, our fighters have the same problems as air force F-15s. On the other hand, if we can get a carrier battle group off Elu, we can do it."

That was better. "Where's the nearest carrier? How fast can we get it there?"

"The *Vinson* and her battle group are about four hundred miles east of Pearl Harbor. She is a nuclear-propelled carrier. Some of her escorts are nuclear-propelled. We don't have to worry about their running out of fuel. They can make a rapid transit at thirty-two knots. *Vinson* carries four fighter squadrons, F-14 Tomcats and F/A-18 Hornets. *Vinson* can handle the job when she gets there."

It sounded wonderful, but there was one critical question. "How long will it take the *Vinson* to get to Elu?"

The captain made a quick mental calculation. "Five to six days, sir."

Jesus Christ! Five to six days! It might as well be five to six years. Brand suppressed the urge to swear and pound the table. He took a deep breath and forced himself to speak calmly.

"Gentlemen, I understand your problems, but we've got to do something. Intelligence reports that the Russians have deployed a second TU-95 regiment into Cam Ranh Bay. They can fly in more troops, and they'll bomb the hell out of Carter. You gentlemen are the experts. Think. There must be something we can do."

There was a long silence. Then the air force colonel spoke reluctantly. "Well, General, I was just talking on SATCOM to Major Banford, the CO of Eagle Force. One of his pilots, Captain Chavez, has an idea. But, sir, it's a really crazy idea."

Brand smiled grimly. "Good, that's what we need, a really crazy idea."

Chapter Nineteen

"The quality of the plane matters little. Success or failure depends on the man who sits in it."
                    —Baron Manfred von Richtofen

44TH SOVIET NAVAL AIR REGIMENT—OFF ELU

The sixteen huge TU-95s of the 44th Naval Air Regiment flew steadily on toward Elu. Captain 2nd Rank Yegor Pavlovsky sat at the controls of the leading TU-95. He glanced out the window of *Number 64* and checked the other three aircraft in his flight. The sun had been up for nearly two hours now. The morning light gleamed off the silver-gray wings and the large red stars of the 44th's aircraft as they flew in four flights of four, one flight after another.

Pavlovsky checked his engine gauges. No problems. All four 14,795-horsepower NK-12M turbine engines were performing perfectly, maintaining a steady 475 miles per hour cruising speed and an altitude of 22,000 feet. He had not expected anything to be wrong. He had flown in TU-95s for ten years. No plane was more reliable. Pavlovsky was proud of his aircraft and his regiment. Forty-eight hours ago they had been operating in the North Pacific, sparring with the combat air patrols from the American aircraft carriers in the Sea of Japan. In those 48 hours, they had deployed 3,600 miles from Vladivostok to Cam Ranh Bay, refueled, rearmed, and flown 4,500 miles toward Elu. Ivashko might boast that his 32nd Regiment was the elite air regiment in the Pacific Fleet, but Pavlovsky knew better. No one could match his 44th.

Now, if his navigator would get them to the damned island. Ivashko would never let Pavlovsky hear the last of it if the 44th had to fly a search pattern. Carefully, Pavlovsky adjusted his trim. *Number 64* was getting a little nose heavy as she burned off fuel. The bomb bay was full of 1,100-pound FAM-500 bombs. He would be glad when he got rid of them. The extra weight of the bombs made his plane a little sluggish, but he had confidence they would do the job. His twelve bombers would deliver 288 FAM-500s, nearly 320,000 pounds of bombs. He did not think Colonel Ulanov was going to need the weapons and ammunition the other four TU-95s were carrying. After the 44th finished dropping its bombs, there were not going to be any Americans left for *Spetsnaz* to fight.

The copilot tapped Pavlovsky on the shoulder and pointed ahead. Pavlovsky peered through the windscreen. In the distance, two white streaks had appeared over Elu, slanting down toward the 44th Regiment. Contrails! Someone was diving down from high altitude. Pavlovsky pushed the intercom button.

"Enemy aircraft sighted, straight ahead, high and diving! Battle stations! Gunners, stand by to engage!"

Pavlovsky brought up his binoculars. Two huge green-and-brown camouflaged aircraft, eight jet engines, a huge vertical tail: American B-52s! But what in the devil's name were they doing? Why were they coming head on? B-52s have no forward firing guns. Could they intend a suicidal ramming attack?

"Break! Break!" He shouted into his radio. "Number one flight break!"

He pulled hard on the control yoke and wrenched *Number 64* into a hard left turn.

EAGLE NINE—OFF ELU

Eagle Nine was diving hard. The old airframe shuddered and shook as five hundred thousand pounds of B-52G plunged down through the thicker, lower air. Captain Ray Chavez was in the pilot's seat. He kept his eyes on his instruments and his hands on the control yoke. He wanted to get down fast, but it would be embarrassing if he pulled the wings off.

Chavez eased the yoke back, and *Eagle Nine*'s nose came up as the huge aircraft leveled off at twenty-two thousand feet and roared toward the column of TU-95s at six hundred miles per hour. Chavez had never seen a TU-95 before, but there could be no doubt. He could see the huge, sixteen-foot, contra-rotating propellers clearly. Nothing else in the world looks like that. Chavez spoke into his radio mike.

"*Eagle Ten,* enemy in sight. I am attacking the first flight. Follow me. You take the pair on the left."

Jim Wesson's voice was clear in Chavez's headset. "Roger, *Nine,* attacking!"

Chavez reached to his right and shoved all eight throttles forward to the wall. The roar of the eight J-57-43Ws deepened as *Eagle Nine* went to full power and roared toward the TU-95s. The Bears seemed to grow larger and larger. Things happen rapidly when you are closing at a combined speed of 1,200 miles per hour. Now, if that kludge of a missile installation only worked.

No use waiting any longer. Chavez pushed a switch

and an AIM-9M Sidewinder's infrared seeker began search. Chavez heard a growling tone in his headset as the Sidewinder's infrared heat seeker locked on. Instantly, he pulled the trigger and the slim, deadly missile roared out from *Eagle Nine*'s right-wing pylon and streaked toward the Russians, its rocket motor leaving a gray-white streak of smoke.

The Russians were breaking formation, two to the left and two to the right, starting to move out of the way of *Eagle Nine* and *Ten*'s head-on attack and to bring their 23-mm guns to bear. TU-95s have no nose guns; their top and belly turrets can fire forward, but their arcs of fire are restricted by the propellers and the wings. Chavez saw yellow-white flashes as the twin AM–23mm cannons opened fire, each turret pouring forty-five 23mm cannon shells per second at *Eagle Nine*. Chavez armed another Sidewinder, heard the tone as the seeker locked on, and launched the missile. The Sidewinder shot toward the second TU-95. He felt *Eagle Nine* shudder as a burst of 23mm cannon shells tore into her fuselage.

The right-hand pair of TU-95s loomed gigantic in the windscreen. Chavez pulled back frantically on his control yoke and tried to climb as the huge B-52G streaked straight for the Russian leader, who was frantically trying to dive. Chavez saw his first AIM-9M Sidewinder streak past the Russian leader, strike the second TU-95, and explode against his left wing root. *Eagle Nine* shot past the leader at 1,100 miles per hour. Chavez could see the big red stars on the wings and the number 64 on the huge silver-gray fuselage. Ray Chavez would have sworn he missed the TU-95 by inches; actually it was at least ten feet. He watched the TU-95's upper gun turret swivel and pour 23mm cannon shells at the B-52G as *Eagle Nine* flashed by. He heard the chatter of four .50 caliber Browning M3 machine guns as his

229

tail gunner returned the compliment, spraying the Russian leader with three hundred .50 caliber full-metal-jacketed bullets in a single four-second burst.

The second TU-95 was staggering, nosing upward, with smoke pouring from the spot where the first Sidewinder hit. There was a bright yellow flash as the second AIM-9M Sidewinder struck the TU-95's midsection. For a second, it seemed to have no effect; then the huge silver-gray aircraft vanished in a colossal ball of orange fire. She must have been carrying bombs, and they had detonated! Chavez pulled frantically at his controls. Too late. *Eagle Nine* roared through the giant ball of flame and smoke. Her huge airframe shuddered and groaned. Fragments of the TU-95 struck and tore gashes in the wings and fuselage. The engines began to lose power as they ingested smoke. Chavez could not hold her steady. *Eagle Nine* began to spiral down, out of control.

44TH SOVIET NAVAL AIR REGIMENT—OFF ELU

Yegor Pavlovsky fought his controls desperately as the gigantic blast wave threatened to tear *Number 64* apart or hurl her out of control. Pavlovsky pushed his throttles all the way forward, and his four Kuznetsov NK-12M engines went to war-emergency power. He noticed the copilot was praying. The Soviet navy officially discourages officers praying, but Pavlovsky did not mind. They needed all the help they could get. The four great, sixteen-foot, dual propellers bit into the air as Pavlovsky fought her nose down, picked up speed, and brought *Number 64* into a shallow dive.

He glanced upward. A huge cloud of dirty gray smoke was still spreading across the sky. The damned B-52 had destroyed *Number 59*. It was clear what the Americans had done. They had mounted air-to-air missiles on their B-52s. Bombers do not carry defensive air-to-air missiles because the airflow around the fuselage prevents the missiles from being launched at fighters attacking from the side or behind. But the Americans were not using their missiles defensively; they were attacking, using their B-52s as fighters, and firing their missiles straight ahead. It was simple, but diabolically clever!

Pavlovsky pulled *Number 64* into a sharp left turn and looked behind him. Number Two Flight was scattered, and he could see only three aircraft. The remaining B-52 flashed toward Number Three and Four Flights. With more time to react, they were turning away as the American roared past. Pavlovsky saw yellow flashes as their 23mm guns opened fire, catching the B-52 in a withering crossfire. He watched as the B-52 passed through and began a wide shallow turn as soon as he was out of 23mm cannon range. It was trailing a thin stream of gray smoke, but Pavlovsky had no doubts. The American was turning to come back and attack again. Something had to be done, or the American would cut the 44th Regiment to pieces with missile fire.

Somebody had to do something. Pavlovsky decided instantly that he was someone. He knew that he was the best pilot in the regiment. It was up to him. He hit his intercom button.

"Weapons Officer, jettison the bombs." He switched to radio. "Tumansky, take command. Take your flight, and Number Three and Four and go on to the island. We must support the army. Carry out the mission at all costs."

"Understood, Captain, exactly so."

Now he spoke to his wingman. "Drop your bombs, Sixty-eight, and follow me. We will protect the rest of the regiment. If this Yankee wants to play games, we will accommodate him."

FAM-500 bombs cascaded downward from the two huge TU-95s. Pavlovsky could feel *Number 64* pick up speed and become more responsive to the controls as fourteen tons of bombs fell away. "Let's go, Sixty-eight. Turning left, now!" The two huge TU-95s turned sharply and headed back toward *Eagle Ten.*

EAGLE NINE—OFF ELU

Eagle Nine shuddered and groaned under the G loads as Ray Chavez leveled out, but B-52s are tough. The giant aircraft held together. Chavez thanked God and Boeing-Wichita. Without the new superstrength wing bolts installed the last time *Eagle Nine* had been at the factory, he would have pulled the wings off! He glanced at the altimeter. It read fourteen thousand feet. He checked the eight rows of engine dials. Number Six was running rough, not putting out full thrust. It had probably ingested debris and was damaged. Under normal circumstances, he would have shut it down and headed for home. But things were not normal. He was the leader of the USAF's first B-52G fighter force and in combat. He pulled *Eagle Nine*'s nose up and began to climb. He had to get back into the fight.

He heard a voice in his headset. "*Eagle Nine,* this is *Eagle Ten.* What's your situation?"

"I'm headed back up, *Eagle Ten.* What's going on?"

"Glad to hear you're still with us, *Eagle Nine.* We got two, maybe damaged a third. Twelve of them are going on toward the island. I'm behind them and coming up to attack again. Two of them are coming back toward me."

"Take that pair out, *Eagle Ten.* Try to stay out of gun range. Those 23mms are nasty. I'll go after the main formation."

"Roger, *Eagle Nine. Eagle Ten* attacking."

44TH SOVIET NAVAL AIR REGIMENT—OFF ELU

Yegor Pavlovsky was thinking hard. He was not sure exactly what kind of missiles the American B-52s were carrying, but they must be infrared homing missiles. The B-52s did not carry missile-directing radars. Probably they were Sidewinders. Pavlovsky had no idea what the exact range of a Sidewinder was, but he knew it would be far greater than the three thousand-yard effective range of his 23mm cannons. He must use countermeasures or he was a dead man, but his infrared flares could only be used behind his plane. No matter, he had to protect his regiment. He pulled *Number 64* into a shallow turn and reversed course, heading back toward Elu.

He could no longer see the American, but he knew the B-52 was coming on. He spoke into the intercom. "Gunner, watch him closely. Tell me instantly if he launches a missile or changes course. Electronic warfare, this is the captain. Stand by for infrared countermeasures, on my command."

Pavlovsky could feel the skin on the back of his neck crawl. What in the devil's name was that B-52 doing?

"Gunner, report. What is he doing?"

"He is coming on, Captain, closing the range, still closing, he's—*launching, Captain! Launching now!*"

"Countermeasures, now!"

Behind *Number 64,* infrared flares burst in bright flashes of heat intended to baffle any infrared missile's heat seeker. Pavlovsky pulled *Number 64* into a diving right-hand turn. Not too far. He must stay with the flare pattern. Something slender, white, and deadly flashed by above the right wing, trailing gray-white smoke.

Pavlovsky heard the voice of his wingman in his headset. "I'm hit, Captain. Starboard engines on fire, I'm going down. The crew is jumping now."

The gunner cut in. "Captain, he's launched again!"

Pavlovsky threw *Number 64* into a climbing, left-hand turn. He could see *Number 68* nosing up, trailing a banner of smoke and flames from her right wing. A Sidewinder streaked toward *Number 68*. The flames were irresistible to a heat-seeking missile. The Sidewinder struck and detonated in a yellow flash. Pavlovsky watched, horrified, as *Number 68*'s right wing was torn away. The huge TU-95 began to roll over and over, then fell toward the ocean below, trailing a huge plume of greasy black smoke.

There was a sudden loud noise. *Number 64* shuddered and vibrated. Pavlovsky fought the controls. He heard the gunner's voice, as calm as if he were strolling in Red Square. "We're hit in the tail, Captain. He's coming on, the bastard's in range now, Captain, I'll get him if I can! Opening fire." Pavlovsky heard the chatter of the 23mm cannons as Gurevich opened fire. He was a damned good man. Live or die, Pavlovsky was proud of his regiment.

He kept *Number 64* turning, fighting to maintain control. She was responding to the controls, but she was sluggish. Now *Number 64* had reversed course and was headed straight for the B-52. The huge green-and-brown camouflaged aircraft loomed larger and larger in Pavlovsky's windscreen. Hang on, keep him in gun range, make him turn, don't let him get by. The two huge airplanes roared toward each other, closing at a thousand miles an hour. The American launched another missile, but it was too close to guide. Pavlovsky's top gun turret hammered away. He could see yellow flashes as the 23mm cannon shells exploded on the B-52's blunt nose.

The American was stubborn. He did not want to turn. Pavlovsky roared straight ahead. Come on, comrade, we will see whose nerve breaks first. At the last desperate second, Pavlovsky tried to turn right. He could see the American, too, was turning hard. But *Number 64* was responding too slowly. The huge green-and-brown B-52 seemed to fill Pavlovsky's windscreen. *Number 64* and *Eagle Ten* struck each other head on at a thousand miles an hour and vanished in a tremendous ball of smoke and flame.

EAGLE NINE—OFF ELU

Eagle Nine was climbing hard. Ray Chavez had all eight engines in full power war emergency only. Water-methanol injection was on. Seven of the eight engines were generating 13,750 pounds of thrust. Number Six was running rough and the over temperature warning light was on. He knew he ought to shut it down. To hell with it! He needed every pound of thrust he could get to catch those TU-95s before they reached Elu. He was gaining on them at two miles per minute, but there were not enough minutes left. He had to make them break up their formation and maneuver.

The Russians were eight miles ahead now, and two thousand feet higher, eight of them, flying in a loose formation. Four others seemed to be faster. They were pulling steadily ahead. They must have been lightly loaded. Chavez shrugged. Eight-to-one seemed like long enough odds to him. He would worry about the leading four after he took care of the other eight. He was painfully aware that he was flying toward the muzzles of sixteen 23mm cannons. Still, he had the range advantage. He could hit them before they could hit him. He armed another Sidewinder and launched.

The Russians knew he was there. He could see infrared countermeasures flares flickering in the TU-95s' wakes. The Sidewinder streaked toward the Russian formation. No one sits complacently and watches an air-to-air missile coming straight at him. The Russian formation broke as the TU-95 pilots made evasive turns. The Sidewinder went streaking through the TU-95 formation but failed to lock on. The damned flares had confused the missile's seeker. Chavez launched again. He was going to have to get closer and the Russians were losing distance as they made their evasive maneuvers.

He saw a yellow flash as the Sidewinder detonated against an engine of one of the TU-95. The huge aircraft staggered and black smoke began to stream back from the damaged engine. The TU-95 began to fall behind the others as it lost power. Another TU-95 throttled back, reducing speed and maneuvering to protect his damaged comrade. *Eagle Nine* was closing rapidly as the two TU-95s slowed down. He could not take the time to go around them. The other TU-95s were almost over Elu. All right, he had eight missiles left. He would blast his way through!

The two huge silver-gray TU-95s were looming larger and larger in his windscreen as *Eagle Nine* closed in. Chavez armed and launched two more Sidewinders in rapid succession. They streaked toward the TU-95s. Chavez saw flickering yellow flashes as the TU-95 gunners opened fire with their twin 23mm tail guns. Tracers flashed past *Eagle Nine*'s nose. Both Sidewinders struck the damaged plane, homing in on the engine fire. The TU-95 began to plunge downward, trailing flame and smoke.

Chavez launched another Sidewinder and saw it strike the second TU-95. The big plane staggered but flew on. Chavez fired again. The Sidewinder struck the TU-95's tail and exploded in a yellow flash. Chavez could see ragged holes in the TU-95's tail surfaces, but still the huge plane flew on.

The TU-95 was looming gigantic in *Eagle Nine*'s windscreen. Chavez hauled on his controls, and *Eagle Nine* shot by the damaged TU-95, a hundred yards to the Russian's left. He could see flames beginning to stream backward from the doomed plane's fuselage. But the TU-95's gunner could also see *Eagle Nine.* The giant green-and-brown airplane filled his sights as he brought his top and bottom gun turrets to bear. The gunner was a brave man. He knew his plane was going down, but he would take the B-52 with him if he could. He pulled his triggers, and four AM–23mm cannons opened fire. To the devil with melting barrels and conserving the ammunition supply! He held the triggers back and poured a thousand 23mm high-explosive incendiary cannon shells at *Eagle Nine* in one long, sustained twelve-second burst.

Ray Chavez saw yellow-white flashes as the twin turrets opened fire. Then, the world blew up. Exploding 23mm cannon shells raked the right side of the flight deck. The cockpit was full of smoke and flying bits of metal and glass. Chavez fought desperately to maintain control as *Eagle Nine* began to shudder and fall off on one wing. Air was howling through holes in the shattered windscreen at five hundred miles per hour. Chavez could barely see. Lights were flashing and alarms were howling. *Eagle Nine* was damaged and on fire in a dozen places. Chavez throttled back and the giant B-52 slowed rapidly. She should have been falling apart, but Boeing builds tough airplanes.

There was no use kidding himself. She wasn't going to make it. Chavez could see the coastline of Elu just ahead. If a pilot can't save his airplane, he must try to save his crew. He pushed his intercom button. "We're not going to make it. I'll hold her level as long as I can.

237

Punch out now!" The navigator and the radar navigator-bombardier sat below Chavez on the lower deck. They acknowledged and ejected. What was the matter with the rest of the crew? He couldn't hold her much longer. Chavez looked to his right. His copilot was dead, hit by two 23mm shells Chavez could see that the whole right side of the flight deck was riddled with 23mm shell holes. His gunner and electronic warfare officer were dead. He was the only living man on the flight deck. *Eagle Nine* shuddered and shook. He was losing control. Time to go. He pushed the button, and his ejection seat fired, blasting him upward and away from *Eagle Nine*'s cockpit. Chavez felt a surge of relief as his chute opened. He glanced below and watched in horror as *Eagle Nine* spiraled down toward Elu, out of control and trailing a banner of smoke and flame across the sky.

Chapter Twenty

"Is our victory certain?"   —Otto von Bismacrk

"Yes, but in war nothing is ever absolutely certain."
                              —Helmuth von Moltke

SPETSNAZ TEAM—ELU ISLAND—THE PLA-
TEAU AREA

Viktor Ulanov was watching and waiting. It was not
something he did well. He was ready and his men were
ready. Where in hell was the damned navy? He was
lying in the edge of the trees where the road made its
final bend and slanted nearly straight up the last six
hundred meters to the plateau. There was very little
cover from here on, but during the night Ulanov had
infiltrated his assault force into the bomb craters left
by the American bombers. It had been done well and
very quietly. With a little luck, the Americans did not
know the leading elements of the *Spetsnaz* assault force
were within less than two hundred meters of their positions. His 120mm mortars were set and ready to fire.
Everything was ready. Now, if this famous Captain
Pavlovsky and his 44th Regiment would only arrive,

they could get on with the attack. The longer things were delayed, the greater the chance that the Americans would be reinforced.

He glanced at his watch. The planes should be here now. He picked up his radio and pushed the button.

"Forty-four Leader, Forty-four Leader, this is *Spetsnaz* Leader. Come in, Pavlovsky, what is your situation?"

For a moment, all Ulanov heard was static. Then he heard a voice in his headset.

"*Spetsnaz* Leader, this is Captain-Lieutenant Tumansky. We are under heavy attack by American B-52s firing guided missiles. Captain Pavlovsky is dead. I am approaching Elu with all surviving aircraft. Where do you want your supplies and the bombs?"

"I am sorry to hear about your captain. Look at your photo map. Bomb the mass of rocks near the entrance to the plateau and the trees two hundred meters beyond them. Drop the men and supplies in the harbor area. Do you understand?"

"Yes, Colonel, I understand. We will— *Look out! He's coming up again. He's launching! Countermeasures now!*"

Tumansky was no longer talking to Ulanov. He had other things to do. Ulanov brought up his field glasses and scanned the sky to the north. There they were, a formation of TU-95s, flying majestically on toward Elu at five hundred miles per hour. As he watched, he saw a gray streak flash up toward one of the TU-95s and the yellow flash of a warhead detonating. Something came into his field of view, a huge, blunt-nosed, green-and-brown camouflaged bomber, pursuing the TU-95s like a killer whale after its prey. He watched, fascinated, as the battle rushed toward Elu and filled the sky above him. He saw a TU-95 burn and fall out of the sky. Was that damned American going to shoot down an entire naval air regiment? No, now the B-52 was trailing smoke and flame, and spiraling down out of the sky. It smashed into the edge of the plateau and vanished in a ball of orange fire.

Tumansky's voice sounded in Ulanov's headset. "Tumansky here, Colonel. We got him. Your cargo and men are dropping in the harbor area now. Surviving aircraft will begin dropping bombs in two minutes. Some of my aircraft are damaged. The attack may not be coordinated as well as you would like."

"I understand. Do the best you can. Out."

He switched to his tactical frequency. "Assault team stand by. Mortar section open fire on my command."

He heard the familiar whining sigh of falling bombs and watched as the 1,100-pound bombs began to detonate in the American positions. The last TU-95 was dropping its bombs. Now! Quickly now, while the bombs were still falling. "Assault team! First Company attack! Mortars. Open fire!"

1ST SPECIAL FORCES GROUP (AIRBORNE)— ELU ISLAND—THE PLATEAU

Goldberg crouched in the bottom of his foxhole. The earth shuddered and shook as the last Russian 1,100-pound bombs detonated. It was far worse than before. The air was full of smoke and dirt, and clods and rocks rained down. The Russian planes had come in high, out of Stinger range. There had been nothing he could do but hang on and pray. Goldberg was defending the rocks. Ten minutes ago, he had had twenty men and four SAWs ready for action. God only knew what he had left now. He could see Garcia in the next hole, snarling and swearing as he crouched behind his SAW, a two hundred–round belt ready in the wicked little machine gun.

The last thing in the world Goldberg wanted to do

was look over the rim of his foxhole. But he had to see. If the Russians knew their business, they would attack right behind their bombs. He had to fire the Claymores and spot the mortar fire if he was going to have a chance in hell of stopping them. He got his glasses in his right hand and his radio's mike in his left and peered over the rim of his foxhole.

For a moment he saw nothing, just the road and dozens of bomb craters. Then something smashed into the ground twenty yards in front of him. Dirt flew, and dense, gray-white smoke began to billow upward. A heavy mortar smoke round. Goldberg pushed the button on his headset. "Talon One, this is Talon Two. I am taking heavy mortar fire just in front of my position. They are laying down a smoke screen and—." He ducked as two more smoke rounds struck. "Give me mortar fire fifty meters in front of my position on my command."

More Russian mortar rounds struck nearby. Several machine guns opened fire and began to spray Goldberg's position with .30 caliber full-metal-jacketed bullets. The smoke was spreading, but Goldberg could still see through the gaps. The landscape was still empty but it wouldn't be long—. Goldberg felt a sudden cold knot in his stomach. Dozens of men in brown-mottled camouflage uniforms were pouring out of bomb craters and charging up the slope, straight at him, automatic rifles in their hands. Garcia's SAW began to chatter as he sent burst after burst of .223 bullets down the road.

Goldberg pushed the button and spoke into his mike. "Give me everything you've got, Talon One, they're coming!"

SPETSNAZ TEAM—FIRST COMPANY—ELU ISLAND—THE PLATEAU
Sharypa crouched in the bomb crater and watched

as the last bombs detonated. He was leading the Second Platoon. He and his men were ready, loaded down with the tools of their trade. Each man had an AKD-74 automatic rifle, ten loaded thirty-round magazines, six hand grenades, body armor, and assorted knives and pistols. He had no doubts that he and his men could deal quickly and effectively with the Americans, if only they could get in close. But Sharypa had been in enough battles to know that that was a very big if, indeed.

The attack plan made Sharypa nervous. Captain Gromov was a good officer in his way, brave enough, tough, but stolid and unimaginative. He went too much by the book. This attack straight up the road was orthodox, but dangerous. Sharypa had seen more than one good man killed in by-the-book attacks. Sharypa preferred tactics with speed and deception. It did not matter. He was not in command, and orders are orders.

He watched as the 120mm mortar smoke bombs began to shroud the American position in a cloud of gray-white smoke. Well, that should help. It is hard to shoot with great accuracy when you cannot see the target. Sharypa did not like waiting. Were they never going to go? He heard the PKM machine guns open fire, then Captain Gromov's hoarse shout, "Come on, boys!" The First and Third platoons swarmed out of the bomb craters and charged up the slope. Captain Gromov was leading them, his 9mm CZ-75 pistol in his hand. Sharypa was not sure that that was smart, but at least Gromov was the kind of officer who leads his men. Second Platoon was the second wave. Sharypa waited until Gromov and his men had gone fifty meters and gave the order. "Come on, comrades, lets go!" The Second Platoon scrambled out of the bomb craters and charged up the slope.

Cord was two hundred yards away, concealed in his hide, his Lee-Enfield in his hands, looking almost due east toward the plateau road and the rocks. He was, for Cord, waiting patiently, slowly scanning the bomb craters through his Mark II scope, looking for targets. He had watched in awe as the huge, silver-gray TU-95s had dropped their bombs. He thanked God he was not with Goldberg in the rocks. There was nothing that Cord could do against heavy bombers flying at twenty thousand feet. But if the Russians really wanted that bloody satellite, they were going to have to go up the road. There was a lot Cord could do about that.

He watched as mortar rounds began to lay down a smoke screen in front of the American position. Any second now. There! There they came, sixty or seventy men in mottled brown camouflage uniforms. Cord was perfectly positioned on their left flank. He would have three or four shots before they knew he was there. Steady down, Cord, pick your targets, and make them good!

A big man was leading the attack, waving a pistol in one hand, and shouting orders. Brave, mate, but not smart. Cord put the vertical post of his Mark II telescopic sight against the big man's side and squeezed his trigger. The big Lee-Enfield roared, and the man went down hard, but he was still moving. Cord worked his bolt with blazing speed and fired gain. The man lay still. A man with a tactical radio on his back was right behind the leader. Cord worked his bolt, aimed, fired, and the radioman went down.

Mendoza was forty yards to Cord's left with his M60 machine gun team. He opened fire, sending short, accurate six round bursts of .30 caliber bullets into the Russian attack's left flank. Cord swung his scope smoothly, picked up a man shouting orders, aimed, squeezed, and fired. The man went down.

Cord saw yellow-white muzzle flashes as two Russian .30 caliber machine guns opened fire. Bursts of .30 caliber full-metal-jacketed bullets tore through the trees and ricocheted off the ground around Cord. The Russians did not know exactly where Cord and Mendoza were, but they knew the area where they must be, and they poured in suppressive fire. Cord saw a cloud of dust and a dark object shot toward him, trailing gray-white smoke. He ducked as the 85mm high explosive RPG-7D round detonated twenty yards away. Those God damned rockets again. What was next? Too right, Cord knew what was next, the heavy mortars. Well, this is what they paid him for. He clenched his teeth, screwed up his courage, and fired precise, deadly, superbly aimed shot after shot at the *Spetsnaz* team.

Victor Ulanov watched through his field glasses as the First Company attacked up the road. It seemed to be going well. Irina Yakoleva lay nearby in a prone position, peering intently through the telescopic sight of her SVD sniper's rifle. She was looking for targets, but there was little to see. The 120mm mortar smoke bombs had shrouded the American position in a cloud of dense, gray-white smoke. The smoke was greatly reducing the effectiveness of the Americans' fire. Here and there, a man had gone down, but most of his men were advancing freely. They were halfway to the rocks, another hundred meters and they would be within hand grenade range. Suddenly Man after man was hit and lay sprawled on the ground. The attack was stalling as his men dove for cover in the bomb craters.

Ulanov pushed the button on the radio headset. "Gromov, what is happening? What is your situation?"

Silence. "Lieutenant Zaitsev. Lieutenant Paktusov, Come in, report."

Nothing. Then he heard Sharypa's voice loud and clear. "The captain's dead, Colonel. A sniper got him. The lieutenants are dead or wounded. We are taking machine gun fire and highly accurate sniper fire from our left flank. It must be coming from those trees two hundred meters to the west. Put the mortars on them."

"Acknowledged, Sharypa. Hang on!"

"Exactly so, Colonel. Be careful, Colonel, that sniper is the devil himself. He——."

"Sharypa? Come in, Sharypa."

Silence. Damn! Either Sharypa was hit or the radio was out. Either way, he had lost communications with his assault element at the crisis of the battle. He must——. Something was happening, a change in the sounds of the battle. He could still hear the spiteful chatter of automatic rifles and light machine guns exchanging fire, but something was different. A cold chill ran down Ulanov's spine. His mortars had stopped firing!

Instantly, he pushed his head set button. "Mortar Section! Come in! Why in the devil's name have you stopped firing? Answer me, Popov!"

"*Starshiy Serzhant* Popov here, Colonel. I have ceased fire in accordance with regulations."

"What do you mean, regulations?"

"Sir, tactical regulations clearly state that when the supply of mortar bombs falls to less than ten rounds of high-explosive bombs per tube, the remaining ammunition shall not be expended without the authorization of the company commander or higher command authorities. I have nine high-explosive bombs and six smoke remaining; therefore, I have ceased fire."

Ulanov suppressed an overwhelming desire to go down to the mortars and kill Popov with his bare hands.

"Fire mission, Popov! Coordinates 498-562. The smoke bombs first, then add fifty meters and fire the HE."

"Understood, Colonel. Do I understand that you specifically authorize the firing of the remaining ammunition?"

"Popov, if you do not stop talking and get those bombs in the air, I will personally send you to the hottest corner of hell!"

Popov shrugged. He was an old soldier. He had been yelled at by colonels before; he would be yelled at by colonels again. It went with the job.

"Exactly so, Colonel! I carry out your orders without question!"

Ulanov wondered what Popov was doing in *Spetsnaz*. He would obviously make a brilliant lawyer. Still, in one way he was right. If they were almost out of mortar bombs, they were in trouble. He must get more ammunition. Who could he spare? Of course!

"Major Mamin, we are almost out of mortar bombs. The TU-95s dropped a fresh supply down in the harbor area. Take the truck and both jeeps and the command section. Get more bombs to Popov as soon as possible. Do not fail. The success of the mission may depend on it. Understood?"

"Exactly so, Colonel! Immediately! I carry out your orders without question!"

Mamin shouted orders. Men ran for the vehicles. Ulanov was impressed. Perhaps Mamin was good for something after all. He turned to Chazov. "Take charge here. I am going up to the First Company to take command."

Chazov took a deep breath. Ulanov knew Chazov was going to say something he did not want to hear. "With all due respect, Colonel, that is most unwise. You are the team commander. You must remain in command. If you are killed leading a company, the whole mission may fail. Give me a radioman, and I will go."

Ulanov did not like it, but he knew that Chazov was right. Sometimes it is easier to be a hero than a good commander. He could not hesitate, he must decide now. The mortars had resumed firing, and the 120mm bombs were already placing smoke to screen the left flank.

"Very well, Chazov, go. Take—." The devil! Who could Chazov take? Ulanov had sent every man in the command section down the mountain with Mamin.

Irina Yakoleva spoke quickly. "I will go with Captain Chazov, Colonel. I know how to operate the radio."

For a second Viktor Ulanov hesitated. He did not want to send a young woman into a firefight. He almost said that, but he decided it was not wise. Someday he might tell Irina Yakoleva she could not do something dangerous because she was a delicate flower of Soviet womanhood, but it would not be when she held a loaded, high-powered semiautomatic rifle in her hands.

"Very well, go. Good luck, Chazov, but good or bad, capture those rocks!"

Captain Chazov and Irina Yakoleva crouched at the edge of the trees, watching as the 120mm smoke bombs rained down to the left. Chazov did not like it. There was not enough smoke to completely block the view from the American position. It would help, but it was going to be extremely hazardous out there.

He and Irina Yakoleva each had a radio strapped to their backs. He hoped at least one of them would make it. Chazov spoke quietly to Irina Yakoleva. "As soon as the mortars switch to high explosives, we go. I will go first. We must not bunch up. You follow on a count

248

of six. If I do not make it, you know the orders. Capture those damned rocks at all costs. Understood?"

"Exactly so, Captain."

Chazov heard a series of booming roars as thirty-four—pound high-explosive bombs began to rain down on the American flanking position. He smiled. "Good! That will make the American snipers keep their heads down. Ready. *Go!*" Chazov shot forward, running as fast as he could while carrying seventy pounds of weapons, ammunition, body armor, and radio.

Irina wished she had not volunteered. How many times had she been told, "Never volunteer for anything!" Too late now, Yakoleva. Two, three,—she knew it was not some faceless American sniper waiting for her. Four, five—Cord was out there. She knew it. She could almost feel him. And this time Cord would kill her if he could. Six! Go, Yakoleva, *go!* She leaped up and ran forward as fast as her long legs would carry her.

Her nerves screamed, but nothing seemed to happen. She began to gain on Chazov. She was not wearing body armor. Russian designers had never contemplated anyone built like Irina Yakoleva when they designed the breast plate. She forced herself to slow down, they must not bunch up. That would—something struck Captain Chazov on his left side. The tremendous impact of the bullet threw him to the left and smashed him to the ground. He lay still. Irina hurdled his body and ran on. She hated to leave a comrade dead or wounded, but Cord would be working his rifle's bolt. To stop to aid Chazov was certain death.

Think, Yakoleva, think like a sniper! A moving target is difficult at two hundred meters but not impossible. Cord would have to lead her by two body widths to hit her. If he fired with his sights centered on her body, the bullet would pass behind her. Cord knew that. He had hit Chazov because Chazov had run all out at a steady pace. That gave Cord a constant lead. She must not do that. If she did, she was a dead woman.

Slower then, now faster, now—she heard the crack of a supersonic rifle bullet passing close to her head. Slower, fast—the ground just in front of her erupted, gravel stung her thighs as the bullet ricocheted away. She began to gasp for breath. Even without body armor, she was carrying fifty pounds, and running in this damned heat was awful.

For a moment, Cord seemed to have stopped firing. Perhaps the smoke was blocking Cord's line of sight. Lovely thought; or perhaps a mortar bomb had landed on him. Even lovelier! Irina Yakoleva suddenly screamed in surprise, pain, and fury. Some one had just pressed a red-hot iron against the back of her left thigh. Irina staggered. God damn you, Cord! She could feel blood running down the back of her thigh. Keep going, Yakoleva, to stop is suicide. Hang on, almost there. She saw heads peering from a bomb crater ahead and made a rolling dive for cover as Cord fired again, missing her by inches. Dirt and grit sprayed her face, but she was there. She threw herself into the safety of the crater.

Irina Yakoleva flew into the bomb crater, smashing into two astounded *Spetsnaz* troopers. For a moment, she lay there gasping for breath. "She's hit," she heard someone say. She felt someone pressing a field dressing against her thigh and tying the bandage in place. She recognized Sharypa's voice. "Easy, Lieutenant Yakoleva, it is not serious. You will have a scar to show that you were in combat, but it is just a flesh wound, you will be all right."

A scar! Irina Yakoleva exploded. She swore expertly and furiously. "Cord, you . . . ." Even the hardened

250

Spetsnaz troopers were astounded. Her command of the Russian language was superb. Cord probably was the devil himself, but it seemed improbable that he had really done some of the things Irina Yakoleva mentioned. Irina paused for breath.

"I am sure this man, Cord, is everything you say he is, Lieutenant, but you did not run up that road to tell us about Cord. What is happening?"

"The colonel sent Captain Chazov to take command. Cord hit him. He is dead or wounded. The colonel says you must attack. He has masked the American flanking position with a smoke barrage, but now we are out of mortar bombs. We must attack now, before the smoke clears. Colonel Ulanov says we must capture the rocks at all costs."

Sharypa did not like that phrase; still, the colonel was right. "Are you to take command, Lieutenant Yakoleva?"

Irina Yakoleva shook her head. "That would be most unwise. The men do not know me. They will follow you, and besides, you have seen far more combat than I have. I will go with you and operate the radio, but you are in command."

Sharypa had been afraid he would hear that. He was brave enough, but he had never wanted the responsibility of command. He knew Cord was waiting for the next man who tried to lead the attack. Still, they had not held a gun to his head when they handed him a senior sergeant's shoulder boards. He looked around. A breeze was beginning to come up. The smoke would not last forever. Now or never. He rolled out of the crater and blew his whistle. The shrill tones cut through the crackle of small-arms fire. "Come on, comrades, let's go! Attack! Follow me!" For a moment it hung in the balance. Then, Dudorov followed him, the three-foot-long, tubular shape of his RPG-7D rocket-propelled grenade launcher ready for action, bellowing, "Come on, men, come on!"

The Second Platoon scrambled out of the bomb craters and charged up the slope. They reached the craters where the first wave was pinned down. Sharypa shouted again and again, "Come on, First Company, attack! Attack!" The men of the First and Third platoons knew Sharypa's voice, and they were proud of their company and of *Spetsnaz*. Men will fight and die for their unit when they will fight for nothing else. They scrambled out of the bomb craters and followed Sharypa toward the rocks.

The Americans knew. Their light machine guns opened final protective fire and bursts of .223 bullets filled the air. Sharypa was filled with the mad mixture of fear and fury that close combat brings. Hand grenade range now. There were two loud explosions as American Claymore mines fired. To Sharypa's left, half a dozen men went down as a blast of deadly steel balls ripped into the First Company's ranks. The snarling rattle of AKD-74s filled the air as the attackers poured assault fire on the American positions.

Now they were in the rocks. Ten meters ahead, Sharypa saw an American fire team firing madly. A 40mm grenade exploded to Sharypa's right. He felt lethal, high-velocity fragments tear into his body armor. He fired back desperately, emptying the thirty-round magazine of his AKD-74 at the Americans, trying to spoil their aim. His AKD-74 clicked on an empty chamber. He was not going to live long enough to reload.

Whoosh! Dudorov had fired. Sharypa saw the streak of gray-white smoke as the 85mm OG-7 antipersonnel rocket grenade shot toward the American position. The five-pound warhead detonated in an orange-yellow flash. The Americans went down. Sharypa reached for a hand grenade. Too late. The American SAW gunner stood up, bloody but determined to take one or two more Russians with him. The muzzle of the lethal .223 machine gun swung toward Sharypa's chest. Then, he heard the roar of a .30 caliber semiautomatic rifle as Irina Yakoleva fired four fast shots at point-blank range. The .30 caliber bullets struck the American gunner and tore through his body armor. He dropped the SAW and went down.

There was a sudden, deafening silence. No one was shooting. Sharypa looked around. Everywhere he looked, he could see the mottled brown camouflage uniforms of *Spetsnaz.* The First Company had seized the rocks. Sharypa shook from reaction. No time to feel sick or wonder how many of his comrades were dead. He was still in command. He turned to Irina Yakoleva. "Call the colonel, Lieutenant. Tell him the First Company has captured the American position. He can send up the Second Company whenever he is ready."

Irina Yakoleva smiled. "With the greatest pleasure, *Starshiy Serzhant,* with the greatest pleasure!"

Captain Carter watched through his field glasses as a fresh force of *Spetsnaz* troops swept forward into the rocks, harassed, but not stopped by his 60mm mortar fire. There was no sign of any Americans retreating from the rocks. Goldberg and all the men with him were dead, wounded, or captured. The flanking teams were falling back toward *War God* and the final defensive position. Carter had no illusions. He was lucky if he had thirty men left. He would fight to the end. Surrendering is not encouraged in Special Forces training, but the Russians were going to win. They would roll over him. One last question. Did Washington want him to blow up the satellite?

Carter beckoned to his radioman. "Get me General

Brand in Washington." The radioman nodded. Carter waited. The radioman frowned. "Captain, all I am getting is noise. They are jamming the SATCOM link." All right, Carter, use your famous initiative. Blow the damn thing—.

The radioman interrupted urgently. "Captain! There's a message for you on Tactical Channel Two, correct cipher and call sign."

Carter grabbed the headset. He heard a voice with an odd nasal twang.

"Talon Leader, Talon Leader. This is Thunderbolt Leader. I am inbound to your position. Estimate arrival in two minutes. Mark your positions with red and yellow smoke. Do you copy Talon Leader?"

Chapter Twenty-One

"The Australian Armed Forces are small, but highly professional. Their personnel, training, and equipment are among the finest in the world."

—*Armed Forces Journal*

NUMBER 82 STRIKE WING—RAFF OFF ELU—
The confectioner was Wing-Leader Robert Marks. He was leading the entire long range striking force of the Royal Australian Air Force into combat. The sixteen General Dynamics F-111Cs had roared skyward from the RAAF base at Amberly just before dawn, disturbing the rest of some of the good citizens of Brisbane who commented vigorously about "bloody flyboys." The F-111Cs were heavily loaded with weapons and fuel, flying a combat mission nearly three thousand miles from base. If the American KC-10 tankers did not show up on time they were going in the drink. This did not bother the confectioner. He described the operation as "a piece of cake." It did not bother him that he had no firm information on the situation of Elu. He would have to improvise his attack plan when he got there. That, too, was "a piece of cake."

He wished they would get to the bloody island. His navigator was handling the navigation, and the autopilot was doing the flying. There was really very little for him to do until they got close to Elu. The green-and-brown mottled camouflaged F-111C roared on, propelled by its two Pratt & Whitney TF30 turbofans, at a steady 570 miles per hour. He was almost dozing when his navigator touched his shoulder and pointed ahead. There it was. Good! Now, to teach the bloody Russians to keep off Australian territory. He began a shallow dive. He would go in low and fast.

He activated his radio. "Talon Leader, Talon Leader, this is Thunderbolt Leader, do you copy?" He repeated the call several times. What were the Yanks doing, having a barbecue? He heard a startled voice in his earphones. "Thunderbolt Leader, this is Talon Force. We copy."

"Talon Force, this is Thunderbolt Leader. I haven't got time to chat. Put your CO on."

"Thunderbolt Leader. This is Talon Leader." Good, but no time to talk.

"Talon Leader, Talon Leader. This is Thunderbolt Leader. I am inbound to your position. Estimate arrival in two minutes. Mark your positions with red and yellow smoke. Do you copy Talon Leader?"

"Roger, Thunderbolt leader. Red and yellow smoke, will comply."

The confectioner switched to his tactical channel and spoke to his crews.

"Thunderbolt Force. Thunderbolt Leader. We are attacking. Friendly forces will be marked by red and yellow smoke. I will make the first pass. Thunderbolt Alfa Flight follow me. Other flights attack at one-minute intervals."

The confectioner and his navigator became extremely busy. They were slowing now, airspeed was four hundred miles per hour, altitude one thousand feet. The edge of the plateau was visible in the windscreen. The map said it was nine hundred feet above sea level, but maps have been known to be wrong.

"Radar on, select air-to-ground mode."

The big General Electric APQ-113 radar in the F-111C's nose began to scan.

Better not use bombs or rockets until he was sure where the Americans were. He had a GE M61A1 Gatling gun with 2,084 rounds of 20mm ammunition in the feed. That ought to attract the Russians' attention. Select gun. "Alfa Flight. Guns only this pass."

He glanced at his heads up display. They were going to clear the edge of the plateau by eighty or ninety feet. Piece of cake. "Talon Leader. Thunderbolt Leader. Attacking."

The four green-and-brown camouflaged F-111Cs flashed cross the edge. Turbines howling, the Royal Australian Air Force shrieked across the plateau into battle.

ELU ISLAND—THE PLATEAU

Irina Yakoleva was scanning the area around *War God* with her field glasses, trying to pick out the American defensive positions. Give them credit, they were well concealed. Perhaps she could—. What was that? Smoke grenades were going off in front of the American position, red and yellow smoke. Suddenly, a large aircraft appeared in her field of view, a jet fighter with a big oval fuselage, high wings, two large inlet ducts, a tall vertical tail—F-111! It was flying seventy-five feet above the ground and coming straight at her!

Irina shrieked loudly, *"Air attack! Take cover! Air attack!"* A bright yellow light appeared at the bottom of the leading F-111's nose as its Gatling gun spat one hundred 20-mm cannon shells per second at the *Spets-*

naz position. Irina was already diving for cover behind the largest rock nearby. In five seconds of concentrated firing the four F-111s poured two thousand 20mm rounds into the rocks. The sound of the explosions was one long, ripping roar. Rock fragments whined everywhere, and the acrid smell of burning explosives filled the air. Irina looked up as the firing ceased and the howling of the jet engines reached an intolerable pitch. Four large green-and-brown camouflaged aircraft shot by, fifty feet above her head. She saw the insignia, a blue ring surrounding a white circle with a red kangaroo in the center. The Royal Australian Air Force!

Irina snapped up her glasses and watched as the F-111s made a hard right, four-g turn. She saw a blue lightning bolt and the aircraft number A8-146 on the leader's tail. She had studied the Australian army and air force for two years. She knew instantly what she was seeing, F-111Cs of Number 6 Squadron RAAF. She could also see the bombs and LAU-3A rocket pods under its wings. They would be coming back! Where was Colonel Ulanov? There, prudently taking cover behind a large rock.

Irina dashed forward, nearly colliding with the colonel as he stood up. "What in the devil's name is this, Lieutenant?"

There was no time to chat, but Colonel Ulanov must be convinced that Irina knew what she was talking about. "F-111Cs, Royal Australian Air Force," she gasped. "Number 6 Squadron, of Number 82 Strike Wing."

The Colonel was impressed. That was certainly a specific answer. Lieutenant Yakoleva was obviously a highly competent intelligence officer. But now that he knew, what could he do about it?

"Colonel," Irina said urgently, "those planes will be

back, and there are more of them! They will attack again and again!"

Ulanov frowned. How could she know that? He started to ask, then heard a steadily increasing, howling whine. Here came four more of the damned things, streaking across the plateau. Haloes of bright yellow-orange fire appeared under the wings of the F-111Cs, and gray-white streaks shot toward the rocks. Rockets! Ulanov grabbed Irina Yakoleva and threw her down. Irina's breath whooshed out as 220 pounds of Colonel and 60 pounds of combat gear landed on her back. She seethed inwardly, and was about to say she was not a child who needed to be protected, when the first 2.75-inch rockets arrived and their 7.5-pound warheads detonated. Each F-111C had launched thirty-eight rockets in twenty seconds. She was suddenly very glad to have any protection she could get.

The explosions died away, and the second flight shrieked by overhead. Some of the *Spetsnaz* troopers fired at them with their AKD-74s, but automatic rifles were not going to stop jet fighters. He must do something, or his team would be blasted to pieces, but what? He had an idea, but it certainly called for heroic measures. Well, was he not officially a Hero of the Soviet Union? He grabbed his radio headset and pushed the button.

"Mortar Section. Mortar Section. Come in, Popov!"

"Popov here, Colonel. Major Mamin has delivered more ammunition. I am ready to fire again, if you have targets."

Thank the devil for small favors! "Fire Mission. Smoke bombs, rapid fire, coordinates 292-558, as soon as possible."

"Exactly so, Colonel, stand by, we—." Popov paused. "Colonel, do you realize that that is your own position? You are ordering me to fire on you?"

Ulanov suppressed the urge to scream. He needed smoke now!

"Yes, Popov, I know! Now, fire those bombs now! That is an order! I take the responsibility. Fire, damn it, fire!"

"Exactly so, Colonel. I carry out your orders without question. Firing now!"

NUMBER 82 STRIKE WING—RAAF OVER ELU—

The confectioner was pulling four g's in a hard right turn that took Alfa Flight out over the edge of the plateau and down over the harbor area. For a minute, he was a very busy man. One defect of an F-111 is that it is hard for the pilot to see well to the sides and to the rear. The confectioner had to fly his plane, lead Alfa Flight, and coordinate the attack. This kept him busy, if not out of trouble. As he pulled the big F-111C around, he could hear his pilots' voices in his headset.

"Charlie Flight. Gun and rocket run. Attacking now!"

"Delta Flight. Preparing for bombing run in sixty sec—. Leader! Smoke shells exploding on and around enemy position. Shall I attack?"

A smoke screen! Now, that was clever! But where are those smoke shells coming from? Have to look into that. "Delta Leader. Thunderbolt Leader. Attack at once. Drop all your bombs on this pass."

"Roger, Leader. Attacking now!"

The confectioner completed his turn out over the harbor and headed north, flying over the plateau road. What was this? A truck was driving up the road, bold as brass. Gun was still selected. The confectioner pulled the trigger. The big F-111C shuddered, as the Gatling gun spat four hundred 20mm high-explosive incendiary shells in a four-second burst. He could see the tracers streaking into the truck. Suddenly, the truck exploded in a huge orange ball of fire. The confectioner fought his controls as the shock wave struck the big F-111C like a giant hand. The airframe groaned and shuddered, but General Dynamics builds tough airplanes, and A8-146 held together. He hoped his pilots in Alfa Flight were alert. A collision at four hundred miles per hour and one hundred feet would ruin his whole day!

Almost to the top of the plateau now. Things happen fast at four hundred miles per hour. Select rockets. Aim for the center of the smoke. Oh, yes, "Alfa Flight, attacking now!"

Thirty-eight rockets streaked out from under A8-146's wings and tore into the rocks below. It was impossible to see if they were hitting anything, but the Russians certainly knew that the RAAF was mad at them. Alfa Flight was turning hard again. They still had Mark 82 Snakeye retarded bombs to deliver.

A new voice sounded in the confectioner's earphones. "Thunderbolt Leader. This is Dagger Leader. I am approaching the area from the south. Am I clear for assault landing?"

About time. "Stand by. Talon Leader. This is Thunderbolt Leader. Friendly Lockheed C-130H aircraft are approaching from the southwest. They will make an assault landing in front of your position. Acknowledge, Talon Leader."

"Talon Leader. Roger. Friendly aircraft landing. You guys are doing a great job, Thunderbolt Leader. You can do all our close air support from now on!"

"Think nothing of it, Talon Leader. It's a piece of cake. Do you copy, Dagger Leader? You are clear to land."

"Roger, Thunderbolt Leader. Dagger Force landing now."

The confectioner watched as three large, four-engined transport planes began their final approach. Time to be sure the Russians kept their heads' down. "Bravo Flight, attack! Put your bombs in the center of that smoke."

"Bravo Flight attacking!"

He watched as the first green-and-brown camouflaged transport touched down on the plateau and braked to a stop. The aft door dropped, and men in green combat fatigues began to pour out. The confectioner smiled. Everything was going smoothly. Piece of cake!

Chapter Twenty-Two

"To introduce into war a spirit of moderation would be absurd. War is an act of violence pushed to its utmost bounds."   —General Carl von Clausewitz

THE CRISIS CENTER—MOSCOW, USSR

Colonel Kirilenko began the briefing. General Galanskov listened intently. Kirilenko pointed to a large photographic map of Elu.

"Colonel Ulanov attacked approximately one hour ago. His objective was to seize control of this large formation of rocks which controls access to the plateau. The Americans made a strong defense, but the *Spetsnaz* attack was successful. Colonel Ulanov holds the rocks."

"Excellent!"

"Yes, sir. But the rest of the news is not so good."

Galanskov had been afraid of that. In combat operations, the news is never all good.

"Shortly after the *Spetsnaz* team seized the rocks, they were attacked by F-111C aircraft of the Royal Australian Air Force. They suffered heavy casualties. Then, the Australians landed troops from three transport aircraft."

"The Australians? Are we certain of this?"

"Yes, General. Lieutenant Yakoleva positively identified the F-111C aircraft as belonging to the RAAF. She is not certain, but she believes that the one hundred fifty troops which landed are from the Australian SAS, their *Spetsnaz.*"

"But why are the Australians attacking us?"

Colonel Kirilenko studied the ceiling for a moment. Then, he replied slowly and carefully. "Well, General, Elu is Australian territory. We have landed troops there without their permission, and we are not allies of the Australians. They are a patriotic and combative people. They feel that we have invaded their territory, so they have decided to strike us a blow."

Galanskov nodded. Put that way, it did make a certain kind of sense. "What is their military capability?"

"This was a maximum effort. The Australians used all their long-range combat aircraft. Even so, they must have been refueled by American tankers. They may decide to repeat the attack, but given that they must return to Australia, maintain their aircraft, and rest their crews, a second attack will not come in less than twenty-four to forty-eight hours.

"In the meantime, Colonel Ulanov has approximately two hundred twenty-five men fit for combat. The Americans and Australians have perhaps one hundred fifty. They are heavily armed with many machine guns and mortars. If Ulanov attacks, he must go across eight hundred meters of flat, open ground with little or no cover. His chances of succeeding are poor."

Galanskov nodded. He had been in combat. He knew what machine guns and mortars can do to troops caught in the open.

"Do we know anything that accounts for the strange actions of the Americans?"

"Yes, General. We have a priority message from the

KGB station in Washington. The American president has suffered a severe heart attack. He may be dead or dying. Their vice-president has assumed command. She lacks experience in military affairs and diplomacy. It appears that the American decision-making process is paralyzed."

This was excellent news, if true, but Galanskov was too old a hand to count on it. Who knows, the CIA might even now be preparing a coup to overthrow this woman. Kirilenko had finished. All eyes turned toward Galanskov. Quickly, he reviewed his options. What had the chairman said? "Do not fail, Stepan Pavelovich." Galanskov did not intend to. Time for an all-out effort.

He beckoned to one of his aides. "Establish a secure phone line. I wish to speak to the commanding officer of the 106th Guards Air Assault Division."

THE CRISIS CENTER—THE PENTAGON— WASHINGTON, D.C.

The hum of conversation in the crisis center stopped abruptly. All eyes were on the vice-president as her party entered the room. The national security adviser ushered her to a seat at the conference table, and the briefing began.

She listened intently as Dr. Oliver, the chairman of the Technical Assessment Committee, described the background and the scientific implications of the situation. Many of the technical details were over her head. She did not have a scientific background. But the main points were clear. The Russians had tested something new and deadly. The experts were unanimous. The United States must have that technology.

Dr. Oliver sat down. General Brand stood up and began the military briefing. He was an impressive figure in his uniform, with five rows of ribbons on his chest. He began his briefing formally.

"Madam Vice-President, gentlemen. Before I proceed, we have just been informed by the Australian embassy that Australia has taken military action against the Russian forces on Elu. The Royal Australian Air Force has conducted air strikes against the Russian troops, and elements of the 1st Australian Special Air Service Regiment have air landed on Elu. The Australians have joined the fight. They request our military assistance."

There was a brief hum of conversation. It was obvious that they all felt this was a favorable development. Brand continued. He was an excellent briefer, but the details of his recommendations were confusing. The vice-president had no background in military affairs or foreign policy. When she had been in the Senate, she had specialized in women's issues and the environment. She had no illusions. The president had put her on the ticket to carry the women's vote in the western states. He had never given her any important responsibilities.

Too much of what Brand was saying was complicated and hard to understand. The capabilities of different kinds of airplanes, the types of helicopters which could operate from the *Wasp*, the size of a Ranger battalion, it all ran together in a blur. It was confusing. There was no way she could become an instant expert, but she could not dodge the decision. It was her responsibility.

It came down, as it always did, to people. Who can you trust? Brand sounded convincing. He appeared to know what he was talking about, and he certainly looked like an experienced soldier. But she had been around Washington long enough to know that appearances can be deceiving. Brand might be a Pentagon politician who knew nothing about real war.

Brand finished his presentation. The alternatives were clear. Either approve Brand's plan, or direct him to try to evacuate Talon Force. Everyone was looking at her. They wanted a decision, and they wanted it now. Well, they would just have to wait a minute. She smiled her best smile.

"Excellent briefings, gentlemen. Thank you. You have presented a great deal of information. I need ten minutes to think it over. I will give you my decision then."

She moved to one of the small side rooms, beckoning to her military aide to follow her. He was an army captain, resplendent in his dress uniform. He closed the door, and they were alone, unless, of course, the CIA had bugged the room. The vice-president went straight to the point.

"Tom, those ribbons General Brand is wearing, what do they mean?"

The captain looked surprised, but he answered quickly. "They are his decorations and service ribbons, ma'am. They show the medals he has been awarded and the campaigns he served in."

"Yes, but what do they mean? What is the red, white, and blue one on top, with the little metal thing in the middle?"

"That is the Distinguished Service Cross, the nation's second-highest award for valor. The metal oak-leaf cluster means he has been awarded that medal twice. The next medal is the Silver Star, four awards. The purple-and-white ribbon is the Purple Heart. He has been wounded in combat twice. The others are service ribbons for Vietnam, Grenada, Panama, Kuwait. The blue-and-silver bar under the ribbons is the Combat Infantry Badge. The silver jump wings mean he has had parachute training."

The vice-president nodded. That told her what she needed to know. Whatever else he might be, Brand was a real soldier. She reentered the crisis center. Everyone looked at her expectantly.

"Gentlemen, I have reached a decision. I am countermanding the president's order. General Brand's plan is in effect. I want a maximum effort. We are going in to win!"

There was a buzz of excitement. Brand was smiling. At least she had one fan in the military. The national security adviser was approaching. He was not smiling. Did he think she had made a mistake?

"Well, Frank, there's your decision. Of course, the president may overrule me an hour from now."

He shook his head. "No, Madam President, that will not happen. Your decision will stand."

"Of course, he can change it if——. What did you say?"

"The president died ten minutes ago, Madam President. No one can overrule your decision. You are the president of the United States."

Chapter Twenty-Three

"Strengthen your position. Fight anything that comes."
> —General William T. Sherman

*SPETSNAZ TEAM—ELU ISLAND—THE PLA-
TEAU*

Colonel Viktor Ulanov hugged a rock and coughed again and again. The acrid smoke from the 120mm mortar bombs burned his eyes and throat. At least, his smoke screen seemed to be working. The Australian air attack seemed to have lost some of its precision. That was just as well. Ulanov devoutly hoped he never saw another damned F-111 in his life. He coughed and swore. His ears were ringing from the repeated blasts of bombs, but it did seem to be quiet. He started to stand up and help Irina Yakoleva to her feet. Then he heard a "whine" as a flight of F-111Cs passed over him at less than a hundred feet.

He was a quick learner. It had only taken one attack for him to learn all he ever wanted to know about retarded bombs. He threw himself down behind the rock, knocking the breath out of Irina Yakoleva again. The ground shook again and again as twenty-four five hundred–pound Snakeye bombs crashed into the rocks and detonated. Ulanov swore bitterly and fluently. The confectioner would have been astounded if he had heard Ulanov. Neither he, or any of his pilots, had even imagined any of the things Ulanov accused them of doing.

The radio was crackling. Ulanov picked up the headset. Sharypa was speaking urgently. "Blue One, this is Blue Four. Come in Colonel, come in Blue One."

"Blue One, this is Blue Four."

Ulanov could hear the relief in Sharypa's voice. "Good to hear you, Colonel. Those jets are the very devil."

Ulanov agreed wholeheartedly, but he knew that Sharypa had not called to chat about F-111s.

"What is your situation, Sharypa. Can you see anything?"

"Yes, Colonel. I am in the trees to the north of the rocks, outside the smoke. The enemy is conducting an air landing, three large, four-engine aircraft landed and deployed about fifty troops per plane. The planes were marked with the same insignia as the fighters. The men took cover in the trees around the satellite. I had my machine gunners fire at them, but the range was over nine hundred meters. I doubt that it had any effect."

Damn! A hundred and fifty men. The damned Australians had reinforced the Americans. Together they must have two hundred men. He would be lucky if he had that many men left fit to fight. Well, he had better assess the situation and inform Moscow via SATCOM. He had a dismal feeling that Moscow was not going to be happy with him.

DETACHMENT—1ST SPECIAL FORCES GROUP (AIRBORNE)—ELU ISLAND—THE PLATEAU

Carter was talking to Washington on SATCOM.

General Brand's voice was loud and clear. Carter finished his briefing. The general was pleased. "That's damned good work, Carter."

It was, Carter thought. They had done well, but he had lost Goldberg and twenty men.

"I've got some good news for a change," Brand continued. "The president has approved our plan. Major, reinforcements are on the way. The navy has a large helicopter carrier, the *Wasp,* on the way to Elu. She operates CH-53E heavy lift helicopters. They can lift the satellite and fly it to the *Wasp,* or if it's too heavy, they can fly off whatever your scientists decide are the key components. Tell Gregory and Walsh to get started on that. Pick out the key components and have a plan to rapidly dismantle the satellite if necessary. *Wasp* also operates CH-46 troop-carrying helicopters. They will evacuate all U.S. and Australian personnel as soon as we are through with the satellite. Got it?"

"Yes, sir. What are the reinforcements, and how soon do they arrive?"

"I don't want to transmit any details. The Russians may be intercepting and reading some of our messages. Let's just say major reinforcements and as soon as possible. Now, what is your situation? Can you hold out until you are reinforced?"

Carter thought for a moment. "I can hold out against what the Russians have on Elu. With the Australian SAS troops, the odds are about even. The problem will be if they reinforce their force before our reinforcements arrive."

"That's the bad news, Carter. Intelligence reports and communications intercepts indicate that the Russians are mounting a major operation. We can't be sure of the details, but we know it's aimed at Elu. We've learned that the Russians call that satellite of yours *War God.* The term, *War God,* occurs frequently in

271

these messages. They are concentrating numbers of large transport aircraft. Our best guess is that they are sending in a *Spetsnaz* battalion. With any luck, our people will get there first. Meanwhile, dig in and strengthen your position. If the Russians get there first, hold them as long as you can."

Carter sighed to himself. He knew what that meant.

SPETSNAZ TEAM—ELU ISLAND—THE PLATEAU

Ulanov was waiting. He had reorganized and reported to Moscow. He had talked to Colonel Kirilenko, one of General Galanskov's senior staff officers. Kirilenko had listened carefully and had asked some shrewd questions, but he had been totally noncommittal. He had only told Ulanov to wait while he reported to the general. Ulanov fidgeted. He hated waiting, but he did not think he was going to like what he was going to hear. General Galanskov did not like failed operations or officers who led them. Oh, well, perhaps he could learn to like commanding a company of border guards in Siberia.

The SATCOM operator suddenly handed Ulanov the headset. He looked impressed. "A message for you, colonel. Colonel-General Galanskov from Moscow. He wishes to speak to you immediately!"

"Ulanov? This is General Galanskov. Kirilenko has briefed me on the situation. Listen, you and your men have done well. There is no way you could have foreseen the treacherous actions of the Americans and the Australians. I am sending you powerful reinforcements immediately. I will not risk transmitting details. There is evidence that the Americans may be intercepting and decoding some of our messages. Hold on until they arrive, and the Americans will be finished. Do you understand?"

272

Ulanov did. For the moment, he was still a hero. "Yes, sir, I understand. This is excellent news."

"This next is not so good. Our agents in Washington report that the Americans have decided to reinforce their troops on Elu. We are not certain of the details, but it is likely to be a substantial force. If they arrive before our reinforcements, you will be outnumbered. If this should occur, remember that this operation is vital to the security of the state. Fight to the last man, if it comes to that. Do you understand, Ulanov?"

Ulanov sighed to himself. He did, indeed.

THE CRISIS CENTER—THE PENTAGON— WASHINGTON, D.C.

Brand was relaxing, sitting at the long conference table, drinking a cup of strong black coffee. He knew he drank too much coffee. He would cut down on his consumption immediately, or perhaps when this *War God* operation was over. For the moment, he felt relaxed. His reinforcements were on the way. *Wasp* was closing in on Elu, stuffed full of helicopters, and *Los Angeles* was moving into position to protect her. The Australians were being very cooperative. Best of all, the new president had personally approved his plans. That stopped most of the sniping and backbiting he otherwise might have had to put up with.

Brand decided he liked the president. She had more balls than half the men in Washington. He would vote for her if she ran again. He smiled to himself. He hoped his wife would survive the shock when he told her he would vote for a woman for president. Still, even old Rangers can learn new tricks.

Brand was starting to feel smug. Then, the reflexes that had kept him alive through twenty-five years of special operations cut in, and he began to worry. When nothing can go wrong, something will. What was that

273

old Japanese samurai saying: "When victory seems certain, tighten your helmet strings"? He glanced up and saw coming rapidly across the room the navy captain who knew all about 688s. Brand sighed; no rest for the weary. He returned the captain's salute.

"General, we have a message from naval intelligence. Forty-eight hours ago the Japanese Naval Self-Defense Force was conducting maneuvers in the Western Pacific. One of their destroyers, the *Hatsuyuki,* made a sonar contact on two submarines moving at over thirty knots. *Hatsuyuki* classifies the contact as Soviet Akula or Victor nuclear attack boats. An hour later, the *Hatakaze* made a second contact. It's most unusual for nuclear submarines to transit at such high speeds, so the Japanese decided to pass the word along. Now, if you project their course, it seems almost certain that they are headed for Elu."

Brand smiled. "All right, Captain, what the hell are Akulas and Victors?"

"Sorry, sir. Akulas and Victors are some of the latest and best Soviet nuclear-propelled attack submarines, their 688s."

Brand could have cheerfully gone all day without hearing that.

"What can we do about it?"

"Nothing, General, except alert *Los Angeles.* Also, we need to be certain what rules of engagement are in effect. If *Los Angeles* detects these submarines in her patrol area off Elu, is she authorized to attack them?"

If there was one thing Brand could do well, it was make up his mind.

"Send a message to *Los Angeles* at once. Tell them to expect company. If those Russian subs show up off Elu, don't screw around. Sink them!"

Chapter Twenty-Four

"I do not know what effect these men will have on the enemy, but by God, Sir, they frighten me!"

—The duke of Wellington

ELU ISLAND—THE PLATEAU

Cord was sleeping the deep and dreamless sleep of the just, or, at least the totally exhausted, when God began to speak to him. As Cord had always suspected, God sounded exactly like Regimental Sergeant Major MacNair. That did not bother Cord, but it was obvious that God was not happy with him.

"CORD, what are you doing lounging about on your bloody backside like the Queen of Sheba? You're on active service, in case that fact has slipped your feeble mind. I'm going to be very annoyed with you if you're not on your bloody feet in ten seconds! The colonel wants to see you, God only knows why."

With these unkind words, God began to kick Cord on the sole of his left boot. This was interesting, because it showed that God was an experienced soldier. He knew better than to wake up sleeping SAS men by shaking their shoulders unless you have first separated them from their rifles, pistols, and knives.

Cord opened his eyes and peered in amazement at the figure towering over him. My God, it was Regimental Sergeant Major MacNair, and the RSM was obviously not happy with him. As usual, Sergeant MacNair was the picture of military perfection. He stood six feet four and had the finest military mustache in the Australian SAS. Even on a combat operation, MacNair looked ready to conduct the queen on a tour of the regimental base at Swanbourne. Cord jumped to his feet. It does not pay to annoy regimental sergeant majors. They are not quite as powerful as God. They cannot sentence you to hellfire and eternal damnation, but they can deliver a remarkably close imitation if they really try.

Sergeant MacNair looked at Cord with obvious disapproval.

"You always were a bloody awful man, Cord, but this is too bloody much! Just look at you! Your boots are horrible! Your uniform is filthy! You haven't shaved for a week! You're a disgrace to the regiment! What have you got to say for yourself, Cord?"

MacNair was clearly ahead on points. Cord chose the only excuse MacNair might conceivably accept. "I've been fighting these bloody Russians, Sergeant Major."

Sergeant MacNair considered this for a moment. "Well, perhaps you have been a little busy,"—Cord started to relax—"But"—Cord had been afraid there would be a but—"why are you standing here babbling, Cord? The colonel wants to see you. Come on. Now!"

*THE CRISIS CENTER—THE PENTAGON—
WASHINGTON, D.C.*

General Brand was sitting at the conference table with the assistant secretary. Brand had managed to get seven hours of sleep, but he felt that he needed at least twenty more to feel human. For once, he was being briefed, not giving the briefing.

"The task force is approaching Elu now. It will arrive in approximately one hour. The C-5Bs carrying the company from the 82nd Airborne Division made the rendezvous and have joined the main formation carrying the 2nd Ranger Battalion. Everything is going according to plan. However—"

Brand could have gone all year without hearing that "however."

"—the CIA and the NSA report major air activity in the Soviet Union. A large number of their long-range transports and tanker aircraft are staging into Cam Ranh Bay. We think that they are carrying troops, and their destination is clearly Elu."

"Do we know how many troops and what units?" Brand asked.

"No, sir. But the CIA says they are using their largest transports, AN-122 Cocks and ANT-124 Condors. One Condor can carry two hundred seventy parachutists. The CIA says they could be *Spetsnaz* parachute battalions, two of them, possibly three, if they're really packing them in."

Two or three *Spetsnaz* battalions! The Russians were getting serious! Well, no one had ever promised him that being a general was going to be easy.

"Get me the task force on SATCOM. I want to speak to Colonel Dolan," he said to his assistant in back of him.

The major looked startled. "I'm sorry, sir, I assumed that you had been briefed. Colonel Dolan was injured when a car hit his motorcycle while he was on his way to the base. He is in the hospital with two broken legs."

At least Maj. Muso Gozen, the second in command,

was a cool and competent officer. "All right, get me the Moose."

The major looked unhappy. "Sir, Major Gozen is not in command."

"Why the hell not? Don't tell me he broke his neck practicing his damned karate?"

"No, sir. Major Gozen is with the task force, but he is not in command. Colonel Steiner, the executive officer of the Ranger regiment assumed command when he heard Colonel Dolan had been injured. He is in command."

Oh, God! Roaring Rudy Steiner! Of all the colonels and majors in the Ranger regiment, Steiner was the last man Brand would have selected to go to Elu. But Brand was stuck. There was no way he could order a full colonel to turn over command to a major.

"All right, get me Colonel Steiner."

In less than sixty seconds, Brand was talking to Colonel Steiner. Brand marveled again at SATCOM. Steiner sounded as if he were in the next room. That was a mixed blessing. Steiner was not called Roaring Rudy for nothing. As usual, he carried out his end of the conversation at a constant shout.

Brand concluded his briefing. "You see, Colonel, you've got to take out the Russians on Elu quickly, before the Russian reinforcements arrive. Do you understand?"

"Affirmative, General."

The formal part of the discussion was over. "Good luck, Rudy," Brand said.

"Don't worry, Jim, we'll get it done. We'll hit those Commie bastards so fast they'll never know what happened!"

Brand sighed as he hung up the phone. The assistant secretary looked at Brand intently. "What's bothering you about Colonel Steiner, Jim? I've looked at his rec-

278

ord. He seems to be a brave and capable officer. Why are you concerned that he is in command?"

"Oh, he's brave, and he's capable. Maybe he's too brave. Steiner isn't afraid of anything. He's aggressive, and he moves fast. He'll attack the enemy immediately. No matter what the odds, he'll go in guns blazing, win or die."

"What's wrong with that?"

"Well, there was another army colonel you could say all that about. Remember George Armstrong Custer?"

COMMAND POST—1ST AUSTRALIAN SAS REGIMENT—ELU ISLAND—THE PLATEAU

Cord saluted Colonel Haldane smartly. Cord was not happy to be speaking to the commanding officer of the Australian SAS. It was not that he disliked Colonel Haldane, but in Cord's experience, when sergeants have long conversations with colonels, it generally means trouble. Cord liked to confine his remarks to "Yes, sir!" "No, sir!" and "Right away, sir!" But Colonel Haldane did not appear angry. Perhaps he had forgotten Cord's famous brawl with those Royal Marine Commandos in that bar in Sydney.

"I would like for you to brief me on what has been going on here, Cord, and would you explain just what you have been telling our new Yankee chums. They seem to believe that you wiped out the KGB, destroyed the Russian navy, and slaughtered a *Spetsnaz* battalion single-handed. I would like to hear the facts."

Cord took a deep breath. He was aware that all the officers and senior NCOs were looking intently at him. He would rather have faced *Spetsnaz* again. "Well, sir, this bloody great Russian satellite came down on Elu and . . ." Cord finished and glanced around. Everyone seemed to be smiling. Cord relaxed slightly.

"I think you did rather well, Cord," Colonel Haldane

said. "You did your duty. The regiment can be proud of you."

Cord was pleased. That from the colonel commanding the SAS meant more to him than a dozen medals from some bloody politician. He would have liked to say something grand in reply, but Cord was no orator. He did his best public speaking with his rifle. "Thank you, sir," was all he said.

"Now then," Colonel Haldane said, "we have to do a little planning. We must rescue Miss Foster and recover your code machine, Cord. Make a sketch map of a safe route to your cave, Cord. I'll send a four-man patrol to take care of things."

Cord did not ordinarily volunteer for anything, but in a way Miriam Foster was his responsibility. "I'll go, Colonel," he said quickly.

"Thank you, Cord, but I need you for another mission. The Yanks are flying in reinforcements in an hour. The American air force will bomb the Russian positions and lay down a smoke screen to protect the drop zone. An American air force officer will be here shortly. I want you to find a good observation position and take care of him. Also, the Russians have heavy mortars. They may push forward observation parties through the smoke. I see you have your Lee-Enfield. Good. If the Russians do that, take care of them. Get Cord a radio, Sergeant Major, and any equipment he may need."

Cord was happily stuffing his fatigues with L2 hand grenades when MacNair returned with the radio. "All set, Cord?" Cord nodded. MacNair reached into his pack. "Here, Cord, I brought you a little present."

Cord took the heavy package and opened it. Twenty boxes of .303 Lee-Enfield cartridges! Cord was overwhelmed.

"You are a bloody awful man, Cord, but you can

280

shoot," MacNair said. Cord was stunned. He had never expected anything like this to happen in his entire life. It was obvious that, even if only for a few minutes, the sergeant major was happy with him. Cord could think of nothing to say.

"Come on, Cord, stop dawdling around. The Americans are waiting!"

ELU ISLAND—THE PLATEAU

Cord had selected his position with great care. It offered an excellent view of the Russian positions and good concealment. Cord, Jackson, and Cap. Ray Chavez lay there quietly, waiting for the American planes to arrive. Cord and Chavez had quickly formed a mutual admiration society. When Cord learned that Chavez had piloted that low-flying B-52 that had saved Cord from making a last stand, he would have cheerfully given Chavez his last beer if he had had any left, but it was the sentiment that counted. Jackson was telling Chavez about Cord's exploits, which were losing nothing in the telling, when Chavez's radio spoke.

"Elu, this is *Eagle One.* We will be arriving over your position in five minutes. Transports are ten minutes behind us. Do you copy?"

"Roger, *Eagle One.* This is *Eagle Nine.* We will mark the target with red-and-white smoke."

"Roger, *Eagle Nine.* Red-and-white smoke. How are you, Ray? We're glad to hear you're still alive."

"I'm fine, Major, but I'm ready to go home. Let's take care of these Russians and call it a week." The conversation turned technical as Banford and Chavez discussed bombing patterns and approach angles. Cord and Jackson scanned the Russian positions through their telescopic rifle sights. The Russians seemed to be quiet and unsuspecting.

Chavez finished his conversation. He pointed upward, to the north. There, against the bright blue sky, Cord could see thin, white lines. Contrails! A dozen B-52Gs were advancing majestically toward Elu at thirty-two thousand feet, unseen and unheard.

Jackson spoke into his radio. Cord heard the tube noise behind him as the American mortars opened fire. Red-and-white puffs of smoke began to bloom in front of the Russian positions.

"Eagle Nine, this is *Eagle One.* Bombs away!"

Cord watched intently. At first, nothing happened. Then Cord heard the whistling-sighing sound of bombs falling. It grew louder and louder as 162 Mark 83 1,000-pound bombs cascaded down from the sky and struck the Russian positions. The roar of exploding bombs filled the air. Even from six hundred yards away, Cord could feel the ground shake and vibrate.

The second wave of six B-52Gs began to drop smoke bombs. Huge puffs of gray-white smoke blossomed in the Russian lines. In seconds, they were shrouded in thick clouds of gray-white smoke. It was an awe-inspiring sight. Even Ray Chavez was impressed. He knew what B-52Gs could do, but this was the first time he had ever seen a B-52 attack from the ground. Cord and Jackson cheered and pounded Chavez on the back. When you are in combat, fighting a skilled and deadly foe, it is wonderful to have that kind of power on your side.

Chavez grinned, and with the air of a stage magician announcing his next trick, pointed to the south. Cord looked and swore in amazement. The largest airplane Cord had ever seen was coming straight at him, five hundred feet above the surface of the plateau. It had an immense fuselage, four gigantic jet engines, and a great, tall I tail. It was not just large, it was bloody huge! And more were coming on behind it.

"That's a Lockheed C-5B. We call them aluminum clouds."

Cord could believe that. He watched as the C-5B swept overhead. Parachutes began to fill the sky. Some of them were gigantic. The Yanks were not only dropping men, but heavy equipment, too. Lots and lots of both. Cord was ecstatic. He loved this display of power. He had always liked Americans. Most of them were decent chaps, even if they do talk funny. His faith was justified.

Chavez listened to his radio. "That's the 2nd Ranger Battalion reinforced by units from the 82nd Airborne. They'll take care of these *Spetsnaz* types."

Cord watched as one C-5B after another roared over the plateau and dropped its loads. He knew that *Spetsnaz* was tough, but he did not think they could handle this. Cord was happy watching the C-5Bs. Perhaps that explained why he got a little careless.

Irina Yakoleva was four hundred yards away, looking for targets through the sight of her SVD sniper's rifle. Sharypa had reported what they had seen. Ulanov was about to use the only effective weapon he had. Sharypa was radioing target coordinates to Popov. The 120 mm mortars would be opening fire in seconds. There was nothing for Irina to do but shoot. The bombing had been too precise. She was sure that the Americans must have directed the bombing from a nearby observation post. If she could locate it and take it out—Ah-hah! There, in a clump of bushes four hundred yards away, was an unnatural movement, branches stirring against the wind. She watched intently.

Slowly, carefully, the bushes parted slightly. She would never have seen it if she had not been alerted. She watched as a rifle barrel slowly inched forward. The entire barrel was encased in wood. A Lee-Enfield! Irina felt the same thrill a big game hunter feels when he sees a man-eating tiger. Cord! She took a deep breath, let half of it out, and began to squeeze the trigger. Cord's rifle muzzle was swinging toward her position. He was looking for targets, too, but he had not seen her yet. Steady, Yakoleva, don't jerk the trigger, squeeze, squeeze——. The SVD roared. Cord and his rifle vanished instantly into the bush. Irina felt a thrill of pride. She did not know if she had killed Cord, but she was sure she had hit him. He would no longer be a threat to the *Spetsnaz* team! Now to get back and report to Colonel Ulanov. He must learn that the Americans had arrived in great force.

Cord was looking for targets. He saw a strange, brown-mottled rock topped by a dark-gold mass of ferns. There was an odd black circle in the center. He concentrated on the image in his telescopic sight. Bloody hell! It was Irene, and she was aiming a rifle straight at him! Cord tried to throw himself to the left, but Irina had already fired. The .30 caliber bullet was there in less than half a second.

Something smashed into the right side of Cord's face. Cord had been hit before, but he had never taken a blow like that. His vision blurred. There was a roaring noise in his hears. His whole body felt numb. Cord gasped for breath. Slowly his vision cleared.

Jackson and Chavez were looking at him anxiously. "You OK, Cord?" Jackson asked. "I don't see any blood. They just hit your rifle."

His rifle! Adrenaline flooded Cord's body. Chavez was holding Cord's Lee-Enfield. There was a ragged foot-long gouge, like the stroke of a giant claw, extending from just back of the grip to the upper edge of the buttplate.

Cord swore bitterly. "Irene, *you bloody slag, you town bike, you filthy scrubber, you quandong bitch!*" He paused for breath. Chavez and Jackson looked at Cord blankly. It was obvious that Cord was angry, but he seemed to be raving in an unknown tongue. Actually, he was swearing in Australian.

Cord took his rifle and examined the mechanism. It seemed to be all right, but he would have to take a few shots to be sure that his sights had not been knocked out of alignment. He swore to himself. He bitterly regretted not shooting Irene the first time he saw her. He would not make that mistake again. If he got the bloody bitch in his sights again, she would be a dead blond.

A strange-looking vehicle was approaching the *Spetsnaz* position. It was larger than a jeep but smaller than a truck. Incredibly, in Elu's awful heat, it had plastic side curtains and a roof in place. A number of radio antennas sprouted from the back. It was marked with the white star that identifies U.S. Army vehicles. Also, incredibly, it was flying a large white flag from the tallest antenna. Colonel Viktor Ulanov peered at it through his binoculars. Ulanov had been warned more than once during his *Spetsnaz* training that the Yankees are wily and treacherous. This was probably true, but it was hard to see this single vehicle as a threat. Perhaps the Americans had repented their evil ways, and wanted to surrender. Ulanov smiled. Only a fool would believe that.

He handed his binoculars to Major Yegor Mamin. Mamin stared through the glasses. "Some kind of American military vehicle, Colonel. Perhaps they wish to surrender."

Oh, well, Mamin might be a wonderful political officer, but as an intelligence officer, he left a great deal to be desired. Ulanov turned to his radio operator. "Call Lieutenant Yakoleva. Ask her to report to me at once."

The vehicle had stopped a hundred yards away. Several machine guns were trained on it. If the Yankees were planning treachery, they would get a rude surprise. A man in a combat uniform got out of the vehicle. He was wearing web equipment and magazine pouches, but he had left his rifle in the vehicle. He came toward the rocks and stopped thirty meters away. He shouted in poor, but understandable, Russian.

"Flag of truce. My commanding officer wishes to speak to your commanding officer."

"One moment," Ulanov shouted, "I will call him." He turned to Mamin. "What do you think, Major? What are they up to?"

"Do not go, Colonel. The Yankees are noted for their treachery. Probably they intend to either kill you or seize you as a hostage, hoping to demoralize our team. I will go in your place if you wish. They cannot know that I am not the commander."

Ulanov shuddered. The offer was brave, but if Yegor Mamin started negotiating with the Americans, World War III would probably start in five minutes. "That is a thought, Major, but do you speak English?"

"No, but I speak Romanian."

"Excellent, but that is not likely to be of much use with the Yankees. I do not speak their language either, but Lieutenant Yakoleva does. Suppose we send her."

"That is an excellent plan, Colonel. She seems clever. Perhaps she can learn the Yankees' plans, and if they kill her, it will anger the men and they will fight harder. Yes, send the Yakoleva."

Ulanov noted, for future reference, that Major Mamin was remarkably compassionate. When Irina Yakoleva arrived, Ulanov pointed at the American vehicle. "What do you make of this, Lieutenant?"

Irina took a quick look. "It is one of the new American High Mobility Multipurpose Wheeled Vehicles. The Americans call them "Hummers." It has four-wheel drive and a diesel engine. The side curtains and the tops are made of a plastic called kevlar. It provides limited armor protection. It comes in many different configurations and can mount many different types of weapons. This one is configured as a command vehicle. You can tell by the radio antennas."

Colonel Ulanov was impressed. Lieutenant Yakoleva's knowledge of foreign military equipment seemed unlimited. Irina did not think it necessary to mention that the Australian army was testing HMMWs and that she had read a report on them last week.

Ulanov explained the situation. "They wish to talk about something. Neither Mamin nor I speaks English."

"I will go, my English is excellent."

"Good, but I must warn you, Major Mamin thinks they intend treachery. You may be in danger, white flag or no white flag."

Irina shrugged. "I am armed, and there can be only three men in the vehicle at the most. Give me two good men as an escort, and I will go."

Ulanov nodded. "Get Sergeant Sharypa," he told the radio operator, "and tell him to bring a rocket grenadier."

Someone shouted loudly from the HMMWV. The man was speaking English.

"What is he saying, Lieutenant?"

Irina blushed slightly. "He is telling his soldier to get a move on and to get the Russian commander out there very rapidly, but he is using many very uncultural words. I do not wish to translate precisely."

287

Sharypa arrived, followed by Dudorov with his RPG-7D.

Ulanov briefed them rapidly. "Let Lieutenant Yakoleva do the talking. Be ready to shoot at the slightest sign of treachery. Lieutenant Yakoleva says this vehicle is lightly armored. If Sharypa shoots, put a rocket into it, Dudorov. Do you understand?"

"Exactly so, Colonel," Sharypa said. "We will defeat any Yankee treachery and bring Lieutenant Yakoleva back safely."

There was another angry shout from the American vehicle.

"Very well, then, go, before this fierce Yankee commander dies of apoplexy."

Irina hesitated. "There is a small problem. I have no uniform. I do not look military. They may laugh at me."

Sharypa smiled. He reached inside his uniform and took out his prized, pale blue beret, with the red-star and gold-wreath badge of the VDV. "Wear this, Lieutenant. The Yankees will see that you are a fierce *desantniki* and tremble in their boots."

Irina laughed and put the blue beret on her head at the rakish angle which is popular in *Spetsnaz*. She stepped forward toward the American vehicle. A man got out of the HMMWV and stood staring at her with hands on his hips. He was tall and powerfully built, with graying blond hair. A silver eagle was pinned to the front of his camouflaged helmet. He wore a large automatic pistol in a holster, but carried no other weapons. His face was red. He appeared to be very angry.

Irina stopped three feet in front of the tall American, being careful not to block Sharypa's line of fire. She saluted politely. Before she could speak, the American spoke in a loud and unpleasant voice. "Just who or what the hell are you supposed to be?"

Irina thought for a moment. He was not staring at

her, he was glaring. Irina was used to men staring at
her. She could attract a lot of attention on an Australian beach when she wore her prized string bikini, but
this man was in a rage. He looked as if he would like
to tear her to pieces. Was he trying to frighten her? If
so, he had the wrong woman. She came from a race of
fighters. Irina's ancestors had lived two hundred miles
north of Moscow for a thousand years. They had fought
the Mongols, the Tatars, the Swedes, the Poles, the
French, and the Germans. It would take more than a
loud, uncultural American to frighten her. She drew
herself up to her full five feet eleven and glared back.
"I am Senior Lieutenant Irina Yakoleva," she said
coldly. "My commanding officer has sent me here to
speak to you. What do you wish to say?"

The American's face turned even redder. Perhaps he
was about to die of apoplexy. Irina would not grieve
if he did.

"Listen, you stupid bitch, I am Colonel Rudolph
Steiner. I am in command of the American forces on
Elu. I came here to talk to the Russian commander, not
to waste my time with some damned woman. Now, take
your senior lieutenant's fanny back and tell him that!"

Irina felt the blood rush to her face. It was her turn
to be angry. She normally spoke English with Australians. Fanny is a much worse expression in Australian
than in American, and he had mocked her hard-earned
army rank. He was obviously a fascist and a warmonger
to boot. She knew some very uncultural words in English, and she was tempted to use them, but she was rep-
resenting the Russian armed forces.

"You requested this meeting, Colonel. I did not. I
am here because my colonel sent me. He does not speak
English and I doubt that you speak Russian. If you
have a message, I will accept it. If not, I have other
duties to perform."

"All right, tell your God damned colonel this. I out-number you five to one. I have tanks and heavy weapons. I will give you fifteen minutes to surrender. If you don't, I'll wipe you out!"

Irina threw back her head and laughed. "You are a fool, Yankee. We are *Spetsnaz*. We never surrender!" With that, she saluted and did an about face with the precision of a Guards officer on duty at Lenin's Tomb. She heard the American colonel swearing behind her. He used many extremely uncultural words, but she did not care. Let him stew! Surrender indeed!

She slipped back into the Russian positions. Ulanov was smiling. "You seemed to have a brisk discussion with our Yankee friend, Lieutenant Yakoleva. What did he want?"

Irina told him. Major Mamin, Sharypa, and Dudorov listened intently.

"So, I did not think I needed to trouble you with his insulting proposal," Irina concluded, "so I said 'We are *Spetsnaz*. We never surrender!'"

Dudorov whooped with glee. He clapped Irina on the shoulder. Mamin shook her hand. Irina started to give Sharypa back his blue beret. Sharypa laughed. "Keep it, Lieutenant. You are the best man in this team."

Ulanov smiled grimly. She was right, of course. They would not surrender. But a lot of them were going to die to prove that what Irina had said was so.

Colonel Steiner was explaining his plan. As usual, he spoke loudly. "It's a simple plan, gentlemen. We smother them with speed and firepower and smash them up before they can react. We have twelve Hummers, half armed with .50 caliber and .30 caliber machine guns, and half with Mk 19 40mm automatic grenade launchers. And we have seventeen Sheridans from

290

the 82nd Airborne with 152mm cannons. The mortars will lay down a smoke screen.

"We will move out at high speed and engage them at short range. They can't stand up to that kind of firepower. The rest of the Second Battalion will follow on foot and mop up. It will all be over in ten minutes."

Steiner paused for a moment. His eyes swept the group. "Any questions or comments?"

Colonel Haldane spoke quietly. "What role do you plan for my men? I'm afraid we don't train for mechanized assaults in the SAS, and we have no combat vehicles."

Steiner would have been happy if the Australian SAS were not there. They were likely to get in the way and claim more than their fair share of the credit. Still, they were allies, and it was their damned island. Better be tactful. "Well, Colonel, what would you suggest? You know your men and equipment better than I do."

Colonel Haldane pointed to the map. "I think we can work our way through these trees to the north and get on their right flank without being detected. Their attention will be focused on you when you attack. We will hit them on their right flank and try to get behind them and cut off their retreat."

It was not Steiner's kind of plan, but it would not hurt anything. "That's an excellent idea, Colonel," he said. "How soon can you be in position?"

Colonel Haldane looked at his watch. The SAS can move fast when they have to. "Give me two hours, Colonel Steiner, and we will be ready to attack."

"All right, two hours it is. Any other questions?"

"Yes, sir," Captain Carter said, "what do you want my men to do?"

"Maintain your position around *War God*. We can't leave it unguarded. The Russians may try something cute."

Carter did not argue. His men needed a rest.

"All right, gentlemen," Steiner said, "check your watches. It is now 13:12. We attack in two hours from now. We'll blow those bastards to hell!"

Rudy Steiner glanced at his watch. Sixteen minutes to go. He was waiting tensely. To him, waiting to fight was much worse than fighting itself. Would that damned minute hand never crawl around the dial?

To his left and right, the 82nd Airborne Sheridans were getting ready, concealed in the edge of the trees. He had thought the Sheridans were unnecessary when he had reviewed Brand's plan, but now that he was on Elu, he was glad that they were there.

They did not look very formidable at first glance. They were small, as modern tanks go, weighing only seventeen tons and standing only ten feet above the ground. But when you looked at them closely, your attention was irresistibly drawn to the huge 152mm cannons protruding from their turrets. They were the largest-caliber cannons Steiner had ever seen mounted on tanks. The Russians would be unhappy when the Sheridans opened fire.

The captain from the 82nd Airborne who commanded the Sheridan company noticed Steiner and came over and saluted. What the hell was his name? Oh, yes, DeBerg. "How are things going, Captain?" Steiner asked.

"Going well, sir. We'll be ready. We dropped seventeen Sheridans. The low-altitude extraction drop is hard on them, but we'll have fifteen ready to go. Meanwhile, Colonel, I have an idea. I'd like to suggest a minor change to the plan."

Steiner frowned slightly. He did not like people who suggested changing his plans. However, a good commander always listens to his subordinates' suggestions before rejecting them. "What's your idea, Captain?"

"Well, sir, Sheridans are good combat vehicles, but they have their strengths and weaknesses. They're fast, we can do forty miles an hour on flat, hard ground, and the M81 152mm guns give us a lot of firepower. But our armor protection is very light. The hulls are forged aluminum. A .50 caliber machine gun will penetrate them at close range. The turrets are welded steel. They are stronger, but any cannon shell will get through. Sheridans have to depend on speed, mobility, and firepower to survive."

Steiner nodded. His attack plan maximized that.

"The 152mm gun is our best weapon, Colonel. We can fire cannon shells or antitank guided missiles from the gun. For this mission, we've loaded mostly 152mm cannon shells, thirty-six of them and two missiles on each Sheridan; 152mm high-explosive fragmentation shells weigh sixty-three pounds. They are extremely powerful.

"My idea is to hold one of my three platoons back and use them like artillery. We could put more than a hundred shells into the Russian position in five minutes. That will cover the advance of my other two platoons and your Rangers. Believe me, Colonel, those 152mm HE-FRAG shells will knock hell out of the Russians."

Steiner smiled. He could use some artillery. "Damned good idea, Captain. Do it! Blast them to hell!"

Colonel Ulanov was waiting tensely. The Americans had not come to Elu to admire the scenery. They would attack as soon as they were ready. He could feel it. Lieutenant Yakoleva's description of the American airdrop had been chilling. At least a battalion of infantry and many extremely large containers. He was probably out-

293

numbered three to one. That did not bother him too much. His men were well dug in, and Russian soldiers fight with dogged determination when they are defending organized positions. But what had been in those large containers? Irina Yakoleva had reported that the American colonel had boasted that he had tanks. That seemed hard to believe, but Ulanov could take no chances.

He had only one weapon that might kill tanks, his RPG-7D rocket-propelled grenade launchers. He had sixteen left. They were now deployed in a classic anti-armor ambush in the bushes and long grass in front of the Russian positions, accompanied by snipers and mortar observers. It was all he could do, but he was nervous. Russian soldiers had not fought tanks since World War II. Would his men panic and run when they saw American tanks coming at them? Well, their grandfathers had stopped the German Panzers. Perhaps they could stop the Americans now.

Two minutes to go. Colonel Steiner stood in his Hummer. Its diesel engine was idling, ready to go. DeBerg was standing in the turret of his Sheridan, looking to the left and right, checking C Company's Sheridans. Steiner could hear him speaking into his radio.

"Company, start engines!"

A rumbling, coughing roar filled the air, as one after the other, the Sheridans' 300-horsepower Detroit Diesel 6V53T engines roared into life.

"Load, HE-FRAG!"

Steiner could hear the klack! of the breech and DeBerg's loader's voice, "HE-FRAG up!" The Sheridans' 152mm guns were loaded and ready to fire.

Sixty seconds. Steiner looked at the nearest Hummer. Long belts of gleaming brass cartridges dangled from the breeches of its .50 and .30 caliber machine guns. The Rangers manning the Hummer looked tense, but ready.

Thirty seconds. Steiner heard the American mortars open fire, and smoke and HE mortar bombs acred upward and dropped toward the Russian positions. De-Berg gestured at Steiner, half a wave, half a salute, and vanished into his Sheridan, slamming the turret hatch behind him.

Fifteen seconds. Steiner felt a sense of elation. The waiting was over. Time to fight. He knew he was not a perfect officer, but he knew his plan was good. He knew the Rangers would follow him, if for no other reason than because he would lead them into combat, not send them to fight. Steiner felt a knot of fear in his stomach. He knew he might be about to die. What the hell, if his number was up, he would rather die leading a Ranger battalion than any other way.

Five seconds! Ten of the Sheridans began to move forward ominously. The other Sheridans fired almost simultaneously; the muzzle blasts of the seven 152mm cannons merging into a single, great roar. Seven heavy HE-FRAG shells shot through the air and detonated in the Russian positions. Huge fountains of dirt and smoke shot upward. DeBerg was right. The Sheridans' 152mm cannons were extremely powerful.

Steiner grinned to himself. He knew they called him "Roaring Rudy" behind his back. There are times when it pays for a soldier to have a loud voice. He filled his lungs and shouted. His voice boomed out over the sounds of battle. "Come on, Rangers, let's go! Follow me!"

Rangers do not indulge much in cheering. Weapons ready, they moved, quiet and deadly, toward the Russian lines.

Dudorov was waiting quietly in the long grass. His RPG-7D was loaded with a PG-7M high-explosive anti-tank rocket grenade. He was glad Sharypa and Lieutenant Yakoleva were with him. You could always count on Sharypa in a tight place, and Dudorov thought Lieutenant Yakoleva was lucky. Perhaps she would bring him luck. If the Americans did have tanks, he would need all the luck he could get.

The plateau was deceptively peaceful. The only sounds were the sighing of the wind through the long grass and the mournful cries of a few sea birds circling overhead. Then, Dudorov heard a sound that no experienced combat soldier will ever forget. Tube noise. The American mortars were opening fire. That was not pleasant, but the next sounds were worse, sounds to freeze an infantryman's blood. The distant, muffled roar of many powerful engines starting and the unmistakable squeal and clack of tank treads. The American colonel had not lied. The Americans did have tanks, and they were coming straight at him.

Sharypa was speaking rapidly into the radio, sending target location data to the *Spetsnaz* mortar section. Something was moving out of the edge of the woods which marked the American position. A tank! Another and another! Dudorov peered through his RPG-7D's telescopic sight. The range must be seven hundred or eight hundred meters, far too long for RPG-7D fire, but he wanted to see what he had to face.

He stared at the magnified image in his sight. He was puzzled. He had studied tank recognition, all RPG grenadiers must. He would have recognized an American M1A1 or M60A3 main battle tank, or a British Challenger or German Leopard II, but this was strange and different. It was much smaller than he had expected, with only five roller wheels, and a squat appearance. But the gun! It was the largest cannon Dudorov had ever seen on a tank. Captain Chazov said you should always know and attack the weak points of the enemy tanks. But what in the devil's name was this?

"What kind of tank is that, Lieutenant?" Dudorov asked.

Irina Yakoleva thought hard. She had never seen a tank like that, but somewhere in a musty file she had seen a photograph of—. "It's an American Sheridan. The Australians tested them when they were fighting on the American side in Vietnam. The Australians rejected it because its cannon rounds are very vulnerable if the hull is penetrated, and the hull is weakly armored. Aim for the hull, Dudorov, aim for the hull!"

Dudorov smiled. You could always count on Lieutenant Yakoleva. She seemed to know everything. Very well, he would aim at the hull, but he would not fire yet. He remembered his training. The biggest weakness of a rocket-propelled weapon is the backblast and the smoke from the rocket motor when you fire. If your position is well chosen, the tanks do not know where you are until you fire. Once you fire, they will probably spot you, and tank crews hate antitank teams with a pure and burning passion. You had better make your first shot count.

The plateau was no longer peaceful. American mortars and heavy cannons were pounding the *Spetsnaz* position. Popov's mortars were firing rapidly, hurling 120mm high-explosive and smoke bombs at the advancing Americans. From the rocks and trees that formed their positions, the *Spetsnaz* .30 caliber PKM machine guns shot burst after burst at the American tanks and infantry. Dudorov could see yellow flashes, as .30 caliber bullets struck the leading Sheridan and ricocheted off its armor. Machine gun and mortar fire were not going to stop the tanks, but it might pin down their infantry and force them to seek cover. That would improve the chances of the RPG teams. Tanks alone are bad enough. Tanks and infantry attacking together are pure hell.

Now, the American tanks were three hundred meters away. Let them get a little closer. There were five of them, moving forward steadily. Fironov's team was to Dudorov's left, Orlov's team to the right. Three RPG-7D teams against five tanks. Long odds. Two hundred and fifty meters, two hundred; Dudorov saw a line of gray smoke streak toward the leading Sheridan. Orlov had fired. The PG-7M HE-AT rocket struck, and its 85mm warhead detonated in a yellow flash of fire on the front of the Sheridan's turret. Nothing happened. The jet of molten metal and white-hot gas had failed to penetrate the armor.

The Sheridan's turret swung menacingly toward Orlov's team. The .30 caliber machine gun mounted next to the tank's cannon began to chatter, sending burst after burst of .30 caliber bullets at the *Spetsnaz* team. Dudorov peered through his RPG-7D's optical sight. The range was less than two hundred meters. The Sheridan was turning toward Orlov's team. The left side of the tank was exposed. Dudorov aimed at the hull, directly beneath the turret, and fired. The PH-7M rocket grenade streaked toward the Sheridan. It struck and detonated in yellow flash. For a second, nothing seemed to happen. Then, the Sheridan shuddered. There was a tremendous explosion, then another, and another. The lance of molten metal and white-hot gas had struck the Sheridan's cannon shells and detonated them. A last, immensely violent explosion shattered the Sheridan's hull and blew the entire turret into the air in a flash of smoke and superheated flame.

Two more Sheridans turned toward Dudorov and ad-

vanced ominously, .30 caliber machine guns blazing.
Sharypa grasped a PH-7M grenade, pulled the safety
pin from the rocket's nose, and slid the long, thin motor
body into Dudorov's RPG. Fironov's team fired, and
a PG-7M rocket grenade burst low against the Sheridan's hull. The Sheridan jerked and ground to a halt.
The rocket had cut the tank's left tread. It was immobilized, but its weapons still worked. Its turret swung toward Fironov's team.

Dudorov aimed at the other Sheridan. In his telescopic sight, it seemed close enough to touch. The
image in his sight seemed to dissolve in orange flame.
The Sheridan had fired its cannon. The heavy HE-
FRAG shell struck thirty yards behind Dudorov. There
was a tremendous blast, and shell fragments whined
overhead. Steady, Dudorov, don't panic, aim! Dudorov
aimed at the front of the hull and fired. The rocket
whooshed out of the launcher and struck just below the
turret. The Sheridan staggered and stopped. The
hatches flew open, and the crew bailed out frantically.
Flame and smoke poured out of the open hatches.

Sharypa was reloading the RPG-7D as fast as he
could. Dudorov looked to his left. The immobilized
Sheridan was firing its .30 caliber machine gun in a
steady series of short bursts, searching for Fironov and
his team. Fironov popped up in a kneeling position, his
RPG-7D over his shoulder, ready to fire. Before he
could pull the trigger, the Sheridan's huge cannon
roared. It was a new and deadly type of round, like the
blast from an immense shotgun. A pattern of deadly
steel balls moving at high velocity tore into Fironov and
his team. The RPG-7D dropped from his dead hands.

Dudorov cursed. He aimed at the Sheridan's hull
through his PRO-7 optical sight and pulled the trigger.
He saw the yellow flash as the warhead detonated, but
nothing happened. The Sheridan's turret began to

swing menacingly toward Dudorov's team. He could see the huge, gaping black hole in the cannon's muzzle.

If he had been alone, Dudorov might have thrown down his RPG-7D and run, but Sharypa was frantically reloading, and Dudorov would rather die right there if it came to that, than run out on Sharypa. Sharypa would already have been running, but Dudorov was depending on him, and *Spetsnaz* troopers do not desert their comrades under fire. Irina Yakoleva was too busy shooting to think. She fired ten rounds of .30 caliber bullets from her SVD at the threatening Sheridan, hoping she might find a vulnerable spot. She snarled in fury and frustration as her bullets glanced harmlessly off its armor. She might as well be blowing kisses at the damned thing!

The Sheridan's turret stopped. The cannon seemed to be pointed straight at Dudorov's head. Sharypa shouted "Ready!" Dudorov fired. The PH-7M rocket shot toward the tank. The American gunner must have fired almost simultaneously. The image in Dudorov's optical sight went black. Something drove the sight back into his face like a blow from a giant's fist. Dudorov was stunned. He could hear Sharypa calling for the mortars to fire smoke. Irina Yakoleva was firing rapidly. Dudorov looked at his RPG-7D. It looked as if giant rats had been gnawing on it. It would never fire again.

Bullets were whining overhead. American infantry had reached the Sheridans and were firing their SAW light machine guns at the team. Dudorov grabbed his AKD-74 and began to fire back. A second wave of American infantry was advancing. A Hummer was in the middle of the group. Dudorov saw the tall, red-faced American colonel standing up in the vehicle, shouting orders, leading his men.

Irina Yakoleva saw Colonel Steiner, too. For a second she felt anger and elation. Then her sniper's instincts took over. First priority! Kill their senior officers! The cross hairs of her telescopic sight steadied on Colonel Steiner's chest. She felt no emotion. The angel of death is no more cool and implacable than a sniper when she fires. Irina squeezed the trigger. Her SVD sniper's rifle roared. The .30 caliber full-metal-jacketed bullet tore through Steiner's chest, killing him instantly. Irina fired the rest of her ten round magazine at the Hummer, hoping to knock it out.

Now 120mm mortar smoke bombs began to burst in front of the Americans. In seconds, they were shrouded in gray-white smoke. Sharypa thought furiously. What could they do? There were too many Americans. Could they—. What was that? There was a momentary lull in the roar of the battle. Sharypa heard the sound again. Tanks! A second wave of Sheridans was advancing. They would not stop them with rifles.

"We can't do anymore here," Sharypa shouted. "Come on, Lieutenant, come on, Dudorov, run for it!"

They ran as fast as they could, keeping low, back toward the Russian lines. Behind them they heard the rumble of engines and the squeal of tracks as the Sheridans advanced.

Major Muso Gozen peered through the drifting smoke, trying to see what was happening. He could tell by the sounds of the battle that something was wrong. The Sheridans had hit or been hit by something— mines, antitank missiles; at any rate the attack was stalled.

His radio crackled. His operator handed him the headset. Gozen heard a hoarse voice over the crackle of automatic rifles and machine guns. "Sergeant Thompson, Bravo Company, Major. The captain told me to tell you the attack is stalled. The Russians got several Sheridans with RPGs and—incoming!" Gozen heard the roar of exploding mortar bombs.

"Jesus Christ, that was close! Sorry, Major. Colonel Steiner's dead. A sniper got him. You're in command."

"Roger, Thompson. Tell your CO to hold on. I'm bringing up Alfa Company and the rest of the Sheridans."

The seven reserve Sheridans were moving forward in a widely spaced line. Gozen identified DeBerg's tank by the ID number painted on the hull. He stepped in front of the Sheridan and gave the stop signal. The Sheridan ground to a halt. The turret hatch clanged open, and DeBerg's head and shoulders appeared. Gozen clambered up the side of the Sheridan.

DeBerg's face was pale, but he did not appear to be panicked. "What's the situation, Captain?" Gozen asked.

"My assault platoons ran into an antitank ambush, RPG teams, I think. Seven Sheridans were knocked out. The other three are engaging the Russians at close range. Your two Ranger companies have come up and are supporting them, but the attack is stalled. I was moving forward to reinforce them. The RPG fire has slacked off. Maybe they've run out of rockets."

Maybe, but better not count on it.

"What are your orders, Major?" DeBerg asked.

"Let's do it by the book, Captain. Basic tank-infantry team attack. I'll assign a rifle squad to cover each of your tanks. Move slowly enough so that we can keep up with you. You take out the machine guns with your cannons. We'll take care of the RPG teams."

DeBerg nodded. "All right, Major, let's go." He spoke to his loader. "Load canister!"

The turret hatch slammed closed. The Sheridan started forward. Major Gozen nodded to himself grimly. It was a simple plan. Now, all they had to do was do it.

Colonel Ulanov peered grimly through his binoculars, trying to make sense of the situation. Smoke from mortar bombs and burning tanks drifted across the battlefield. His RPG teams had done well, but they had paid the price. The huge American tank guns were deadly at close range. Only three teams had come back.

Some of his men were cheering as they watched the Sheridans burn, but Ulanov did not deceive himself. There were many Sheridans left, and a full battalion of infantry. The Americans would attack again. It would be hard to stop them, perhaps impossible. Where in the devil's name were the reinforcements General Galanskov had promised?

They were moving through the smoke now. Major Gozen moved with DeBerg's Sheridan, staying close, but not too close. Gozen knew that infantrymen do not like hostile tanks. The Sheridans would draw fire like magnets as they closed in on the Russian lines. He threw himself down as a pair of 120mm mortar bombs burst thirty yards away. Fragments struck DeBerg's Sheridan and ricocheted off its armor. The Russians were firing blindly into areas where they knew the Americans had to be. Gozen took no comfort in that. If it happens to hit you, an unaimed round will kill you just as dead as one aimed with incredible precision.

It seemed a bit unfair that the Sheridan crews were protected by armor while Gozen and his men had nothing but their shirts. He banished that thought as unworthy. His ancestors had been samurai in Japan for a thousand years before they came to America. If there

303

is such a thing as a hereditary warrior, Gozen was it. If he was going to die, he was going to die. Besides, they were passing a burning Sheridan. The crew had not gotten out. Gozen lost all desire to be a tanker.

The smoke was thinning. They were coming out into the sunlight. The damned rock formation was two hundred yards ahead. The Russians were in a bad mood. Storms of machine gun and automatic rifles beat against the Americans. DeBerg's Sheridan suddenly fired. The seventeen-ton tank shook and vibrated and rocked back on its tracks. Hundreds of steel balls struck a *Spetsnaz* PKM machine gun crew like a giant shotgun blast. The Sheridan fired again. The gunner was using his 8-power telescopic sight. At two hundred yards he could not miss. A 152mm HE-FRAG shell struck another Russian machine gun position and exploded with tremendous force. Rocks and dirt shot skyward. The machine gun abruptly quit firing.

Ten Sheridans were firing now, blasting the Russian lines with their heavy 152mm shells aimed with deadly precision. The volume of fire from the Russian position slacked off as machine gun after machine gun was knocked out. It was an unfair fight. The Russian machine guns could not hurt the Sheridans. One round from a Sheridan's 152mm cannon was all it took to destroy a machine gun crew. Gozen felt sorry for the Russians, but not too sorry. After all, their machine gun teams were trying to kill him and his men, and no one had ever told him that war was fair.

The Rangers and the Sheridans were beginning to gain fire superiority. Weapons blazing, they closed in on the Russian positions.

Colonel Haldane was seething quietly. He was ten minutes late. It could not be helped. His men were moving quietly through the trees. In Vietnam the Viet Cong had called the Australian SAS "the phantoms of the jungle." Anyone who earned that nickname from the VC moves quietly indeed, but speed and quiet movement do not go hand in hand. At the moment they were waiting, while MacNair and Cord cleared a two-man observation post protecting the Russians' right flank. Haldane could hear the roar of battle to the south. It did not improve his disposition.

MacNair appeared in the trees ahead and gave the all-clear signal. The SAS slipped forward through the trees until MacNair signaled halt. Haldane eased his way forward until he was crouched by MacNair. The RSM pointed to the south. Forty yards away, Colonel Haldane could see a camouflaged machine gun position and several foxholes. They were occupied by men in mottled brown camouflages uniforms. *Spetsnaz!* They were on the right flank of the Russian position. The Russians were looking to the front and to the south. It was a pardonable error. Being attacked by a battalion of Rangers and a company of tanks attracts your attention forcibly; but it was likely to be a fatal error.

The SAS squadrons positioned their M60 machine guns and waited tensely. Haldane looked for Cord. He was lying prone a few yards away, studying the Russian positions through his mark II telescopic sight. Haldane moved quietly to Cord's side and pointed to the Russian machine gun team. Cord nodded and aligned his sights. Haldane looked to the left and right. Number Two Squadron and Number Three Squadron would make the attack. Everything was ready. Haldane touched Cord's shoulder lightly.

Cord took a deep breath, let half of it out, and squeezed the trigger. His Lee-Enfield roared. The Russian machine gunner went down instantly. Cord worked his bolt with blurring speed. The Lee-Enfield roared again. The Russian assistant gunner fell across the

PKM machine gun. The SAS opened fire, pouring burst after burst into the startled Russians. The assault teams moved forward and in seconds L2 hand grenades were bursting in the Russian positions. Taken by surprise, outnumbered and outgunned, the *Spetsnaz* platoon disintegrated and fell back on the main Russian position. Behind them, the SAS pushed forward, weapons blazing.

The situation in the rocks was a fair approximation of hell. The huge American tank cannons fired shell after shell, and the plunging fire as their mortar bombs rained down out of the sky was almost as deadly. The *Spetsnaz* team fought on grimly, with the total determination of Russian soldiers defending their last position, but Ulanov knew they were losing. You do not stop tanks with rifles. Suddenly, Ulanov heard heavy bursts of firing to the north. No one had to tell him what that meant. Flank attack! Ulanov knew what he had to do, but it was the bitterest decision of his life. Command is often like that. He filled his lungs and shouted. "Break contact! Break contact and fall back!"

Sharypa spoke rapidly into the radio. "Popov! Final protective fire! Do it now!"

The *Spetsnaz* team fired rapidly at the advancing Americans and Australians to pin them down for a vital minute. Popov's 120mm mortar bombs began to fall, screening the withdrawal. The *Spetsnaz* team began to stream out of their positions and to retreat toward the trees to the east. Ranger fire teams began to advance through the smoke into the rocks. In a minute or two it was over. The Americans and Australians controlled the only entrance to the plateau.

Chapter Twenty-Five

"We must hold our minds alert and receptive to the application of unglimpsed methods and weapons. The next war will be won in the future, not in the past. We must go on, or we will go under."

—Gen. Douglas MacArthur

ELU ISLAND—THE PLATEAU

Carter finished briefing Gregory and Walsh. Gregory nodded. "We understand, Captain. As soon as the *Wasp* gets here, the CH-53E helicopters will lift *War God* and fly it out to the ship. If that's not possible, we are to remove the key components, and they will be flown out. Just one question, how much weight can a CH-53E lift?"

Carter was proud of himself. He had not forgotten to ask about that. "A single CH-53E can lift sixteen tons. If you can get two slings on it, two CH-53Es could lift thirty-two tons, but that's the limit. It isn't practical to try and lift a new kind of load with three or more helicopters."

Gregory shook his head. "Then lifting the entire satellite is out of the question. We don't need the entire satellite anyway. A lot of it, the structure, the propulsion system, and the communications are pretty ordinary stuff. What we want is the laser, the laser's power supply, and, maybe, the control computers. That's where the advanced technology is. If we get those components, we'll have everything that's important. Do you agree, Laura?"

"I'm sorry, what did you say?"

Gregory repeated himself. Laura agreed. Gregory stuck his head inside one of *War God*'s access hatches and began to plan.

Laura Walsh appeared indifferent. She seemed listless and preoccupied. Carter was concerned. Perhaps it was only natural. Nothing in her life had prepared her for suddenly being thrust into a combat operation. Carter decided to try to cheer her up. She was vital to the success of the operation, and besides, he liked her, even if she did think he was a trifle dense.

"Don't worry, Dr. Walsh. It's all going to come out all right. *Wasp* will get here, and we'll take the key components back to the States. Think of the fun you will have playing around with it."

Laura smiled slightly. "Call me Laura," she said. "I'm sure you're right, Captain. The operation's going to be a big success. That's not my problem. It's me. A week ago, I would have told you I was Wonder Woman, tough as nails and afraid of nothing. Now, I know different. I never imagined anything like the battle, the machine guns, the mortars and the bombs, people getting killed. I was scared to death. I was literally shaking with fear. I've found out that I'm a coward, and I don't like it."

Carter smiled. That made Laura angry. He could at least have showed a little sympathy. "It's all right for you," she said. "Men like you, and Cord, and Jackson, you're not afraid. You're brave, but I'm not. I'm sorry. I don't like it, but I'm not."

Carter began to laugh. He laughed harder and harder. Laura was furious. She had told him the truth. Now he was laughing at her, enjoying her humiliation. Finally, he stopped.

"Laura, that's ridiculous! I'm scared, Jackson's scared, even Cord is scared. We're all scared. Anyone who isn't afraid of bombs and machine guns isn't brave, they're crazy. Welcome to the club! Being brave is just doing your job no matter how scared you get. I haven't seen you running away, screaming. Don't worry, you're as brave as any of us."

Laura smiled again. She hoped that it was true. Anyway, it was nice of Carter to have said it.

Gregory emerged from *War God*. "I think I've got it figured out," he said. "First, we take out the laser, then the power supply, and then anything else that looks useful. But we are going to have to open the forward doors. There's no other way to take out the laser and the power supply, the access hatches are too small. I think I see how to open her up. Do you want to take cover while I do it?"

There was no hesitation this time. Carter and Laura Walsh remembered the access doors vividly. They took cover. Gregory reached inside *War God* with an insulated probe. "Here we go!" He touched something. There was a muted hum of machinery, and *War God*'s forward doors swung open.

PLESETSK COSMODROME—PRIMARY CONTROL CENTER

Svetlana Snastina was sleeping on a cot in one corner of the control center. She was dreaming that she had met a charming young physicist who thought that she was wonderful. He was telling her all she had ever needed to know about high-energy particles. It was clear that they were going to win the Nobel Prize together and live happily ever after, when some fiend began to shake her shoulder.

Captain-Engineer Cherenavin was speaking urgently. "Wake up, Comrade Snastina, wake up! Comrade Sukhenkiy says something is happening. Please come to your console at once."

Svetlana got up and moved quickly to her control console. Vladimir Sukhenkiy was standing by the console. He did not waste words. He simply pointed at the display. Svetlana peered at the glowing letters on the screen. This was interesting. The flight control computer was active despite the command to shut down. The display changed as a new message was received and decoded:

—PLESETSK—WAR GOD FLIGHT CONTROL—NONSTANDARD UNAUTHORIZED ATTACK SEQUENCE OR TEST APPARENTLY UNDERWAY—LASER AND PRIMARY POWER SYSTEM READY—NO TARGET DATA OR FIRING AUTHORIZATION RECEIVED—INSTRUCTIONS?-

Sukhenkiy spoke quietly. "This started about three minutes ago, Svetlana. The Americans have opened *War God*'s forward doors. They are apparently trying to either test or disconnect and remove the laser. Can you do anything to stop them?"

Svetlana slipped into her chair and began to think furiously. Whatever they were doing, *War God*'s flight control computer was interpreting it as the start of a firing sequence. Very well, she would show them! Quickly, she typed a message on her console keyboard:

310

—WAR GOD FLIGHT CONTROL—PLE-
SETSK—EXECUTE FIRING SEQUENCE—
ACCEPT PLESETSK COMMANDS ONLY—
FIRING PATTERN TEST SIX—AUTHORI-
ZATION PASSWORD—SVETLANA-DEEDS
OF GLORY—FIRE ON MY COMMAND-

The coded message flashed upward from to Plesetsk
to *Cosmos 2009* and was instantly relayed to *War God.*

—ACKNOWLEDGED-READY—FOR   DI-
RECTED ATTACK SEQUENCE-

Svetlana reached for the Initiate Attack button. For
a second, she hesitated. She had never killed anyone.
She was about to do so now. War, to her, had always
been the abstract battle of machine versus machine in
the void of space. This was as personal as pulling a trigger.
   A vision flashed into her mind, that bitch, Laura
Walsh, in her whore's dress, triumphantly exhibiting
Svetlana's laser to a roomful of fawning American officials. Svetlana pushed the button.

ELU ISLAND—THE PLATEAU

Andy Carter and Laura Walsh stood in front of *War
God*'s open forward doors. Laura was peering intently
at the laser. Carter watched her work. Carter only
vaguely understood what he was seeing, but it was fasci-
nating to see it just the same. This was what it was all
about. He was here on Elu because of this thing. It gave
him an eerie feeling to stand in front of *War God*'s laser.
It was like looking down the barrel of a giant cannon.
   Gregory was doing something at the back of the laser,
working on the power supply. Suddenly, there was a

low-pitched, humming noise, and the laser mirror moved smoothly in its pointing gimbals.

Laura was startled. "Are you activating anything, Ed?"

"No, I was just checking the power supply connections. I—." Suddenly the humming became louder and louder, deepening in pitch. There was a loud crackling noise, and an electrical smell filled the air. "Get down!" Gregory shouted. "Hit the dirt, get down!"

Laura froze. Carter did not hesitate. He threw both arms around Laura and hurled her to the ground. He heard an earsplitting, ripping, cracking sound. He looked up. A ten-foot-diameter, pale blue beam of light was shooting out of *War God*'s laser, pointing straight ahead from the huge cylinder. The beam stopped, and the laser mirror swung smoothly to a new pointing angle.

"Run!" Gregory shouted. "Run, get back against the side. Quick! Run!"

Carter did not stop to ask questions. He pulled Laura to her feet and dived for *War God*'s side. He heard the ripping, cracking sound as the laser fired again. He dragged Laura farther back, staying close to *War God*'s side. He did not know what would happen to a man caught in that pale blue beam. He had no desire to find out. He hugged *War God*'s side as the ripping, crackling noise filled the air and the pale blue beam raved out again and again. Carter was fascinated by what he saw. It was like a giant swinging an immense, blue sword around his head in deadly arcs. No wonder the Russians had named it *War God*.

Suddenly, the laser stopped firing. There was a deafening silence. Then, Carter heard Gregory shout. "Keep down! I'm going to pull the control cables. There, now they can't fire the damned thing again." Thank God for small favors. Carter would be extremely happy if he never saw another high-frequency laser in his life.

Gregory emerged from *War God*'s side as Carter and Laura Walsh stood up.

"What the hell happened?" Carter asked.

"The Russians must have detected that the forward doors were open and that we were working with the laser. They commanded it to fire in a pattern that swept out a hemisphere. If you hadn't moved fast, they would have gotten you; but once you were behind the laser, you were safe. It's interlocked, so that it can't fire to the rear and hit its own structure. But if you had been in the path of the beam, you would have been killed. You wouldn't be dead yet, but you would have been hit by a fatal dose of gamma radiation. Nothing could be done about it. You would have died in a few hours."

Wonderful! It gave Carter a strange feeling. He was used to people trying to kill him. It went with his job; but the thought that some Russian ten thousand miles away had pushed a button and nearly killed him was particularly unnerving. It did bring up one question.

"I thought you and Laura said the laser wouldn't work in the atmosphere, and that's why the Russians had to test it in space. I'm no rocket scientist, but it sure as hell seemed to be working perfectly a minute ago."

Gregory smiled. "I guess I wasn't precise. The laser will work perfectly in the atmosphere, but air absorbs gamma radiation. You couldn't attack a target in space with a gamma ray laser mounted on the earth's surface. The energy would be absorbed before it got there. At three or four thousand yards, it's probably harmless; but at two or three feet it will fry you. In space, there's no air to worry about. There, you could probably kill a satellite or a missile at fifty thousand miles or more. Anyway, I think I've pulled its fangs."

Laura did not look happy. The thought that someone ten thousand miles away had just tried to kill her was particularly unpleasant. Investigating *War God* no longer seemed like a wonderful adventure. She forced herself to put it out of her mind. She had a question. "Ed, you said you pulled some cables. How did you know which cables to disconnect?"

"I found what has to be a local control panel for testing. It's connected to a black box that must be the control computer. There are four cables running from the computer to the base of the laser. Commands to the laser must go through those cables. When they're disconnected, the Russians can send all the commands they want to, and the laser won't respond. Listen, Laura, this panel has a lot of labels and instructions on it. You read Russian. Take a look, and tell me what it says."

Laura wriggled into one of the side access hatches.

Carter was left outside, listening to the conversation and admiring Laura's wriggle.

"I want to get the laser disconnected from the power supply before we do anything else," Gregory said. "See that switch? I think it controls the flow of power from the nuclear reactor to the laser power supply. I'm going to shut it off. That should shut down the laser power supply. Once that's done, I'll disconnect the power supply from the laser, and we can get ready to take the laser out. What do you think, Laura?"

Laura shrugged. She knew a great deal about lasers, not nearly so much about the rest of the satellite. Gregory was the expert there. She looked at the legends on the panel. Gregory's analysis looked good.

"It sounds good to me, Ed. Let's do it."

"All right. Reactor power switch off."

Carter heard a crackle of electricity. Instantly, an alarm began to wail. Then, Carter heard a strange woman's voice speaking emphatically in a foreign language. The alarm continued to wail. The woman spoke again.

"Jesus Christ!" Laura shrieked. "Svetlana Snastina!"

Carter was baffled. He had heard of Jesus Christ, of course, but who or what was Svetlana Snastina?

"Put the power back on, Ed! For God's sake put it back on! It's antimatter! They're using antimatter, and we've just cut the containment field power! Get it back on, Ed!"

Gregory did not stop to argue. Instantly, he pushed the switch back to the on position. "Reactor power switch on." The alarm stopped wailing. The woman's voice spoke again. Then, everything was still, except for the muted hum of *War God*'s equipment. "All right," Gregory said, "everything seems to be back under control. What was all that about, Laura?"

"We cut off electrical power from the nuclear reactor to the laser's power supply. It holds antimatter. The antimatter is contained by a powerful electromagnetic field. The alarm was to warn us. Nothing happened because they used a fail-safe design. The emergency power batteries took over, but they can only supply the required power until they are drained. I don't know how long that would be. It might be minutes. It could be a few hours. But when the batteries run down, there's going to be one hell of an explosion."

Gregory looked dubious. "Are you sure, Laura? Couldn't there be any other explanation?"

"I'm absolutely certain. That recorded voice you heard was a Russian engineer, Svetlana Snastina. I've met her. The little bitch is one of their leading high-frequency laser experts. She probably led the team that designed the laser. What she said was 'Emergency! Emergency! Condition Red! Primary containment power to the laser power supply is off. Antimatter fuel is loaded. Containment power is now being supplied from emergency batteries. Restore primary containment power immediately! If this cannot be done, evacuate the launch complex immediately!' Then, it just repeated until you switched reactor power back on. I don't think there can be any doubt, Ed."

"No, you're right." Gregory whistled softly. "Evacuate the entire launch complex! They do expect one hell of an explosion. Better get on the SATCOM and find out what the great thinkers in Washington want us to do. I'm pretty sure I can disconnect the laser from its power supply. That's OK. But do they really want us to put that power supply on the *Wasp?* If we do, and we lose antimatter containment power, there won't be any *Wasp.*"

Andy Carter and Laura Walsh stepped into the cover of the lush green trees behind *War God*'s rear and started for the command post. It would have been unwise to stroll along in the open. The Russians were less than a thousand yards away, and it would not do to irritate an alert Russian machine gunner. Carter was burning with curiosity. He had not wanted to ask questions when Gregory and Laura were working. Now seemed like a good time.

"Laura, what is this antimatter you and Ed were talking about? Why is it so important, and why are you afraid it will blow up?"

"Do you know what antimatter is?"

"Well, it's something you read about in science fiction. Antimatter universes, that sort of thing, but you and Ed are talking like it's real."

"It is real. Everything is made up of atoms, the trees, the ground we're standing on, the air, the entire earth. The matter around us is made up of atoms. All of these atoms are made up of three types of subatomic particles: protons, neutrons, and electrons. The protons and neutrons are the heavy particles, eighteen hundred times more massive than electrons. They are at the center of the atom in the nucleus. The electrons orbit around the nucleus like the moon around the earth. The proton has a positive electrical charge; the electron has a negative charge. Neutrons have no charge. All the matter we think of as normal is this way, made up atoms consisting of protons, neutrons, and electrons. Do you understand that?"

"Of course," Carter said, and he did. After all, he had passed chemistry at West Point. Only with a C, of course, but he had passed. Laura nodded. It was good that he was not totally illiterate.

"But, there is another kind of matter. There is a particle like an electron, but with a positive electrical charge. We call it a positron, or an antielectron. They are not imaginary. Anderson detected them in 1932. Similarly, there are antiprotons, particles just like a normal proton except that they have a negative charge, and there are antineutrons. The antiparticles form atoms of antimatter, with antiprotons and antineutrons in the nucleus and orbital antielectrons. There is nothing unnatural or unstable about antimatter, Andy. In fact, some scientists think that half the matter in the universe is antimatter, but, under natural conditions, it can't exist here on earth."

Carter was puzzled. "All right. I've never heard of these antiparticles, Laura, but I'll take your word for it. But if antimatter is natural and stable, what's the big deal, and why can't it exist on earth?"

"Because," Laura said softly, "if an electron encounters an antielectron, or a proton encounters an antiproton, they will annihilate each other, and the mass of the two particles will be completely converted into pure energy." She paused for a second. "And it will be gamma ray energy, Andy, pure one hundred percent gamma ray energy."

"Jesus Christ! And *War God*'s weapon is a gamma ray laser!"

"That's right, and the amount of energy released in matter-antimatter mutual annihilation is immense. We think that hydrogen fusion in our hydrogen bombs is powerful, but it converts less than one percent of the fusing matter into energy. Matter-antimatter mutual annihilation will convert one hundred percent of the colliding mass into pure gamma ray energy. We can make small amounts of antimatter in our laboratories. It disappears almost instantly when it contacts normal matter. But the Russians have discovered a way to make antimatter in quantity and store it for long periods of time. That's what's inside *War God*'s laser power supply right now, pounds of antimatter. All they have to do is react small amounts of antimatter with normal matter and they generate enormous amounts of pure gamma ray energy to power the laser. No wonder the God damned thing is so powerful."

Carter shook his head. "That just can't be, Laura. I've seen Ed touch that thing with tools and with his hands. If the power supply is made of antimatter, wouldn't that cause an explosion?"

"No, you don't understand. The laser power supply isn't made of antimatter, it contains antimatter. The outer shell is normal matter. The antimatter is inside, in a vacuum, contained by powerful electromagnetic fields. The fields keep it from touching the normal matter container. But if the power to maintain those electromagnetic fields goes off and stays off for a few seconds, the antimatter will contact the normal matter container walls, and you'll have one hell of an explosion."

"Just how powerful, Laura?"

"I don't know exactly. There are too many factors involved, but very powerful. You wouldn't want to be within miles of *War God* if that thing detonates. It could conceivably destroy the whole island."

SPETSNAZ TEAM—ELU ISLAND—THE PLATEAU

Major Yegor Mamin sat in the *Spetsnaz* command post fighting to stay awake. The heat and the humidity were awful. To a man born in northern Russia, Elu was an excellent imitation of hell. Colonel Ulanov was asleep. With Captain Chazov wounded, Ulanov had had no choice but to leave Mamin in command. It was true that Ulanov had ordered Mamin to call him instantly if anything happened; but for the moment, Mamin was in command of the *Spetsnaz* Team.

A light blinked on the SATCOM radio. The operator put on his headset, listened, and spoke to Mamin. "Message from Moscow, Major. A Colonel Kirilenko wants to speak to the commanding officer. Shall I wake the colonel?"

Mamin shook his head. He did not particularly like Ulanov, but an exhausted colonel would be of little use to anyone. Mamin was not afraid of responsibility. At least, he could take a message. He took the headset.

"Major Mamin here."

"Mamin? Has something happened to Colonel Ulanov?"

"He is asleep, Colonel. He is very tired. However, I will call him if you wish."

"That will not be necessary, Mamin. You are the acting commander; that is satisfactory. I have a message from General Galanskov. The scientists say that the Americans are inside *War God* investigating the equipment. You are ordered to do anything you can to stop

319

or delay them. Do not, of course, damage the satellite. Do you understand the order?"

Mamin swore to himself. Just how in the devil's name were they supposed to do that, send the Americans a threatening letter? "Exactly so, Comrade Colonel. We carry out General Galanskov's orders without question."

Mamin considered the options. The only weapons the *Spetsnaz* team had which could reach *War God* with accurate, sustained fire were the 120mm heavy mortars. It had been clever of Ulanov to bring them. Mamin was not an expert on mortars. He was not sure if they could do what Moscow wanted. Well, he could find out.

He spoke to the radio operator. "I am going down to the mortar position. I will have a radio with me. Call me at once if anything happens."

SPETSNAZ TEAM MORTAR POSITION—ELU ISLAND

Sergeant Popov looked around quickly as Major Mamin approached. The devil! It was the *Zampolit!* Well, there was nothing for him to complain about. The mortars were dug in and camouflage, and the men were at work improving the position and checking the ammunition resupply. Still, a visit from a political officer usually means trouble. Popov saluted smartly as Mamin came toward him.

"*Starshiy Serzhant* Popov reports to the *Mayor.*" Mamin returned Popov's salute. He did not know Popov personally, but he knew the type well. Popov was an old and experienced soldier. As they say in the Russian army, "He had eaten bread cooked on every kind of stove." He would carry out orders to the letter, but he would not assume any responsibility he could avoid.

Mamin put on a friendly smile. "At ease, Sergeant.

320

I need your advice on the employment of the mortars. You, after all, are the expert."

Popov relaxed. He knew he was being flattered, but he knew 120mm mortars forward and backward, and he had memorized the regulations governing their employment. No *Zampolit* could catch him out when it came to mortars. He listened intently as Major Mamin explained the problem.

"I understand, Major. We cannot use high-explosive mortar bombs. The fragments would damage the satellite. We could fire smoke. That would harass them a bit, but if they are determined, it will not stop them. But there is something else. Look here, sir."

Popov led Mamin to a cargo canister full of mortar bombs which had been carefully placed fifty meters away from the 120mm mortars. Mamin glanced at the bombs. They did not appear to be different from the ready bombs near the mortars.

"These came in the ammunition resupply that the navy aircraft dropped yesterday, Major. They came from Vietnamese army inventory. They sent us a little surprise. Look here, see the purple bands on the bombs? These are chemical bombs, blood gas to be precise. It will kill anyone without a gas mask in sixty seconds. It is very effective. We used it in Afghanistan. I assume you do not care if we kill a few Americans?"

Mamin smiled grimly. "Not at all, Popov. The more you kill, the better I will like it. Kill them all, if you can. How soon can you open fire?"

"Well, sir, regulations clearly state that chemical bombs can only be used on the specific authorization of a senior officer."

Mamin smiled again. He would have bet a thousand rubles that Popov would say that. "Is a major senior enough for you, Sergeant, or shall I call the colonel?"

Popov saluted smartly. "That will not be necessary, Major. I carry out your orders without question!"

He turned to his section. "Fire mission! Prepare to fire chemical bombs!" The mortar crews ran to their weapons, pulling on their ShMS gas masks as they ran. The loaders ran to the chemical bomb container and began to carry the 120mm gas bombs to the mortars.

Popov put on his own ShMS. His voice was distorted by the mask, but it was understandable. "Ready to fire gas bombs in sixty seconds!"

ELU ISLAND—THE PLATEAU

Gregory was working inside *War God*'s forward doors. He was studying the huge laser and the large bolts that attached it to *War God*'s structure. He had a set of metric torque wrenches in his kit bag outside. They ought to handle the bolts. He was getting enthused. The laser was a wonderful thing. He could hardly wait to get it back to the States and test it. He was less happy about the power supply. If Laura was right, it was a very dangerous thing, indeed. Well, perhaps the boys in Washington would have some words of wisdom for him.

He stepped out into the sunlight. A soft breeze was blowing from the southwest. Thank God. It made things a little cooler. He saw Laura coming back from the command post and waved to her. Suddenly, without warning, he heard a sound like a giant coughing. Incoming mortar fire! Gregory threw himself down flat. He heard twin thuds as the mortar bombs hit the ground. He waited for the blasts, but nothing happened. Duds? He heard soft popping noises, as if very small explosive charges had fired. Maybe they were smoke rounds. He risked a quick glance. Nothing. He heard two thuds as more bombs struck, burying themselves half way into the hard ground. Again he heard the soft popping

322

sounds and saw the sides of the bombs split open. He saw an odd shimmer in the air, as if something nearly transparent was moving toward him, carried by the breeze.

Then he knew. Gregory leaped to his feet. Too late. The odorless, colorless gas had reached him. His eyes and throat were suddenly burning. He tried to run, but his muscles were convulsing, and he fell to the ground. He saw Laura staring at him from thirty yards away. She did not know what had happened.

Gregory took one last, deep breath. The gas seared his lungs. With his last ounce of strength, he shouted desperately: "Gas! Gas! Run Laura, run! Ga—." He lost consciousness. In a few seconds, he was in a coma. Sixty seconds later, he was dead.

Laura ran as fast as she could, holding her breath desperately. Her heart was pounding, there was a roaring in her ears, and her lungs were burning. Her body was telling her she must breath or die. Her mind knew that to breath might be to die horribly, as she had seen Ed Gregory die. She staggered on, fighting to resist the terrible temptation to breathe. She collapsed and fell hard. The breath whoosed out of her body as she instinctively gasped for air. She lay there, gasping, waiting in horrible anticipation. She did not know what poison gas felt like, or how fast it acted. Nothing happened. She was breathing Elu's hot and humid air, nothing else, thank God!

She forced herself to get up and stagger on. Carter had to know the Russians were using gas. She was out of shape for running in one hundred degree heat and ninety percent humidity. She was about to collapse again as she reached the command post. A Special

Forces corporal she did not know caught her as she was about to fall again.

"Gas!" Laura gasped. "The Russians are using poison gas. Tell Captain Carter. Gas!"

The corporal did not waste time in conversation. He reached into a pouch on his belt, took out a gas mask and hood, and pulled them over his head. As soon as his mask was in place, he shouted, "Gas! Gas!" Laura saw other soldiers putting on gas masks and taking up the warning cry. Laura watched, feeling alone and isolated. They were taking her warning seriously, but what about her? She tried not to panic, but it was hard. How fast does gas spread? She looked back toward *War God*. She saw nothing, but the damned stuff was invisible. What could she do? Was any place safe?

She felt hands on her shoulders and turned around. Andy Carter was there, wearing a mask and hood. He held out something in his hands. His voice was distorted by the mask, but his words were clear. "Here, Laura, this is an M40 gas mask. Put it on. That's right. Here, let me help you with the straps. Now, take a deep breath, breathe out hard. It's all right now, just breathe normally, and tell me what happened."

Laura gasped out her story. ". . . then he had convulsions and he died. He died trying to save my life. I feel horrible. God damn those Russians! How can they do a thing like that?"

Carter had no answer. His mind was concentrated on what he had to do. Thank God he had enough sense to bring chemical warfare equipment. If the Russians were using nerve gas, gas masks alone would not do the trick. He went to a nearby equipment canister and pulled out an M43A1 Detector Unit and an M42 Alarm Unit. He connected the two units and activated them. Together, they constituted an automatic chemical agent alarm system. If there was gas in the area, the

M43A1 would detect it, and the M42 would flash a light and sound an audible alarm. The alarm remained silent. Good, no gas in the CP area.

Now, for the bad part. Carter had been through chemical warfare training, and he had paid attention. Ever since the Russians had used chemical weapons in Afghanistan, he had known that someday his unit might be hit with them. He thought he knew his protective equipment and how to use it. He was about to find out if he was right. He was not sure what kind of gas the Russians had used. Laura's description of Ed Gregory's symptoms could indicate a blood gas or a nerve gas. If it was a blood gas, Gregory was dead. If it was a nerve gas, he would die soon unless someone administered the antidote. Someone had to go find out. Carter did not want to go. He would much rather face machine guns than poison gas, but he was the best-trained man available. Someone had to be him.

He took his protective gear from the canister and began to put it on. He pulled on the protective socks and overboots and his glove liners and protective gloves. Next, he put on the protective suit and sealed it. The charcoal-impregnated polyurethane suit liner and the Buytl rubber gloves and boots, combined with his M40 gas mask and hood, should protect him against any known chemical agent.

Carter was now in Mission-Oriented Protective Posture 4, the highest degree of chemical warfare protection a U.S. soldier can achieve. He was also hideously uncomfortable. The suit did not provide air or cooling. It merely shut Carter off from the outside air except for the air he breathed through his gas mask filters. In Elu's heat and humidity, wearing MOPP 4 was cruel and unusual punishment, but it was not nearly as bad as what happens to you when you are hit by nerve gas and are not wearing MOPP 4.

Carter picked up the alarm and walked slowly toward *War God.* He must exert himself as little as possible. He was in serious danger of passing out from heat prostration. Don't panic, Carter, slow and easy does it.

He reached *War God.* Gregory lay a few feet away. The warning light on the M42 Alarm Unit began to flicker, indicating that there was a low concentration of gas in the area. Carefully, Carter knelt down by Gregory and felt for a pulse. There was none. Gregory's face and lips were a bluish purple color. He was obviously dead. A blood gas, then, hydrogen cyanide or cyanogen chloride. It did not matter much. Both will kill you very dead very quickly.

Carter opened his M43A1 Chemical Agent Detector Kit and took out the sampler-detector. He crushed the test ampoules and wet the test spots on the special test paper. He waited until one of the test spots changed color. He was right. The test indicated blood gas. He waited a little longer, keeping his eyes on the nerve gas spot. It would not be amusing if he unsealed his suit only to find that the Russians had used more than one kind of gas. The spot did not change. Blood gas only.

Carter walked slowly back to the command post. He noted approvingly that everyone was still masked and that several more automatic alarms had been set up. He gave the command to unmask and went quickly to Laura Walsh. "I'm sorry, Laura, Ed was dead. There was nothing I could do for him. They're using hydrogen cyanide. Your M40 mask will protect you from that. You have to get back to *War God* and disconnect the laser. I'll get some of the combat engineers to help you."

Laura was already pale. She turned paler and began to tremble. She remembered the look on Ed Gregory's face when he died. She would cheerfully have gone to hell rather than go back to *War God* and face that damned gas. "I don't know if I can do that, Andy. I'm scared to death of that stuff."

"You've got to go, Laura. The rest of us can do what you tell us to do, but you're the only one who knows what to do. If we don't get that damned laser, a lot of good men have died for nothing. You've got to go."

Damn him! But he was right. She trembled with fear, but she put her M40 gas mask back on. "All right," Laura said, "I'll go."

RAAF AMBERLY—NUMBER 82 STRIKE WING—RAAF

The confectioner was sleeping deeply, but not peacefully. He was dreaming that his wife and his girlfriend had met by chance at a party and were beginning to compare notes. It was only a matter of time until—. He awakened with a start. Someone was knocking insistently on his door. He flicked on the light. Bloody hell! Three o'clock in the morning!

"What is it?" the confectioner snarled. At least it was a polite snarl.

"Sorry to disturb you, Wing Leader. The air marshal is on the secure line. He says he must speak to you immediately."

Bloody hell, what now? The confectioner pulled on his shoes and staggered to the ops room. He picked up the phone and managed a semipolite "Marks here, sir."

"Ah, yes, Bob. I am sorry to disturb you. Let me say first that you and your squadrons did an outstanding job on Elu. The Americans cannot say enough about the air support you provided them."

"Thank you, sir," the confectioner said. He was pleased, but he did not think the air marshal had called at 3:00 A.M. just to tell him that. He waited for the penny to drop.

"Bob, we have just received word from the Americans that the Russians are preparing a major strike against our forces and the American forces on Elu. Large numbers of transports and combat aircraft are flying into Cam Ranh Bay. Our intelligence people confirm this. It looks like an all-out effort. The Americans have asked us for all possible support, and, of course, the Australian SAS is on Elu, too. I know you and your men are tired, and your F-111Cs need maintenance. But we need a maximum effort. Can you have all available aircraft in the air at dawn this morning?"

The confectioner thought for a moment. His aircrews were tired. F-111Cs are complex machines with many moving parts and complicated electronics systems, difficult to maintain. His ground crews were working round the clock, getting the Wing's aircraft ready to fly again. It would not be easy, but Number 82 Strike Wing could do it. "Piece of cake, sir," the confectioner said.

Chapter Twenty-Six

"The purpose of a United States Navy nuclear attack submarine is to strike fear and terror into the hearts of our enemies."   —Adm. Hyman Rickover

USS LOS ANGELES—NORTHEAST OF ELU

Los Angeles was appraoching Elu from the northeast. For nearly three days, she had been sprinting and scanning, advancing for an hour or two at thirty knots, then slowing to a crawl for a half hour while her sonar operators conducted a thorough search in all directions. They had detected nothing of any importance.

Everything had worked perfectly during her long run toward Elu, but Comdr. Carl Pedersen was not a happy man. No submarine captain who has to make a long, high-speed run under combat conditions ever is. *Los Angeles* was a 688 class submarine, and they are very quiet, indeed, but not at thirty knots. Pedersen had been running at eight hundred feet, where water pressure would minimize propeller cavitation noise, but he could do nothing about the noise from the reactor-cooling water pumps. At any speed above fifteen knots, they must be working steadily, pumping cooling water in and out of *Los Angeles*'s SG6 nuclear reactor.

The closer *Los Angeles* got to Elu, the more nervous Pedersen became. It was all too easy to imagine a Soviet Victor waiting in *Los Angeles*'s path. It would be moving slowly and quietly, listening intently, with a salvo of 26-inch advanced antisubmarine torpedoes ready in her tubes.

It was time to slow down. Roaring up to Elu at thirty knots would be an elaborate means of committing suicide, and Commander Pedersen was not the suicidal type. He ordered Engineering to slow to twelve knots. The control rods slid deeper into the reactor, and *Los Angeles* began to slow as steam pressure dropped and her propeller began to turn more slowly. Now, the reactor cooling pumps were shut off. At this speed, enough cooling water was circulated by natural convection currents to make the pumps unnecessary. *Los Angeles* became very quiet, indeed.

Now, it was time to deploy the BQR-25 towed sonar array. Pedersen gave the order, and the three hundred–foot-long linear array slid smoothly out of the fairing on the right side of the hull. Soon, the long, thin cylindrical array was being towed along, a thousand feet behind *Los Angeles*'s stern.

Pedersen ordered the helmsman to turn *Los Angeles* so that the towed array faced toward Elu. At eight hundred feet, *Los Angeles* was in the middle of the deep sound channel. Pedersen glanced at the instruments which displayed water temperature and salinity. Sonar conditions were almost ideal. If there were something there to detect, *Los Angeles*'s sonar should detect it. Slowly, the data came up on the Mark 117 Fire Control System display screens. Nothing. Pedersen sipped his coffee. What next? If he were the skipper of that Russian Echo class submarine, what would he do? Perhaps patrol quietly, at very low speed, north of the island. He ordered another course change to align the towed array to scan north of Elu. If that were the case, then—.

The leading sonar operator spoke suddenly. "Possible contact, Captain. At long range. Approximate bearing 140."

Pedersen glanced quickly at the Mark 117 FCS weapons status display. *Los Angeles* had only four 21-inch torpedo tubes. That was one of the few tactical weaknesses of the 688 class. She carried several types of torpedoes and missiles in her torpedo room, but only four could be loaded and ready to fire at any one time.

The weapons display indicated that all four tubes were loaded, Harpoon submarine-launched antiship missiles in One and Two, and Mark 48 Advanced Capability torpedoes in Three and Four. If the contact were a submarine, only the Mark 48 ADCAPS were likely to be useful. Harpoons cannot be used against underwater targets. They would be effective against a submarine only if it were on the surface.

"Positive contact, Captain. Nuclear-powered submarine running deep and at high speed." Data was flowing into the Mark 117's computers. They were analyzing every detail of the signal and plotting the possible target's course. The initial plot came up. A line extended from the contact toward Elu. It was not precise, but it was enough. There were no friendly submarines within a thousand miles of Elu. Pedersen turned to the navigator. "Give me a ROUTE CALC to intercept the contact, speed not to exceed twelve knots."

He pushed the intercom button. "Torpedo room, this is the captain. Unload Harpoons from One and Two. Reload with Sea Lance missiles." The navigator finished his calculations. *Los Angeles*'s blunt bow swung smoothly towards the predicted intercept point. *Los Angeles* was headed into battle.

70 LETTS USSR—NORTHWEST OF ELU

70 Letts USSR was moving steadily toward Elu, her 6,300 tons being driven at thirty knots by her twin nuclear reactors. *70 Letts USSR* was a Victor III, one of the newest and deadliest nuclear attack submarines in the Soviet navy. Her name meant 70th anniversary of the Soviet Union. Her captain and her crew were proud of their boat and excited by their special mission.

Captain 2nd Rank Kirichenko stood in *70 Letts USSR*'s control center, studying the situation plot. *70 Letts USSR* was fifty miles from Elu now. He must make his decision soon. It would be dangerous to get too close to Elu while still making thirty knots. The question was how close to get before slowing down. The admiral had stressed the critical importance of the mission; it would not do to be too cautious. Pallitsyn, in *Krasnogvardets,* had already reduced speed to ten knots and was deploying his towed array for a complete sonar scan. Well, let him. It made no sense for the two Victors to move together. Pallitsyn was a competent officer, but at times he acted like an old woman, not a Soviet attack submarine commander.

Kirichenko glanced up. Someone was looking over his shoulder: Lieutenant Seregin, the *Zampolit.* Kirichenko smiled. Seregin was not so bad as political officers go. It would not hurt to impress him favorably. It would be excellent if his report stressed Captain Kirichenko's skill, aggressiveness, and devotion to duty.

"We are almost there, Seregin. Look at the board. There is Elu. Here we are. Shortly, we will slow down and start patrolling. We are ready for action. All tubes are loaded. We have Type 68 wire-guided homing torpedoes in One and Two, Type 65 antiship homing torpedoes in Three and Four, and self-defense decoys in Five and Six, just in case there is a Yankee submarine out here. As you can see, we are ready for anything."

Seregin was impressed. Kirichenko appeared to be carrying out the mission in a bold, but well-prepared manner. "Excellent, Captain. You are carrying out the admiral's orders in an exact and precise manner. He will be pleased."

Kirichenko smiled to himself. *Yes, and your masters at the KGB will have nothing to complain about. That thought made up his mind. 70 Letts USSR* would stay at thirty knots a while longer.

KRASNOGVARDETS—NORTHWEST OF ELU

Ten miles to the north, *Krasnogvardets* was running quietly at ten knots. Her reactor cooling pumps were shut down, and Captain 2nd Rank Pallitsyn was deploying her towed array from the housing in *Krasnogvardets*'s stern. *Krasnogvardets* was a Victor III, like *70 Letts USSR*. She did enjoy one advantage. During her last overhaul, her propellers had been replaced with the new Toshiba models. She was now much quieter than before. *70 Letts USSR* had not received the new superquiet propellers. It made a significant difference. *Krasnogvardets* was much quieter and harder to detect at low speeds.

This made Captain Pallitsyn happy. He believed that the captains of quiet submarines have the best chance of surviving to write their patrol reports. Now, the towed array was fully deployed three hundred meters behind *Krasnogvardets*'s stern. Pallitsyn watched as his sonar operators began their search. *Krasnogvardets* means Red Guardsman. Pallitsyn often used the name to remind his crew that they must always be on their guard. Perhaps they were a bit tired of hearing it, but he did not care. If there were American 688s off Elu, it was critical that *Krasnogvardets* detect them before they detected her.

USS LOS ANGELES–EN ROUTE TO ELU IS-LAND

Commander Pedersen studied the situation display intently. The contact was still roaring along toward Elu at thirty knots. He touched a key, and a circle appeared about the Own Ship symbol which showed *Los Angeles*'s position. The circle indicated the maximum range of the Sea Lance UUM-125 missiles that were now loaded and ready in tubes One and Two. The Hostile Submarine symbol, which indicated the contact's position, showed it moving steadily closer and closer inside the circle. Pedersen made a quick calculation. Preparing the torpedo tubes for firing made a certain amount of unavoidable noise. Firing the Sea Lances would make more, but at thirty knots, the contact was unlikely to hear it. The self-induced noise of moving a large submarine through the water at thirty knots would greatly reduce the contact's passive sonar performance.

The contact was less than forty miles from Elu. He might slow down and go quiet at any minute. Time to make a decision. That's what the navy paid him to do.

He spoke to the leading sonar operator. "What have we got, Chief?"

"The computer says it's a Soviet nuclear attack submarine, either a Victor or an Akula, Captain."

Pedersen nodded. Computers are wonderful things, but he still believed in human judgment. "What do you think, Chief?"

The sonar operator smiled. The Swede was the kind of captain he liked. "Well, Captain, its got two reactors and one shaft with two tandem four-blade co-rotating propellers. It's a Victor III, can't be anything else."

That was enough for Pedersen. For once, somebody

in Washington had had the intelligence to issue sensible rules of engagement. He did not need anyone's permission to fire. He pushed the intercom button. "Torpedo room, ready One and Two for immediate firing."

The outer doors of torpedo tubes One and Two slid smoothly open. The two Sea Lance missiles waited silently in their protective capsules as the final checks were made. On the weapons status display console in the attack center, the ready lights came on. Pedersen gave the order. "Fire One!"

"One Fired!"

He waited twenty seconds. Sea Lances are complex weapons. Be sure that Number One is working before Number Two is fired. Now! "Fire Two!"

"Two Fired!"

The first Sea Lance shot smoothly forward from Number One torpedo tube. A sensor calculated its forward motion. When it had cleared *Los Angeles*'s long, black hull, the solid propellant rocket booster ignited, and its guidance system steered the missile toward the surface. It reached the surface and broached, rising rapidly on a pillar of spray and fire. Twenty seconds later, Number Two emerged and followed Number One at supersonic speed. The two Sea Lances roared toward their present target, arcing through the sky on ballistic trajectories toward what appeared to be an empty spot on the bright blue water below.

The booster motors burned out, and the missiles nosed over and began shallow dives toward the ocean below. Timers ran down, and the activate commands flashed to the warhead sections, where Mark 50 antisubmarine homing torpedoes waited, silent and menacing. The torpedo batteries activated, and their sonar systems and guidance units warmed up. A command flashed to each torpedo's Stored Chemical Power System. Inside each SCEP, electrical squibs fired and melted a solid block of lithium, which began to react with the liquid sulfur hexaflouride to generate intense heat. Steam began to flow to the torpedo propulsion systems.

As the Sea Lances dropped toward the ocean, deacceleration panels opened and slowed the missiles rapidly. Squibs fired and blasted the protective nose fairings away. As the Sea Lances neared the surface, the Mark 50 torpedoes were released. Number One struck the water and vanished below the surface in a huge white cloud of spray. Twenty seconds later, Number Two followed. Now, both torpedoes were in their element. Their guidance units steered them toward the predicted intercept point. Each torpedo moved in a sinusoidal, snakelike search pattern, its sonars listening passively for the target.

Positive contact. Machinery noises ahead, slightly to starboard. Both Mark 50s went to the homing mode. The full-power command flashed to the propulsion systems, and they shot toward their target at maximum speed.

70 LETTS USSR—EN ROUTE TO ELU ISLAND

Captain Kirichenko looked at his situation plot. *70 Letts USSR* was thirty miles from Elu now. Time to reduce speed. He ordered Engineering to reduce speed to ten knots. The reactor control rods slid deeper into the twin reactors, steam pressure in the turbines fell, *70 Letts USSR*'s two massive, four-bladed propellers began to turn slower and slower, and her great, gray hull began to slip quietly through the water, six hundred feet below the surface.

As she slowed, the self-generated noise from her machinery faded to a whisper, and her passive sonar performance improved. *70 Letts USSR*'s sonar operators scanned intensely for any sound that might indicate a hostile submarine was in the area. Nothing, all displays were clear. Kirichenko considered deploying *70 Letts USSR*'s towed array sonar. If American submarines were approaching Elu, that would be the best—.

"Captain," the sonar officer suddenly shouted, "torpedo running, intercept course, bearing 156, high-speed approach!"

Kirichenko stared at his displays in horror. What in the devil's name was happening? There was no sign of a contact. Where in hell had the torpedo come from?

"Captain, second torpedo running! Bearing 156. High-speed approach!"

No time for deep thought.

"Helmsman, turn into them, course 156! Torpedo room! Ready Five and Six for immediate firing!"

70 Letts USSR's blunt bow began to swing toward the oncoming torpedoes. In the torpedo room, the crew tried desperately to get tubes Five and Six ready to fire. Too late. The first torpedo struck *70 Letts USSR* on the bow. The Mark 50's shaped charge warhead was designed to pierce the thick, tough hulls of modern Russian submarines. The warhead detonated, and a white-hot lance of superheated gas and molten metal penetrated *70 Letts USSR*'s hull. Her hull rang as if she had been struck by a giant sledgehammer. Instantly, the torpedo room began to flood. Great gouts of bubbles flowed out from the hole in *70 Letts USSR*'s gray hull. Water poured in, driven by the immense pressure at six hundred feet.

Desperately, Kirichenko ordered full power, while the planesman fought to keep the bow up. The chief engineer blasted high-pressure air into the rapidly flooding torpedo room. The men there died almost instantly, but they were all going to die if *70 Letts USSR* continued to flood and control was lost.

The second Mark 50 was confused by the sonar return from the vast cloud of bubbles pouring from *70 Letts USSR*'s damaged hull. It passed over her huge, gray hull and shot on past the stricken submarine. As it emerged from the bubble cloud, its sonar had no target. Smoothly, the torpedo's computer attack logic steered the Mark 50 into a 180-degree turn and began the target reacquisition search pattern. *70 Letts USSR* was very noisy, indeed, as her crew fought for survival. The Mark 50 reverted to the homing mode and sped back toward *70 Letts USSR*. It struck just below the conning tower. The warhead detonated. The white-hot lance of flaming gas and molten metal pierced the hull and shot into the control center, killing some of the crew and knocking out vital equipment. High-pressure water began to pour into the control center. The forward compartments were flooded with hundreds of tons of water. Her crew lost control, and the long, gray hull began to go down rapidly by the bow, trailing a huge plume of bubbles. Kirichenko took one last despairing look at his depth and pitch gauges. There was nothing he could do. *70 Letts USSR* was going deeper and deeper, the angle of her bow increasing steadily, as she began her last dive to the ocean floor eight thousand feet below.

KRASNOGVARDETS

Krasnogvardets was still running quietly at ten knots. Her towed array was fully deployed, and Captain 2nd Rank Pallitsyn and his control center crew were watching their displays. There was nothing to see but Kirichenko, boiling along in *70 Letts USSR* like a drunken Cossack. Kirichenko was a likable fellow, but he took too many chances. Pallitsyn had atended the Leningrad Academy of Submarine Warfare. He had never forgotten the words of the chief instructor in submarine-versus-submarine combat. "When you are fighting another submarine, it is like two men armed with razor-sharp sabers stalking each other in a pitch-dark room. The man who makes the first mistake is a dead man." Well, if there was an American 688 out there, her captain had a very sharp saber, indeed.

"Captain," his sonar officer said, "contacts! Two short sounds, about twenty seconds apart, bearing 126. Each contact lasted approximately three seconds."

"What do you make of it, Marensko?"

"I'm not certain, Captain, but it sounded like booster rocket motors firing under water, something like our own SS-N-16s."

Pallitsyn felt a chill. *70 Letts USSR* could not possibly have gotten a long-range sonar track while steaming at thirty knots, and Kirichenko could not have launched his long-range SS-N-16 antisubmarine missiles without it. Besides, it did not seem possible that *70 Letts USSR* could be on that bearing. There was only one probable explanation, and Pallitsyn did not like it.

"Anything else, Marensko?"

"No, Captain, nothing—wait. *70 Letts USSR* has reduced speed. I can no longer detect her."

At last, you are showing some sense, Kirichenko. Let us hope it is not too late. There was nothing Pallitsyn could do but watch his displays and wait. The seconds crawled by. Then, he saw a white flash on the display screen.

"Explosion, Captain, bearing 184! Someone's blowing high-pressure air. Second explosion, same bearing."

The sonar displays faded. There was nothing to see but the occasional flicker of random ocean noise. The seconds ticked slowly by. Finally, Marensko spoke. "Breaking up noises, Captain, bearing 184."

70 Letts USSR was gone, Pallitsyn would have bet his last ruble on that. Bad as that was, it gave him one critical advantage. He knew that there was an Ameri-

339

can submarine along bearing 126. He did not think that the American could know that he was there. He checked his weapons status display. He had Type 68 wire-guided torpedoes in tubes One, Two, Three, and Four and self-defense decoys in Five and Six. Pallitsyn smiled grimly. *Krasnogvardets* was ready. All right, Yankee, let's see whose saber is the sharpest.

Krasnogvardets's blunt, rounded bow swung slowly around, and she began to creep slowly, quietly, toward the American.

USS LOS ANGELES

"Breaking up noises, Captain," *Los Angeles*'s leading sonar operator said. "We got her."

Commander Pedersen nodded. He pushed the intercom button. "This is the captain speaking. We just engaged and sank a Soviet Victor class nuclear attack submarine. Congratulations to all hands for a job well done."

Now to find that damned Echo and take care of her. The Echo would not be moving fast when they found her. She would be moving very slowly to minimize machinery noise. *Los Angeles* had two more Sea Lance missiles left in her torpedo room, but they needed a noisy target for a long-range attack. Better not count on the Echo's captain being cooperative. Pedersen made his decision.

"Reload One and Two with Mark 48 ADCAPS."

With four advanced capability antisubmarine torpedoes in her tubes, *Los Angeles* would be ready for the damned Echo when they found her. Quietly, *Los Angeles* resumed her search pattern.

KRASNOGVARDETS

Krasnogvardets moved quietly toward her contact at ten knots. Pallitsyn and his control center crew watched their displays intently. Nothing so far, but the American must be there. He must have moved after launching his missiles at *70 Letts USSR,* but there was no way to predict in which direction. The American would be moving very quietly, and therefore, very slowly. Pallitsyn sipped a mug of scalding hot tea and worried. Every intelligence report he had ever read said that American attack submarines are some of the quietest in the world and have highly trained, expert crews. It was not a reassuring thought.

He was tempted to do something, but anything he might do, speed up, risk active sonar pinging, could be fatal. As the old Russian proverb goes, "When the cat's on the roof, the mice should be quiet." Slow and quiet were the best tactics for *Krasnogvardets.* The minutes crawled by. Pallitsyn poured himself another cup of hot tea. It was beginning to look like the American had given him the slip. He was considering a course change when Marensko spoke softly. He was almost whispering, but the sonar officer's voice was hoarse with excitement. "Probable contact, Captain, dead ahead. A nuclear-propelled submarine, on the same course we are on, moving at low speed and running very quietly."

Aha! There you are, Yankee, dead ahead and moving away. Thank the devil for small favors. A nuclear submarine's sonar performance is at its worst when searching dead astern. *Krasnogvardets* had a nearly ideal tactical position. Now, to exploit it. Let's get ready, but get a little closer.

"Torpedo room, prepare all torpedo tubes for immediate firing."

All right, ready, but better be certain before we fire. "Any change, Marensko?"

"No, Captain. We are gaining on her very slowly, but it is a positive contact, Captain. I am certain it is a submarine."

Better be sure which submarine. Pallitsyn knew it would not enhance his chances for promotion if he sank *Leningradski Komsomols* by mistake.

"Could it be *Leningradski Komsomols,* Marensko?"

"No, sir. Those old Echos are too noisy. *Leningradski Komsomols* could not run that quietly for a million rubles. The contact is stronger now, a single shaft with a single multibladed propeller. It is an American attack submarine, either a 688 or 637 class. I can't tell which, but I would bet my pension on it. It is one or the other."

Pallitsyn smiled grimly. When you are hunting man-eaters in the jungle, it matters little whether you find a lion or a tiger. He glanced at the weapons status display. All tubes were ready for firing. Now, to swing the saber.

"Stand by to fire Three and Four on my command. Reload immediately with Type 68 torpedoes."

"Captain," Marensko said suddenly, "she's changing course and turning toward us. I think she is reversing course. She will be coming straight at us."

Of course. The American is running a search pattern, looking for *Leningradski Komsomols.* But now, one of the best submarine sonars in the world would be pointing straight at *Krasnogvardets.* He was losing his advantage as the American turned. No time to waste!

"Fire Three and Four."

Krasnogvardets's long gray hull vibrated as the two long, heavy Type 68 torpedoes shot out of the torpedo tubes and moved toward the American submarine, trailing their guidance wires behind them.

USS LOS ANGELES

Los Angeles began to answer the helm and change course. Commander Pedersen was beginning to believe that the damned Echo was tied up at the dock on Elu, giving her crew shore leave. Suddenly the leading sonar operator spoke. "Possible contact, Captain, bearing 02. Sounds like a submarine running at low speed."

Instantly, Pedersen was alert. Anything on bearing 02 had been directly astern of *Los Angeles* until she turned. He did not hesitate. "Torpedo room, prepare all tubes for immediate firing." The outer doors of *Los Angeles*'s four torpedo tubes swung smoothly open. He watched as the ready lights came on.

"Positive contact, Captain. Nuclear submarine, it's got one shaft with two tandem, four-blade, corotating propellers. It must be another Victor III, but there's something funny about the contact. It's so faint that he must be at long range, but there isn't any convergence distortion. That indicates she's close."

Pedersen thought this over. *Los Angeles* was now headed straight for the contact. Perhaps if he turned ninety degrees and used the towed array, he could—. Then, it hit him like a hard right to the stomach. Toshiba propellers! A Victor III with the new superquiet Japanese propellers. The Victor could be only a few thousand yards away and ready to—.

"Captain! Torpedoes running. Close in, slow speed, bearing 02!"

Jesus Christ! He who hesitates is lost. Make him maneuver and break his guidance wires. "Fire One," Pedersen ordered. "Launch noisemakers. Launch bubble generators!" And pray to God it's not too late!

The long, green Mark 48 ADCAP torpedo shot from the torpedo tube and accelerated toward the contact. Two noisemakers tore through the water, emitting noises like the biggest, fattest target imaginable. The bubble generators began to spew out huge clouds of bubbles which screened *Los Angeles* from the Victor's sonar.

"Target acquired," the weapons officer said. The Mark 48 ADCAP had locked on to the target with its own sonar. All right, give them something to worry about. "Go active. Full speed. Cut the wire!" The command flashed along the Mark 48 ADCAP's guidance wire. Its sonar began to send pulse after pulse of sound into the water, and it began to home on the return from the Victor's hull. In its propulsion section, the throttle opened and otto fuel poured into the engine at the maximum possible rate. The torpedo cut its guidance wire. It was no longer controlled from *Los Angeles.* It was on its own now, an underwater guided missile, shooting through the water toward its contact at nearly sixty knots.

KRASNOGVARDETS

Krasnogvardets was moving steadily toward the contact. Pallitsyn watched his displays intently. His Type 68 torpedoes were running quietly at twenty knots. The contact was showing no detectable reaction. It was beginning to look like he might take the American by surprise. Then Marensko spoke suddenly. "He's launched, Captain! Torpedo running, bearing 126. Right at us! Noisemaker decoys! Bubble generators!"

The devil! "Weapons Officer! Torpedoes full speed! Fire defensive salvo!"

"Torpedo approaching rapidly. The damned thing must be making sixty knots! Active pinging. Its locked on and homing, Captain!"

"Helmsman, hard starboard. Planesman take her up to four hundred feet. Engineering, full power immediately!" *Krasnogvardets* turned hard to the right and her bow pointed upward. Pallitsyn waited and sweated. His noisemakers and bubble generators were deployed and going. He could hear the hull creak as *Krasnogvardets* shot upward and the external pressure decreased. He had done everything he could do. Now, if only he could shake that damned thing that was screaming

344

through the water toward *Krasnogvardets* like a demon from hell.

Pallitsyn could not see the Mark 48 ADCAP's guidance unit scanning the scene ahead. There were two superb new targets which had appeared from nowhere. That fainter target dead ahead was the real target. The target was turning, speeding up, and moving toward the surface. The torpedo turned left, moved towards the surface. It struck *Krasnogvardets* aft, on the port side. Its heavy warhead, designed to pierce the hull of the newest and toughest Russian submarines, detonated and tore a large hole in *Krasnogvardets*'s hull. High-pressure water began to pour into the reactor room, and a huge column of bubbles began to spew upward toward the surface.

Krasnogvardets's reactors went into emergency shutdown. Pallitsyn desperately ordered full speed on emergency power. The chief engineer switched to the emergency battery, but the battery could only drive *Krasnogvardets*'s 6,300 tons at 4 knots. The chief engineer began to blast high-pressure air into the reactor room in a desperate effort to control the flooding. There was nothing else he could do but pray.

USS LOS ANGELES

Los Angeles was turning hard starboard as *Krasnogvardets*'s Type 68 torpedoes passed through the bubble clouds and came on menacingly toward their target. They were running at high speed and closing the range rapidly now. Desperately, Pedersen launched two more noisemakers. The first torpedo took the bait. There was a tremendous shock as it struck the noisemaker and detonated less than a hundred yards from *Los Angeles*'s long black hull. The shock wave struck *Los Angeles* hard. Men were thrown to the deck, red warning lights flashed everywhere, and alarms wailed in every compartment.

The second torpedo's sonar was temporarily blinded by the blast. It missed *Los Angeles* by less than a hundred feet. Pedersen could actually hear its propellers whirring as it passed by. As the torpedo's sonar cleared, it saw that it had lost the target. It searched diligently ahead. No contact. It turned 180 degrees and went into a sinusoidal search pattern. Contact. The target was directly ahead. It shot forward. Suddenly, it struck something invisible but solid. Its contact piston functioned, and its warhead detonated.

Pedersen was attempting to assess damage when the second shock wave struck. *Los Angeles* shook and vibrated, but this detonation was farther away, and the shock wave was weaker. Thank God for that! *Los Angeles* probably would not have survived another shock like that. There were minor leaks and the diving officer was having trouble maintaining trim, but *Los Angeles* was surviving. The water around *Los Angeles* was beginning to clear as the noisemakers faded into the distance.

Now that he knew that he was not going to sink, Pedersen remembered that he was in the middle of a battle.

"Sonar. Report! What's going on?"

"Towed array is gone, Captain. That last torpedo most have hit it. Contact on bearing 02. Submarine blowing high-pressure air. Flooding noises. She's moving upward at low speed. We must have hit her."

Pedersen felt a moment's pity. The Victor was badly damaged and struggling for her life. But he could not afford pity. Her hull was still intact. She might launch more weapons at any moment. He could not risk his ship and crew. He gave the order to his weapons officer. "Fire Three and Four. High-speed approach."

346

"Three and Four fired!"

Two more Mark 48 ADCAPs shot from *Los Angeles*'s hull and raced toward *Krasnogvardets*. Pedersen watched as the torpedo symbols crawled across *Los Angeles*'s displays and merged with the symbol of the stricken Victor. The torpedoes struck *Krasnogvardets* just under her conning tower. The two heavy warheads detonated and ruptured her pressure hull completely. Pallitsyn and his control center crew were killed instantly. All control was lost. *Krasnogvardets*'s hull flooded, and she began to break up as her shattered hull started sinking toward the bottom of the Pacific, eight thousand feet below.

Chapter Twenty-Seven

"In war, you will usually find that the enemy has three courses of action open to him, and of these three, he will usually adopt the fourth."

—Helmuth von Moltke

29TH ATTACK REGIMENT—OFF ELU

Colonel Ivan Iskaziev sat in the pilot's seat of the leading Sukhoi SU-24. The big, two-tone gray camouflaged plane droned on toward Elu, propelled by its twin Tumanskii R-32B engines at a steady six hundred miles per hour. Behind Iskaziev's plane, the other twenty-three aircraft of his regiment followed in a loose column of flights of four. Eight of his thirty-two aircraft had been forced to turn back. That was unimportant. Twenty fully armed SU-24s should be enough.

Iskaziev felt numb with fatigue. His regiment had been in the air nearly eight hours since they left Cam Ranh Bay. There was no room for error in the mission plan. He must reach Elu and make his attack quickly. The transports were twenty minutes behind him. The devil alone knew what would happen if they missed the island.

Iskaziev's weapon systems—navigation officer tapped him on the shoulder. There, ahead on the horizon, there it was. Iskaziev's fatigue faded as adrenaline flooded his system. He punched a button on his communications control panel and set his radio to a special frequency. He spoke into his headset.

"North Star, North Star, this is Red Star Leader. Report situation and status."

North Star was the very latest version of the Bear, so new that it had been given a new type number, TU-142. The TU-142s did not carry bombs or missiles. Their huge fuselages were crammed with the latest electronic surveillance equipment and radars. North Star was at forty thousand feet, scanning the air and sea space around Elu for two hundred miles in all directions. If hostile aircraft were over Elu, the TU-142 would detect them.

"Red Star, North Star here. Two unidentified aircraft at thirty-four thousand feet over island, approximately forty miles ahead of you. Targets are not Soviet aircraft. You are authorized to engage and destroy."

"Acknowledged, North Star. Red Star attacking!"

Time to fight! The weapons system officer was already checking out the four long-range AA-9 air-to-air missiles which hung under the SU-24's wings. The missile-ready lights came on.

"Radar on, air-to-air mode."

The big, multimode radar in the SU-24's nose began to scan, sending out 200-kilowatt pulses again and again. Instantly, two strong blips appeared on the radar display. Two large aircraft were orbiting over Elu at thirty-four thousand feet. North Star was to the west of the island. There were no friendly aircraft over Elu. Iskaziev armed his missiles. They must be the Sidewinder-armed B-52s he had been warned about. He would take no chances. He would attack at long range.

The range was thirty-two miles. Iskaziev pushed the button. The big SU-24 shook and vibrated as the two AA-9 missiles roared forward from under its wings. Flickers and flashes appeared on the SU-24's radar scope. The enemy had detected Iskaziev and was trying to jam his radar. Too late! The missiles were away, and they were guided by infrared homing. No radar countermeasures could stop them.

Two bright specks of fire appeared on the horizon. One of them blossomed into a ball of orange flame. One of the blips vanished from the SU-24's radar display. The second target had slowed and was headed downward. Iskaziev could take no chances. He launched his second pair of missiles. The big AA-9s roared toward the target. Iskaziev saw two more bright yellow flashes, then a ball of orange fire as the target exploded. He studied his radar display. Nothing. No more targets. The Soviet air force controlled the sky over Elu.

Iskaziev spoke into his microphone. "Target in sight. 29th Regiment attack by flights at sixty-second intervals. First Flight, follow me!"

Iskaziev pushed his throttles forward. The big Tumanskii engines roared as they went to maximum power. Iskaziev pushed his controls forward, and twenty-four deadly gray planes slanted down out of the sky toward Elu.

ELU ISLAND—THE PLATEAU

Laura Walsh was working inside *War God* when she heard the steadily increasing, howling whine of jet engines. She looked quickly out one of the access hatches. Four jets were streaking across the plateau, a hundred feet above the ground. They seemed to be coming straight at her. Laura thought they were Australian F-111Cs. That was a pardonable error. Seen head-on, SU-24s and F-111Cs look very much alike.

Bright yellow lights began to flicker under each plane's nose, and halos of orange fire appeared under their wings as the aircraft began to blast the American positions with 23mm cannon shells and 57mm rockets. Laura did not have to see the red stars on their wings to know that they were hostile.

The sound of the explosions was one long, ripping roar. Rockets and cannon shells were striking a hundred yards to the left and right of *War God*. To the east, Laura could see other flights of SU-24s preparing to attack. She was filled with rage. Four days ago, she had never met a Green Beret or a Ranger. Now, they were her friends, the men who were keeping her alive, and the Russians were killing them.

She had to do something, but what? All right, Walsh, you're so God damned smart, don't sit there and shake, fight with your brain! Laura cringed as another four SU-24s howled overhead, but she moved quickly to *War God*'s internal control panel. She stared intently at the neat rows of buttons and their Russian labels. Yes, that might work. As the scream of jet engines built up again, Laura pushed three buttons in sequence, Emergency, Defensive Systems, and Activate.

Instantly, *War God*'s flight control computer flashed into life. Was *War God* under attack? Data poured in from *War God*'s attack sensors. There were hostile projectiles approaching.

—ARM WEAPON—PREPARE FOR FIRING—ATTACK TARGETS 1, 2, 3, AND 4-

The laser swung and pointed smoothly. Matter and antimatter blazed together in the laser power system, and Laura heard the ripping, crackling sound as *War God* fired.

Captain Pavlyuk was leading the Fourth Flight. The four SU-24s passed over the rocks and howled toward the woods to the west. He could see the satellite's huge silver cylinder near the edge of the trees. Suddenly, a pale blue beam of light flashed from the satellite and illuminated Pavlyuk's SU-24 as *War God* struck at the speed of light. Billions of watts of perfectly focused gamma ray radiation struck the SU-24. Its electrical and electronics systems were destroyed instantly as wires failed, transistors shorted, and power supplies exploded.

Pavlyuk pulled on his controls frantically. No use, he was sitting in an unguided missile. The SU-24 flashed over the trees and struck the ground at six hundred miles an hour. It vanished in a huge ball of orange flame as its bombs and fuel exploded. There was another blast, and another, and another as the other three SU-24s of the Fourth Flight struck the ground and exploded.

Colonel Iskaziev was stunned. What in the devil's name was happening? The entire Fourth Flight seemed to have committed simultaneous suicide. Something was terribly wrong. He did not hesitate. He spoke rapidly into his microphone.

"All Red Star Flights, break off attack immediately. Reform. Rendezvous thirty kilometers north of the island."

Iskaziev listened as his flight leaders acknowledged the order. Then he spoke again. "All Flight Leaders, did anyone see what happened to the Fourth Flight?"

"Fifth Flight Leader, Colonel. All Fourth Flight aircraft were illuminated by a beam of blue light. It looked like a searchlight. There was no visible damage. They just flew into the ground. The blue light came from somewhere in the American positions Fourth Flight was attacking."

Suddenly, Iskaziev's heart froze. He knew! The laser! The triply damned laser. Somehow the Americans were using *War God*'s laser against him. It was certain death to continue the attack. Instantly, he was on the radio again. He must contact Moscow. He could not do it directly, but the TU-142 had a SATCOM radio.

"North Star, this is Red Star Leader. Emergency! The Americans are firing *War God*'s laser at my planes. I have lost four SU-24s and their crews. I have broken off the attack. Contact Moscow. Tell them they must do something about the laser. Tell them to hurry. The transports will be here in fifteen minutes."

"Red Star Leader, North Star. Your message understood. We are contacting Moscow headquarters via SATCOM immediately. Stand by."

Almost immediately, Iskaziev was at the rendezvous point. Things happen fast at six hundred miles per hour. The SU-24s of his regiment were orbiting in a wide, shallow turn. He made a quick visual check. All the SU-24s still had bombs and missiles attached to their underwing pylons. No one had panicked and dropped his weapons when the regiment had broken off the attack. Good. He still had twenty fully armed aircraft. The 29th Attack Regiment was ready to attack again, if only Moscow could do something about that damned laser.

PLESETSK COSMODROME—PRIMARY CONTROL CENTER

Svetlana Snastina was dozing in front of her console in the control center. She awakened with a start as the Attention alarm on her console buzzed. Something was going on. There was a major change in *War God*'s weapon system status. The laser was firing again and again. Quickly, Svetlana scanned her displays. *War God* thought it was under attack and was defending itself in the emergency mode. A light on her console indicated that the local control panel had been activated. That was the source of the emergency commands. One of the Americans had done it. Svetlana would have bet her last ruble that it was Laura Walsh!

Quickly, she pushed the Override button. she typed a message into the computer.

—LOCAL CONTROL PANEL MALFUNC-
TIONING—ACCEPT ORDERS ONLY FROM
PLESETSK—PASSWORD—SNASTINA-
DEEDS OF GLORY-

She pushed the transmit button.

29TH ATTACK REGIMENT—ELU ISLAND

Iskaziev waited impatiently. His fuel supply was dwindling and the transports were getting closer by the minute. Whatever happened, the transports must get through. The devil alone knew what would happen if he had to delay the drop. Seconds dragged by. What were they doing in Moscow, parading in Red Square?

He contacted each of his remaining flight leaders one by one, asking for their fuel and weapon status. It was not really important, but he wanted to hear their voices. Attack pilots must be prepared as a matter of course to face missiles, antiaircraft guns, and hostile aircraft. But his men had just seen eight of their comrades killed by a beam of blue light. Iskaziev would not blame them if they were frightened and demoralized, but he detected no sound of panic in their voices. He was not surprised. He knew his men, and he was proud of his regiment.

"Red Star Leader, this is North Star. Moscow says that *War God*'s laser is disabled. It is impossible for the Americans to fire it at you again. Moscow says you must

354

resume the attack immediately. The transports will arrive in nine minutes."

That was excellent news, if true. Moscow certainly sounded confident, but they were not going to sit in an SU-24 and fly into range of that deadly laser beam. He was, but there was no choice. Iskaziev spoke into his headset.

"North Star, your message acknowledged. Red Star preparing to attack now. All Red Star Flights, we will attack west to east this time in a column of flights. I will lead. Second Flight, follow me in two minutes. Other Flights, follow Second Flight at one-minute intervals. Acknowledge."

The last thing in the world Iskaziev wanted to do was fly toward that deadly laser, but they paid him to command an attack regiment, and the function of an attack regiment is to attack. He pushed his throttles forward and the two big Tumanskii R-32B engines roared as they went to maximum power.

Iskaziev brought the big gray SU-24 around in a precise right turn and headed toward the western edge of the plateau. The rest of his flight followed smoothly. Radar on, ground attack mode. He would cross the edge of the plateau and attack at fifty feet. That would take the Americans by surprise, and minimize their time to react. He watched tensely as he and his flight hurtled toward Elu at six hundred miles per hour and the edge of the plateau seemed to expand and fill his windscreen. It would not do to make any mistakes. If he struck the ground at these speeds he—.

"Red Star Leader, this is North Star. Come in Red Star."

What in the devil's name did the TU-142 want now? This was the wrong time for distractions.

"Red Star Leader here. I am attacking now, North Star. Can your message wait?"

"No, Red Star Leader. Something is wrong with your attack coordination. Your Second Flight is not maintaining its assigned interval. Radar shows he is too close and accelerating. You will arrive over the target simultaneously. The risk of collision is high. Take immediate corrective action!"

The devil! What was happening. Iskaziev glanced in his rearview mirror. He saw what he expected to see, four SU-24s, but North Star was right. They were much too close and closing fast. What was the Second Flight doing? He was about to use his radio when a subconscious alarm made him look in his rearview mirror again. The four planes were much closer now. He could see details clearly. Something was wrong. The four planes were high-wing, two-seat, two-engine monoplanes, with tall, single vertical tails, but there was something strange about the shape of the jet engine inlets. They were not rectangular like an SU-24's, they were rounded like those of—F-111s!

"Break! Break! First Flight Break! Hostile aircraft dead astern and closing!" he shouted, and pulled the big SU-24 into a hard right, four g, climbing turn as 20 mm cannon shell tracers blazed by his canopy.

NUMBER 82 STRIKE WING—RAFF—OVER ELU

The confectioner had his sights on the SU-24 leader's wingman. He had approached Elu flying at fifty feet above the ocean's surface, where multiple radar returns from the waves would confuse the Russian radar. He had insinuated Blue Flight neatly into the Russian column. Now his afterburners were on. His two big Pratt & Whitney TF30s were producing maximum war emergency power as Blue Flight closed on the leading flight of SU-24s at eight hundred miles per hour. The Russians showed no sign of knowing the Australian F-111Cs were there. Piece of cake!

That's right, mate, keep on straight, level and happy, now. Suddenly, the leading SU-24 broke, turning up and to the right. Instantly, the confectioner pulled the trigger. His 20mm GE M61 Gatling gun spat a hundred 20mm cannon shells per second at the gray SU-24. The wingman's SU-24 exploded in a ball of orange flame. A second SU-24 was burning and going down out of control. The confectioner's wingman had done his job.

The confectioner pulled his F-111C around to the right as hard as he dared. It would be a pity if he pulled the wings off at eight hundred miles an hour and fifty feet. He was sure both his wife and his girlfriend would miss him. A8-146 shook and shuddered, but she held together. The confectioner was not going to be drawn into a dogfight. He had no time for that. He must disrupt the Russian attack. Now he had reversed course and was roaring straight toward the oncoming column of SU-24s.

The two formations flashed together and passed through each other at a combined speed of 1,400 miles per hour. He and his wingman fired together. The 20-mm tracers streaked through the oncoming Russian formation. The confectioner could see the SU-24s turn and break from their formation in the face of the Australians' surprise attack. They were pulling hard, high g turns to the left and right, and most of them had jettisoned their bombs as they tried desperately to lighten their planes for air-to-air combat.

The confectioner roared straight at the last two Russian flights. One of their flight leaders was being stubborn. He did not break, but kept on, headed straight toward the green-and-brown Australian F-111Cs. The confectioner saw a halo of yellow fire bloom under the oncoming SU-24's nose as its pilot triggered his six-barreled 23-mm Gatling gun and sent seventy 23-mm cannon shells per second at the confectioner and his wingman.

Red and green tracers crisscrossed as the F-111Cs and the SU-24s sped toward each other at 1,400 miles per hour. The Russian was stubborn. So was the confectioner. They flashed past each other. The confectioner would have sworn that they missed each other by six inches. Actually, it was at least six feet.

Suddenly, there was nothing ahead of the confectioner's flight but blue sky and blue water. They had flown through the SU-24 formation and passed over the eastern edge of Elu. The confectioner discovered that he had been holding his breath. He took a deep breath and pulled A8-146 into a right-hand turn. Yellow Flight was about to attack the Russians from the west with AIM-9L Sidewinders. Better be sure that he was—.

"Break, Blue Leader, break! He's on your tail!"

The confectioner did not waste time thinking. He zoomed and reversed his turn as green 23-mm tracers flashed past his canopy. A8-146 shuddered as the Confectioner pulled the hardest possible left-hand turn. He lost speed. He intended to. The SU-24 overshot and flashed by. Now to get into a shooting position. The confectioner went into the scissors, pulling two fast turn reversals intended to force the SU-24 out ahead of the F-111C. The Russian pilot tried to counter by turning hard in counterreversals, but the confectioner was the better pilot.

He got his sights on the gray SU-24 and squeezed the trigger. The F-111C's Gatling gun fired in one long continuous roar, like a giant piece of canvas being ripped apart, as it poured one hundred shells per second into the SU-24. The confectioner saw rapid, winking yellow flashes as the 20mm high explosive–incendiary shells tore into his target and detonated. Gray-white smoke began to pour from the SU-24's engines, but it was still under control. The confectioner fired another three second burst of 20mm HE-I. The SU-24 exploded in a great ball of fire.

The confectioner looked around quickly. Another gray SU-24 was spiraling downward, trailing smoke. As he watched, the two-man Russian crew ejected from their doomed plane. Another plane was going down, trailing a banner of flame and smoke. Green-and-brown camouflage. He had lost an F-111C, and there were no parachutes.

He looked at his round counter. He had started the fight with 2,084 rounds of 20mm cannon ammunition. He had less than four hundred left. He glanced at his fuel gauges. Damn! Fighting on afterburners consumes fuel at a terrific rate. He was dangerously low, just enough fuel to reach the American tanker aircraft and refuel if he were lucky. He spoke quickly into his headset.

"Thunderbolt Force, this is Thunderbolt Leader. Break off and head for home immediately!"

The confectioner turned left and headed west. The Russians were not attempting to pursue the Australian F-111Cs. They were regrouping over Elu to cover their transport aircraft. Well, it would have been nice to sweep the Russians from the sky; but this was combat, not a fairy tale. Eight against sixteen is long odds. At least he had thoroughly disrupted their attack and saved the SAS and the Americans from a hard pounding, but it had not been easy. This time, even the confectioner did not think it had been a piece of cake.

ELU ISLAND—THE PLATEAU

War God's laser stopped firing. Laura looked around. There were no more of the gray camouflaged planes to fire at. Laura took a deep breath to steady her nerves.

She felt a strange mixture of emotions. She was proud of herself. She had proved to herself that she was not a coward. She had used one of the deadliest weapons ever devised by men and fought her battle with it. But she also knew that she had killed the men in those gray planes. By pushing three buttons, she had killed them just as dead as if she had taken a pistol and shot them right between the eyes. That made her feel a little sick. She would have to live with that.

Suddenly, Laura heard the sound of jet engines. A long line of huge planes was sweeping in from the west, flying over the harbor area. As Laura watched, parachutes began to appear below and behind the first plane. Laura could see the red star on the plane's side. Time to fire the laser again. She pushed three buttons in sequence, again Emergency, Defensive Systems, and Activate. Nothing happened. Quickly, she pushed them again. She heard a chime from *War God*'s internal control panel. A light had come on in the lower right hand corner of the panel. Laura looked at the two words under the light: Command Override. There was nothing she could do. The Russians in Plesetsk had won this round. Laura watched helplessly as the huge Russian transport planes roared over Elu, filling the sky with parachutes.

106TH GUARDS AIR ASSAULT DIVISION ELU ISLAND

Colonel Viktor Ulanov was awakened instantly. What was that noise? Jet engines! He looked quickly to the east, then swore bitterly. Four F-111Cs were coming straight at him. He snapped up his field glasses. Something was strange. The planes were not firing and they were not painted in green and brown but in two shades of gray. The four planes screamed overhead firing their cannon and launching rockets into the American positions. He was not good at fighter aircraft recognition. He did not have to be. As the gray jets flashed overhead, he saw the bright red stars on the wings and heard bombs exploding.

Sharypa was pointing to the west, yelling gleefully. Ulanov swung his glasses in that direction. A large column of huge, gray, four-engined transport planes was flying majestically toward the harbor area. Ulanov did know transport aircraft. He recognized Soviet ANT-124s; he had jumped from them before. As he watched, a stream of parachutists began to jump from the first aircraft, followed by large loads supported by multiple parachutes. His men were laughing and cheering. Ulanov found he was cheering, too, as the giant aircraft soared over Elu, dropping steady streams of men and equipment. Let's see how the Yankees do against the VDV!

ELU ISLAND—THE ROAD TO THE PLATEAU

Cord led the six-man reconnaissance patrol down the old trail. Cord went as carefully and quietly as he could, his Owen gun ready in his hands. Cord didn't think there was any way the Russians could know about the trail. You could not see it from the road, and there was no reason to suspect that it was there. Still, better safe than sorry. It would be very unpleasant to take a chance and learn that you were wrong when you heard the spiteful chatter of PKM machine guns opening fire. Being ambushed can ruin your whole day.

The ground was rough and uneven, hard going for men carrying sixty pounds of weapons and gear. At least it was a bit cooler. The evening sea breeze was beginning to blow as the sun started to set. If Cord's memory was correct, they were close to the second bend in the road. If they moved through the trees to the edge of the road, they would be able to see down into the village and the harbor area. They needed to learn what all those Russians were up to. That was the object of the exercise, or as Sergeant Jackson had quaintly put it, "The name of the game." Americans were decent chaps, but they certainly did talk funny.

Cord reached the trees at the edge of the road. He looked carefully up and down the road. No Russian patrols. Nothing, all clear. He signaled, and Jackson came quietly forward, followed by a thin, wiry oriental American whom Jackson had introduced as Sergeant Nguyen. He was the Special Forces team's intelligence sergeant. Nguyen, Jackson had assured Cord, knew everything. Perhaps so, but so far, Nguyen had said absolutely nothing. Cord did not mind. He did not care for men who liked to chat while on patrol.

Jackson and Nguyen joined Cord. They needed to cross the road to be able to observe the entire harbor area. Cord was getting ready to go when he heard the sounds. He froze instantly. Engines! He could hear the rumbling roar of diesel engines, many engines, and now the unmistakable squeal and clack of tank treads. Combat vehicles were moving up the plateau road, many combat vehicles.

Something came around the bend in the road. To Cord, it looked like a tank, a small tank, true, but still a tank. It was painted a dull, nonreflective green. It had a small gun turret which mounted a short-barreled, large-caliber cannon. On a rail mounted above the cannon barrel there was a three-foot-long rocket, or guided missile. Cord did not like it. He did not need to see the red star painted on the hull to know that it was hostile.

"What the hell is that thing, Nguyen?" Jackson whispered.

"*Boyevaya Maschina Desantvaya,*" Nguyen said quickly.

"Say what?" Jackson asked.

362

"It's a BMD, a Russian armored airborne combat vehicle. It's an infantry fighting vehicle, like our Bradleys, but it's designed for air assault operations. It can be parachute dropped from transport planes. It's a late production model. That's a 73mm cannon in the turret and a Sagger AT-3 antitank missile mounted above it."

Sergeant Nguyen seemed fascinated by what he saw. Cord was not. He could have lived a long and happy life without ever having seen a BMD. But there was more than one BMD to see. As Cord watched, another and another came around the bend until a column of the damned things was crawling up the road, like a line of giant green insects.

The first BMD was passing them now, less than fifty feet away. They held perfectly still. The Russians could not hear them over the noise of their vehicles, but the BMD crews were bound to be alert and scanning the terrain around them. Any movement might be detected and draw fire. Cord was not sure just what a BMD's 73mm cannon could do at close range, and he was not eager to find out.

"What do those markings mean, Nguyen?" Jackson whispered.

"The white parachute with a plane on both sides and the red star between them means it's a Soviet VDV air assault division vehicle. The insignia on the turret, the red star and the red flag surrounded by a gold wreath, is the Guards Badge. It means that this is a unit from a Guards air assault division, elite troops with a distinguished combat record. Guards units are the best troops in the Russian army."

Cord was impressed. Sergeant Nguyen did seem to know everything. He probably knew the bloody drivers' names, but nothing he had said made Cord happy. He counted the BMDs as they passed. "I make it nine," he said.

Jackson and Nguyen nodded. "That's how many there should be," Nguyen said. "There are nine BMD's in an air assault company."

"Here come some more of the God damned things," Jackson said. "No, that one's different. What the hell is that?"

Nguyen peered intently. Cord looked, too. It was bigger than a BMD, and it looked strange. It was like a tank, but it had no gun turret. Protruding from the front of the dull green hull was a large, extremely long-barreled cannon. It was painted with the same markings as the BMDs. If anything, it looked far more unpleasant than a BMD.

Nguyen spoke with the air of a bird watcher who has just seen a rare and remarkable bird. "That's a Russian *Aviadezantnaya Samochodnaya Ustanovaka-85,* an ASU-85 airborne armored assault gun. It mounts a high-velocity 85mm cannon. There are thirty-one of them in a Russian air assault division."

"Jesus Christ!" Jackson said. "You mean we're up against a whole God damned Russian division?"

"No," Nguyen said. "I wouldn't say that. There weren't nearly enough parachutes for a division. I'd say it's probably a Guards air assault regiment, a third of a division, reinforced, of course. They will have a total of about fifteen hundred to two thousand men and one hundred thirty armored combat vehicles."

Four ASU-85s rumbled by. More BMDs came around the bend. Like a swarm of armored ants, the dull green vehicles moved slowly but steadily up the plateau road.

Jackson whistled softly. "OK, we've seen enough. We'd better get on the radio and tell Major Gozen we're about to be hit by a God damned elite armored regiment."

"I don't think so, Frank," Nguyen said. "That's just

364

one battalion. They will want to bring up the whole regiment before they attack. Besides, it's starting to get dark. They won't attack at night. A BMD's night vision equipment isn't all that good. No, they'll wait and attack us in the morning when they're ready."

Lovely, Cord thought. It sounded like he should spend the next few hours writing his will.

U.S.-AUSTRALIAN FORCE COMMAND POST—ELU ISLAND

Despite the eighty-five degree heat, Major Muso Gozen felt a chill. He did not doubt what Jackson and Nguyen had told him. He had heard the rumble of engines and the squeal of tracks in the background as their voices came over the radio. A Guards air assault regiment! That meant 1,500 to 2,000 men. Even with the Australians and the Special Forces troops, he would be outnumbered two or three to one. But that was not the problem. They had forgotten that Russian airborne troops are armored infantry, not paratroopers. A Guards air assault regiment would have well over a hundred armored combat vehicles, BMDs, ASU-85s, the works. How in hell were he and his men going to stop them?

The Moose was a professional's professional. He could recite the Table of Organization and Equipment of a Ranger battalion without a second's hesitation. He had fired every type of weapon in the battalion and knew the capabilities of each perfectly. That was what worried him. The 2nd Ranger Battalion's only antitank weapons were its ten M47 Dragon missile systems.

They were considerably better than nothing, but Major Gozen did not like Dragons. Although officially classed as medium antitank weapons, their warheads weighed only 5.4 pounds. That would probably be enough to take out a BMD if the Dragon hit it.

That was the problem, getting hits. Dragons are steered by commands from an AN/TAS-5 optical/infrared tracker attached to the missile launcher. The missile trails wires behind it as it flies toward the target. The tracker senses the position of the missile relative to the target. Corrective steering commands are sent to the missile via the wires. All the gunner has to do is keep his tracker's cross hairs centered on the target. In theory, you get a direct hit every time.

In practice, it's not so simple. In order to save weight, the Dragon's designers had made the gunner part of the launching system. The front of the Dragon's launcher tube is supported by a bipod. The rear of the tube is supported by the operator's hands and right shoulder. If the gunner does not remain perfectly still and hold the launcher tube firmly, the cross hairs will move and the missile will miss or crash into the ground.

It can work. Gozen had seen Dragon operators score ninety percent hits firing missiles on training ranges. But that was in peacetime when no one was shooting back. Remaining perfectly still and icy cool when people are shooting at you is not easy, and Gozen knew the Russians would be shooting back. If he had been Chief of Staff, Dragons would have been replaced by something better years ago. Well, Dragons were what they had. They would have to fight with them.

He turned to Colonel Haldane. "Do you have any antitank weapons with you, Colonel?" he asked.

"I'm afraid not, Major. We thought we were going to fight *Spetsnaz*. We did not anticipate an antiarmor action."

That was the problem, none of them had.

"How about you, Carter?"

"Not really, Major. We have two Browning M2 .50 caliber machine guns. They may penetrate a BMD's armor at close range."

Better than nothing. Well, at least they had Sheridans.

"How many Sheridans are operational, DeBerg?"

The 82nd Airborne captain looked thoughtful. "Seven ready right now, maybe another one or two in a few hours. We're taking parts from damaged vehicles where we can."

"All right," Gozen said. "The only way the Russians can get their armor up on to the plateau is up the road. We'll set up an antitank ambush in and around that big formation of rocks. That's the cork in the bottle. With the Sheridans' antitank missiles and the Dragons, we'll stop them there."

Gozen was not at all sure that they were going to stop them, but a commander has to sound confident.

Captain DeBerg looked unhappy. "I'm sorry, Major, there's a problem with that plan. The Sheridans' MGM-51A Shillelagh missiles are highly effective, but they have a dead zone. We can't guide the missile until it's flown twelve hundred fifty yards. After that, we have a very high hit probability out to the maximum range of fifty-seven hundred yards. But we simply can't engage targets with the Shillelaghs at less than twelve hundred fifty yards. If you want us to fight at close range, we will be restricted to using our 152mm cannon. That will work. I've studied BMDs and ASU-85s. They are lightly armored. Our 152mm high explosive–antitank shells can knock them out. We can do it either way. I can look for positions for long-range missile fire, or fight them close in with the guns. Whatever you decide, Major."

Gozen thought for a few seconds. It was going to be bad when the Russians attacked. One of the worst things light infantrymen can be asked to face is an armored attack. His Rangers were superb troops, man for man, as good as any in the world. From what he had seen, Carter's Special Forces troops and the Australian SAS were just as good. But even the best troops can get what the Germans call "Panzer Fever," the fear and panic that can sweep through a force which is attacked by enemy armor when they have none. Direct, visible support from the Sheridans would stiffen his men's morale.

"All right," Gozen said. "We'll fight them at the rocks. Bring your Sheridans in close, DeBerg."

He turned to his Ranger officers. "Have the antitank sections get the Dragons out of the equipment containers and check them out. We'll select fighting positions for the Sheridans and the Dragon sections while the light lasts. Let's go."

The officers dispersed to their units. For a few minutes, Gozen was alone except for his radio operator. Gozen felt almost peaceful. He had made the hard decisions and come up with the best plan he could think of. It was all settled now. In the morning, the Russians would attack, and they would fight them.

Gozen looked at the lush green trees and the splendid colors of the sunset. He would fight and face death tomorrow, but his ancestors had done that for a thousand years. It would be wrong to say that he was not afraid, but he knew he would do his duty.

A disquieting thought slipped into his mind. Gozen was an avid student of military history. He remembered another elite force that had defended a narrow road against heavy odds. In 480 B.C., 300 Spartans had fought to hold the pass at Thermopylae against 150,000 Persians who were invading Greece. The Spartans fought with incredible skill and courage until finally the Persians rolled over them, and the Spartans were killed to the last man. Somehow, Gozen did not like the comparison.

Colonel Haldane finished briefing the SAS officers and senior NCOs. Outwardly Haldane was calm. Inwardly he was seething with frustration. They were going to lose. There were too many armored BMDs and not enough antitank weapons. The damnable thing was that he could do nothing about it. The soldiers of the 1st Australian SAS Regiment were some of the finest in the world, but they had no antitank weapons. Good as his men were, they were not going to kill BMDs with rifles, machine guns, or hand grenades.

Someone was standing in front of him. It was Regimental Sergeant Major MacNair. The RSM did not salute. After all, they were in the field and in combat, but his military bearing was impeccable as usual.

"Sir," MacNair said, "I've been thinking. We have to do something about those bloody Russian BMDs."

That was glaringly obvious, but Colonel Haldane had served with MacNair for many years. MacNair was not given to making stupid remarks "Too right we do, Sergeant Major. Just what do you suggest?"

MacNair held up a rectangular canvas bag with carrying handles on one side. He grinned wickedly. "Charges, sir! We've got plenty of these five-kilogram demolition charges. We'll just put in a couple of detonators and fire the charge with an L2 hand grenade and primacord. My old granddad was at Tobruk with the 9th Australian Division back in 1941. He swore they blew up German Panzer Mark IIIs and Mark IVs by throwing explosive charges under them. Those were twenty- and thirty-ton tanks. These bloody Russian BMDs can't be any tougher than that!"

Colonel Haldane thought for a second. Obviously, MacNair was right. A five-kilogram demolition charge contains eleven pounds of C4, an extremely powerful explosive. If detonated under a BMD, it would certainly blow the BMD to hell. There was one obvious problem with MacNair's scheme. The BMD crews were going to be extremely annoyed when people tried to throw charges under their BMDs. Each BMD carried three .30 caliber machine guns specifically to shoot people the crew found annoying. The SAS men who tried to throw the charges under the BMDs were very probably going to be committing suicide. Still, he could think of nothing better.

"Very well, Sergeant Major. We'll do it. Call for volunteers. I'll inform Major Gozen of our change in plan."

"Right, sir. With your permission, I'll lead the party."

Colonel Haldane nodded and left the area. All of the SAS men in the area became very busy checking their equipment. No one looked at the RSM.

"All right, now," MacNair said, "Lovat, Frazer, Blake, Smith, Monash, Hughes, Blackburn, Elliot, Wade, special detail, follow me."

Cord continued to check his rifle diligently. He permitted himself a faint smile. It looked like he had managed to dodge the bullet this time. But it would be a cold day in hell when the RSM forgot Cord.

MacNair looked around with an eagle eye. "Just don't sit there on your bloody backside grinning like a hairy ape, Cord. Come on. We have charges to rig!"

43RD GUARDS AIR ASSAULT REGIMENT— ELU ISLAND—THE ROAD TO THE PLATEAU

Colonel Viktor Ulanov sat in the boxlike armored hull of the BMD-2KSh. It was the command version of the BMD and carried radios and senior officers instead of cannons and missiles. It was a bit cramped and smelled of oil, but Ulanov did not care. The sights and sounds of a regiment of BMDs filled him with quiet elation. He knew what a Guards air assault regiment could do. If the Americans did not know, they were about to find out.

He sipped a cup of scalding hot tea and listened as Colonel Artyshenko finished briefing his three battalion commanders. The 43rd Air Assault Regiment's commander was a small man, but he radiated authority.

"The American positions are eight hundred meters away. The key to their defense is this formation of rocks. The Third Battalion will lead the attack supported by the ASU-85s. I will be with the Third Battalion. The Second Battalion follows the Third. As we reach the plateau, the Third Battalion moves to the left of the rocks, while the Second Battalion goes to the right side. We will surround the Americans and annihilate them. First Battalion remains in reserve. It will attack only on my command.

"Now, the weakness of the plan is this damned narrow road. Only one or two BMDs can move along it at one time, so we are forced to attack in a column until we reach the plateau. Then we can fan out and surround the enemy. We will use the ASUs to place a heavy fire on the Americans as the BMDs move up the road. That will help, but do not deceive yourselves. If the Americans have any kind of antitank weapons, we are going to lose vehicles. We must not let this stop the attack. Once we attack, keep moving at all costs. If vehicles are knocked out, they must not block the road. Following vehicles are to push them off the road and keep on going. Are there any questions?"

The senior battalion commander spoke. "Yes, Comrade Colonel. When do the dismount groups leave the BMDs and fight on foot?"

"That is impossible to predict. It depends on how the fighting goes. I delegate that decision to the battalion

371

commanders. Use your own judgment. Any further questions?"

"None, Comrade Colonel, we carry out your orders without question!"

Colonel Artyshenko turned to Viktor Ulanov. "What do you think, Ulanov? You know the terrain, and you have fought these Americans and Australians."

"The plan seems excellent. Given the situation, there is no other choice but to attack up the road. It will be difficult forcing our way on to the plateau, but once we have done that, the Americans and Australians are doomed. They are well trained and well led, but the best light infantry in the world stand no chance against an air assault regiment. I do have one question, Colonel. What do you want my *Spetsnaz* team to do?"

"I do not think it wise to mix your men and mine in the attack, Ulanov. They have not trained together. Confusion might result. Hold your present position until we have seized the rocks. Then, bring them forward to secure the rocks while my regiment makes the final attack across the plateau."

Ulanov thought for a moment. You might say it was not a glorious role, but his men had fought and had bled enough. Let the Guards have the glory. "Very well, Colonel, as you say."

"Very well, comrades," Colonel Artyshenko said. "Go back to your units. Have the men complete their final precombat checks, and then get some sleep. In the morning, the Guards will settle this affair."

THE CRISIS CENTER-MOSCOW, USSR

General Galanskov sipped his tea and listened to the briefing. It seemed to him that he had been drinking tea and being briefed for the last hundred years. Perhaps the devil was punishing him for his sins. At least, this time most of the news was good.

372

Colonel Kirilenko was briefing. "The 43rd Guards Air Assault Regiment has landed on Elu. They are checking out their vehicles and preparing for combat. They will move up the road tonight and wait for dawn near the top. They will attack as soon as the light is good. They will attack in a column of three battalions of BMDs supported by ASU-85 assault guns. They will seize the rock formation, then spread out, overrun the plateau, and destroy the enemy."

Galanskov nodded approvingly. Given the terrain and the forces involved, it seemed to be an excellent plan.

"Is there any sign of an American reaction?" he asked.

"None, except the American warship, the *Wasp,* is now within four hundred miles of Elu. It will arrive there tomorrow."

"What are the capabilities of this ship?"

Kirilenko was an army officer. That was not his department. He turned to Captain Bezobrazov. The naval intelligence officer stepped to the table and turned on the slide projector. An excellent color picture of a large warship appeared on the screen.

"This is the USS *Wasp,* a large amphibious assault ship. It—"

Galanskov frowned and pointed at the picture. Bezobrazov stopped instantly.

"There is some error here," Galanskov said. "This is not some kind of amphibious ship. It is clearly an aircraft carrier."

Captain Bezobrazov sighed. Explaining naval affairs and warships to Soviet generals was not always easy.

"Yes, sir," he said tactfully, "it does indeed resemble an aircraft carrier, but it cannot operate conventional naval aircraft. Catapults are required to launch such aircraft from a ship, and the *Wasp* has no catapults.

The large flight deck is used to launch and recover helicopters. The *Wasp* can carry as many as forty to fifty United States Marine Corps helicopters, CH-46s, CH-53s, and AH-1Ws. The *Wasp* is designed to carry, land, and support United States Marines."

Galanskov did not like the sound of that. "How many marines?" he asked.

"Approximately one thousand nine hundred, General, and they would have heavy tanks and powerful artillery. Fortunately, they are not on board. The *Wasp* was on a special mission before she was diverted to Elu. It was on a goodwill tour to Singapore, Australia, and New Zealand. Our agents have confirmed that the *Wasp* is not carrying a combat unit of U.S. Marines."

"Why are they sending a ship with no combat capability to Elu?"

"The *Wasp* is fully loaded with helicopters. Part of her mission was to transport and support a group of United States Army helicopters for demonstrations and maneuvers with the armed forces of allied nations."

Bezobrazov glanced at his notes. He was a naval officer. He knew nothing about U.S. Army helicopters. "These include American army UH-60B and AH-64A helicopters. The Yankees like to sell their military equipment to their trusted allies. It increases their influence with these countries, and it makes money for them. For example, these American army helicopter units conducted several maneuvers with units of the Australian army while the *Wasp* was visiting Australia."

Captain Bezobrazov paused for emphasis. He wanted to be sure that Galanskov understood what he would say next. "The important point, General, is that while most of the Marine Corps helicopters were unloaded to make room for the army models, the *Wasp* does have a squadron of U.S. Marine CH-53E heavy lift helicopters on board. They can lift *War God*, or its key components, to the *Wasp.* Then, they and the U.S. Army helicopters can evacuate all the American and Australian personnel from Elu."

Galanskov understood all too well. "Then this ship, the *Wasp,* is the key piece in the game. If it reaches Elu, the Americans can carry off *War God.* Checkmate! They will have won the game."

Captain Bezobrazov nodded. "Exactly so, General."

"This must not be allowed to happen. Contact the submarine *Leningradski Komsomols.* Confirm the attack order. *Leningradski Komsomols* is to sink the *Wasp* as soon as it comes within missile range."

Chapter Twenty-Eight

"There are only two kinds of ships in the world, submarines and targets."   —U.S. Navy Submarine Service
proverb

LENINGRADSKI KOMSOMOLS—OFF ELU

Captain Khrenov woke with a start. Someone was rapping urgently on the door of his tiny cabin. He glanced at the clock. He had been asleep for less than an hour. No wonder he felt dazed with fatigue. This had better be important. If not, he was going to kill someone.

"Yes, yes, what is it?"

"Captain." It was Lieutenant Samsonov's voice. The communications officer was excited. "A message is coming in from Moscow via Pacific Fleet headquarters. Highest priority! It is being decoded now. I think it is the attack order."

That got the adrenaline flowing! Khrenov rolled out of his bunk and went rapidly to *Leningradski Komsomols*'s control center. Lieutenant Shpagin handed him the message.

"Attack order, Captain. From Moscow via Pacific

Fleet headquarters. An American warship approaching Elu has been detected by our ocean surveillance satellites. She is an amphibious warfare ship, a forty thousand–ton helicopter carrier of the Wasp class. She is 180 miles to the north of us."

Khrenov poured himself a cup of scalding hot tea. He needed to clear his head.

"She is steaming alone? No escorts?"

"None detected, Captain. She appears to be steaming alone."

Khrenov did not like the sound of that. It was extremely stupid of the Americans to send this ship to Elu without escorts, if that was what they had done. He did not believe the Americans were stupid. They had been known to escort their carriers with 637 or 688 class attack submarines. The sooner he sank the American ship, the better.

He punched up the Wasp class on the intelligence computer. Interesting. The Wasp class did not carry long-range antiaircraft missiles, but she did have three Phalanx systems. Very well, how many missiles to launch? A forty thousand–ton warship would not be easy to sink. He had four SS-N-3C missiles left; he would launch them all. That would attract the Yankees' attention!

Very well, do it! Khrenov ordered a passive sonar search in all directions. His sonar operators scanned slowly and carefully, listening for any sound which might indicate the presence of another submarine. At last the sonar officer reported. "All clear, Captain. No contacts."

Khrenov nodded to Lieutenant Shpagin. "Sound Battle Stations, Pavel. Weapons Officer, stand by to launch Three, Four, Five, and Eight."

He pushed the intercom button. Khrenov's voice rang through *Leningradski Komsomols*'s compartments. "Stand by for surface—action-guided missiles, battle surface!"

Compressed air roared into the ballast tanks and forced hundreds of tons of water out into the sea. *Leningradski Komsomols*'s long gray hull moved upward, and she surfaced in a mass of frothing, white bubbles.

Khrenov did not dare to be on the surface without using his air search radar. He remembered the American bomber with the Harpoon missiles vividly.

"Radar, start search."

He waited tensely. *Leningradski Komsomols* might have to dive at any second.

"All clear, Captain, nothing detected."

No reason to delay. "Man the bridge!"

The lookouts rushed up the ladder to the bridge and began scanning the horizon. Khrenov was right behind them. The lookouts called, "All clear!"

Khrenov swept the horizon with his own binoculars and confirmed the lookouts' report. Conditions were good. Visibility was excellent in the clear morning sunlight. The sea was calm. A breeze was blowing from the west, creating some small waves, but they would not interfere with a missile launch.

"Commence launch operations!"

Leningradski Komsomols's hull vibrated as the front of the conning tower rotated and exposed the missile guidance and tracking radars. The four huge missile launchers slowly elevated upward to twenty degrees and locked into the firing position. The final countdown had begun.

Khrenov began to sweat. He must stay on the surface for the next twenty minutes. While the conning tower was rotated and the missile launchers were elevated, he could not dive. *Leningradski Komsomols* was vulnerable now. All he could do was launch the missiles as soon as possible.

USS LOS ANGELES—OFF ELU

Thirty-two miles to the north, a long black teardrop shape slipped quietly through the water. *Los Angeles* was running at antenna depth. Only a few feet of her gray-and-white-mottled Type 18D periscope-antenna mount protruded above the surface. 688 class submarines are some of the quietest submarines in the world, and *Los Angeles* was running very quietly, indeed. Her sonar operators were operating her huge BQQ-5 sonar in the passive mode, listening for any sound that might indicate that they had detected the elusive Soviet Echo class submarine. The electronic intercept antennas on the Type 18D mount were listening intently for any signals in the radio-frequency bands.

Lt. Comdr. Paul Jones had the con. He sat in *Los Angeles*'s attack center, sipping a cup of coffee strong enough to float nails. He glanced at the sonar displays on the Mark 117 Fire Control System. Nothing. *Los Angeles* had been searching steadily for eight hours with no contacts. The captain of that Soviet Echo was either very good or very lucky. His boat was inherently noisier than *Los Angeles,* but so far, he had eluded detection. Perhaps, if they—.

The leading sonar operator spoke suddenly. "Commander, I've got something. Possible contact. It's beyond the first convergence zone. Sounds like a submarine blowing ballast tanks. Approximate bearing 190."

Bingo! "Helmsman, course 190."

Los Angeles's bow turned menacingly toward the contact. Jones began to worry. Should he stay near the surface or haul down the periscope and go deep? If the Echo was surfacing, he should probably stay at antenna depth. If—.

"Commander, this is ESM. Positive intercept. Soviet Snoop Slab air search radar operating in search mode, bearing 192. Snoop Slab is carried by Soviet Echo IIs and—." The electronic support measures operator's voice suddenly stopped. Jones's nerves crawled, but he resisted the temptation to ask questions. Svenson was one of the best electronic technicians on the boat. He knew what he was doing.

"Commander"—Svenson's voice was hoarse with excitement—"positive intercept. Soviet Front Door missile tracking and Front Piece missile guidance radars operating, bearing 192. Echo II class submarine on the surface, operating in missile launching mode."

"Battle Stations!" Jones glanced at the Mark 117 FCS weapons status display. All four of the 21-inch torpedo tubes were loaded, Harpoon antiship missiles in One and Two, Mark 48 ADCAP torpedoes in Three and Four. He stared at the situation display.

A line radiated outward from the Own Ship Position symbol along the intercept bearing. A diamond-shaped Friendly Surface Ship symbol indicated *Wasp*'s position two hundred miles to the north. No doubt about it, the Echo was going after *Wasp*. Time to do something, and do it quick!

Jones had no range data. Electronic intercepts give excellent bearing data but little range information. However, Harpoons can be launched in the Bearing ONly search mode. The best indications were that the Echo was not less than thirty miles away or more than sixty. The Harpoons could handle that. He checked the engagement planning display and gave the attack order.

"Prepare to fire One and Two. Bearing Only Launch Mode, bearing 192. Start search at twelve miles."

The Mark 117 Fire Control System generated the guidance data and sent it to the torpedo room, where the two UGM-84 Harpoon missiles waited in their metal-and-plastic capsules. The data were stored in the missile guidance units. The outer doors of the torpedo tubes opened smoothly. In the attack center, the missile-ready lights came on.

"Fire One and Two!"

"One fired! Two fired!"

The metal-and-plastic capsules shot forward and out of *Los Angeles*'s torpedo tubes. As they cleared the long, black hull, lanyards pulled taut and the capsule steering fins deployed. The unpowered, buoyant capsules steered upward at a thirty-degree angle toward the surface. The capsules reached the surface, and sensors detected broach. The capsule nose caps separated, and the tail sections were jettisoned. The Harpoons' solid-propellant rocket boosters fired, and the missiles roared upward, trailing gray-white smoke.

As the Harpoons left their capsules, their fins and wings extended. The boosters accelerated the missiles to six hundred miles per hour, burned out, and fell away. The J402-CA400 jet engines started. As the missiles reached one thousand feet, they nosed over into a forty-five degree dive, pulled out, and roared down the bearing line, skimming low over the ocean at six hundred miles per hour. A minute later, their PR-53/DSQ-58 homing radars clicked on and started search, scanning repeatedly ahead.

The seconds ticked by. The radars scanned steadily, following their programmed search pattern as the missiles flew along the bearing line. Then, the Harpoons' radars detected a target ahead. The radars locked on, and both missiles roared toward the target.

LENINGRADSKI KOMSOMOLS—OFF ELU

Khrenov was fuming. Missile Number Three was being stubborn and refusing to transfer to internal power. He needed to launch all four together for a coordinated attack, but the waiting made his nerves crawl. He was still on the bridge on the top of *Leningradski Komsomols*'s conning tower. He hated being on the surface in a combat zone, but his SS-N-3C missiles could not be launched when the submarine was submerged. Would they never get that damned missile ready?

Suddenly, the electronic warfare officer was shouting over the intercom. "Captain, radars detected! Hostile cruise missiles incoming, bearing starboard 12, terminal homing mode!"

Khrenov's heart froze. There was nothing he could do, not one chance in a thousand, but he had to try. "Emergency! Lower launchers! Secure conning tower! Prepare for emergency dive!"

There was momentary confusion as *Leningradski Komsomols*'s crew shifted from preparing to launch to preparing to dive. Orders were shouted and equipment activated. The huge missile launchers were unlocked and started to lower slowly back into the hull. The front of the conning tower began to rotate back to cover the missile guidance radars, but too slow, too slow. Thirty or forty seconds had gone by, and the Harpoons were coming at ten miles per minute.

Khrenov snapped up his binoculars. There they were, two gray-white circles, two Harpoon missiles, coming straight at him. The electronic warfare officer activated his countermeasures, but *Leningradski Komsomols* was a perfect target, a single vessel in the middle of a broad ocean area. She had no guns or antiaircraft missiles to defend herself.

Khrenov watched in horror as the first Harpoon shot straight at *Leningradski Komsomols*'s bow. The missile struck at the base of the empty forward missile launcher. Its five hundred–pound, steel-cased warhead penetrated and detonated. Khrenov ducked as jagged steel fragments tore into the conning tower.

The second Harpoon struck the bow, and penetrated into *Leningradski Komsomols*'s forward torpedo room. The warhead detonated, and *Leningradski Komsomols*'s hull shuddered and was rocked by explosion after explosion as the warheads of her torpedoes detonated. Flame and smoke began to pour out of gaping holes in the bow.

Lieutenant Shpagin's voice crackled over the intercom. "Captain, fire and explosions in the forward torpedo room. The control center is flooding. Primary power is out. We can't hold her. She is going down by the bow!"

If a captain cannot save his ship, he must try to save his crew. Khrenov's voice rang through *Leningradski Komsomols*'s compartments for the last time.

"Abandon ship! This is the captain. Abandon ship!"

Chapter Twenty-Nine

"The Spartans ask not how many the enemy may be, but only where they may be found."

—Aegius of Sparta

2ND RANGER BATTALION—ELU ISLAND— THE PLATEAU

Major Gozen scanned the road carefully through his field glasses. He could see nothing except the road itself and the lush green tropical trees that bordered it. It would have been a peaceful scene except for the bomb craters which pockmarked the landscape. It was really a nice day. The sun was shining. The sky was blue. A soft breeze was blowing from the west. The temperature had dropped to a bearable eighty degrees. Elu seemed peaceful and deserted. Gozen did not deceive himself. Concealed in and around the rocks, his men were waiting, quiet and deadly, their weapons ready. And he knew that the Russians were massed around the turn of the last bend in the road.

Gozen heard a sound over the sighing of the breeze, faint at first, then louder and louder, like the sound of distant thunder. Engines starting! Dozen of engines.

The Russians were coming. Well, let them come. He had made all the preparations he could think of; there was nothing left to do but fight.

Something came slowly around the bend. It was nine hundred yards away, but Gozen could see it clearly in his field glasses. It was dull green, angular, and ugly, and it had a long-barreled cannon protruding from the front of the hull. An ASU-85! Another came round the bend, and another, and another. They advanced slowly for about fifty yards, then pulled off to the sides of the road, two to the left and two to the right. All four 85mm cannon muzzles were pointing up the road. Major Gozen would have sworn that all four were pointed straight at him.

He watched as the barrels of the guns moved slightly. The gunners were making their final sight adjustments. Now, the long cannon barrels stopped moving and stared ominously at the American positions. Gozen saw bright yellow flashes as the first four twenty-one–pound high-explosive shells screamed into the rocks at 2,600 feet per second and detonated. Fountains of dirt and a hail of rock fragments filled the air. Now, the ASU-85s began to fire steadily, rhythmically, four shells every twenty seconds. The Russian 85mm SD-44 cannon is not the newest cannon in the world. It was designed during World War II to counter the deadly German 88. The performance of the two cannons is very similar. The 85 mm was designed to tear targets to pieces, and it does it very well.

Bravo Company was defending the rocks. They were well concealed and dug in, but they could not stand much more of this. Time to strike back. Gozen was with Alfa Company. Alfa Company's three Dragon teams were concealed in the grass and bushes nearby. Gozen gave the open-fire signal. The Dragon operators popped up, resting the missile launchers on their bipods and supporting the missile container tubes over their right shoulders. The first Dragon gunner fired. Gozen heard the muffled roar of the recoilless gas generator as it fired and ejected the missile from the launch tube.

The Dragon missile shot toward the ASU-85s at 375 feet per second, trailing its guidance wires behind it. Pairs of small rocket thrusters inside the missile fired, each generating 265 pounds of thrust for .7 seconds to sustain the Dragon's initial velocity. Six, five,—Gozen could see the ASU-85s cannon muzzles start to traverse smoothly to aim at this new threat,—four, three—would that creeping, crawling thing never get there?— two, one—Gozen saw a yellow-white flash as the Dragon's warhead struck the ASU-85 just to the right of its cannon barrel. A lance of white-hot gas and molten metal penetrated the ASU-85's frontal armor. For half a second, nothing seemed to happen. Then, the ASU-85 blew apart spectacularly, as thirty-six ready rounds of 85mm cannon ammunition detonated in a series of violent explosions, and orange flames and greasy black smoke poured out of its shattered hull.

Two more Dragons were on the way. Gozen could see the missiles making small, quick course corrections as the AN/TAS-5 trackers corrected their aim. Steady now, steady, keep those damned cross hairs on target! Keep them on—. Gozen saw three bright yellow flashes as the remaining three ASU-85s fired together. The three 85mm high-explosive shells screamed into the Ranger Dragon teams' positions in less than a second. One shell struck the ground directly in front of a Dragon launcher and detonated, filling the air with shrieking steel fragments. The three-man Dragon team died instantly. Deprived of guidance signals, the Dragon lost control and dove into the ground fifty feet from the ASU-85s. Its warhead detonated futilely.

The third Dragon team had better luck. Their missile

struck low, but the warhead's detonation cut the ASU-85's left-hand track apart. It was not destroyed, but it could no longer move. Moving as rapidly as they could, the two surviving Dragon teams discarded the empty launching tubes and clamped their trackers onto plastic tubes containing fresh Dragon missiles. But the ASU-85s had the range. They began to fire as rapidly as their loaders could throw rounds into their guns and close the breech blocks, each gun firing an 85mm shell every ten seconds. The twenty-one–pound shells screamed into the Ranger positions. Explosion after explosion blasted the Ranger antitank teams. A hail of steel fragments cut a second Dragon team to pieces.

The third team fired again. Their Dragon shot from the launcher tube and streaked toward the ASU-85s. More 85mm cannon shells screamed into the Ranger position. The ground shook and trembled. The acrid smell of burning explosives filled the air. With superhuman determination, the Dragon gunner kept his cross hairs on the target. The Dragon struck, and its warhead detonated. The ASU began to smoke and burn. Gozen could see the hatches fly open as its four-man crew bailed out.

Something was happening at the bend in the road. A squat, dull green shape moved around the bend and started up the road toward the rocks. It was not an ASU. Gozen could see a small turret mounting a cannon and a guided missile. A BMD! Now another and another came around the bend. For a few seconds, that was all; then, three more squat, dull green shapes followed the first group, and then, three more. Nine BMDs, a Guards air assault company. This was it. The Russian commander had started his main attack.

Simultaneously, 120mm heavy mortar bombs began to rain down on the American positions. The *Spetsnaz* team's weary mortar section had been reinforced by six fresh 120mm mortars and crews from the Guards air assault regiment's mortar company. The thirty-four–pound, high-explosive 120mm mortar bombs began to detonate in a steady stream of explosions, filling the air with flying dirt, dust, and rock fragments.

The Sheridans were to the north of the rocks where the Russians could not see them. They were the only effective mobile antiarmor force Gozen had. Time to use them now. Gozen took his radio headset. "Airborne Leader, this is Black Beret. This is the main attack. They're hitting us with everything they've got. Bring up the Sheridans. Counterattack!"

Gozen heard DeBerg's voice. "Black Beret, this is Airborne Leader. Hang on, we are on the way." DeBerg continued, but he was no longer talking to Major Gozen. "Load, HE-AT! Airborne units, this is Airborne Leader. Attack. Airborne!" Over the radio, Gozen heard DeBerg's gunner, loader, and driver shout "Airborne!" in unison. He knew that same word was echoing through the other Sheridans.

To an outsider, particularly someone who was not a soldier, it would have sounded like a meaningless ritual, but it was not. "Airborne" is the watchword of the 82nd Airborne Division. Gozen smiled grimly as he heard it. DeBerg was reminding his men of their famous unit. However the battle went, no one was going to be able to say the 82nd Airborne had let the Rangers down on Elu.

DeBerg had better hurry. More squat, dull green shapes were coming around the bend, and nine more BMDs were moving up the road. Four more ASU-85s followed, moving quickly into firing positions. Now, more BMDs came round the bend.

The ASU-85s continued to pound the Ranger positions in the rocks. The BMDs were not firing yet. Gozen knew they were conserving ammunition. Each BMD carried forty rounds of 73mm cannon ammunition in an automatic loader. They were saving that until they got in close.

Gozen heard the rumble of engines and the squeal of tracks behind him. DeBerg's 82nd Airborne Sheridans were coming up. They stopped and opened fire, their M81 cannons hurling sixty-pound 152mm shells at the Russians. For half a minute, the Russians were taken by surprise. Gozen saw a 152mm shell detonate on the side of a BMD's turret, knocking it completely off the hull. The decapitated BMD lost direction and nosed over into the ditch at the side of the road. Another BMD began to burn spectacularly, and an ASU-85's hull was penetrated and shattered as its cannon ammunition exploded.

But now, the Russian weapons were trained on the Sheridans. The BMDs and ASUs began to fire rapidly, blasting 73mm HE-AT shells and 85mm High Velocity–Armor Piercing projectiles at DeBerg's Sheridans. And now, Gozen saw orange flashes and puffs of gray smoke around the turrets of several BMDs. They were launching their rocket-propelled AT-3 Sagger antitank missiles at the Sheridans. The Saggers streaked toward the American tanks, trailing their guidance wires behind them.

Gozen saw an AT-3 missile detonate just below the turret of a nearby Sheridan. The Sheridan shuddered and then exploded in a series of shattering blasts as its 152mm shells detonated. Another Sheridan was burning, flames and smoke spewing from a jagged hole in its hull. The Sheridan's hatches were open. Maybe some of the crew had gotten out alive. The battle was deadly. The lightly armored Sheridans and BMDs were pounding each other with weapons designed to destroy sixty-ton main battle tanks. It was like eggs smashing at each other with sledgehammers. Any blow that landed was lethal.

A dozen shattered, burning BMDs and ASUs lined the road, but the rest were coming on. Gozen glanced behind him. Three of the Sheridans were still firing. The rest were knocked out. The first BMDs reached the end of the road and moved out onto the plateau. Bravo Company's Dragon teams opened fire from the rocks. The first two BMDs blew up as the M47 Dragon missiles struck and detonated, but the other BMDs pressed on, moving ominously toward the Rangers concealed among the rocks. The BMDs opened fire. Their 73mm cannons and .30 caliber machine guns were blasting away, pouring a storm of fire into the American positions.

1ST AUSTRALIAN SAS REGIMENT—ELU ISLAND—THE PLATEAU

Cord crouched in the long grass watching the BMDs rumble by. Cord was MacNair's Number Two. MacNair was the logical man to throw the charges. He was larger and stronger than Cord. Cord had the three spare charges. He would pass them to MacNair as soon as he threw the first one. The BMDs had not noticed the Australians. That did not surprise Cord. The Russians' attention was fixed on the Americans in the rocks, and a buttoned-up BMD does not give its crew the finest visibility in the world. But Cord knew that this would change very rapidly when the charges started to go off.

MacNair pointed. A BMD was coming by, looming up out of the smoke, less than twenty feet away. Cord wondered why he had left the family sheep ranch to lead a life of adventure. His father had told him it was foolish and that Cord would come to regret it. Shows you should always listen to your old dad.

MacNair pulled the pin on the L2 hand grenade and

390

threw the charge under the BMD with a form that would have done credit to the best slow bowler in Australian cricket. Several years crawled by. Then, there was a shattering explosion, then another, and another. MacNair had succeeded in getting the charge under the BMD's automatic loader. Forty 73-mm cannon shells detonated in rapid succession. Cord ducked as pieces of BMD rained down from the sky. Maybe old MacNair wasn't crazy after all.

Another BMD loomed up out of the smoke. Its gunner was in an extremely bad mood. His .30 caliber coaxial machine gun spat burst after burst of full-metal-jacketed bullets at Cord and MacNair. Only one thing saved them. They were in the BMD's dead zone. One of the design flaws in the BMD is that the turret cannon and machine gun can only be depressed three degrees below the vertical. The Russian gunner could not lower the muzzle of his PKT machine gun enough to hit them. But there were other BMDs coming. Better get this one now!

MacNair armed and threw his second charge, but he staggered as he threw it, and it went wide. There was a shattering explosion, but nothing happened. The BMD came on. MacNair was down. Cord could see a splash of blood on the left leg of his fatigues. That made Cord angry. Cord did not love MacNair, but he respected him, and, by God, MacNair was his RSM! Cord ran at the side of the BMD. The gunner was still firing his machine gun, but he could not hit Cord now. Cord was back in the BMD's dead zone.

Cord pulled the pin on his first charge and wedged it between two of the BMD's roller wheels, then threw himself down. There was a thunderous explosion. The BMD's track was cut, and the two roller wheels sheared off. The BMD ground to a halt. The bloody gunner was still shooting. Cord had one charge left. He would fix the bloody bastard. Who dares, wins! Cord ran at the side of the BMD. His last charge was in his hands. He reached the side of the immobilized BMD and shoved the charge under the barrel of the 73mm cannon. He pulled the pin and dove for the ground.

The charge detonated and eleven pounds of C4 blasted the BMD. The turret was shattered. Smoke began to pour out. Cord had no charges left. It was time to get RSM MacNair and get the bloody hell out of there. But first things first. Cord unslung his rifle. The weight of the Lee-Enfield in his hands was reassuring. That was just as well. Over the roar of battle, Cord heard a metallic clang. The hatches in the rear of the BMD's hull had been thrown open. Four determined-looking Russians were leaping over the side, clutching AKD-74 automatic rifles in their hands.

Most people, including even experienced soldiers, would have given Cord no chance at all, one man with a hand-operated, bolt-action rifle against four men with automatic rifles. But a few old Australian or British soldiers who knew Lee-Enfields might have smiled. Without thinking, Cord exploded into that deadly technique called "Ten rounds rapid." The Lee-Enfield seemed to exploded into flame as Cord fired and worked the butter-smooth bolt with blinding speed. A good man with a Lee-Enfield can fire ten aimed shots as fast as can be done with any rifle in the world, and Cord was a good man. Full-metal-jacketed 174 grain bullets were tearing through the Russians as they hit the ground. Aimed shots kill. The BMD's dismount group fell to the ground and lay still.

Time to get out. Cord threw two smoke grenades in the general direction of the other BMDs and yelled at the top of his lungs, "Break contact! Break contact!" He grabbed MacNair by his web equipment straps and began to drag him back toward the SAS position in the trees. Lovat and Blake came running out of the smoke. Cord looked behind him, but there was no one else. They had gotten five or six BMDs, but they had lost six men. In the cold equations of tactics, that was a good trade, but those six men were Cord's friends. And Cord knew all too well that the loss of six BMDs would not stop the Russians. He swore bitterly under his breath as they dragged MacNair back to the SAS lines.

2ND RANGER BATTALION—ELU ISLAND— THE PLATEAU

More and more of the dull green Soviet armored combat vehicles had reached the plateau and were closing in on the rocks. In a minute, the dismount groups would leap from the BMDs and start the final assault. The Rangers and the 82nd Airborne Sheridans had done their best, but they were not going to stop them. Too damn many BMDs!

Gozen had not wanted to risk the SATCOM radios in forward positions. He had left them with Carter. Gozen spoke into his tactical radio's headset. "Talon Leader, this is Black Beret Leader. Get on the AN/PSC-3 SATCOM, and contact General Brand. Tell him we can't hold them. We don't have enough anti-armor weapons. Most of the Sheridans have been knocked out. We are being overrun. Ask him for orders. Should we attempt to destroy *War God* or any of its components? Can *Wasp* send helicopters to attempt evacuation of survivors? Hurry, we haven't got much time!"

"Roger, Black Beret Leader, wait."

It was perfectly good radio procedure, but what else was he going to do? More and more BMDs and ASU-85s were moving up and onto the plateau. One large group was moving to the east of the rocks, a second was moving to the west. He would have to pull out Bravo

Company if he could. Otherwise, they would be surrounded and wiped out. As Gozen watched, the Russians began to fire 120mm mortar smoke bombs into
and around the rocks. They were blinding Bravo Company's gunners before the final assault.

Gozen saw the rear hatches slam open in the rear of
the BMDs. Four Guards air assault soldiers leaped from
each BMD, clutching their AK 74 rifles and RPK-74
light machine guns in their hands. Time was running
out for the Rangers. What the hell was Carter doing?

Carter's voice came through Gozen's headset. "Black
Beret Leader, this is Talon Leader. I have contacted
General Brand. There is interference on the channel,
but his reply is clear. He says, 'Do not try to destroy
the satellite. Tell Major Gozen to hold on. Fight to the
last man.' "

Well, that was clear enough, and it certainly sounded
like General Brand.

"Anything else? What about evacuating survivors to
the *Wasp?*"

"The general did not mention that, Major. He did
say something else, though. It was a personal message
to you. It's some kind of code. He said, 'Tell the Moose
to hang on, I'm sending in the cavalry.' "

Gozen blinked. Had Carter gotten General Brand's
message wrong? If it was a code, it was one that Gozen
did not know. The cavalry? Well, Gozen was in no position to be particular. He would take any damned help
he could get!

FLIGHT DECK—USS WASP—OFF ELU

Wasp was steaming toward Elu at a steady twenty-
four knots. Her flight deck was crowded with men and
helicopters as she prepared to launch. Comdr. Roger
Douglas was *Wasp*'s aviation boss. He was responsible

for all flight deck operations, including the launching and recovery of all helicopters.

At the moment, Douglas was suppressing the urge to shriek and scream. It was not that the army helicopter pilots were incompetent. In fact, they were highly skilled, but they had never flown in a mass launch from a moving ship. The opportunity for spectacular accidents was mind boggling. There were no opportunities for rehearsals. Everything would have to be done right the first time.

Commander Douglas made one last visual check of the flight deck. The army flight crews were standing quietly by their AH-64A helicopters. The AH-64As were the ugliest helicopters Douglas had ever seen. They were angular, squat, and painted a hideous army dull olive drab and dark green camouflage pattern. Actually, they were modern, powerful machines, and their army crews seemed to love them. All Douglas wanted was to get them all off his flight deck and safely into the air.

Douglas moved to the lead army helicopter. Lt. Col. Chuck Stuart was standing by his AH-64A. Like his men, he was wearing a CWU-27P fire-resistant flyer's coverall and SPH-4 flight helmet.

"Mornin,' Commander," Stuart said in his soft Tennessee twang. "Are we ready to launch yet? It sounds like things are gettin' a bit rough for our side on the island."

"Right, Colonel," Douglas said. They were as ready as they were ever going to be. Time to go over it one last time. The AH-64A's army radios would not internet with the *Wasp*'s navy models. The launch would have to be controlled with hand signals.

"I'll stand by your helicopter, Colonel, and give you the takeoff signal. I'll have a petty officer standing by each of your squadron's helicopters. They will give your pilots a clear-to-takeoff signal as soon as the helicopter is airborne and clear of the flight deck. As soon as you are clear, make a quick ninety-degree turn port. After that, you are on your own. Good luck with your mission. Any questions?"

Colonel Stuart smiled. He thought "petty officer" was the most hilarious military title he had ever heard. Well, it was the navy's ship. They could call their people whatever they liked. He thought for a moment. "I do have one question, Commander, just to be sure I've got it straight. Which way is port?"

Douglas shuddered. "To the left, Colonel, to the left!"

Stuart nodded. "All right, let's saddle up and go." He climbed into the pilot's seat of his AH-64A.

Douglas looked along *Wasp*'s flight deck. All the army flight crews were in their ugly helicopters. Time to do it. He gave the start-engines signal. Colonel Stuart nodded. The starters whined, and the two 1,696-horsepower General Electric T700-GE-701 gas turbine engines howled into life. Douglas pointed forward. Go! Stuart threw him a salute.

The screaming whine of the engines intensified as Stuart went to full power. The heavily loaded AH-64A lifted straight up for fifty feet, then tilted forward as Stuart went to full pitch. The AH-64A whined forward over *Wasp*'s bow and immediately turned left out over the blue water. A second AH-64A followed, then another, and another, until twenty-one olive drab and dark green helicopters were airborne and headed for Elu at 180 miles per hour.

43RD GUARDS AIR ASSAULT REGIMENT— ELU ISLAND—THE PLATEAU

Colonel Artyshenko's command BMD-2KSh ground onto the plateau. Artyshenko peered through the vision slots in his dome-shaped cupola. It had not been easy. Twenty or more BMDs and ASUs were lying, shattered and burning, along the road. Give them credit. The Americans and Australians had fought like the very devil, but the Guards were winning. No matter how brave men are, they do not stop armored fighting vehicles with rifles.

The Third Battalion of the 43rd was in position to the west of the rocks. The Second Battalion was to the east. Time to bring up the First Battalion from its reserve position and finish off the Americans once and for all.

Artyshenko pushed the button on his headset. "First Battalion Leader, this is Artyshenko. Bring your battalion up and attack to the west. Push the attack, but remember, do not damage the satellite. Acknowledge!"

Artyshenko heard the First Battalion commander's voice clearly over the roar of battle. "Exactly so, Colonel. First Battalion moving up and attacking now!"

Artyshenko looked to the west. A company of the Third Battalion was beginning to fan out and move toward *War God.* They would soften up the Americans who were there. The First Battalion would finish them off and mop up. Then, they would——. What in the devil's name was that? Something was coming straight at him, flying low and fast over the tops of the trees to the west, like a monstrous olive drab and dark green dragonfly. He saw another coming, and another.

There was an orange flash from the right side of the first thing. Artyshenko saw something flashing toward him at supersonic speed. It struck the top of the BMD-2KSh directly on the cupola. There was an intense explosion, and a white-hot jet of gas and molten metal sprayed the inside of the command BMD. Colonel Artyshenko died instantly. He never knew what hit him and blew his vehicle apart, but it was an AGM-114 Hellfire missile.

2ND SQUADRON—6TH CAVALRY BRIGADE (AIR COMBAT)—ELU ISLAND—THE PLATEAU

Lt. Col. Chuck Stuart led the first flight of AH-64A helicopters across the plateau. Behind him, the other AH-64As of the 2nd Squadron of the 6th Cavalry Brigade followed in a column of six flights of three. Ahead, he could see three BMDs burning. Stuart was not surprised. You seldom need to hit anything more than once with a Hellfire missile. The Hellfire's twenty-pound high-explosive antitank warhead had been designed to destroy fifty ton Soviet main battle tanks. Its effect on a lightly armored eight-ton BMD was certainly spectacular.

He did not have time for another missile launch on this pass, but a gun attack would do. He stared at a BMD through the monocle of the Integrated Helmet and Data Display Sighting System mounted on his helmet. Automatically, his gunner's Target Acquisition/Designator Sight swiveled to point at the BMD. Fire control data flowed to the AH-64A's computer.

Underneath the AH-64A's nose, the M230A1 30mm automatic cannon turned rapidly and began to smoothly track the target. Stuart's gunner pushed the switch. The AH-64A vibrated as the M230A1 spat twenty M778 30mm cannon shells at the BMD in a precise, two-second burst. Stuart saw a dozen yellow flashes as the swarm of 30mm cannon shells struck the BMD. It began to burn and explode.

There were more vehicles clustered around a rock formation ahead, and many more were moving in a large column up the plateau road. Stuart had been warned that there might be American Sheridans in the area. He punched up the four-power magnification view from the TADS. He had better be sure before he started shooting.

Stuart saw small, round, centrally placed turrets with guided missile launchers mounted above the cannon barrels. BMDs! He designated a BMD with his IHADSS monocle. The AH-64A vibrated as the 30mm cannon fired again, and twenty 30mm cannon shells shrieked toward the BMD at 2,600 feet per second. The BMD exploded in a ball of orange flame as its 73mm cannon shells and Sagger missiles detonated. The other two AH-64As of Alfa Flight blasted the massed BMDs with bursts of 30mm cannon fire.

Alfa Flight flashed over the mass of dull green BMDs, turbines howling. Stuart pulled his AH-64A into a hard right turn. Behind him he could see numerous fires and explosions as Bravo and Charlie Flights attacked with their 30mm cannons blazing.

Stuart lead Alfa Flight in a sweeping right-hand turn out over the harbor area and around in a three-quarter turn until the three olive drab and dark green camouflaged AH-64As were flying low and fast up the plateau road. The last, straight stretch of the road was crowded with BMDs and ASU-85s. Stuart had never imagined there could be so many targets in one place.

But the party was over. The 2nd Squadron's sudden slashing attack had taken the Russians by surprise. Now, they were reacting. Stuart saw a series of sparkling yellow flashes run along the line of vehicles as the BMDs began to fire back with their PKT .30 caliber machine guns. Green tracers filled the air and clawed at the onrushing AH-64As. That did not worry Stuart. His squadron's AH-64As were protected by metal-and-plastic armor designed to resist and survive hits by .50 caliber machine guns and 23 mm cannons. They were very unlikely to be knocked out by .30 caliber machine gun fire.

But Stuart knew that .30 caliber machine guns were not the only air defense weapons the BMDs carried. Each was equipped with a shoulder-launched SA-7 *Strela* antiaircraft missile, and one of the crewmen was trained to use it. The SA-7 was the Russian equivalent of the American FIM-92A Stinger. Intelligence said that the SA-7 was not nearly as good as the Stinger. Stuart devoutly hoped that they were right. He had a sinking feeling he was about to find out.

The AH-64A Apache's designers had considered the infrared homing missile to be one of the worst threats their helicopter would have to face on the battlefield. The AH-64As incorporated passive design features to minimize infrared radiation and active infrared countermeasures. The hot exhaust gases of each of the twin General Electric T700-GE-701 turbo shaft engines were channeled through a McDonnell Douglas Black Hole infrared suppression system, which drew in cool outside air and mixed it with the hot exhaust gases in three secondary exhaust nozzles. This cooled the hot gases and significantly reduced the AH-64A's infrared signature. The secondary nozzles were angled outward to prevent the guidance unit of an infrared homing missile from looking directly up the exhaust ducts and viewing the hot internal engine components.

These were built-in features. They worked all the time. In theory, most infrared homing missiles would not be able to lock on. But theories have been known to be wrong. The AH-64A also carried a Saunders AN/ALQ-144 infrared jammer mounted on the top of the fuselage just behind the rotor mast. An M130 Chaff/Flare dispenser was mounted on the left side of the fuselage. It carried thirty infrared flares to confuse and blind infrared homing missiles.

All this seemed complicated and redundant, with backups for backups. Perhaps some of it was unnecessary. You would have had a hard time convincing Chuck Stuart of that. He was about to be shot at with infrared homing missiles, and he wanted all the protection he could get. He activated the AN/ALQ-144 infrared jammer. It consisted of a multicolored, glass-enclosed, superheated ceramic block. When commanded to do so, it would emit immensely powerful pulses of infrared energy.

These thoughts raced through Stuart's mind in five seconds as his AH-64A whined toward the column of Russian armored vehicles that jammed the road. He laser-designated the rearmost BMD and launched a Hellfire. The missile shot forward. From the left and the right, two more Hellfires streaked toward the mass of dull green vehicles as the other two AH-64As in Alfa Flight launched.

Now the three helicopters were flashing over the Russians. Stuart spoke into his microphone. "Alfa Flight, discos on, now!" Stuart triggered his own AN/ALQ-144 infrared jammer. To the human eye very little happened as the "disco light" jammer began to flash. But in the infrared spectrum, the AH-64As were emitting immensely powerful, blinding pulses of infrared light. Stuart glanced in his rearview mirror. The three BMDs had been struck by Alfa Flight's Hellfires. They were burning and exploding. That was not surprising. Hellfires seldom miss, and their twenty-pound warheads usually kill what they hit.

Stuart flinched as he saw orange flashes from several of the undamaged BMDs and long, slender objects trailing gray smoke shoot up toward the AH-64As. SA-7s! He triggered his M130 flare launcher, and two infrared flares flashed and burned behind his helicopter.

The guidance units of the Russian SA-7s lacked the sophistication of American Sidewinders and Stingers. Their guidance units were confused and blinded by the

AH-64A's countermeasures. They shot harmlessly past Alfa Flight's three helicopters. Stuart breathed a sigh of relief. The Russians' only real air defense weapon had been neutralized. Each of his AH-64As had gone into combat carrying sixteen Hellfire missiles and four Stingers. They had approximately three missiles for every Russian armored combat vehicle, and Hellfire hits and kills eighty to ninety percent of the time. He almost wished there was some way the Russians could give up and surrender. Now, it was going to be a slaughter.

29TH ATTACK REGIMENT—OFF ELU

Capt. Pavel Ozhimkov was a stern and humorless man in his late twenties. Few people liked Ozhimkov, but most people admired him. He was completely dedicated to flying and to doing his duty. There were jokes in the 29th Regiment which said that Ozhimkov was married to his SU-24 and performed various unlikely and unprintable acts with it. But even the men who told the jokes would have admitted that Ozhimkov knew more about SU-24s than their designers and was one of the finest pilots in the regiment.

Ozhimkov knew all this, but all he felt at the moment was burning shame. The 29th Regiment had gone on its first combat mission in forty years, and he had not been with them. He had been forced to abort by a faulty fuel pump, and to sit on the ground while the 29th roared up from Cam Ranh Bay and flew into battle. It had been the worst day in his life.

The mechanics had worked around the clock trying to get some SU-24s ready to fly. By robbing parts from one plane to fix another, they had been able to get one flight of four SU-24s in the air. It made Ozhimkov feel a little better that the colonel had chosen him to lead the flight. The mission was critical but simple. Fly to Elu, contact the TU-142 on station, be vectored to this

402

American ship, the *Wasp,* and sink it at all costs. Ozhimkov had never attacked a ship before, but each of the two-tone gray SU-24s in his flight was carrying six 1,100-pound laser-guided bombs. A forty thousand–ton ship must be a giant target, and laser-guided bombs seldom miss. He was confident that his SU-24s could sink it.

It would not do to be overconfident. It was possible that there might be some of those damned Australian F-111Cs in the area. Well, each SU-24 was carrying AA-9 air-to-air missiles under its wings. It did not matter, anyway. Only death would stop Ozhimkov from attacking. He checked with his navigator. They were within a hundred miles of Elu.

Suddenly, there was a voice in his earphones. "Red Star Six. Red Star Six! This is Polar Star. Come in. Emergency! Acknowledge."

The devil! It was the TU-142. What was happening now?

"Polar Star, Polar Star, this is Red Star Six. What is the emergency?"

"Red Star Six, the Guards air assault troops on Elu report that they are under heavy attack by approximately two dozen heavily armed helicopters. They are suffering heavy losses and must have air support at once!"

"Message acknowledged, Polar Star. Are you ordering me to divert to Elu and engage these helicopters?"

"Exactly so, Red Star. Drop your bombs and proceed to Elu on afterburners. Do so at once! The situation is extremely critical!"

"Polar Star, Red Star Six. If I drop my bombs, I will not be able to carry out my mission to attack and sink the American ship *Wasp.* I was told that sinking this ship had the highest possible priority."

"Those orders have been countermanded by direct

orders from Moscow. Carry out my orders immediately, Red Star!"

Very well, comrade, it is your responsibility.

"Acknowledged, Polar Star. Red Star Flight Six, this is Red Star Flight Leader. Jettison bombs. Retain AA-9 missiles. Go on afterburner now!"

Ozhimkov pushed the bomb-release switches and the 1,100-pound bombs fell away. Now he pushed his throttles forward and switched on his afterburners. The rumble of the big Tumanskii R-32B engines changed to a roar as the four big SU-24s accelerated, faster, and faster, until they were flying toward Elu at 1,400 miles per hour.

2ND SQUADRON—6TH CAVALRY BRIGADE (AIR COMBAT)—ELU ISLAND—THE PLATEAU

Lt. Col. Chuck Stuart watched the battle with grim satisfaction. His seven flights were operating independently now, weaving and crisscrossing over the battlefield, launching their deadly Hellfires and strafing the Russians mercilessly with their M230A1 30mm cannons. The plateau was littered with shattered, burning BMDs. Many crew members had managed to get out when their vehicles were hit, but Stuart noted with approval that his crews were ignoring soldiers on foot and concentrating on killing vehicles. He was not surprised. Stuart knew, with absolute certainty, that the 6th Cavalry Brigade was the finest helicopter combat unit in the world, and his 2nd Squadron was the best squadron in the 6th. He considered sending one flight at a time back to *Wasp* to rearm. No, they had plenty of Hellfires. He would—.

What the hell? Stuart heard a warning tone in his helmet earphones. Simultaneously, a light flashed on his Radar Warning Receiver. The RWR had detected radars operating over Elu, and AH-64As do not carry radars. He flicked on his radar jammer and scanned the sky around him. Nothing.

Suddenly, he heard a voice in his earphones. "Saber Squadron. Fast movers! Fast movers! From the west, fast and low! Look out Charlie Flight! They're right behind you!"

Stuart hauled on his controls and pulled number 25386 into a hard right turn. He knew there were no friendly jets over Elu. These must be Russian SU-24s. The fight was no longer one sided.

29TH ATTACK REGIMENT—OVER ELU

Captain Pavel Ozhimkov led his flight of four SU-24s in a long, screaming dive toward Elu. As they dropped down from thirty-six thousand feet toward sea level, the increased drag of the thicker, lower-altitude air began to slow them down. Ozhimkov leveled off at a thousand feet. He checked his air speed indicator. He was doing eight hundred miles per hour. He could see the western edge of the plateau ahead.

Ozhimkov spoke to his weapon systems/navigation officer. "Radar on. Terrain clearance mode."

The weapon systems/navigation officer pushed a button, and the big radar in the SU-24's nose began to scan. "We will clear the edge by thirty meters, Captain."

"Very, well. Radar, air-to-air mode."

"Air-to-air mode. Switching now!"

The SU-24's radar began to emit rapid 200-kilowatt pulses as it scanned for targets. Almost instantly, the radar display was alive with targets, perhaps twenty of them. They were moving at one hundred to two hundred knots, and flying at a hundred feet or less. Helicopters! There could be no doubt. And there were no friendly helicopters over Elu.

"Red Star Six Flight, hostile helicopters ahead. No friendly aircraft ahead. Weapons free! Attack!"

The four SU-24s flew toward Elu at maximum speed. Ozhimkov glanced at his radar display. There were three targets dead ahead. He looked up. He could see the sunlight glinting off rotor blades. He armed an AA-9 missile and fired. The missile streaked toward the target. His wingman launched, and a second AA-9 streaked toward the targets. Suddenly, Ozhimkov's radar display was filled with streaks and flashes. The Americans were trying to jam his radar. It made no difference. The AA-9s were guided by infrared homing units which were far larger and more sophisticated than those of the Russian SA-7s. Both missiles locked on the left-hand helicopter. Its pilot was turning hard, but too late. The AA-9s struck, and the helicopter vanished in a ball of fire.

Ozhimkov found himself flying straight toward the leader. He recognized that angular, ugly silhouette. An American AH-64A, the finest attack helicopter the Americans had. While he was thinking, he pulled the trigger. The big SU-24's six-barreled Gatling gun roared into life and sent three hundred 23mm high explosive–incendiary cannon shells at the AH-64A in one sustained four-second burst. Ozhimkov could see dozens of bright yellow flashes as his 23mm HE-I shells struck the AH-64A and detonated. The ugly American helicopter rolled over and went down, trailing smoke and flames. Two down!

Red Star Flight flashed over the plateau and out to sea. Ozhimkov led his flight in a wide, shallow turn, back toward Elu. Quickly, he spoke to his crews.

"Reduce speed. Wings to full forward sweep position. Ready to resume attack. Careful, comrades, we surprised them that time. They will be ready for us now. They are American AH-64A attack helicopters. They can carry air-to-air missiles. Take no unneeded chances. Ready? Go! Red Star Flight attacking!"

2ND SQUADRON—6TH CAVALRY BRIGADE (AIR COMBAT)—ELU ISLAND—THE PLATEAU

Lt. Col. Chuck Stuart watched as the four big, two-toned gray jets roared out to sea. He did not need to see stars on their wings to know that they were hostile. He also knew that time was short. They would be back soon. His AH-64As were now the hunted, not the hunters. They had shot Charlie Flight to pieces. Now they would try to get the rest of the 2nd Squadron. There could be no grand tactics in a fight like this. Each flight would have to fight as best it could. The Russians' overwhelming speed advantage would let them choose the time and the place.

They might not like the party when they got there. The 2nd Squadron's AH-64As were flying with two improved air-launched FIM-92B Stingers on each stub wing tip, and Stuart felt sure that if they could hit an SU-24 with their M230A1 30mm cannon, they would tear the damned thing to pieces. They would—.

"Heads up, Saber Squadron! Fast movers attacking from the east. Look out Alfa Flight, two of them, headed right for you!"

Stuart pulled his AH-64A around, turning into the attack. If they were using infrared homing missiles, he did not want them on his tail. Besides, an AH-64A cannot shoot backward. He armed his Stingers. There they were! Two big SU-24s closing fast.

He launched two Stingers in rapid succession and watched them streak toward the leader. A missile flashed from under the SU-24's wings. Stuart triggered his M130 Chaff/Flare dispenser and prayed. Either his prayers or his flares worked, perhaps both. The two big Russian missiles flashed harmlessly by to one side. Stuart's Stingers struck the leader. Their warheads detonated. The gray SU-24 staggered, rolled, and went down out of control. It struck the ground and exploded in a huge ball of fire. But the other Russian was coming on, straight for Stuart.

There was no time to fire another missile. Stuart stared at the oncoming Russian through the monocle of his helmet mounted IHADDS. His M230A1 30mm cannon swiveled smoothly and roared into life, hurling 30mm cannon shells at the oncoming SU-24. He could see a halo of yellow fire under the SU-24's nose as the Russian pilot fired his 23mm Gatling gun. There was a loud, metallic bang, as a 23mm cannon shell struck the left stub wing of Stuart's helicopter. The AH-64A shuddered but flew on.

Stuart saw a cluster of yellow-white flashes as his 30mm cannon shells tore into the SU-24's nose. Those shells were designed to destroy armored vehicles. They literally blasted the SU-24's fuselage apart, and the flaming fragments exploded in all directions.

Stuart started to breath again. He looked around him quickly. He saw another SU-24 crash and explode, but one of his AH-64As was going down in flames. One SU-24 was left. He had a yellow stripe on his tail. He must be the flight leader. It was Ozhimkov, but Stuart had no way of knowing that. He was on Alfa Two's tail, passing by Stuart's left side, firing bursts from his 23mm Gatling gun at Alfa Two.

It was a well-executed attack, but Ozhimkov was a jet pilot. He had forgotten that the AH-64A's 30mm cannon is not fixed like a jet fighter's gun, but swivels like the turret of a tank. As the big, gray SU-24 shot by, Stuart's M230A1 fired twenty 30mm cannon shells into the SU-24's side. Stuart could see the yellow-white flashes of detonating cannon shells and fragments flying as the SU-24 disintegrated in midair.

Stuart looked around quickly, but the sky was empty. He spoke into his microphone. "Saber Squadron. All fast movers are shot down. Resume attack on hostile armor."

He laser-designated another BMD and launched a Hellfire. The 2nd Squadron helicopters were no longer the hunted. They were the hunters again.

SPETSNAZ TEAM—ELU ISLAND—THE PLATEAU

Colonel Viktor Ulanov watched in horror as the American AH-64A helicopter roared over the battlefield and attacked the 43rd Guards Air Assault Regiment again and again. The destruction was incredible. The American missiles seemed to kill every Russian vehicle they struck. Ulanov and the *Spetsnaz* team were south of the rocks, waiting to move in and occupy them when the Guards gave the word. Ulanov knew that that message would never come.

The American helicopters did not seem to be paying any attention to men on foot. They were concentrating on killing vehicles, but this might not last for long. Their automatic cannon would be deadly if they decided to attack the *Spetsnaz* team, and he had no effective antiaircraft weapons.

Their only chance was to get off the plateau, and get off quickly. It was a bitter decision, but there was no other choice. Ulanov gave the orders. Moving quickly in small groups, the *Spetsnaz* team began to move off the plateau and down the road. Ulanov checked to be sure that none of the wounded were left behind, and moved toward the road. There seemed to be some kind of disturbance ahead. Someone was shouting louder and louder. The devil! It was the damned *Zampolit!*

Major Mamin had his pistol drawn and was yelling at Sharypa and a small group of soldiers. "This is treason! No one will leave the plateau! I will execute the first one of you who tries to do so."

"Major," Sharypa said, "it is Colonel Ulanov's direct order. The men are only doing as they have been told."

"I do not believe you, Sergeant. A Hero of the Soviet Union would never give such a cowardly order!"

Ulanov was getting a little tired of Major Mamin. He brought his AKD-74 rifle to his shoulder and took aim. Damn! Dudorov had moved quietly behind Major Mamin and was in Ulanov's line of fire.

Mamin waved his pistol and started to say something else. Dudorov was remarkably fast for such a big man. In one smooth motion, he smashed the steel buttplate of his rifle against the back of Major Mamin's head. Mamin slumped to the ground. He was unconscious. Ulanov was not surprised. Anyone Dudorov hit seldom needed to be hit again.

Dudorov was kindhearted. It never occurred to him to leave Mamin there for the Americans. He put Mamin's pistol back in its holster and fastened the flap. He hoisted the unconscious Major over one broad shoulder and started down the road. Ulanov followed him. Slowly, wearily, the *Spetsnaz* team started back down the plateau road.

2ND SQUADRON—6TH CAVALRY BRIGADE (AIR COMBAT)—ELU ISLAND—THE PLATEAU

Stuart made a final pass over the plateau. He could see groups of shattered, burning dull green BMDs and ASU-85s everywhere he looked. None of the Russian vehicles seemed to still be in action. Either they had been knocked out by 2nd Squadron's deadly Hellfires, or their crews had abandoned them, realizing that the fight was hopeless. Through his PNVS, he could see groups of Russians on foot moving down the plateau road toward the harbor. He could have ordered his crews to blast them with their 30mm cannons, but they

410

were no threat to anybody anymore. He had no stomach for slaughtering helpless men. Let them go.

He brought his battered AH-64A to a hover almost over *War God.* Old number 25386 was a damned tough machine. He would write McDonnell Douglas a letter of appreciation if he ever had the time. He reduced power, and the big AH-64A settled down on the ground. Stuart stared at the huge silver-gray satellite. So that was what it was all about. He opened his canopy panel and climbed out. For a moment, the area appeared deserted. Then, swarms of men appeared from nowhere and came running toward him. He was glad he recognized American uniforms and Fritz helmets. They were some of the fiercest-looking men Stuart had ever seen, and every one of them was a walking arsenal.

He was in danger of being beaten to death as the laughing, cheering men pounded him on the shoulders. He gathered that the 6th Cavalry Brigade was popular at the moment. He was saved by a stocky oriental major.

"I'm extremely glad to see you, Colonel. I'm Major Gozen. That was a damned fine show! I'll buy you a case of whatever you're drinking when we get back to the States."

"That's very kind of you, Major. George Dickel's Old Number 8 sour mash will be fine," Stuart drawled, "but, I'll insist you help me drink it. Meanwhile, the navy is shrieking and screaming that we have got to evacuate this place immediately. They will send marine CH-53E helicopters as soon as you give the word. They have some crazy idea the whole island is going to blow up."

"They may not be wrong. At least, our scientists think it may happen. Let's get those CH-53Es here as fast as we can."

Stuart nodded and turned toward his helicopter.

"Colonel, just one more thing," Major Gozen said.

"If the 2nd Ranger Battalion is ever in trouble again, we will send for the cavalry!"

Lt. Col. Stuart smiled. As he got into his AH-64A, he was whistling an old tune. Not many people would have recognized it, but Major Gozen was a student of military history. It was the old Civil War army song, "If you want to have a good time, join the cavalry."

Chapter Thirty

"Those who serve the state must be prepared to make great sacrifices."
                                                        —Lenin

THE CRISIS CENTER—MOSCOW, USSR

General Galanskov sat in the crisis center listening to the briefing. He felt a cold knot in his stomach. The messages from Elu were clear. The Americans and the Australians had won. *Spetsnaz* and the Guards air assault troops had tried hard, but they had failed. The Americans were dismantling *War God*. Soon, they would use their heavy-lift helicopters to fly the laser and the other key components to the *Wasp*, evacuate their personnel, and sail merrily off.

Galanskov imagined reporting this to the chairman and shuddered. Perhaps they would not shoot him. The new government liked to pretend it had retained some of Gorbachev's reforms. On the other hand, perhaps they would shoot him. The chairman believed in old-fashioned methods. What had he said? "One other thing, Stepan Pavelovich, do not fail!" But he had no cards left to play. But wait, perhaps he did. He beckoned to one of his aides.

"Get me a secure line to the primary control center at Plesetsk. I wish to speak to Comrade Chief Test Conductor Vladimir Sukhenkiy immediately."

PLESETSK COSMODROME—PRIMARY CONTROL CENTER

Sukhenkiy took the phone. It was trouble, he could smell it. Colonel-General Galanskov was not calling him, personally, to discuss the price of tea in Moscow.

"Sukhenkiy here, Comrade General," he said cautiously.

Galanskov went straight to the point. "Things have not gone well on Elu, Sukhenkiy. The Americans still hold *War God*. They have a large ship which carries heavy-lift helicopters off Elu. I am afraid that they will lift the satellite or its critical components to the ship. Our forces on Elu will not be able to prevent this. That must not be allowed to happen. We must stop them at all costs. The security of the State is involved. Do you understand, Sukhenkiy?"

"Yes, General, I understand."

"Good. You said earlier that you believed it was possible to destroy the satellite by remote command from Plesetsk. Can you do this?"

Sukhenkiy sighed. He had been afraid it would come to this. He desperately wanted *War God* back at Plesetsk for study and analysis, but there was no arguing with Galanskov's logic. The Americans must not get *War God*'s technology.

"Yes, General. Comrade Snastina has a plan which I believe will work. You will recall the technical briefing. *War God*'s laser is powered by matter-antimatter annihilation. The antimatter is contained in the laser power supply by powerful electromagnetic fields. The electrical power for this comes from *War God*'s nuclear reactor. Shut off the power, and in a few seconds there will be an extremely powerful explosion."

"Excellent, but how powerful? Will it destroy *War God* completely?"

"General, it will destroy *War God* and everything around it for several kilometers. It may very well destroy the entire island."

General Galanskov was pleased. Perhaps he had not failed after all. "How soon can you do this, Sukhenkiy?"

"We can send the commands via *Cosmos 2009* immediately, but there is a delaying factor which must be considered. *War God* is a fail-safe design. We must load the antimatter when the satellite is on its booster rocket two hours before launch. We were always concerned about an accidental explosion on the launch pad. If *War God*'s reactor goes out, the antimatter containment system automatically switches to the emergency batteries. There is no way to prevent this. They will maintain the containment fields for a while. When their power is exhausted, then the explosion will occur."

"Very well, Sukhenkiy, send the commands at once."

"I do not understand, General. Surely I must wait until our men have been evacuated from the island?"

There was a cold, grim silence. Then Galanskov spoke. There was a tone of deadly authority in his voice. "There is no way to evacuate them, Sukhenkiy, and there is no time. I bitterly regret the sacrifice of their lives, but there is no alternative. I accept the responsibility. Send the commands at once. That is an order!"

Sukhenkiy felt sick, but he had been in the army. He knew that there are times when men's lives are expendable when the stakes are high, and the Americans must not have *War God*.

"Exactly so, Comrade General. I carry out your order without question."

Sukhenkiy hung up the phone and sighed. *War God* was almost like one of his own children. To think of destroying it was very hard, but it must be done. Very well, do it now!

He walked quickly to his control console. Svetlana sat there, monitoring the displays. She looked up as he approached.

"Orders from Moscow, Svetlana. They are from General Galanskov, himself. We must destroy *War God* to keep it out of the American's hands. Is all in readiness?"

Svetlana nodded. "The commands are loaded in the computer, ready for transmission. This is equivalent to a destruct order. The two-man rule applies. I will enter my password."

Her fingers moved over the control board keys.

Sukhenkiy watched as the words came up on the control console display.

SNASTINA—DEEDS OF GLORY-

He entered his own password.

SUKHENKIY—RED STAR-

Svetlana nodded and reached towards the Execute button. Suddenly, she stopped. "Have all our men been evacuated from the island?"

Sukhenkiy sighed again. She would not like the answer, but he had never lied to Svetlana. He was not going to start now.

"No, Svetlana, and they cannot be. There is no time. We must send the final order immediately."

Svetlana turned pale. She would have destroyed every American satellite in space with a smile, but they were talking about men's lives, hundreds of Russian lives. Her finger stopped halfway to the Execute button. "But, it will kill them all. We cannot do this!"

"We must, Svetlana."

Still, Svetlana hesitated. Sukhenkiy nodded. Svetlana was a young woman, with a long and, one hoped,

a happy life ahead of her. He was getting old. If someone had to bear the guilt for the rest of their life, let it be him. He reached past Svetlana's hand and pushed the button.

"Execute!"

The order flashed up from Plesetsk to *Cosmos 2009* and was relayed down to *War God*. The flight control computer decoded and analyzed the message. It realized that it had been ordered to destroy *War God* and itself, but computers do not care. It merely checked the names and passwords and confirmed that they were correct. Confirmed. An order flashed to *War God*'s nuclear reactor, commanding shutdown in the fail-safe mode. There was a crackle of electricity inside *War God*'s huge hull as the emergency batteries cut in and began to supply power to maintain the antimatter containment fields. Now, it was only a matter of time.

Chapter Thirty-One

"No man is an island entire of its self; . . . Any man's death diminishes me, because I am involved in mankind; therefore never send to learn for whom the bell tolls; it tolls for thee."   —John Donne

THE PLATEAU—ELU ISLAND

Major Gozen and Captain Carter watched as the huge Marine Corps CH-53E helicopter started its engines. First one, then two, then three 4,380-horsepower General Electric T64-416 turboshaft engines whined into life. The huge seven-blade main rotor began to turn faster and faster, and the thirty-five ton helicopter lifted smoothly into the air. Gozen was impressed. As a Ranger officer, he was used to helicopters, but the marines' Sikorsky CH-53E heavy-lift helicopters dwarfed the standard army models.

As the CH-53E lifted off, the sling that attached *War God*'s laser to the bottom of the huge olive-drab helicopter stretched taut. The CH-53E pilot went to full power, lifted *War God*'s laser off the ground, and flew off to the east, toward the *Wasp*.

Gozen felt an odd combination of elation and relief.

It was over. This was what they had fought for. The Rangers and the Green Berets had done their job. Now, it was up to the rocket scientists. He only hoped it had all been worth it.

A hundred yards to the north, other CH-53Es were loading American and Australian troops, fifty at a time. Major Gozen was impressed. The pilots and crews of Marine Heavy Helicopter Squadron 364 obviously knew their business, and their huge helicopters were ideal for moving men and equipment rapidly. Another hour, and the American-Australian force would be gone from Elu. Provided of course, that they had an hour. Gozen was acutely aware that he was standing twenty feet from something that was probably more powerful than a hydrogen bomb. And it might be about to detonate.

He wondered how much time he had. If anyone on Elu could tell him, it would be Laura Walsh. She was inside *War God*'s silver-gray cylindrical hull, running tests that might give him a clue. Laura emerged from *War God*'s interior. She was carrying a mysterious black box and frowning slightly. Gozen sincerely hoped that the news was not bad. He was sure his ancestors were wonderful people, but he was in no particular hurry to meet them.

Laura paused by the two officers. Another huge CH-53E helicopter whined overhead, loaded with troops and headed for the *Wasp*. "How does it look, Dr. Walsh?" Gozen asked, as the Ch-53E's engine noise faded away. "How much time do you think we've got?"

Laura frowned again. "It's hard to be precise, Major. I lack some critical data. However, I have investigated the emergency backup batteries. They are high-capacity nickel-cadmium units. I have measured their charge and the current flow. I would estimate that detonation of the power supply will occur in approximately three hours, plus or minus one half-hour. If we are off Elu in two hours, we will be safe."

Major Gozen sighed with relief. "That's excellent, Dr. Walsh. We will have completed our evacuation of Elu in less then an hour. Then the Russians can have it and detonate their damned power supply if they want to."

Laura looked concerned. "What about the Russians, Major? How will they get off the island? Is there a Russian ship nearby?"

Major Gozen shook his head. "No, the navy says the nearest Russian ship is fifteen hundred miles away. It will be at least forty-eight hours before it gets to Elu."

"That won't do any good," Laura said. *War God*'s power supply will detonate in three or four hours. Anyone who is still on Elu when that happens will be killed."

"I'm sure you're right, Dr. Walsh," Gozen said, "but it is not anything we are doing. The NSA says the detonation was ordered from Moscow by Colonel-General Galanskov. He must have known that there was no way to evacuate his people when he gave the order. I'm sorry, but I don't see anything we can do about it."

"We have to do something, Major. We have to try. The Russians are soldiers. They were ordered here to do a job, just like you and your men. Surely, you can't hate them for that. I can't believe you want to see them die!"

Major Gozen thought for a moment. Then he spoke quietly. "Dr. Walsh, I don't hate anyone, and I don't train my men to hate anyone. I am an American soldier. I don't make the political decisions. The national command authorities sent us to Elu to fight the Russians, and we did. If they had sent us here to fight the French or the Norwegians, we would have done it. If I could have accomplished our mission without killing anyone, it would have made me happy. I'm sorry that the Russians are going to die, but I still don't see that there is anything we can do about it."

Laura spoke impatiently. "Yes, there is! I'm no military expert, but I can see that there is. *Wasp* is a very big ship, and these CH-53E helicopters can carry fifty men at a time. All we have to do is use them and evacuate the Russians to the *Wasp*."

That was a startling thought. Major Gozen thought hard for thirty seconds. "Well, Dr. Walsh, from a purely technical point, you are right. The *Wasp* can carry that many more people, and the CH-53Es can fly them off. I will contact the captain of the *Wasp* and see if he will agree. But that still leaves one big hole in your plan. As far as we know, the Russians are not aware that *War God* is going to blow up, or what will happen when it does. And the last time they saw American helicopters, they were not very friendly. If they see sixteen CH-53Es flying towards them, I'm afraid they will open fire with everything they've got. How do we convince the Russians that we are suddenly the good guys who are trying to save them?"

Laura smiled. "I understand, Major. Well, I'm willing to put my money where my mouth is. I speak fluent Russian, and I understand *War God*'s antimatter power supply. Give me a jeep, and I will go talk to them. I believe I can convince them."

Major Gozen smiled. "I believe you probably can, Dr. Walsh. You are extremely persuasive. But you are a civilian. Will the Russians believe you are speaking for the U.S. military commanders?"

Andy Carter grinned. He believed firmly in never volunteering for anything, but there are times when a man must rise above his principles. "You're right, Major. I'd better go with Laura. I'll wear my green beret and look military as hell. That ought to help convince them."

421

"All right, Captain, go ahead. Do you want an escort?"

"No, sir, I want to look as nonthreatening as possible. We'll go by ourselves."

"All right, Captain. Get going, but be careful. Those Russians are not going to be in a happy mood. Good luck!"

Carter nodded. He was certain that he and Laura were doing the right thing. But he was a soldier; she was not. He could put himself in the place of the Russians guarding the road down from the plateau. They would be nervous, wary of another American attack. They might shoot at an American vehicle the instant they saw it, white flag or no white flag. It would be a pity if their mission of mercy ended in a hail of fire from Russian PKM machine guns.

Chapter Thirty-Two

"The enemy of my enemy is my friend."   —Afghan
                                            Proverb

*SPETSNAZ TEAM—EL ISLAND—THE HAR-
BOR AREA*

Colonel Viktor Ulanov sat on a rock feeling depressed. Like many Russians, he was normally cheerful;
but when he was gloomy, he was very gloomy, indeed.
He knew it is the duty of a commander to cheer up his
men and keep up morale, but he could think of nothing
cheerful to say. They had done their best, but they had
lost. The American helicopters and Rangers had been
too much for them. It was useless to think of a counterattack. The American helicopters would slaughter them
as they tried to go back up the road to the plateau. He
was not going to do that. Even if they shot him when
he got back to Moscow, he would not throw away his
men's lives on a suicidal attack.

He glanced around him. Nothing he saw made him
cheerful. The command group was a little worse for
wear. Major Mamin was nursing his sore head, Chazov

his sore ribs, and Irina Yakoleva was sitting down, resting her leg, as she idly cleaned her SVD sniper's rifle.

There was a sudden stir of motion. Ulanov looked up. Someone was coming rapidly from the direction of the road. It was Sharypa. "Colonel," Sharypa said, "there is a jeep coming slowly down the road. Two men in uniform and a woman in civilian clothing riding in it. One of my corporals speaks some English. He says they say they want to speak to our commanding officer at once and that it is very urgent."

Now what? He did not think he and the Americans had anything to talk about, but why not? He had never heard that Americans believe in blowing themselves up in car bomb attacks. Two men and a woman did not sound like much of a threat.

"Very well. Let them come through our lines and bring them here. I will see what they wish to say."

Sharypa saluted and was off. Ulanov alerted the command group. Mamin seemed in a bad mood. Ulanov was not surprised. Anyone Dudorov hit was going to feel it for a long time. They watched as the jeep drove up slowly. Sharypa was following it. Ulanov looked at the occupants. One man was an American army officer, the driver was a private. The woman was quite pretty. They all seemed dirty and the worse for wear. Well, Ulanov was no picture of military splendor himself. Combat is hard on men and uniforms.

The Americans got out of their jeep. Irina Yakoleva stepped forward. Ulanov noticed that she held her SVD sniper's rifle cradled in her arms. The muzzle was not pointing at the Americans and her finger was not on the trigger, but it was close. She was ready to fire fast if she had to. Ulanov smiled. If the Americans intended treachery, they would have to deal with the Yakoleva.

Irina stepped forward. "I am Senior Lieutenant Irina

Yakoleva. This is Colonel Ulanov. He is in command. He does not speak English. I will translate."

The American stared at Irina in an odd way, as if he could not believe his eyes. Irina shrugged. Perhaps tall blonds are rare in America. The American saluted Colonel Ulanov politely and began to speak. Irina translated rapidly.

"I am Captain Andrew Carter, 1st Special Forces Group, United States Army. I am second in command of U.S. forces on Elu. My commanding officer has authorized me to speak to you."

"Very well, I am Colonel Viktor Ulanov. I am in command of the Soviet forces on Elu. What do you wish to say?"

"Colonel, you and your men are in extreme danger. I have come to offer you our assistance."

Ulanov was puzzled. Was the American threatening him? That made no sense. "If you attack us, we will fight," he said quickly. "We will not surrender."

Carter shook his head. "We are not threatening you, Colonel. It is the satellite. *War God*'s weapon is a high-power laser. It is operated by an an extremely powerful power supply. That power supply is going to detonate. It will be like the explosion of a hydrogen bomb. Everyone who is on Elu when that happens will die. We have a ship and transport helicopters available. We are willing to evacuate you and your men."

Ulanov was skeptical. "A power supply will do this, Captain? How is that possible?"

Carter pointed to the woman standing by his side. "This is Dr. Laura Walsh. She is a scientist who works for the American government. She can explain better than I can."

The woman began to speak. Ulanov was startled. She was speaking excellent and fluent Russian. She sounded knowledgeable and authoritative, but it was hard to believe what she said. "Those are the facts, comrades," she concluded. "Are there any questions?"

Ulanov could not think of any. He needed a minute to think. "Excuse me, Captain, I must confer with my officers."

"Certainly, Colonel, but do not take too long. The clock is running."

Unpleasant thought. Ulanov and his officers moved a few yards away. He did not want the Americans to hear what they said. He needed to think. Let the others speak first. "What do you make of it?" he asked.

Major Mamin sneered. "A pack of lies! Fairy tales to deceive children! Antimatter, who has ever heard of such a thing?"

"I have," Irina Yakoleva said quickly. "I read an article in *Pravda* a few months ago. It said that many Russian scientists believe that the great meteor which struck Siberia in 1908 was made of antimatter. That is said to account for the immense power of the explosion, and to explain why no fragment of the meteor has ever been found. It would have been completely destroyed by contact with normal matter, as this woman, Walsh, has said."

"I, too, have heard this theory," Captain Chazov said. "It was an extremely powerful explosion, Colonel. It blew down large trees more than thirty miles from the point of impact."

Wonderful! And they were less than four miles away from a large amount of the damned stuff! But two questions were still unanswered. "Very well. Thank you for your opinions. Let us talk to this Carter some more."

They moved quickly back toward the Americans. Ulanov spoke quietly. "We have listened carefully to you and Dr. Walsh. But, there is something I wish to know. Suppose there is a an antimatter power supply

426

in *War God.* How do you know that it is going to detonate?"

Irina Yakoleva translated quickly. Carter nodded. It was a fair question.

"United States intelligence agencies have intercepted and decoded messages from inside the Soviet Union. Russian scientists at Plesetsk received orders from Moscow to detonate *War God*'s power supply. Those orders were given by Colonel-General S. P. Galanskov of the GRU. The scientists replied within a few minutes that the command had been sent. The power supply will detonate as soon as *War God*'s emergency batteries run down. You will be happy to know that General Galanskov regrets that you will all be killed."

General Galanskov! Even in Elu's heat, Ulanov felt a chill. He no longer had any doubts. The Americans were telling the truth.

"I believe you, Carter, but I have one more question. You say you are in danger at this very moment. We have just been fighting hard, trying to kill each other. Why will you Americans risk your lives to save us?"

"We are all soldiers, Colonel," Carter said softly. "You fought for your country, and I fought for mine, but it is over. There is nothing left to fight for. We have removed some components from *War God* and taken them to the *Wasp.* We do not dare to try to take *War God,* itself. If the power supply detonated on board *Wasp,* the ship would be totally destroyed. We see no reason why brave men should die for nothing because they wear blue berets instead of black or green. That is the truth, Colonel. Our helicopter crews have volunteered to take the risk. We are ready to start flying you and your men off Elu at once. Now, I must ask you for an immediate decision. The risk is increasing with every second that passes."

Ulanov hesitated for a second. They might shoot him

427

him when he got back to Moscow, but he would die to save his men if it came to that. "Very well, Captain, what are your precise conditions?"

Carter smiled. "There are no conditions, Colonel. You are not surrendering, we are rescuing you from, let us say, a natural disaster. There is one thing I must ask, however. You will understand that we cannot take several hundred armed Russian soldiers aboard a U.S. Navy ship. You may keep your weapons, but all ammunition must be left on Elu. Our helicopter crews will check your men before they board the helicopters."

"Very well, Captain," Ulanov said quietly, "I accept your offer. I will give the orders immediately."

"No!" Mamin shouted suddenly. "This is treason, Ulanov. You cannot do this!"

Ulanov turned toward Mamin. The KGB officer's face was flushed with anger. He had drawn his 9mm Markov PSM pistol from its brown leather holster. The black, round muzzle was pointing straight at Ulanov's chest.

"You are a traitor, Ulanov. You are going to die!"

"Do not be insane, Major. What good will it do for us all to die here. Why should we all die for nothing?"

Ulanov was thinking furiously. His rifle was slung over his shoulder. His pistol was in his holster. If he reached for either, Mamin would fire instantly.

"Words cannot save you, Ulanov," Mamin shouted, his voice hoarse with anger. "Surrendering your command is treason. You will die now!"

The muzzle blast of the shot fired at point-blank range was stunning. There was another blast, and another, as Irina Yakoleva fired her SVD semiautomatic rifle as fast as she could pull the trigger. Half a dozen .30 caliber full-metal-jacketed bullets tore through Mamin's body at 2,700 feet per second. The shock was tremendous. The 9mm PSM automatic slipped from

Mamin's nerveless fingers. He fell heavily. He was dead before he hit the ground.

Ulanov turned back toward Carter. The American looked startled. His hand was poised near his pistol holster.

"Do not be concerned, Captain. This has nothing to do with you. I accept your offer. Let us begin the evacuation immediately."

Carter nodded. The Russians appeared to have an extremely decisive method of settling disagreements between officers, but that was not his concern. He went to his jeep and took out a flare gun. He loaded it and quickly fired a red and then a yellow flare.

"The helicopters will be here in five minutes, Colonel."

"Very well, Captain, I will give the orders."

Ulanov turned to Irina Yakoleva. "That was quick thinking and fast shooting, Lieutenant. I owe you my life. I will buy you a bottle of the best vodka when we get back to Moscow."

Irina shook her head. "I will not be drinking vodka when I return to Moscow." She looked down at Mamin's bullet-riddled body. "They will probably shoot me for this. If not, well, perhaps I will learn to love Siberia."

Ulanov smiled. "Call the medical sergeant, Captain Chazov. Lieutenant Yakoleva is obviously suffering from this damned heat. As we all know, Major Mamin died heroically, leading a counterattack against the American Rangers. I intend to recommend him for a medal."

"Exactly so, Colonel," Chazov said. "I will be glad to sign the citation as an eyewitness."

The sound of helicopter rotor blades filled the air. One after another, a long line of giant U.S. Marine Corps CH-53E helicopters touched down in the harbor area. The Russians quickly boarded the giant helicopters. Ulanov and Carter waited until all but the last helicopter was airborne.

They and the *Spetsnaz* command group climbed aboard. The big olive drab helicopter lifted off, its turbines whining, and headed out to sea toward the *Wasp*.

An eerie quiet settled over Elu. On the plateau, *War God* was alone again, but not for long.

Chapter Thirty-Three

"God and soldiers we adore, in time of danger, not before."
                                    —John Churchill

SURVIVORS OF LENINGRADSKI KOMSO-MOLS—OFF ELU

Captain 2nd Rank Viktor Khrenov clung to the life raft. Approximately sixty officers and men had escaped from *Leningradski Komsomols* before she went down. They had managed to inflate two sixteen-man life rafts and get them into the water. Space in the life rafts had to be reserved for the wounded and injured. Able-bodied men must depend on their life belts and hang on to the rafts. Anyone who drifted away would quickly be lost in the vast expanses of the Pacific.

The water was not cold. They were probably not going to die of exposure. Perhaps it would have been kinder if the water temperature had been freezing. Then they would have died quickly and painlessly. Their emergency food and water would last six or seven days. Then they would start to die of thirst and starvation. Not a pleasant way to go. Their only chance was to be picked up by a passing ship. Khrenov did not deceive himself. There was not one chance in a thousand that would happen.

Someone on one of the rafts was yelling and pointing. A slender object was cutting through the water two hundred meters away. Khrenov's stomach clenched. Not sharks! No, it was strange, like a mottled gray post rising out of the water. The water around the base of the thing began to froth and bubble. A long, teardrop-shaped black hull rose smoothly from the ocean. It was a submarine. Its conning tower was amazingly small and slender, and a diving plane protruded horizontally from each side of the conning tower. Khrenov had never expected to lay eyes on one, but he knew what it was— a U.S. Navy nuclear attack submarine, a 688.

A hatch opened in the top of the slender conning tower. Two sailors came out and began to scan the horizon with binoculars. It was all so familiar that Khrenov almost laughed. Now, an officer came up through the hatch and stared at Khrenov and his men. Khrenov felt a chill of apprehension. The *Zampolits* had always sworn that the Yankees were merciless and cruel. Had they come to be sure that there were no survivors?

The officer had a microphone in his hand. His amplified voice rang out, but he was speaking in English. Khrenov did not understand. Lieutenant Sphagin could speak English. "What is he saying, Pavel?"

Lieutenant Sphagin translated quickly. "He says that he is Commander Jones, the executive officer of the submarine USS *Los Angeles*. They cannot take us on board. They do not have space enough for sixty men. He says we should not be concerned. Several large CH-53E helicopters are on the way from the USS *Wasp*. They will pick us up and fly us to the *Wasp*. The fighting is over. He says we will be well treated and returned to the Soviet Union. They will dive now. His captain does not like to stay on the surface."

Khrenov was chuckling as the *Los Angeles* cleared her bridge, and the long black hull vanished below the surface. He began to laugh, harder and harder, until his whole body shook. The devil liked to have his little jokes. Khrenov had done his damndest to sink the *Wasp* and had lost his ship trying. Now the *Wasp* would save him! He roared with laughter.

FLIGHT DECK—USS WASP—OFF ELU

Wasp was steaming steadily northeast, her seventy thousand horsepower driving her through the water at twenty-four knots. She was already ninety miles from Elu, but *Wasp*'s commander was not about to slow down. He was not sure whether he believed in antimatter or not, but he was not about to take any chances.

The last giant CH-53E from Elu was landing on *Wasp*'s flight deck. Miriam Foster led her parishioners out of the huge fuselage. The natives treated Miriam Foster with great respect. It was obvious to them that they had underestimated Miriam. Anyone who could call down these huge birds down from the sky and calmly fly around in them was obviously a being of great power.

Laura Walsh stood with a small group of American and Russian officers just aft of *Wasp*'s island. They were talking and Laura was translating smoothly. She was surprised that somehow she had become a member of an exclusive club that included the Special Forces, the Rangers, the SAS, and *Spetsnaz*. They were quite willing to talk to her and listen to her opinions. Apparently, when she had fired *War God*'s laser at the attacking SU-24s, she had become a combat veteran and joined the club.

"That was a very well executed attack your Rangers made, Major Gozen," Ulanov said. "Your use of the Sheridans was a big surprise. We did not expect that."

"Your antiarmor ambush was very effective, Colonel," Major Gozen said. "Your use of your RPG-7s showed great tactical skill."

"I have very good men," Ulanov replied. "Most plans work well when you have good men to execute them."

Laura shook her head in amazement. Soldiers! A few hours ago, they had been fighting furiously. Now, they were like football coaches after a big game, calmly talking over the key plays. She would never understand them.

Twenty feet away, Irina Yakoleva sat with Cord. They were talking and laughing. Cord was showing Irina his .303 Lee-Enfield, pointing out the fine points of its bolt action and the telescopic sight. Irina rolled up one leg of her faded blue jeans to display a long and shapely leg. There was a bandage on the back of her leg, just above the knee. It seemed that Cord had shot her there with his rifle. They both seemed to find that hilarious.

Now, Cord was pointing to a long fresh scar in the wood of his rifle's stock. Irina ran her finger along the groove and smiled. Yes, she had almost gotten Cord. They both laughed again. The fact that they had tried hard and nearly killed each other seemed to be remarkably amusing and to create some strange bond between them. Laura sighed again. No, she would never understand soldiers.

Colonel Ulanov spoke somberly. "Tell Major Gozen that I have the utmost respect for him and his men. They certainly did their duty on Elu. He can be proud of his men and his unit."

Major Gozen nodded. "Thank him, Dr. Walsh, and return the compliment. Say that his men fought bravely and well. I am sorry so many good men died, his and mine."

Captain Carter spoke for the first time. "They fought for their country. We fought for ours. Let's just hope that there was some point to it, that it was all worth it in the end."

"It was," Laura said quietly.

They all looked at her, startled for a moment. Her translation was so smooth that they had almost forgotten that she was there.

"It would be very bad if one country dominated space. It wouldn't matter if it were the United States or the Soviet Union. With that much power, the leaders of that country might get overconfident and take chances. Then we might have an all-out war. We can't afford to take a chance on that. Nobody won completely on Elu, and I think that's a good thing, a damned good thing. The balance is preserved. That's the important thing."

"Perhaps you are right, Dr. Walsh," Major Gozen said quietly. "The balance is preserved, at least until the next time."

Laura was about to say something else when *Wasp*'s loudspeaker system burst into life.

"Now, hear this! Now hear this! All personnel on deck go below immediately! I say again, all personnel on deck go below immediately!"

Laura did not need to ask what was happening. The NSA was still intercepting and decoding *War God*'s telemetry messages to Plesetsk. *War God*'s power supply was about to go.

ELU ISLAND—THE PLATEAU

War God lay alone on the deserted plateau. Its emergency batteries were nearly drained. In a few more seconds, they would no longer be able to maintain the anti-matter containment fields. The flight control computer shut down power to the telemetry data link transmitter.

That would enable *War God* to survive for a few seconds more. That was its final option. There was nothing more it could do. Destruction was imminent. If the computer had been human, it would have cursed or prayed. But computers do not care. It waited calmly for complete destruction.

Within the laser power supply, the electromagnetic antimatter containment fields flickered and went out. For half a second, nothing happened. Then, no longer confined, the antimatter touched the unprotected normal matter of the power supply. There was an intense, brilliant flash of yellow light as antimatter and normal matter vanished in mutual annihilation. In a fraction of a second, *War God* was no longer there. Not a single one of its atoms still existed. The dazzling ball of yellow fire expanded, giving off intense bursts of gamma radiation.

To an observer in space, it would have seemed as if a small piece of the sun had suddenly appeared on Elu. Most of the plateau vanished in less than two seconds. The blast wave spread incredible destruction across the island. In a few seconds more, the explosion was over. All the antimatter had been consumed and converted to pure energy. All that was left of Elu was the bare, blackened rock, smoldering and smoking in the bright sunlight.

Chapter Thirty-Four

"A large meteor struck the isolated island of Elu in the Southwest Pacific."   —*The New York Times*

"A RAN helicopter crashed on HMAS *Darwin* during maneuvers in the Southwest Pacific. The resulting fire caused severe damage. . . ."   —*Sydney Morning Herald*

"Admiral Orlov announced the tragic loss of the submarines *70 Letts USSR* and *Krasnogvardets* during recent maneuvers."   —*Pravda*

"Two Air Force B-52G bombers were lost during a SAC exercise south of Guam. General Kramer stated that this demonstrates the need for increased production of the B-2 bomber."   —*Washington Post*

"The 2nd Ranger Battalion returned to Fort Lewis, Washington after a rapid deployment exercise in Australia."   —*Seattle Times*

A cold spring breeze was blowing over Moscow. It was warm and pleasant inside the Kremlin conference room where a small, select group was assembled. They had sipped wine and vodka and nibbled caviar and crackers. Now, they listened attentively to the chairman as he spoke. For once, he seemed almost jovial. Perhaps it was the vodka, or simply that even the chairman got tired of glaring icily at people all the time.

He read from the sheet of paper in his hand. "Colonel V. Ulanov, for personal bravery and skillful command of his unit in classified combat operations, is awarded the Order of Aleksandr Nevskii."

Everyone clapped politely.

"Captain 2nd Rank V. Khrenov, for heroic actions while in command of the submarine *Leningradski Komsomols,* is awarded the title of Hero of the Soviet Union and the Gold Star Medal.

"Sergeant M. Sharypa and Corporal I. Dudorov, for heroic actions in classified combat operations, are awarded the Order of Glory, Second Class.

"Lieutenant I. Yakoleva, for sustained heroism in classified combat operations, is awarded the title of Hero of the Soviet Union and the Gold Star Medal.

"Dr. V. Sukhenkiy and Dr. S. Snastina, for outstanding technical accomplishments and support to the Soviet armed forces, are awarded the title Hero of Socialist Labor and the Hammer and Sickle medal.

"Major Y. Mamin, who died heroically in classified combat operations, is awarded the Medal for Valor."

Svetlana Snastina peered nervously at Vladimir Sukhenkiy. She had never been in the Kremlin before and certainly never received a medal from a high government official.

"I do not understand," she said softly. "I thought that when we were forced to blow up *War God* that we were defeated and the Americans had won. Now, it seems that we were victorious and the Americans lost, and everyone is receiving medals. I do not understand it at all."

Sukhenkiy smiled. "It is the way the world works, Svetlana. The Americans may have carried off some components of *War God,* but they did not get the power supply. Many important people were involved in directing and planning the operation: the army, the navy, the GRU and the KGB. None of them will admit that they failed in any way. We have declared victory, and the medals and awards are symbols of this. Enjoy your medal, think how proud your mother will be."

Svetlana smiled. That was certainly true. Her mother had never understood why Svetlana was interested in such weird things, instead of meeting nice young men, getting married, and having children. Her mother still would not understand what Svetlana did or why she did it, but she would be pleased. Svetlana shrugged. She still did not really understand politics. She would be happy to go back to working on lasers.

The chairman finished making the presentations. General Galanskov stepped forward. Russians love drinking toasts. Galanskov was not about to miss an opportunity.

"Comrades, I have not come here today to make a speech, but to give an order. Let everyone fill his glass. Now, a toast. To those of you who built *War God,* to those of you who fought for *War God* and kept it from falling into the hands of the Americans, I salute you. The Soviet Union is proud of you!"

Everyone drank and applauded. The ceremony was over. Irina Yakoleva filled her glass with ice-cold vodka and sipped it slowly. It certainly would not do to drink too much during her first hour as a Hero of the Soviet Union. She felt a glow of satisfaction. This would certainly help her military career. The next old-fashioned senior officers who started to tell her she could not do something because she was a weak and delicate woman, would choke on their words when they saw the Gold Star Medal of a Hero of the Soviet Union pinned to her uniform.

She noticed that all the army and GRU people seemed to be collecting around her. Perhaps it was time for another toast. Well, one more glass of vodka would not hurt her.

"Irina Yakoleva!" General Galanskov's voice cracked like a whip. "I am astounded at your decadent and careless behavior! You are here to be honored by the Soviet people and you behave in this disgraceful and shameless manner. Why are you out of uniform?"

Irina's mind raced. What had she done? Out of uniform? She was wearing her best parade—walking out dress uniform. It was true that she had had it tailored a bit here and there to show off her excellent figure. If General Galanskov objected to that, he was the first man who ever had.

"No excuse, sir!" she said.

"Fortunately, the problem is easily corrected," General Galanskov said. "You are wearing the shoulder boards of a senior lieutenant, Captain Yakoleva. By chance, I happen to have a pair of captain's shoulder boards in my pocket. Here, put them on at once!"

Irina blushed. It was an old army joke, but a good one, and it is one that the victim seldom minds. Everyone clapped her on the shoulders and congratulated her. Sharypa and Dudorov put her new insignia of rank on her shoulders and saluted her with incredible precision. They could not have done better for a marshal of the Soviet Union. That meant a great deal to her, more than the chairman's speech and Colonel-General Galanskov's congratulations. The ceremony was breaking up. People were leaving. Irina was pleased to see that Colonel Ulanov was standing there. They should not part without saying good-bye after all they had been through together.

"Let us go and have a drink or two together, Captain Yakoleva," Ulanov said. "It is very bad luck not to wet down your new shoulder boards when you have just been promoted."

"Exactly so, Colonel. But, if you do not mind too much, could we drink at my apartment? I have an excellent bottle of vodka there. I am afraid that there are times I drink a bit too much when I am off duty. If I am alone tonight, I fear I may drink too much. But, if I am with a trusty comrade, one whom I have been in battle with, we will talk of what we have done, divide the bottle, and all will be well."

Colonel Ulanov smiled broadly. "Never let it be said that Viktor Ulanov let a comrade down. Nothing would please me more! Let us go at once to your apartment, and drink to your promotion."

THE OVAL OFFICE—THE WHITE HOUSE— WASHINGTON, D.C.

It was a pleasant spring day in Washington. The president was enjoying herself. She was genuinely interested in people. She always liked handing out awards to people who have earned them. She read from the list in her hand. "Brig. Gen. James E. Brand, the Distinguished Service Medal for outstanding service during recent military operations, classified citation.

"Lt. Col. Muso A. Gozen, the Distinguished Service Cross, classified citation.

"Capt. Andrew J. Carter, the Distinguished Service Cross, classified citation.

"Capt. Raymond L. Chavez, the Distinguished Flying Cross and the Air Medal, classified citation.

"Sgt. Franklin R. Jackson, the Distinguished Service Cross, classified citation.

"Dr. Laura A. Walsh, the Medal of Freedom, classified citation.

The president paused for a moment, and beamed at her audience.

"Not everyone who deserves to be honored could be here today. To honor them, I would like to present two more awards which honor them. Lieutenant Colonel Gozen, congratulations on your promotion, and your new assignment. I would like your first official act as the commanding officer of the 2nd Ranger Battalion to be to accept for your battalion, the Presidential Unit Citation."

She turned to Cord. He was a marvel of military perfection in his dark blue dress uniform. He was nervous, but it was worth it. Even Regimental Sergeant Major MacNair had never met the president of the United States.

"Sgt. John H. Cord, Number 2 Squadron, 1st Australian SAS Regiment. With the complete approval of the Australian government, I award the Presidential Unit Citation to the 1st Australian SAS Regiment. Please accept this award for your regiment."

Everyone was looking at Cord. He was almost paralyzed with stage fright. He stepped forward, took the award, and saluted smartly. He managed to force out "Thank you, Ma'am." That was an oration for Cord. He still did his best public speaking with his rifle.

The ceremony began to break up. The army men and Cord gravitated together. Laura Walsh was pleased to see that she seemed to belong to that select group.

"Congratulations on your promotion, Moose," General Brand said. "The 2nd Ranger Battalion couldn't have a better CO. Now, we have got to wet down those new silver oak leaves. It's bad luck if we don't. I want you all to come along and have a few drinks on me."

No one seemed to have the slightest objection.

BLOCKBUSTER FICTION FROM PINNACLE BOOKS!

THE FINAL VOYAGE OF THE S.S.N. SKATE   (17-157, $3.95)
by Stephen Cassell
The "leper" of the U.S. Pacific Fleet, SSN 578 nuclear attack sub SKATE, has one final mission to perform—an impossible act of piracy that will pit the underwater deathtrap and its inexperienced crew against the combined might of the Soviet Navy's finest!

QUEENS GATE RECKONING   (17-164, $3.95)
by Lewis Purdue
Only a wounded CIA operative and a defecting Soviet ballerina stand in the way of a vast consortium of treason that speeds toward the hour of mankind's ultimate reckoning! From the best-selling author of THE LINZ TESTAMENT.

FAREWELL TO RUSSIA   (17-165, $4.50)
by Richard Hugo
A KGB agent must race against time to infiltrate the confines of U.S. nuclear technology after a terrifying accident threatens to unleash unmitigated devastation!

THE NICODEMUS CODE   (17-133, $3.95)
by Graham N. Smith and Donna Smith
A two-thousand-year-old parchment has been unearthed, unleashing a terrifying conspiracy unlike any the world has previously known, one that threatens the life of the Pope himself, and the ultimate destruction of Christianity!

Available wherever paperbacks are sold, or order direct from the Publisher. Send cover price plus 50¢ per copy for mailing and handling to Pinnacle Books, Dept.17-436, 475 Park Avenue South, New York, N.Y. 10016. Residents of New York, New Jersey and Pennsylvania must include sales tax. DO NOT SEND CASH.